ROUGH RED

MARTIN SYLVESTER

VILLARD BOOKS NEW YORK 1990

Library of Congress Cataloging-in-Publication Data
Sylvester, Martin.
Rough red/by Martin Sylvester.
p. cm.
ISBN 0-394-57687-X
I. Title.
PR6069.Y43R6   1990
823'.914—dc20   89-39502

9 8 7 6 5 4 3 2
First American Edition

AST DAY, FIRST DAY

THE PAIN WAS LIKE A DEAD WEIGHT ON HIS CHEST . . .
A face appeared, an oval of sharper focus against a misty background shot through with jagged lights. Maria, his wife, her eyes huge, was telling him something . . .

An English *doctor? Why?*

Above him, reflected sunlight danced on the high bedroom ceiling. He closed his eyes, fingers groping for the smoothness of gold. The sounds of the village seemed to come in waves, from far away. Was he hearing them, or were they memories? The uneven rattle of hooves—that must be from the past, when he was young, when the streets were still cobbled. Now he could hear distant music, shouts, and laughter from the English colony: all summer it went on, a perpetual holiday . . .

Another face—Antoni! Now he can tell him about . . . no, no, Antoni was in America. That was a piece of bad luck.

Who, then?

The English doctor. His hands were cool, and skilled. A glass appeared, half full of cloudy liquid. The doctor tilted it carefully against his lips, but he could feel the wetness trickle down his chin. He heard a voice saying that the pain should soon diminish—the doctor, speaking in careful Spanish . . .

He was aware of a pillow being pushed behind his head, but his thoughts had returned to his problem.

Perhaps the doctor could help him . . . if he could be trusted. Perhaps he must *trust him—what other way was there?*

His fingers pulled at the ring on the third finger of his left hand. Seeing this, the doctor bent to help him.

"Déselo . . ." Give it to . . . He could hardly get the words out. Could the doctor hear him? Yes, he was nodding gravely.

"Es importante . . ." He wanted to say more, but the pain was stronger, crushing his strength, his will.

Perhaps, if he slept for a while . . .

HURSDAY

"THIS IS THE LIFE!" I TOLD MYSELF.

Midday: and the temperature at La Sauvegarde was in the high nineties, according to the thermometer that hung in the shade of the vine shelter: by this afternoon it was bound to climb over the hundred mark. The sun bore through the vine leaves, making patches of brilliant, luminous green on the pages of my book. In the fields which surround the house, there was no sound except the tinny rasp of crickets and the sighing of the large white cows which loitered mournfully on the already close-cropped brown grass, their heads hung low with boredom.

I lifted my book again, a *roman policier* featuring Inspector Maigret. I make a point of reading some French while on holiday—it's useful for my work, and it pleases Claudine. But it's still an effort, and I get annoyed at myself for feeling childish when I have to ask her to explain a word or phrase. Of course, when we're at home in Church Street, Kensington, it's the other way 'round, but she doesn't seem to mind. I think women have a stronger sense of their own identity than men.

A crunching of footsteps on gravel, a tinkling of ice in glasses, and I lowered the book. It was she, my beautiful dutiful wife.

"Darling!"

"Some iced *pamplemousse, chéri.*"

"Wonderful!"

"Where are the girls?"

"By the pool, frying as usual. Shall I take that to them?"

"Oh no, I will do it. *Bouge pas.*"

My eyes followed her stylish, Gallic perambulation across the courtyard to the pool enclosure. Yes, this was the life. I drank some iced grapefruit juice, and forced my attention back to the book, but no, it was too much like hard work. Ships and men rot in port, and that includes wine merchants: after nearly two weeks at La Sauvegarde, I could feel the first barnacles along the waterline. Not that I hadn't enjoyed myself so far—that wasn't it—but you need to train and prepare for the life of leisure, and with an ailing business to prop up I was out of practice. Also, it must be admitted that being on holiday with two teenage daughters does have disadvantages, however much one loves the little darlings and delights to watch them growing up. Sylvie is fifteen, and Nichole thirteen: as our old farmhouse is well off the beaten track, they're stuck here, and never go out unless I drive them. So Claudine and I are never alone. Worse, she's distracted by them, and makes me feel surplus—selfish, I know, but time is roaring by, and when you've got these hot, hot afternoons . . .

But here she comes, back from the pool enclosure to sit with me. The cane chair creaks as she settles into it.

"I don't know how they can stand being out all day in this heat," I said.

"Ah, but they are both so *bronzée*!" Claudine said fondly. "Now they can go back to school and everyone will say, oooh, where have you *been*?"

"Oh, they'll all be just the same," I said. "That's what summer holidays are for—sun, and . . . so forth."

"Then one does not want to be a poor pale thing, an exception," Claudine said. "You know how much a young girl hates to be that."

"You know best, darling," I said, suppressing a yawn. "Tell me—what's on the program for this afternoon?"

"Program?"

"Well, you know—plans. Any plans?"

"You want to go out somewhere?"

"No, not really. No, I don't think so . . ."

"Well, then . . ."

"I thought, perhaps . . . a siesta."

"Why not. And I will perhaps be with the girls by the pool."

"Oh."

"You think they prefer to be by themselves?"

"Well, no, I'm sure they love to have you with them. But . . ."

"Yes?"

"So do I, darling."

She didn't reply, so I looked up. Her eyes were hidden by sunglasses, but her lips were curved in a smile. "In the good old days," I said, "we used to have wonderful siestas in that room, the shutters closed to keep the heat out, dust dancing in the chinks of sunlight. Long lazy times, the sort that make you feel nothing else matters. Have you forgotten?"

"My William," she said, "of course not!"

"Well, then . . ."

"If the girls were not here, it would be like that, I promise."

"But they are. All right, I know—they're at the age when giggles break out at any suggestion of you and I disappearing to spend some time together. The sooner they get boyfriends and interests of their own to fill their heads with, the better."

Claudine put her hand on mine. "This will not be long, for Sylvie," she said thoughtfully and, it seemed, a little sadly.

No, it was no good. Siestas were not on, not at present: I knew that, really. We were never one of those frank, full frontal families where everybody wanders in and out of the bathroom in the nuddy, and parents brightly announce that they're just off for an hour's lovemaking so please don't disturb. Something off-putting about that life-style, I always thought: goes with clumpy sandals, Müesli, and camping in Scotland.

"Shall I tell you what I propose for lunch, *chéri*?" Claudine said.

"Yes, darling," I said, "please do." Though circumstances sometimes work against us, we are in sympathy, and I knew it was likely to be something special. She told me. It was. "This is the life!" I assured her. She left to get on with it, pleased at having managed the beast.

A simple repast, really: just a little block of local *pâté de foie gras truffée,* a green salad with walnut oil dressing, a selection of cheeses, and to finish, chilled lemon sorbet: she'd put a splosh of Calvados in mine. We usually have sweet Monbazillac with rich *pâté,* but I'd run out, so we had a Gewürztraminer instead—not so good, but okay for a change. After which, we went our separate ways. An advantage of our rambling old farmhouse is that there are innumerable corners to escape to: I think holidays are hell if you can't avoid the herd and be unsocial when you feel like it. Claudine and the girls went off to the pool, and I took the local paper—the *Sud Ouest*—and set up a deck chair at the far end of the terrace where there's a good view down the valley. I had a blue umbrella for shade, a straw hat to tip over my eyes, and one of the small cigars I sometimes use to impose a mood of relaxation.

There's not much in these local papers. Some Spanish strawberries had been ambushed—well, that's how it translated. I avoided some heavy stuff headed *Economie: mauvais indices*— we get enough of that at home.

I began to fold up the paper. It was at that moment that my eye caught a two-column advertisement with a box around it, and a name I knew. Translated, it said:

> CATHERINE ANNE GORDON
> Persons having any information as to the where-abouts of Mlle. Catherine Anne GORDON, last seen on the evening of Saturday 31 July at CUBZAC, are urgently requested to address themselves to Maître Robert LEFARGE, *notaire* at . . .

I didn't need to look at the address—I already knew it: Maître Lefarge was our *notaire.* I also knew Cubzac, which was our nearest village of any size, and had been there with Claudine and the girls on Saturday 31 July because it was the evening of the annual fête, a big affair beginning with a parade of schoolgirl majorettes, followed by fireworks at the old bridge, fairground sideshows, and dancing. I didn't know Catherine Anne Gordon or anything about her, except that she sounded Scottish and had frantic parents trying everything they could think of to trace her. They'd have to be frantic to employ Maître Lefarge—a fussy, self-important little lawyer whose ability to bungle the simplest of transactions was legendary.

Well well. A missing mademoiselle. If that ever happened to me, I'd . . . I'd . . . well, what would I do? Something . . . or other.

I let the paper slide to the ground, pulled the straw hat further over my eyes, and went to sleep.

I was woken by a rending noise. It sounded as though a maniac was on the loose with a chain saw.

Sitting up, I stared down the valley to see if I could locate the source of the disturbance. On the track which connects us to our neighbor's farm half a mile away, I could see a helmeted figure on a small motorbike. Small, but very noisy: the two things seem to be related. It was headed up the valley toward us, bucking and skidding dangerously on the flinty surface, going much too fast. Urgent dispatches? No—just our neighbor's son coming to show off his new pride and joy, doubtless. I got up, stretched to ease the creases which the deck chair had impressed upon me, and went to the poolside to alert the girls.

I needn't have bothered. They were already fully alerted, giggling and buckling bikini straps. Their nest at the far end of the pool was strewn with magazines and bottles of lotion; they rose from it like birds disturbed by a hunter.

"I was going to warn you that François is on his way here," I said, "but I see I needn't have bothered."

"What does he want?" hissed Sylvie, making faces at Nichole, who was emitting suppressed shrieks like a boiler about to burst. They huddled together, clutching towels, playing at panic. Were these the same razor-tongued creatures who could cut me down to size whenever they felt like it?

I wasn't going to let them off. "Come to see you, I expect. And to show off the new bike. You'd better go and bring him in. Perhaps he'd like a swim."

Claudine rose from the sidelines. "I will bring some lemonade," she said. "Go on, Sylvie! You too, Nichole. *Allez-y!*"

"You go, maman," Sylvie said, drooping.

"Don't be ridiculous. *Allez!*"

They left together, towels around their shoulders, sunglasses stuck on the tops of their heads. I looked at Claudine. We could hear the girls giggling and twittering all the way across the courtyard—in French because they go to the Lycée in London and it's as natural to them as English.

"*Ça commence,*" Claudine said. Yes. Sylvie now, and then— in a couple of years or so—Nichole would follow. The end of childhood. I don't know why, but I hadn't been prepared for it. Known, but not felt.

"*Mon pauvre homme,*" Claudine said, putting her hand on my shoulder. Was it that obvious? Anyway, some years yet before I became a grandfather.

"I'll come with you to the kitchen," I said.

Passing through the hall, we saw the girls silhouetted by the open front door: beyond, astride his motorbike, helmet casually hooked on one arm, was the dark, youthfully muscular figure of François, right hand still on the twist grip of the throttle, zoom, zoom. The scene was as still as a painting: nobody moved or spoke. Claudine waved and went on to the kitchen; I advanced to the door. He cut the engine.

"*Bonjour,* François."

He took his hand from the throttle, shook mine. "*Bonjour.*" He had a lot of dark hair, a grave expression, and an aura of masculinity much stronger than his sixteen years. No spots. He put his hand back on the throttle.

"Lemonade in a moment," I said, but there was too much silence going on for anybody to hear me. I left them to it.

By the time the lemonade was ready, the kids had managed to get themselves to the poolside. I put the tray down, and François handed each of the girls a glass with formal politeness. He spoke then, but got only the most monosyllabic response. Hoping they'd come to life if I left, I went back to the kitchen to collect Claudine, and we settled ourselves at the far end of the terrace where I'd been reading the newspaper, safely out of range of these teenage trials.

The paper was still on the ground next to my chair. I picked it up.

"Maître Lefarge is in the news," I said, pointing to the notice. Claudine glanced at it, then took the paper from me and read it a second time, carefully.

"What can have happened?" she said, frowning.

"To the girl? Sounds as if she went missing at the fête. It doesn't say how old she was or give any description: could be any age from a tiny tot to a maiden aunt. Typical of Lefarge to leave out vital information. But somehow, I've got the feeling she's about Sylvie's age—girls in their teens are strange creatures, unknown quantities, full of surprises, aren't they. Like ours over there. Or perhaps I think that because I'm still stunned by the spectacle of Sylvie lost for words."

"I never think," Claudine said, "of Cubzac *en fête* as dangerous. Some silly boys drink too much, perhaps, and fight with each other. But for the girls, no. Never."

It was true. Cubzac is a sleepy little place: a straggle of houses, a few indifferent shops for necessities, a little café, and a large church, all clustered around the old stone bridge over the wide but shallow, weedy river. The annual fête is the one big event of the year, heralded for weeks in advance by banners strung across the road. CUBZAC EN FÊTE!!! they shout in huge, shaky lettering, as if the whole performance hadn't taken place the year before, and the year before that, back into prehistory, probably. We went for the fireworks, which the French are specially good at, but there was never anything new. No—not true: this year there'd been—

"Perhaps she joined the drum majorettes and went off to see the world," I said. "You know—like the Foreign Legion."

Claudine was still frowning.

"You really take this seriously," I said, "don't you."

"But of course! A young girl missing—that is serious!"

"Well yes, darling—but there's probably some quite harmless explanation. A misunderstanding about where to meet. Or she went off with a boyfriend, and he crashed the bike. Something like that. In hospital with concussion, that's my bet."

"That is *harmless*?"

"Well, it's quite normal, not criminal—that's what I mean. An accident, that's all."

"But William—today is Thursday, and she has been missing since last Saturday—*five days ago* . . ."

"She may have turned up by now. We only know she was still missing when that notice was sent in to the *Sud Ouest,* say two days ago."

"All right—missing for three days, then. That is not much better than five, *hein*?"

"True. It would have to be quite a bad accident to put her in hospital, out cold, for three days."

"And the boy's parents—they would know. They would tell the girl's parents."

"If they knew who she was, and where to find them. But if not, they've probably seen this notice and contacted Lefarge . . . look, darling, this is all guesswork, and fairly pointless. I just wanted to show that it could easily be an accident, nothing more. There's no reason to suppose that our daughters are at risk from a lurking sex maniac."

"Lurking?"

"Hanging about, you know—*un homme furtif*, whatever. Let's drop it, shall we, and have some tea? I wish I'd never shown you the thing; you've got too lively an imagination."

"And two young girls," Claudine said severely.

I sighed. Once she gets an idea into her head . . . "Tell you what I'll do," I said. "First thing tomorrow, I'll drop in on Lefarge, and see what it's all about. Almost certainly this girl will have turned up. Then you'll be able to relax again—okay?"

Claudine nodded. "Thank you, *chéri,*" she said. "I would like that."

Well, I had nothing better to do. And to be honest, I was quite intrigued myself. "Right," I said. "Meanwhile, shall we see what scenes of depravity are taking place around the pool? Young François seems to me to have most of what it takes to sweep a girl off her feet, and we'll have to . . ."

"Yes," Claudine said, "yes. He *has* grown up, hasn't he."

She spoke in a reflective tone. I looked at her sharply. She looked back at me, smiling slightly—all right, but in such a way . . .

"Good God!" I said.

"*Chéri?*" she said innocently.

"Nothing. Time for tea."

FRIDAY

"*BONJOUR, MAÎTRE.*"

"*Ah, M'sieu Warnair! Comment allez-vous?*"

The lawyer's office was not the town house favored by English country solicitors, but a modern bungalow on the outer fringe of St. Pierre de Chignac, the overgrown village where we pay our rates and do our shopping. I had arrived at half past nine, early enough, I hoped, to catch Lefarge before he built himself in for the day behind piles of documents.

There was no one else in the bleak little waiting room, and I wasn't kept more than the fifteen-minute minimum that Lefarge's dignity demanded, before being permitted to pass into the presence. I sat, now, squashed into a small leather reproduction antique chair, looking across the broad desk at Lefarge, who sat impressively in a much larger one. Behind him was a wall of books. To my cynical eye, they'd always seemed suspiciously new and unused—bought by the yard, I suspected, to intimidate his peasant clients and justify his outrageous fees. Lefarge was the sort of lawyer who, first, could transfer the wrong parcel of land to the wrong client, and, second, could try to charge everybody all over again for putting right his own mistake. I know: it happened to me.

Civilities concluded, I explained that I'd come in response to his advertisement. Had the girl turned up?

Malheureusement, Lefarge said, she had not. It was an affair of the most distressing kind. The unfortunate parents . . . but perhaps I had information that would be of assistance?

Perhaps, I said. But would he describe the girl—how old was she?

For answer, Lefarge opened a drawer of his desk, and produced a photograph. He passed it across the desk.

A holiday snapshot, no more, but it was clear enough. It seemed that my guess about the girl's age had been roughly correct. She was standing by a car, smiling into the camera, blond hair blowing clear of a small-featured, still childish face. She wore a loose white pullover and tight blue jeans. The smile was enigmatic. There were mountains in the background.

Seventeen?

Yes, said Lefarge, she is seventeen; the only daughter of an English family. The father is a doctor.

Of medicine?

Un médecin, oui—c'est ça.

And she disappeared at the Cubzac fête?

Lefarge gave me an outline. The family had been on holiday in Spain, where they had a *maison secondaire.* It was their custom to drive there, spending some time in France on the way out and on the way back. This time, they had come back through the Dordogne, booked for two nights in Périgueux at the Hôtel du Périgord, and on the second evening, a Saturday, had driven out to the fête at Cubzac, to see the fireworks. The village was very crowded with spectators, and so it was arranged that, if they became separated, they would meet at their car at a certain hour.

But the girl didn't turn up?

Exactly. The parents waited for some time. Then the doctor went to search for his daughter—the crowd had by then thinned out, as many people went home when the fireworks were over. But he could find no trace of her. After waiting another hour, they returned to the hotel. But *mademoiselle* was not there, either.

So they went to the police?

Naturally! But, alas, police researches failed to produce her. They tried the hospitals?

But of course! As you would expect. And a description has been circulated to every *gendarmerie* in the *Département*. Result—zero.

I was silent, thinking it over. No motorbike accident, then. More of a mystery than I'd supposed.

So, they came to me, Lefarge said importantly. A recommendation, I believe . . .

I thought: not such a big deal—I'd never heard of a *notaire* in Cubzac itself, so Lefarge was the nearest. But it had been a sensible move to appoint a local agent to handle the affair—just bad luck that they were landed with Lefarge.

Has anyone else replied to the advertisement? I asked.

Apart from yourself, M'sieu Warnair, no. I regret that there is no further information on the affair. But now, perhaps you have something to tell me?

Not exactly, no.

But . . . then this is a consultation on your own account? You wish for advice? Lefarge said, leaning forward. Oh yes—he could be sharp enough when he smelled an opportunity for charging fees. But I was forewarned, and had prepared a blocking move. No no, I said, absolutely not.

Then . . . ?

My wife and I were discussing your notice in the *Sud Ouest* and decided that I should call on you to see if we could be of assistance. We, too, were at the Cubzac fête, with our two young daughters. One of us may, perhaps, have seen something that would assist the inquiry, without perhaps realizing the significance of what we saw.

Ah. Lefarge leaned back in his chair. Most kind, he murmured. There was a pause while he sifted the situation for economic advantage. Then he brightened.

His clients, he said, had not yet left the district. They would, without doubt, be most interested to meet you, M'sieu Warnair—and Madame Warnair—to discuss the affair. Also grateful, he added.

Oh yes, I thought, oh yes. Gratitude equals money.

I will be pleased to arrange such a meeting, Lefarge said. At your house, perhaps? At your convenience, of course.

Well, I thought, well. I suppose it was all leading up to this. And it isn't a bad idea—I can't say it is, even if Lefarge is going to make his percentage on it.

Yes, I said, we would be glad to meet your clients, my wife and I. But Maître Lefarge . . .

M'sieu?

Please be sure not to raise their hopes. The meeting may not, probably will not, advance the inquiry at all. It may well be quite useless, except, perhaps, that we may offer a little comfort. You understand?

Entendu, M'sieu Warnair. I understand perfectly, and you are of course quite right—it will no doubt be a great comfort to Doctor and Madame Gordon to discuss this tragic affair in their own language with compatriots. When would a meeting be convenient?

The sooner the better, I said. This afternoon would be fine. There's no telephone at my house, but if you will invite them just to turn up any time this afternoon, or this evening, we'll be there.

Bon! Alors, je vous remercie mille fois . . . Lefarge rose, rubbing his hands.

The pleasure is all mine, I said. *Au 'voir, Maître.*

There's a David Hockney painting which exactly captures the luminous blue of swimming pool water, shot through with shimmering reflections like silver eels, sunlight caught in the rippled surface. I floated weightlessly on an air bed, watching more silver eels writhing on the bottom of the pool, all around the black rectangular shadow of my raft. On my back, the sun was about as hot as I'd known it at La Sauvegarde. We're about fifty miles inland from Bordeaux, where Claudine's parents live: they're wine trade people—that's how I met her—with old-established offices on the prestigious Quai des Chartrons. Fifty miles is the ideal arm's length for in-laws: we get on very well, but Claudine's mother can't understand why we choose to spend our holidays in a tumbledown old farmhouse, miles from the shops, and surrounded by dirty and dangerous woods and fields where animals do disgusting things in full view of the terrace.

"What's the time?" I called.

"What?" Sylvie's voice, from the sunbathing nest.

"Time!"

"Half past three."

"Thanks."

The Gordons might be here soon, if Lefarge managed to tell them the right address. Claudine had seemed quite pleased about that, though she could hardly not be, as she'd been the one who wanted to follow this thing up. Tomato salad with garlic bread for lunch, with ten degree *vin ordinaire*—then I'd finished up the lemon sorbet. That's all you need, really, in this hot weather. And for this idle life . . .

Was that a car? Sounds echo so much in this valley; you can't be sure where they're coming from. Yes, surely it *is* a car . . .

"William!" Claudine calling from the house.

"Okay!—I'm coming."

I rolled off the air bed and swam to the steps. Oops—no clothes on. Where's my towel? Quick rub and wrap, then into the hut. Emerge decently clad in shorts, shirt, and espadrilles. Voices in the courtyard—the Gordons already?

Passing through the tall gateway which closes off the pool area, I saw Claudine coming to fetch me. "They're here," she said needlessly. I knew how she felt—strangers, an event which called for a united reception. "I'm with you, darling. Let's sit on the terrace—I'll bring a couple of extra chairs."

I crossed the courtyard to greet the couple who stood there. Dr. Gordon stepped forward, his hand held out. "Alex Gordon," he said. "Hope we've come at a convenient time—my

French isn't up to much, but I understood from our lawyer that any time this afternoon would suit you."

"He got it right for once," I said. "This is fine—glad you could come."

"Ah," Gordon said, "like that, is it? I wasn't much impressed with him, but we had to get a move on—no time to ask around. You know him, then?"

"I shouldn't really have said that. We use him ourselves, and he's straight, which is something. But he's not much more than a pen pusher—you have to tell him exactly what you want done and make sure he understands, or you can find yourself with a large bill for time wasted," I said.

"Mr. Warner, you're a godsend!" Gordon had a quick, nervous smile. He was a lively man of medium height, mid-forties, athletic build, healthily tanned, his movements energetic and precise. Although little of his dark hair was left, he was one of those men whom baldness suits and seems a natural state. "This is Sheila," he said, and then, to her: "We're in luck, darling—only been here two minutes and already Mr. Warner is giving us just what we need: I had doubts about Lefarge, remember?"

I took her hand, which was as limp as her husband's had been firm. Sheila Gordon was, or had been, a very pretty woman—that was obvious. But now her prettiness hung by a thread: faint marks that would soon become permanent lines were showing around her eyes and mouth, and her blond hair looked faded. She smiled at me, but it seemed an effort, and her eyes quickly slid away as I smiled back. But of course, the strain of these last few days must have been very hard to bear.

"We're very grateful to you, Mr. Warner," she said, taking her husband's cue.

"Please!" I said. "I do hope Lefarge gave you my message. I haven't anything particular to tell you, and I didn't want you to drive up here with high hopes and be disappointed. All I suggested was that it might help if we were to meet and compare notes, as we—Claudine and I and our two girls—were all at the Cubzac fête and just might have noticed something useful. That's all. And please call me William. Shall we sit on the terrace, over there?"

"Would you like tea, perhaps?" Claudine asked. "Or fruit juice?"

"I think, tea—if it's not too much trouble," Sheila Gordon said. "Thank you . . ." She looked to her husband for help.

"Claudine," he supplied.

"Of course," she said. "I'm sorry . . ."

"Let's sit," I said. "You go ahead, Sheila, and I'll bring two more chairs."

Claudine led her away, and Dr. Gordon followed me into the barn, where we keep spare chairs, and took one from me. I said:

"I'm very sorry about what's happened. With a house here, and a French wife, I feel kind of responsible—it's my patch, as it were."

He stopped and turned, the chair gripped easily in brown hands, and gave me his quick, nervous smile. "That's nonsense, of course. We're entirely to blame—I should have made sure we didn't get separated. It was during the fireworks—there was a real crowd down by the bridge, and a lot of people were dodging about, looking for a better place to watch from. One moment we were all together, the next . . . Cathy had gone. Of course, I just thought she'd turn up again when the fireworks were over."

"I'd have thought the same. In fact, we must have been close at the time—were you near the little wharflike cobbled lane that leads down to the weir?"

"We were on it—yes."

"Well, we must get my girls in on this—they might have seen your daughter. Did you bring a photograph?"

"I've brought a pack of holiday snaps," Gordon said.

"Good. Well, let's have some tea, and then get down to it, if you'd like to. You've heard nothing since I saw Lefarge this morning?"

"Nothing at all."

I led the way out of the barn. "The worst I've ever known to happen at any of these village fêtes is that some of the lads have too much to drink and make a nuisance of themselves—nothing more. Rural France is still one of the safest, most civilized parts of the world, I believe."

"So I thought," Gordon said, "so I thought." We went down the steps to the terrace, and he stopped to take in the view. "Beautiful spot!" he said, "beautiful. Are those your cows?"

"No. It's our field, but we let our farmer neighbor use it in return for keeping an eye on the house—it means we've got animals to look at, and we don't have to worry about upkeep."

He nodded. "I've got a little place in Spain," he said. "Not like this—it's a village house in a place about fifty miles south of Barcelona. Had it for years: it's small, but it's in a group with a communal bar, swimming pool, all that. Ten-minute walk to the beach. I suppose, as you've got this, you never go down to Spain."

"As a matter of fact, I do: I've an agent in Barcelona and, as it's only a day's drive from here, I quite often take a break from holiday and drop in on him, to see what's new."

"An agent?"

"I'm a wine merchant. I operate from Kensington Church Street: mostly French wines, but there's some good stuff coming out of Spain these days, and Alastair—my agent—tells me where to find it."

"It sounds," Gordon said, "like the ideal existence. Lucky chap!"

"Oh, it's a lot less ideal than it sounds. I spend most of my life at a desk, sifting through price lists and invoices."

"Don't believe a word of it," he said, flashing me his smile. "In any case, I don't want my illusions shattered. Some people have got to have the ideal existence, or there's nothing for the rest of us to look forward to."

"Yours can't be bad, surely," I said. "At least you must feel a lot more useful to your fellow man than I do—I'm promoting cirrhosis of the liver, but you're curing it. You're a GP, I suppose?"

"A surgeon, actually," he said. "Consultant at Guildford General."

"My apologies," I said. "Lefarge described you as *Dr.* Gordon, so I assumed . . ."

"I couldn't begin to explain in French why surgeons in the UK give up being Doctor and revert to Mister," he said, "even if I could in English. Here comes your wife with the tea. And speaking of wives—just a word about Sheila . . ."

"Yes?"

"She's taking this very hard indeed, and it might be best if we left her with your wife after tea, while we went off to show your girls the photographs of Cathy. If that would be all right with you?"

"Of course. Claudine will look after her—she's very sympathetic."

"You understand, then. I'm most grateful, William."

"No problem, Alex."

We picked up our chairs again and went to join the ladies at the table.

But in the event, it was Sheila who put an end to the small talk around the tea table by asking me where we'd been, and what we'd done, the evening of the Cubzac fête. During the discussion that followed, I ran the whole of that evening through my mind, looking for clues to the girl's disappearance. Playing detective, if you like—well, the professionals hadn't so far been much help.

We'd arrived at about half past eight and, after parking the car just outside the village so as to be sure of getting away easily after the fireworks, had strolled about, watching the last of the stalls and sideshows being set up. As dusk began to fall, we installed ourselves at a table outside a little café beside the

church, where a graveled area had been roped off as a shooting
gallery. The targets were pinned up on boards against the end
of the ancient stone church, and live ammunition was being
used, not just air rifles. Try that in England, I remarked to
Claudine, and the vicar would have a fit!—real bullets!—a
single piece of rope to stop passersby from wandering in front
of the targets and getting riddled!—look, there's a dog going
through and they're not even bothering to stop shooting! Really!—you Frogs are completely mad where firearms are concerned! Claudine shrugged. Such a fuss, she said, and anyway,
now they are putting up lights to warn people. Oh yes, I said,
a couple of rusty old bicycle lamps—terrific! Anyway, we
finished our drinks and moved on. Just around the corner was
a stall where live ducks were crowded into a small pen under
the glare of a spotlight: if you could throw a plastic ring over
the neck of one, it was yours. The ducks were rushing to and
fro in a panic. Back home, I started to say, the NSPCA . . . No
I'd be wasting my breath, she wasn't interested. We passed on
to another booth where I shot Ping-Pong balls off air jets and
won a black plastic spider which I gave to Nichole, who
shrieked and dropped it. I think it was just after that when we
heard martial music approaching down the lane behind the
church, and followed the crowd to find a vantage point.

It was almost dark, and the first thing we saw was a dark blue
Transit van with booming loudspeakers mounted on top, and
silver stars painted all over it. Space had been left on the sides
for silver lettering—LES FAUVETTES. A few yards behind, in
the wake of the loudspeaker van, was the head of a column
of baton-twirling high-stepping majorettes, keeping strictly
to the beat of the martial music, their faces rigid with self-
consciousness. Cries of encouragement came from friends and
relations in the crowd. The girls wore blue tunics with short
flared skirts, white Stetsons, and fringed white cowboy boots.
Their batons had lights at each end which made dazzling circles in the dark. They passed us in descending order of size,

from girls old enough to have hoarse-voiced admirers among
the spectators, down to tots of six or so. *"Adorable!"* breathed
the crowd as the little creatures stamped and twirled and occasionally broke ranks to run and catch up. *"Adorable!"* breathed
Claudine, clutching my arm. I didn't feel it, myself, but then
I've got a thing about the American influence spoiling the
essential Frenchness of France.

But we all enjoyed the fireworks. We filed past the glare of
the booths and down a dark alley beside the river, from which
there was a good view of the old bridge. There, we stood
shoulder to shoulder with all of Cubzac and several hundred
tourists and local visitors to see the rockets soar and burst, the
mortars send up their star shells, the catherine wheels whiz into
disks of golden fire, all reflected in the wide black water. As
a finale, a procession of canoes appeared, carrying flares to
weave a cat's cradle of flame as they swung in and out of the
bridge's five arches. Everyone cheered and clapped. Then the
flares went out, the streetlights came on again, and most people, including us, went home.

Not without dissent, though. Sylvie announced that she and
Nichole were just going over the bridge to the disco for a few
minutes and would meet us at the café afterward. It was a
try-on, of course.

"Ah non! Absolument pas!" Claudine told her.

"But maman . . ."

"Je t'ai dit—non!"

They didn't press it, knowing perfectly well that they hadn't
a hope of persuading us. Claudine and I were united in our
opposition to the disco, which was located in a sectional tin
shed set up for the occasion on a flat piece of ground on the
far side of the river, strung about with colored lights, almost
splitting with the weight of decibels being released inside, and
under the control of a couple of swarthy characters with gold
teeth and sideburns like gorse bushes. Girls were invited in free
of charge, but once in, only a determined snatch squad of

parents would have been able to get them out again. Dancing in the village square, in the open—that we allowed and sometimes took part in, but the tin shed was forbidden territory. So, that was it; we went home and were in bed by eleven.

In the discussion around the tea table, I hadn't liked to make too much of the disco shed: it seemed better to talk to Alex about it later, without Sheila being there. But we all seemed to focus on it, and Alex said:

"Of course, I went in there."

"You did?"

"Yes. I tried to ask the chap on the door—he looked like a gypsy—if an English girl had gone in. He either couldn't or wouldn't understand, so I pushed past and went in. He didn't try to stop me."

"Can't be the first time he's had parents pushing in. What was it like?"

"I went right through the place—it was all flashing lights and a really hellish din going on, but I can say definitely that Cathy wasn't there."

"What time was that?"

"Well, we waited in the car for twenty minutes before I went to look for her. The disco was the last place I went to, so it must have been about forty minutes after the fireworks finished."

"They were due to start at ten, and were a few minutes late, say five past. They lasted, I'd say, a quarter of an hour, including the canoe procession. Twenty past ten. You got back to the car when?"

"Call it half past."

"Half past ten. Twenty minutes' wait, that's ten to eleven. Another twenty minutes' search, that would make it ten past eleven that you arrived at the disco shed."

Alex nodded. He said, "We keep coming back to that. Do you think I ought to concentrate on it?"

"I think it ought to be checked out again," I said. "That

wouldn't be too difficult—that disco is a regular feature at most of the fêtes around here. But if your daughter did go there, the character on the door would have known—there's no other way in or out, I happen to know that. It's as tight as a fortress, to stop the boys getting in without paying."

"I could ask if the police have already checked," Alex said.

"I think you should," I said. "What do you think, Claudine?"

"I think perhaps it is not so bad as it looks, the disco," she said with a sideways glance at Sheila. "I think, when Sylvie is a little older, and a boy wants to take her, I will let her go."

"Yes," I said, "but all the same . . . I think it's got to be checked out, don't you agree?"

"I think," Sheila said abruptly. "I think . . ." Her voice died. We all tried not to look at her. "I think," she said, "that we must . . . must . . . try everything." She had struggled to get the words out, and now tears were streaming down her cheeks. "I'm sorry," she sobbed, "so stupid . . ."

"Oh my dear!" Claudine said, jumping up and going around behind Sheila's chair. "Come with me," she said gently, "come inside. I have some tissues . . . come!"

She persuaded Sheila out of her chair, and led her away.

"I'm afraid you were right," I said to Alex.

"I suppose I should have come by myself," he said, "but I didn't want to leave her on her own at the hotel." We'd both jumped up ineffectively when Claudine started to lead Sheila off, and now stood watching as the pair of them went up the steps into the house. "Perhaps this would be a good time to talk to the girls?" I suggested.

"Might as well. Yes, thanks."

We walked together up the steps to the courtyard, and across to the pool gate.

"Get some clothes on, girls," I called. "We want to talk to you."

From the open gate I saw them stirring. I waited. Beside me, Alex glanced through the gate, and then looked aside. He started to say something, stopped himself, and then began again:

"While we're waiting . . . no, it's a silly question."

"What?"

"It doesn't matter." Something in his voice made me look up. His face wore a curious air of defiance. What was this all about, all of a sudden? "Go on, ask me!" I said, intrigued.

"Well, I was just going to say, do you let them go topless on the beach?"

It wasn't the sort of question I'd expected, and I had to suppress a laugh: he sounded so serious. "What beach?"

"Well, wherever you go."

"Oh, I see. *Let* them? I don't think it would occur to me to stop them, if it's that sort of beach."

"Oh," he said. "As simple as that."

"You don't approve?" I said, slightly nettled.

"It may sound old-fashioned, but I'm afraid I don't. For one's own daughter, at least. On *display*, practically." The emotion was more obvious now.

Maybe, I thought, he's got some kind of hang-up or obsession. Well, it was nothing to do with me. "I know what you mean," I said, "but after the first shock and surreptitious goggle from behind the dark glasses, you get used to it, don't you find? Then it seems unnatural to see girls wearing little strips of cloth across their chests, I think."

Alex shrugged, made a face, but said nothing. Evidently he didn't agree. I wondered what his daughter was like, who had inspired this strength of feeling in him. It seemed to go beyond the normal fatherly possessiveness over a pretty daughter. "Well," I said, "I think my girls are decent now. We can go in."

"I'm sorry," he said. "I didn't mean to sound critical. Forget it, please."

"It's already forgotten," I said lightly, though it wasn't. Maybe I'd be able to make sense of it later. We went through the gate into the pool compound, and I introduced Alex. The four of us sat on the long bench outside the changing room. I explained the situation, and Alex produced the photographs. He passed them around, and for the second time, I tried to guess what she was like, this girl with the long fair hair and enigmatic smile. Sheila was in some of the pictures: even in those happier times before her daughter's disappearance, she had the look of a woman who was enduring rather than enjoying life; she seemed to find it difficult to smile for the camera, and had often been caught with her face half turned away, or with a hand shielding her eyes. But mostly the pictures were of the girl, Cathy, on her own, posed against holiday backdrops of Spanish village, harbor, beach, and of course the mountains I'd seen already.

"Your only child?" I asked, to make sure Lefarge had got it right.

"Yes," Alex said.

"And she's seventeen?"

"Yes."

"I suppose, then . . ." I was going to say that these pictures might be of the last family holiday, but stopped myself just in time. Choosing words more carefully, I said: "I suppose she's getting to the age when she'll be going off on holiday with friends?"

Alex hunched his shoulders, dropped them again. "Perhaps," he said, shuffling the little pile of pictures on his lap.

"You think you'll be glad to get them off your hands, but when the time comes . . ." I said. Sylvie and Nichole made loud sobbing noises. I ignored them.

"Something like that," Alex said. He wasn't being forthcoming—perhaps I was being flat-footed. But I was trying to work around to a direct question—how had he got on with his daughter? It was crucial, obviously. If he wanted me to help, I had to know that.

"I suppose you've had the usual problems," I said. "I don't know whether they're better or worse with an only child."

"Problems?" Alex said, shooting me a quick glance. "Well yes, of course. As you say, the usual ones."

"But no real rows? Nothing that might make her want to take off? I only ask because—"

"We were very close," he said shortly, "very close."

"Of course. Well, let's see about these pictures."

The girls had been passing them back and forth, and commenting in whispers, gasps, and bursts of suppressed laughter: even under the shadow of the guillotine, they'd find something to giggle at, and it was pointless to remonstrate. "Well?" I asked severely.

Sylvie, spokesperson, said:

"We think perhaps, yes . . ."

"Yes? You recognize her?"

"We think so, Papa."

"Come on, then! Where do you think you saw her?"

"By the bridge. After the fireworks, when we were walking back to the car."

Not so surprising, I thought—they were of the age to notice other girls, especially their clothes. But how sure were they?

"Be careful about this," I warned them. "Now—what was she wearing, the girl you saw?"

Sylvie riffled through the snapshots, selected one. She held it out to me. It was the one I'd been shown at Lefarge's office, with the backdrop of mountains, the girl in loose white pullover and tight blue jeans. "Like this," Sylvie said.

Could be coincidence, of course. But—

"That is what she was wearing at the fête," Alex said, leaning past me to look at Sylvie. She gazed back at him, her face serious, her clowning forgotten for the moment. "That's why I gave Lefarge that picture," Alex added. "It's the only one with her in that pullover—it was quite nippy up there."

"Crossing the Pyrenees?" I asked.

"Yes. On the way home."

I turned to Sylvie. "Was she coming off the bridge?"

"No, Papa. Going the other way, almost the only one."

Everyone else was on the way home. But Cathy Gordon wasn't—she was going *on* to the bridge, away from where her parents' car was parked. Had she got lost, taken the wrong turning in confusion? But the disco shed was over there . . . I looked at Alex. Of course he knew that—he'd been there. I said:

"Was she alone?"

"I think so."

"Anything else you can remember?"

"I don't think so. We noticed her because, you know, you *would* . . ."

A girl that stood out in a crowd. Heading . . . where?

"I'm most grateful to you, Sylvie, and Nichole," Alex said, leaning forward again. It must take something, I thought, to smile as he was doing at such a moment.

"I'm sorry," Sylvie said to him. Her eyes were big with sympathy, I noticed. Odd how they save it for strangers.

Alex was subdued by what the girls had told us. We'd left them to get back to sun-worship, and now sat at the terrace table, in silence. I felt I'd said enough, if not too much, already, and that I ought to take a back seat now: I sat, slumped in the cane chair, watching one of our dapper little lizards sunning himself on the top of the terrace wall. Diamond-shaped head tilted to watch me, he lowered himself onto his belly, and raised each long-fingered hand in turn, vibrating it to catch the cool evening air that was beginning to drift down the valley.

After a few minutes, I heard voices and footsteps on the gravel path behind me, and turned to see Claudine approaching, arm in arm with Sheila. She has a talent for girlfriends, and Sheila was clearly under the spell. Alex and I got up and saw them into chairs, and then, when we were all seated, Alex cleared his throat and gave a matter-of-fact résumé of what Sylvie had said.

Sheila took it well. I suppose almost any news is better than being kept in suspense. "What happens next?" she asked, of nobody in particular.

"William thinks I should chase up the police, and of course that must be right," Alex said.

There was a short silence before Sheila said:

"Can you manage that, darling?"

"Do you mean—is my French up to it?" Alex said. "Well, I've managed so far."

"I suppose so," Sheila said doubtfully. I thought: she doesn't seem to have much confidence in him. *Why?*

"William will be glad to do it," Claudine suddenly announced. *"N'est ce pas, chéri?"*

Oh. The fact was, I didn't know how far I wanted to get involved in the Gordons' problems, especially if it meant more waiting around at lawyers' offices and in police stations. But Claudine wasn't giving me any choice.

"Of course, if you'd like me to," I said.

"No, really—I'm sure I can manage," Alex said.

"It's not just his French, but his time: he's already long overdue," Sheila said to me apologetically.

"Ah yes," I said, "the hospital."

"My registrar can cope for another day or two," Alex said.

"Please, Alex! If Mr. Warner really doesn't mind," Sheila pleaded. Alex merely glanced at her, didn't respond. I felt Claudine's foot nudge mine under the table.

"Do call me William," I said. "No, of course I don't mind."

Alex had a number of nervous mannerisms, a sign of bottled up energy. He was biting his lip. Then he made a face, converted it to a smile, and said:

"All right. I mean, it's very kind of you, and it would be a great help."

"It's his work, you see," Sheila put in. "He's got a very full list, and . . ." Her voice trailed away uncertainly.

"No need to explain," I said. "I can imagine." In fact, I couldn't imagine any job important enough to drag me back to England if I had a daughter missing in France, but that, of course, may explain why I'm a wine merchant and not a surgeon.

"Sheila exaggerates," Alex said.

"No," Sheila said, "it's true, Alex, you know it is."

"I'm not going to argue about it," he said sharply.

"I hope not," Sheila said, "especially as William's already said he'll—"

"All right, Sheila! I've agreed to it," Alex said. He made it sound as if he were doing her a favor. "But I'll be coming out again very soon," he added.

"We'll have to discuss when," Sheila said to me. "But if you'd see the police for us, I'd be most grateful, William."

"I'll do it tomorrow morning," I said. Claudine smiled approvingly. Sheila leaned across the table and clasped my hand gratefully. Alex merely nodded thanks.

After the Gordons had left, Claudine took my arm as we walked back through the hall to the courtyard. "I hope this turns out to be a good idea of yours," I told her.

"But William! You are not cross with me?"

"They're an odd couple," I said. "She wanted me to help, but I got the feeling that he wasn't so sure. Why not, do you suppose?"

"Oh, but they are both so worried," Claudine said. "And, you know, a man does not accept help easily. I think that is all."

"Well, I hope you're right."

I went for a last swim before changing for the evening. Sylvie and Nichole were leaving for the house, their arms full of leisure equipment.

"Has he gone?" Sylvie hissed.

"Yes, they've gone; there's no need to sound like a punctured python. What did you think of him?"

"Mmmm," Sylvie said. "Those eyes, Papa. That smile . . ."

"No, seriously."

"Papa—I just *told* you . . ."

I stared at her. "You can't mean it. He must be *my* age!"

She shrugged, and started off across the courtyard with her burden. Her voice floated back on the evening air:

"Some men have just, you know, *got it* . . ."

I could have asked what she meant, but it would have been a big mistake: they never tell you that. I plunged into the pool instead.

SATURDAY

SO THE NEXT MORNING I WAS BACK IN ST. PIERRE DE Chignac, ringing the bell of the *gendarmerie.* I had to ring twice before the door was opened. Without their hats, the police look much more like the rest of us—I've noticed that before—and I thought I recognized the brown eyes and large but neatly clipped mustache. There was recognition on his part, too.

My name is Warner, I said: you came to my house, La Sauvegarde, a couple of years ago. We had a burglary.

Ah yes, I remember, he said, opening the door wider. Come in. You have had another burglary?

No no, it's about another matter, I said. I would like to see, if possible, the inspector. I've come on behalf of the parents of the English girl who is missing.

Ah. You have information?

Yes.

Wait here, if you please. I will inform the inspector.

I sat on a hard plastic chair in the waiting area. There were notices on the walls—police raffles, announcements of football matches, lists of articles lost and stolen. But nothing about a missing English girl.

A movement caught my eye. Through the open door of an adjoining office, I saw a youth in jeans and leather jacket sprawled in a chair before a steel table on which stood a bulky, old-fashioned typewriter with a sheet of paper curling from the top. No one else was visible. The youth looked away, but I'd caught the expression on his face, the sullen stare of the under-world at bay. My friend with the mustache had been taking a statement, I decided, straight onto the old typewriter, until interrupted by my ring at the door. Wasn't he afraid the bandit would run for it? Then I noticed the handcuffs—yes, well, he'd have to take the table with him.

A door opened. I sat up, and then subsided again. Is it only in France that the police do their own housework? He was obviously a gendarme, this new arrival, in spite of his pale blue tracksuit: he worked his way into the room behind a mop, polishing the plastic-tiled floor. I lifted my legs so that he could pass the mop underneath. *"Merci!"* He chased the mop around the rest of the waiting area and then into the office, where he arrived at the bandit's chair. *"Allez-oop!"* he commanded. The bandit raised his legs and was mopped under. Then we were alone again. A wall clock said ten fifteen.

At ten twenty, the inner door opened a second time, and my friend with the mustache appeared and beckoned. The inspector would see me now.

I sat in the tiny office, and explained my mission. The inspector was politely sympathetic, but it took only a minute or two for me to realize that a Gallic shrug hovered behind his words. As far as he knew, there was, unfortunately, no news of any advance in the affair. A description had indeed been circulated: perhaps a poster would follow: that was not for him to decide but a matter for the people higher up. Certainly he would pass on the information I had given him: I could rest assured that the best use would be made of it. But of course, it was well known that the girl had been at the fête, that was not in question.

But, I said, the point is that my daughters saw the girl walking *away* from where her parents' car was parked. In the direction of the discotheque . . . that was significant, surely?

They would decide, the inspector said. I had his assurance that all necessary inquiries would be made. Everything neces-sary would be done.

The parents are very distressed, I said. It *is* necessary, is it not, to follow up this new information, however slight it may seem?

Your daughters are certain of this? he asked. That Mademoiselle Gordon was walking toward the bridge?

Yes yes, I said, as I told you, they are quite certain. They recognized her from a photograph in which she is wearing the same clothes that she wore at the fête—*but they did not know this when they picked out the photograph*. That's how we can be sure they are certain.

And the age of your daughters, you said, is . . . ?

Thirteen and fifteen.

Thirteen and fifteen. Yes.

I'm sure we can believe them. But even if they were mistaken, there can be no harm in questioning the owner of the discotheque, can there?

I will pass on what you say, *m'sieu*. Meanwhile, please assure your friends that everything necessary will be done to bring this unfortunate affair to a happy conclusion.

I drove home to report to Claudine.

"He kept saying that," I told her. "Everything *necessary* would be done . . . Of course, what he means is, if the girl doesn't turn up meanwhile. That's what they're hoping. Perhaps I ought to call on 'the people higher up,' but I think I'd just get the same treatment. Sympathy, but minimum action. They're probably overworked, of course, like police forces everywhere. And they probably think, though they wouldn't like to say so, that there are plenty of normal reasons for a seventeen-year-old girl to give her parents the slip. No crime's been committed, you see."

Claudine finished tossing salad, and licked oil from her fingers briskly. "A little more pepper," she said. I passed her the grinder, and she gave it three or four forceful turns over the salad bowl. Trouble was on the way, I could see that. "What else could I have done?" I asked.

"*La pauvre,*" she said, mainly to herself.

"Sheila? Yes, I'm sorry for her too, of course. But we don't know these Gordons, not really. They're probably okay, but things may not be quite what they seem on the surface, and it may be best to let the police handle it. She's certainly a bit of a wet blanket, and I'm not sure if . . ."

"William! *C'est pas gentil, ça! Mon Dieu!*"

"Oh come on, darling. I mean, of course I'm sorry for her, for them both, but be realistic! She's one of life's victims; you can see it a mile off. They can drag you down with them, people like that."

"I never," Claudine said, coming to stand over me where I sat at the kitchen table, "I never expect to hear this. You think she is a *blanket*—"

"A *wet* blanket, darling."

"—so you will not help her. *Je m'étonne!*"

"That's not quite what I said."

"No? You mean you *will* help her?"

I explained again, patiently, that it wasn't really our affair, and that I thought I'd now done all I could. Well, it wasn't, and I had.

Claudine didn't reply. I got up, and carried the lunch things out to the vine shelter, feeling aggrieved. This is what I got for galloping off to do her bidding, indulge her whims. The usual reward of chivalry—no sooner do you get back from one crusade laden with holy grails than you get packed off again in search of bigger and better ones. I finished laying the table and sat at it, scowling. I would be true to mine own self, in the future—then this sort of thing wouldn't happen. Claudine had really pushed me too far this time.

"William—" Here she was, at the table.

"What."

"I'm sorry, *chéri* . . ."

Oh no you don't! I know that one—the soft, sneaky way to get things done when he's refused to be commanded. It's useless, madam—I'm my own man again. Not even a repeat of last night's

*performance is going to budge me this time—you see, I know you
enjoyed it as much as I did. Ooh and aah you went—and you
meant it. So we negotiate on equal terms; I'm not to be bullied or
blackmailed . . .*

"You see, *chéri,* I 'ave promised her . . ."

*Even puts on more French accent when she's wheedling—knows
I like it . . .*

"What 'ave you promised, fatal *femme?*"

"That you will help, *chéri.*"

"Oh yes? But how far—to the ends of the earth? I've already
been twice to St. Pierre."

"No, listen, *chéri—*"

"I'm listening."

"Just to find out if Cathy went to the disco, if the police will
not."

"But they may, they said so."

"You told me what they said—if *necessary.* And by the time
they do it, it may be . . . *too late.*"

"Uh-huh."

"*Chéri!*"

"Stop saying that! And anyway, how would I go about it?
It's not so easy, you know."

"Ah! I knew you'd agree."

"I haven't. How?"

"I will explain," Claudine said, uncovering a dish which she
had placed between us. *Endives braised in butter! Oh my God
. . . how could I refuse her, now?*

"Really, you know, it should be very simple," she said.

It was as if there'd been a time warp, and the Cubzac fête was
happening all over again. We sipped our drinks in descending
darkness outside a café, wandered past brightly lit stalls to the
shooting booth, where I won, not a black plastic spider this
time, but a pink plastic doll with orange hair. Shortly afterward, we heard the martial music of the majorettes. And here

they came, Les Fauvettes, marching in strict time behind the loudspeaker van, lighted batons whirling in the dusky street, white boots stamping on the tarmac. But this time, the village we were in was called Ste. Eulalie. And we had the Gordons and young François with us.

It was Claudine's idea to bring François. As Sylvie was going to be there; no persuasion was necessary.

A mortar went off with a tremendous bang, and star shells shot into the night sky, exploding into silver constellations which lit our upturned faces with flashes like lightning. Then another, and another.

"You wouldn't notice, would you," I said.

"Notice?"

"What was going on around you."

"No."

I looked for François and the girls. All three were there, just where I'd last seen them. But they might just as well not have been.

Rockets were taking off now, several at once. Something touching about rockets—up they go with high hopes, a moment of glory, and then a little charred stick comes rattling down. A hand touched my elbow—I turned and saw Claudine with Sheila.

"Can you see the discotheque?" Claudine asked.

"Yes, over there, among the trees. You can see the colored lights."

"Ah yes. I hope it's the same one."

"Always is, according to François."

"Well, I hope he is right. When shall we go?"

"As soon as the fireworks have finished. Alex and I will go with François and the girls, and you bring Sheila. Okay?"

"*D'accord.*"

It was Sylvie's wish come true, and sooner than she or anybody else had expected. She looked around once, gave a slightly nervous smile, and then was towed by François through the doors into the glare and boom of this teenagers' paradise. Nichole, by my side, looked on enviously.

Was I a lunatic, sending my darling daughter into a place from which, exactly one week ago, someone else's daughter had vanished without trace? Well, of course, we didn't know that for certain. And Cathy Gordon, *if* she had gone in there, had been alone, without a sturdy chap like François to look after her. I couldn't see how Sylvie could come to harm.

I turned my attention to the doorkeeper. He was a dark and wild-looking gypsy in blue jeans and red-checked shirt, with a face so deeply lined that it could have been sculpted with a knife. A mass of black, glossy, curly hair hung over his forehead, and more of the same erupted along each cheek in tangled sideburns. Brilliant black eyes scanned each of his juvenile customers briefly but thoroughly as he took their money and let them pass.

"Well, Alex," I said, "there you are. I'll be right behind you."

"William!" Claudine said indignantly.

"I'm not sure my French is up to it," Alex said.

"Ah." It seemed that I was to be honored with the lead in this distinctly dodgy enterprise. "Well, if you'd rather I was spokesman . . . suppose we all approach in a block. That should help to get us some attention, don't you think?"

Alex reached into his jacket pocket, took out the photograph of Cathy, and handed it to me. We advanced on the doorkeeper, who seemed not to notice us.

"*Bonsoir!*" I said.

He paid no attention, but shifted some money from a greasy leather bag to the back pocket of his jeans.

"M'sieu!" I said loudly. He turned his head to glance at me. I held out the photograph, and began to explain. This was an English girl, missing since last Saturday, when she'd been seen walking toward his discotheque. These were the anxious parents, hoping for his kind assistance. Had he by any chance—

"*Comment?*"

I tried again, shouting against the background boom of rocking teenagers. If he could hear me, he wasn't admitting it.

This is important, I shouted. We must speak to you or to your partner.

He turned, and bellowed into the discotheque. There was an answering cry, and a foxy-faced youth appeared. The doorkeeper tossed the leather moneybag to him and gestured to us. "*Allez.*"

I walked beside him, saying how much we regretted the interruption of his work, but hoping he would understand the parents' anxiety, etcetera. He shrugged, and strode on. We reached a streetlight some thirty yards away from the disco shed: he stopped and held out his hand for the photograph. I passed it to him. He gave it a cursory glance. Did he recognize it?

"*Non,*" he said.

Claudine burst into impassioned French, imploring him to look more closely, think again, imagine what he would feel if his own daughter—

"*Non. Je ne l'ai pas vue. Jamais de ma vie.*"

He handed the photograph back to me and strode away. After a few steps he broke into a jog, and we stood there helplessly, watching him snatch the leather bag away from the foxy youth and take up his position at the door again.

"Well, that's that," I said. "I'm afraid he led us over here as the quickest way to clear us off his doorstep. If he did recognize Cathy, he isn't going to say so—he's only interested in keeping out of trouble."

"I'm afraid this was not a good idea," Claudine said. "I am sorry, everyone."

"Oh no," Sheila said, "oh no. Please don't say that."

"Well anyway," I said, "that's it. We might as well go back to the cars, and wait for the kids to finish bopping."

Half an hour later, after the Gordons had driven off, Claudine said:

"Here they are, *chéri.*"

I looked up, through the windscreen and saw the figures of François and Sylvie, hand in hand, silhouetted against the lights of the village. So it had gone well for them, then . . .

"There are three of them," Claudine said.

"Three?" I looked again. She was right. Behind the two familiar figures trailed a third, a stranger. Male, was all I could tell at this distance and against the light. But unmistakably *with* them—I could see heads turning as they chatted together.

I got out of the car and went to meet them, Claudine following. Yes, it was a youth of about François' age. We came face to face, and François waved a hand at him.

"*Robert,*" he said, "*mon copain.*"

"*Bonsoir m'sieu, madame,*" Robert said. We all shook hands.

"Robert's got something to tell you," Sylvie said dramatically.

"He has? About Cathy?"

"Yes! He saw her! And that's not all, he—"

"Hang on," I said. "Let's go and sit in the car, and he can tell us himself. After you, Robert."

SUNDAY

WE'D AGREED ON A WORKING BREAKFAST—COFFEE and croissants in the garden of the Hôtel du Périgord, where the Gordons were staying. It was a *jardin intérieur,* a little oasis of green at the back of the hotel; all around was the subdued hum of Périgueux waking up to a Sunday morning. We sat at a small white table under the shade of a blue-and-white Kronenbourg umbrella, watching goldfish drift lazily about the ornamental pond. A single waitress hurried in and out of the hotel with trays of coffeepots and silver dishes of fresh, crusty bread, her heels clicking busily on the crazy paving. Little was visible of the other breakfasters, mostly single businessmen, except for hands emerging from behind newspapers to grasp coffee cups. There was an almost religious silence, which forced us to mutter together like conspirators—which, in a way, we were.

François had been asked, while in the discotheque with Sylvie, to make what inquiries he could among his friends who might help trace Cathy. He'd been supplied with a copy of the snapshot to show around. We hadn't great hopes that he would come up with anything, as Alex himself had been into the disco shed the evening she disappeared and was sure she hadn't been there. But he'd come up with the goods, in the shape of his friend Robert, another farmer's son with an eye for the girls.

Robert's story was simple, but clear. He'd been at the Cubzac fête that previous Saturday, but his current girlfriend was away on holiday with her family, and he lacked a partner. He hadn't had much hope of finding a spare girl at the disco—they were usually heavily outnumbered by the boys—but had gone anyway, strolling along by himself and feeling blue. As he approached the disco, he saw a fair-haired girl standing on her own and a little to one side—waiting for someone, he thought. Yes—she was very like the girl in the snapshot: he noticed her for two reasons: one, she didn't look French, and two, she was very pretty. Personally, Robert said with the air of a connoisseur, he was attracted to foreign girls—they were . . . *different*. So, after a few moments of indecision, he approached her and invited her to come into the disco with him.

The girl smiled, but she shook her head. Robert asked if she was waiting for someone, but she didn't seem to understand. Oh yes, he thought she'd understood his invitation, he'd gestured to reinforce what he said. But she couldn't understand any more than that, and just kept shaking her head. So he tried her in English—the only foreign language he had learned at school. She smiled again, but all she said, Robert repeated, was No Sank Yew. Eventually he gave up, and walked back to the disco on his own.

Then, as he was buying his ticket, a car arrived. The girl seemed excited, and jumped up and down, waving. The car stopped; she ran toward it and got in. He thought there was only the driver in it, a man. He couldn't see enough to give a description: although there was a streetlight nearby, the interior of the car was in shadow, and all he could see was an outline. The car turned around, making the tires screech on the road. Then it drove off the way it had come.

What sort of car? Well, it was foreign, he noticed that.

Did he note the make? Yes, it was a Renault 5, a red one.

But a Renault 5 isn't a foreign car—it's French!

That wasn't what he meant, Robert said—he meant it was foreign because it had foreign registration plates.

Did he know where from?

It also had a disk with *E* on it.

España.

* * *

Alex signaled the waitress for more coffee; I felt that he was doing this more as a distraction than because he really wanted it. Claudine and I had had the night to think through what Robert had told us, but the Gordons, I could see, were stunned, not knowing what to think, or say. Taking the news at face value, it was hard to avoid the conclusion that their daughter had dumped them without warning and had gone off with a boyfriend. Worse, it had been prearranged—an elopement, in effect. And, worse still, she hadn't even bothered to send them a word of explanation or apology, although she must have known how worried they would be.

"Well," I prompted, "what next? Perhaps you'd like to be left alone to talk it over—it looks like a family affair rather than a crime. I suppose that's a good thing, on the whole, though I know how you must feel about it."

"Perhaps that would be best," Alex said, visibly pulling himself together. "We need a little time to—"

"No!" his wife said loudly. She was immediately embarrassed by her own voice, and said, more quietly, "No. I'm sorry, I didn't mean . . . I don't quite know what I'm trying to say. It isn't right, Alex, to tell them to go, just like that. I'm so grateful to you, Claudine, and William, for all you've done. But—"

"Sheila, I wasn't telling anybody to do anything," Alex said quite sharply. "It was William's own suggestion, and I think it makes sense. We need to talk this over, just you and I."

"But Alex," Sheila said, her voice rising again, "we're in a foreign country; we don't know anybody, and Cathy's still missing! What can we do by ourselves? We need help; you know we do!"

"Come over to La Sauvegarde when you've had time to think it over," I suggested. "We'll do anything we can, of course."

Claudine said: "We will be there. But I think, perhaps, you

will not want to waste time. A week has already passed, you know."

"Yes!" Sheila said. "A whole week! And we don't know where Cathy is, or what's happening to her. We must do something, *now*, not just talk. I can't . . . it's the uncertainty . . . I'm sorry, but not knowing, that's the worst . . . Oh, it's unbearable."

I thought, she's not far from a nervous breakdown. We were all looking at Alex, mainly so as not to witness Sheila's distress. He'd already shown some reluctance to involve us in his problem any more than he had to—I'd have felt the same in his place. But Sheila had abandoned any such inhibitions.

"We're at your disposal," I said. "That's all I can say."

"We're most grateful," Alex said. He seemed to stick there.

Well, come on, I thought—are we going to talk about it, decide what to do next, or not? It wasn't what I'd expected of Alex, this air of indecision. Perhaps he was the sort who needed to be on his own when making plans. Used to the calm of the consulting room. No—surely a surgeon needs, more than anyone, the ability to make quick decisions. Before the heartbeats weaken, the blood drains away, the breathing slows to zero. Out of his element, perhaps. Or—

"Would you mind if I asked you what you suggest?" Sheila said to me. Her pale, worried face looked into mine, entreating. Her brief burst of energy had faded; someone, she seemed to plead, must take over again. I looked across at Alex, but he nodded—I was the one. All right then—let's get on with it.

"Did Cathy have a boyfriend at your holiday place—anyone special?"

"She's too young for that," Alex said.

"But Alex," Sheila said, "several boys wanted to take her out."

"That's not what William means," Alex said.

What did he think I'd meant, exactly? "Did she go out with any of them?" I said patiently.

"Yes."

"To eating places, dancing, all that?"

"Sometimes," Alex said.

"Oh Alex—hardly ever," Sheila corrected him. "He was worried about her," she added. "It's a rather free life out there. You have to be careful."

"I am sure you do," Claudine put in.

"Yes, of course," I said. A picture was beginning to emerge, but it was hard going. They didn't seem to be exactly in tune, these two, as far as their daughter was concerned. "Did you think she had a thing about any of these boys?"

"No," Alex said. "As I said, she was too young for anything serious."

"But she was seventeen. It could have seemed serious to her."

"We didn't notice anyone in particular," Sheila said, glancing at her husband.

"No," he agreed.

"Well, it's a mystery, then. Because it does look as though she's gone off with someone. Doesn't it?"

Alex lifted his coffee cup to his lips, and took a sip. He made a face and put it down again. "I'll have to go down and look for her," he said. His face was grim.

"No, Alex," Sheila said immediately. "No. You can't."

"I think I'm the best judge of that," Alex said.

There was an embarrassing silence, during which they avoided looking at each other. It was clear that there was some deep private disagreement, which they were reluctant to discuss in public.

"What's the problem, exactly?" I asked, feeling that someone had to knock their heads together, and that I'd earned the right to do it. "There must be someone else who could take over your operations in an emergency like this?"

"Yes, of course," Alex said.

"But Alex, it would be much better if you went back home and left this to someone else," Sheila said. "You're needed there; you know you are."

"Sheila, I have to look for Cathy," he said irritably.

"Someone else could do that," she said.

"Who? The police?"

She was silent. I thought: Well, why not the police?

"It's not a police matter," Alex said. He looked at Claudine, and obviously feeling some explanation was unavoidable, said: "As William said, it's just a family affair. I don't want Spanish police blundering about, making a bigger mess of things. Nor does Sheila. Do you, darling?"

"Oh, I don't know," Sheila said miserably.

From the far side of the table, Claudine caught my eye. I knew what she was thinking. Oh *no*! That was my first reaction. Why should I do something like that for people I hardly know?

But then, what would actually be involved? A buzz down to Barcelona to call on Alastair and his new wife—no hardship, that, but a trip that had become one of the most looked-forward-to routines of my business calendar. A day or two of driving about Santa Margarita, doing a little detective work in bars and restaurants. It shouldn't be difficult to locate the girl. I'd rather enjoy the break from family life, in fact—after two weeks of idleness, I was ready for that.

"It would be easy for me to go," I said. "As I told you, I've an agent in Barcelona—more of a friend, in fact. I never need much persuasion to pay him a call." Across the table, Claudine nodded and smiled. *Good boy!* "Then in a few days, depending on how I get on, you could hop on a plane and fly down."

"Oh, I couldn't possibly let you do that," Alex said.

"Do you really mean it?" Sheila said. "Does he, Claudine?" She sounded frantic with relief, if that's possible. I nearly put in a disclaimer—I'm no expert in this sort of thing, please don't expect too much—but it wouldn't have been kind to dampen her enthusiasm.

Alex said: "Thank you, William, but I think not."

"You'll go down to Barcelona yourself? Well, of course—"

"No!" Sheila said loudly.

"Sheila, darling—"

"*I don't want you to go,*" she said emphatically.

He stared at her; again I was aware of the undercurrent of tension between them. Then he dropped his gaze, and said: "All right, then."

"We're very grateful to you, William," Sheila said quickly, clinching the deal. "Aren't we, Alex?"

"Very grateful," Alex said, not looking it. Then he pulled himself together, managed a smile, and added: "Sorry—it's all rather a strain. I really am very grateful."

That seemed to be final. "Well," I said, "if it's decided, I'd better go and telephone, make arrangements," I said. "The sooner I get off, the better." I rose from the table with a certain spring in my movements.

The fact is, while all this had been going on, I'd had a bright, brilliant idea. There are threads in my life which tend to unravel, upsetting the perfect balance of warp and woof. Here was a perfect opportunity for weaving that woof back in.

Ginny!

What would have happened to romance if the telephone had never been invented? Personally, I'd have rather enjoyed the old tradition of surreptitious notes, preferably handwritten in fine copperplate on scented deckle-edged paper, but who would have carried them, now that faithful servants are extinct? Let's be duly grateful, then, for British Telecom and its French equivalent, the PTT.

I stepped into the telephone booth and pulled the door closed. It was hot and stuffy in there, and smelled of stale sweat. Ignore it, I told myself sternly. Love conquers all.

But first, I was going to have to conquer Evan, Ginny's lawful spouse. As it was Sunday, he'd almost certainly be at home with her, at their small but desirable Regency residence in Wiltshire. I strongly suspected that it was his purchase of that house that persuaded Ginny to live with him again after their earlier separation—that, and his being made a senior barrister, a Queen's Counsel. Apart from these banal attributes—rich, successful, and available—he was entirely unworthy of her. Unfortunately, I wasn't in a position to offer any alternative, so she passed out of my life for a while. Over a year went by before we discovered that our previous long-term liaison hadn't died but had only been dormant, and we began to see each other again. And things were working out, although they might never be so good as in that glorious epoch when she'd been living on her own in a flat in South Kensington, within easy reach of Church Street. Those had been the days!—or rather, the evenings, and also the lunchtimes. Now, we had to wait for opportunities such as this one—they didn't come up as often as I would have liked, and I didn't want to waste it by a careless mistake, such as getting Evan on the other end of the line without a plan prepared.

I thought for a few moments, and then had the answer. Ginny was still a free-lance journalist—possibly the worst in the world, but Evan would have no idea about that—nothing that didn't have a direct bearing on his career toward legal stardom made any impression on his parchment hide. Picking up the receiver, I placed a person-to-person call to Virginia Duff-Jones in far-off Angleterre, reciting the number I knew by heart.

Who from? the operator asked.

Time magazine, I said—Paris office.

"*Ne quittez pas.*" I waited.

An unnecessary precaution, as it turned out. I heard Ginny's voice answering the call.

"*Time* magazine? Yes, it's me they want. Put them on, please."

"You're through, caller."

"Hello?"

"This is Ginny Duff-Jones," she said formally.

"I hope you're not going to be disappointed," I said.

"What? Who's that?"

"It's me," I said. "William. I'm ringing from France—I've had an idea, and—"

"*William!* What are you doing at *Time* magazine?"

"That was just a ploy in case Evan answered. Can you speak?"

"You're *crazy* to ring on Sunday! As it happens, he's not back from his jog, but he'll be in any minute. Ring me tomorrow, darling, when he's up at the flat."

"Jogging, is he?" *People keel over, doing that* . . . "Keep him at it, Ginny—a little more every day is the thing, I'm told. But if he comes in before we've finished, I'm still *Time* magazine, right?"

"William darling, listen—"

"You're being offered an assignment, writing a piece on Barcelona, Europe's new capital of high life. Got it?"

"Are you 'round the bend?"

"I'm going to be there from this evening for several days, and I want you to come. The magazine article is your cover story. It's all worked out—all you've got to do is step on a plane. I'm dying to see you!—it's a chance not to be missed. Say you'll come, Ginny!"

"Oh William! But how can I?"

"Very easily. Evan's in London all week, isn't he?—pontificating in halls of justice. He won't miss you. But I do."

"It's not so easy."

"Why not?"

"Well, you see, there are the dogs . . ."

"*Dogs?* For Christ's sake, Ginny—I'm offering you nights of bliss in Barcelona and you're wittering on about dogs! Put them in kennels, that's what people do."

"Oh, I couldn't do that. They'd hate it."

"Well, something. There must be a way."

"I suppose Molly might have them. For how long?"

"Let's say the inside of this week. You could fly down tomorrow, and I'll meet you at the airport."

"I'll have to ask her. Listen—I think Evan's coming in—I'll have to ring off."

"Tell him *Time* magazine rang. Prepare the way. And Ginny—I'll ring you early tomorrow. When does he leave?"

"The eight-fifteen train."

"Perfect! I'll ring you at nine. Find out about flights. I can picture you already, coming through the barrier! I can't wait!"

"Nutcase. But ring me, William darling. 'Bye."

Molly. It all depended on Molly. Whoever she was.

I got out my notebook, and looked up Alastair's number. He had a flat in the center of Barcelona and ran his wine agency from there, not needing a shop window as all his transactions were on paper, with the trade. I'd last seen him in the spring, my preferred time for visiting Spanish vineyards after the blending had been done, and before the coast roads filled up with tourists. In August, he might well be on holiday, I realized.

But he wasn't. And their spare bedroom was at my disposal.

"Are you sure?"

"Of course."

"Just for tonight. Then I'll get myself installed in a hotel."

"Don't think of it. Stay with us."

"I may have to move on down the coast—a village called Santa Margarita. D'you know it?"

"Been through it—a pretty little place. Can I ask what it's got for you?"

"I'm doing an errand for some people we met—their daughter's missing, and we think she may be there with a boyfriend."

"Really!—are you starting a detective agency?"

"Something like that. Tell you all about it this evening."

That's it, then. All fixed up. I stepped out of the booth into sparkling sunlight.

Back at the Hôtel du Périgord, I was just in time to see the Gordons off. They were in a hurry, having realized that they could catch the night ferry from Le Havre and be back in Guildford for Monday morning.

"We're so grateful for all your help," Sheila said, giving me her limp handshake. "Aren't we, Alex?"

"Of course," Alex said. He sounded as though he might be having second thoughts—perhaps felt guilty for having allowed himself to be persuaded into taking off like this—but it was too late now: the wheels were in motion. "I've told your wife where I can be contacted," he said to me. "And I wanted to ask you, as soon as there's anything at all to suggest where Cathy might be . . ."

"I'll keep you posted," I said, "news or not."

"I'd appreciate that very much. And there's one other thing I wanted to say. If—when she's located, I'd like to talk to her myself, first. I wouldn't like it if the police . . ."

"No no, I quite see that. It'll take careful handling—she's at a very vulnerable age."

Alex looked relieved. Had he forgotten that I'd teenage daughters of my own? "You'd better get going," I said. "You've got a hard day's drive if you're going to catch the boat. Try not to worry too much—I'll keep you posted."

Final good-byes were said, and then they drove off, Alex at the wheel, Sheila turning for a last wave. Then they turned the corner and were gone.

"Oh!" Claudine said, "the poor things! Now you must go, *chéri*—you also have a long drive. What about Alastair—did you get him? You were away for ages!"

"I got him," I said, thinking fast, "eventually. It's all fixed—they can put me up." We walked along the pavement to the Citroën and got in. "How are you going to manage without a car?—it's all been so sudden, I hadn't thought of that."

"Madame Reynaud will take me shopping," Claudine said.

"Ah yes. You'll both enjoy that."

"You do not mind to go?" Claudine said, looking at me across the car.

"How could I refuse?" I said, engaging gear.

"Oh, I am sorry! I did not think you would mind. I thought perhaps it would be like a little holiday, you know, *un p'tit escapade*. And for such a good reason."

I'd meant to notch up a sneaky advantage point, but she'd

disarmed me. "You were right," I admitted. "Two weeks of
the lotus life is about my limit—I was ready for this. Well, we'd
better get a move on. I'll drop you off at La Sauvegarde, grab
a bag, and be off. It shouldn't take long to find this silly girl,
and then I'll be back, batteries recharged, and ready for the
celebration banquet. Champagne, of course, and one of your
classics to remind me I'm home."

"*Filet de boeuf poêlé?*"

"Exactly, my darling. How well we understand each other.
With *endives à la dauphinoise.*"

"But naturally!" Claudine said.

"And a good Médoc."

"Not a St.-Émilion?"

"Well, perhaps, but . . ." We had it perfected by the time
I'd delivered her back home.

Midday, and the sun was hammering on the windscreen as I
drove due south. My car was the latest of a succession of
Citroëns, a big silver CX fitted with air-conditioning, but even
with the cooling system at full blast, it could barely cope with
this heat. On the cassette player, old man Bach was doing his
best to distract me. Nothing grabs me like a Bach fugue, unless
it's early jazz, like Jelly Roll Morton or Louis Armstrong in his
Red Hot Pepper days. Polyphonic Man, I am—I love the drive
and interweave of themes against a strong background beat.

It's four hundred miles to Barcelona from La Sauvegarde,
but an easy trip because much of it is motorway, and by four-
thirty I was at La Jonquera, the Spanish frontier. A Spanish
policeman waved me past with a flick of the wrist, and the road
under my wheels changed from *autoroute* to *autopista*. I
floored the accelerator, and the brown, parched mountains on
either side reeled past. The sun had lost its heat, and I tilted
the visor up to see better. Coming this way, I always look out
for the Osborne bull, a giant cutout shape with upturned horns
that stands on a hill overlooking the *autopista*, advertising a

make of brandy. That black silhouette marks the real Spanish
frontier for me.

At half past six, I was in Barcelona. I drove slowly down the
Ramblas, already crowded with evening strollers, plunged into
the furious traffic swirling around the statue of Christopher
Columbus on his tall column like Nelson's and along the
waterfront where millionaires' yachts are moored. Alastair's
flat was near the civil governor's palace, a massive classical
block with urns and balustrades on top, guards with machine
guns in front. I couldn't see their eyes behind the black sunglasses, but their heads turned as I swung into the little street
behind, named after General Castaños. There were no cars
parked anywhere in the street, and a patrolling armed guard
began to walk in my direction as I pulled up outside Alastair's
flat, his right hand on the pistol grip of his gun. I hoped the
safety catch was on.

I opened the door, climbed out, and rang the bell beside the
name A. MacInnes to show the approaching guard why I was
there. After a short pause, a girl's voice spoke out of the entryphone.

"*Quién?*"

"Pilar?" I said.

"*Sí.*"

"It's William. I think I'm about to be machine-gunned."

"Oh good!" she cried. Hopefully she didn't mean it. "We
did not expect you so soon." All was explained. "Welcome!
And wait there—I will come down."

The guard had taken a quick look at the Citroën, and was
now coming up to me, waving his free hand dismissively. He
wore a dark olive-green jacket, fawn trousers, and was
equipped with a holstered automatic and a truncheon in addition to his light-weight machine pistol. Under the peak of his
cap, the dark glasses flashed at me. I find foreign police unnerving, and I hoped Pilar wouldn't be long, as my Spanish is
minimal.

He said something—clear off! probably.

"English," I said to gain time. *"No hablo Español . . ."*

Then the door opened, and Pilar came out.

It isn't fair, the way girls get preferential treatment from policemen. After all, there are plenty of female terrorists about. But that's the way of the world, and this policeman wasn't one to stand against it. Pilar spoke: he smiled, made a lordly gesture, and swaggered off. Of course, I would have done the same. Alastair's new wife had that effect.

"Is okay," she said, smiling at me. "How are you, William?" She put up her cheek and I kissed her, right and left. "Very well," I said. "And you, Pilar?—you look wonderful." So she did: a shapely girl, taller than average, with more hip than the English are used to but which looked just right on her; large dark eyes in an open, mobile face; a mop of dark curly hair. And as I'd already found after meeting her for the first time on my visit here in the spring, a personality that reached out to you, warmth apparently without reserve or calculation. Alastair, I thought, had struck lucky.

"Come!" Pilar said. "Alastair is here—he was on the telephone when you arrive. He will be so pleased you are here already." I scooped my bag off the back seat, locked the car, and followed her.

The flat was on the top floor. We went up in the tiny lift, a wire cage that wouldn't have been overgenerous for a couple of canaries. The building was nondescript, a featureless piece of the street. But inside, Alastair and Pilar had made themselves a glossy pad, with marble floors, an all-white kitchen, modern furniture, and subtle lighting. The Spanish seem to feel at home with modernity in a way that makes me regret our British obsession with nostalgia and antiques.

Alastair was still on the telephone in the little study off the living room, but popped his head out of the door as he heard us, to wave hello. I walked across to the living-room window: the flat was level with the flat roof of the civil governor's palace, and across it there was a view over a sea of roofs punctuated by baroque domes and Gothic spires to the circular backdrop of mountains which compresses Barcelona against the Mediterranean. I didn't know whether it was the quality of the light or the sounds or the smells that affected me, but it all felt very foreign in a way that France never does. As if to confirm my feeling, a drunken voice rose up from the street, hoarsely attempting the wavering complexities of flamenco singing: other voices shouted him down, and the performance died amidst a burst of laughter.

"William—hello!" said Alastair from behind. I turned, and we shook hands automatically like seasoned Europeans. "Sorry about that," Alastair said, "some clients expect you to jump whenever they snap their fingers, even on Sunday. But you'll understand that. Is your car parked down in the street?"

"Yes."

"Better move it before the duty guard gets restive. I'll come with you—there's an underground car park nearby in the Gothic quarter, and it'll be safe there. You can't leave a car on the street these days—the buggers will break your windows to nick half a pair of socks, and if you leave nothing inside, they still break them to teach you not to be mean."

"Is not so bad!" Pilar protested. "In London, I think it is worse."

"It's happening everywhere," I said to placate her. "But I think I'll tuck it safely away. I might not be so lucky this visit as I was last time."

"Okay," she said. "Don't be in a hurry—I think I make a *paella.*" She walked into the kitchen.

"Oh my God," Alastair said under his breath. I followed him along the corridor. As the front door closed behind us, I said:

"Is that bad? I love *paella.*"

"So do I," he said, "but Pilar won't release it from the kitchen until it's exactly right, and that means about midnight.

Never mind, we'll have the bottle of Vega Sicilia I've been keeping for you."

"Vega Sicilia! Really? I thought it was unobtainable—all sold before it's even made."

"That's the *reserva*, a favorite of Winston Churchill's. What I've got hold of is the lesser version, Valbuena. Still, if you haven't had it before—"

"I haven't. This is very good of you, Alastair."

"Say no more, friend and client. Where's the bloody lift? Someone's forgotten to shut the gates—we'll have to walk down."

He led the way, puffing slightly. Always a big man, he'd put on more weight lately, since his marriage. But he was younger than me, still well on the safe side of forty, his curly dark hair without any trace of gray—too young to settle into a middle-aged outline. Perhaps Pilar preferred him this way—many European women like their men to look well fed, meaning prosperous.

We emerged into the street. The Citroën was still there, with all its windows. Well, it'd be a brave villain who broke into a car in this street, under the muzzle of that machine gun. Alastair waved to the guard, who nodded gravely; we climbed into the car and I drove off.

"Go left around this next corner," Alastair said, "and into the main boulevard. Then turn right up the Vía Laietana—don't worry, I'll tell you when we get there." Lights were coming on as Barcelona nightlife got under way, and already people were everywhere, strolling in groups, often arm in arm, through the warm evening air. "Here," Alastair directed, and I swung right to where a sign said APARCAMIENTO SUBTERRÁNEO. I had to go down three levels to find a vacant place.

Back at street level, we walked through the crooked streets of the Barri Gotic, the old Barcelona, taking the most direct route back to the flat. "Don't do this if you're on your own,"

Alastair said. "Somebody else I know got mugged only last week: that makes three this year. But two large blokes together, we should be all right. Well—what's it all about, then?"

"Looks like an elopement," I said, "if that word still means anything. Missing Teenager's Secret Love—that's my guess. Her father's a surgeon, and they have a house at Santa Margarita. On the way home through France a week ago, they went to our local fête, and the girl disappeared. She was seen getting into a car with Spanish plates, driven by a bloke. Since then, nothing. I'm going to have a shot at locating her, while her father dashes back to Guildford General to check on his patients."

"I see," Alastair said. "How well do you know these people?"

"You mean, why am I doing this?" I said. He nodded. "Well," I said, "to be honest, I was bored, and I rather enjoy a mystery."

"So you do," he said, "I remember now. Not the first time, is it—you nearly got yourself killed a couple of years ago."

"I collected a bullet hole, that's true. But this isn't the same, not at all—there's nothing risky about it," I said. We walked past an ancient, blackened stone wall on which vandals had sprayed VISCA CATALUNYA LLIURE!!! "How can people expect to gain support for anything by ruining a medieval wall?" I said.

"Long live free Cataluña," he translated. "Separatist slogans are everywhere these days. Did you notice that all the Spanish road signs have been taken down? Everything has to be in Catalan, now. If you speak Spanish in a shop, they often answer in Catalan. It's become an obsession. And, of course, Barcelona is the capital of the Catalan region—we're right in the thick of it. Sometimes, on my off days, I think we're going to have to move out—it's getting beyond a joke."

"Move out! Where to? What does Pilar think about that?"

"She's torn. It's difficult for her: she was born here, and her family is here: she's been brought up to think of the central government in Madrid as an octopus with too long tentacles. She wants Barcelona to have more say in running its own affairs. But she doesn't like fanatics any more than I do, and when the bombings started—you heard about those?"

"It was in the papers back home, yes. Bombs in offices closed for the night, in empty shops, and so on."

"Small bombs where people weren't meant to get hurt, just to draw attention to the cause—that was it. There's also been a spate of polite bank robberies to get funds—'Stay quite still *señores, señoras*—we have no wish to harm anyone. Just hand over the money—*muchas gracias.*' Sooner or later there'll be a mistake, and people will be killed. It's a dangerous game, but here they've always played at revolution—it's a tradition."

We had stopped in a cramped little square so that I could admire the floodlit facade of an ancient church. Pigeons looked down at us from their roosting places on the heads of saints and martyrs; one, more restless than the others, circled above our heads, ghostly in the lamplight.

"Who's behind it? Just fanatics?"

"Some fanatics. Some intelligentsia—university lecturers, students, media people, who keep the whole thing on the boil by talking about patriotism, but who wouldn't plant a bomb themselves. And businessmen who see profits to be made. This is a big, go-getting, rich city, nicely placed to take advantage of being on the best trade route from Spain to the rest of Europe. The more control Barcelona can take away from Madrid, the richer it's going to get. In those circumstances, a lot of people are tempted to become Catalan patriots."

We walked on. "Where would you go?" I asked. "This is a good area for you, winewise—there are interesting developments going on in the Penedès region at present, more so than in Rioja, I'd say. And the range is wider here—reds and whites of improving quality, plus nearly all the champagne. I can't think of anywhere in Spain I'd rather be, if I were you."

"It's a shame," Alastair said, "and that's a fact. But you're not here to get loaded with my troubles—forget it. Let's get on home and take a trip away from Cataluña, into the Vega Sicilia. That should blow away the blues."

"Ah," I said, "so it should. Lead on, MacInnes!"

And so, for the record, it did. If you see it, buy it. *Salut!*

$\mathcal{M}$ONDAY

AFTER THE MIDNIGHT *PAELLA,* NO ONE WAS IN A hurry for breakfast. The faithful Braun folding alarm clock that I travel with woke me at eight: at half past, after I'd shaved and dressed, there were still no signs of life from Pilar and Alastair. So I made sure I'd got my wallet, notebook, and passport and quietly let myself out of the flat. I had to get some cash from a bank, find a telephone, and phone Ginny at nine.

In the street, the air was cool and fresh, but with a delicious sense of heat to come. I nodded at the armed guard but got a stony stare in return. I walked to the end of the street, around the corner, and down the main boulevard where there was a branch of the Catalan bank, Caixa Catalunya, and also a post office from which I could make my call.

The bank was just opening, and my Visa card secured me a comfortable wad of pesetas. I moved on to the post office and collected a ticket for a telephone cubicle. Behind each double-glazed door, lit like exhibits in a museum, a variety of com-municants sat, mouthing silently at their instruments. I found my cubicle, took my seat, and dialed Ginny's number. This time, I could be carefree about the call—Evan's London train had left more than half an hour ago at eight fifteen, and he was safely out of the way . . .

"Hello?" barked a male voice.

Too late, I realized my mistake. *Bloody British Summer Time!*
. . . It would still be only eight o'clock over there.

Mysterious calls not good! Better dissemble, not hang up! Quickly assume Wiltshire colonel voice!

"Hallooeew? Richard?"

"No Richards here," Evan barked. "What number d'you want?"

"Four seven three three niner. What're you?"

"Four seven three three oh."

"Oh?"

"Yes, oh."

"Oh. Wrong number."

" 'Fraid so."

"Sorry. G'bye."

Ring off. *Phew!*

I went for a stroll along the harbor wall to soothe my nerves. The harbor had everything going for it today—water sparkling, boats bobbing, white hulls gleaming, all that. I stood to watch the cable car crawling up to the gardens of the Miramar, suspended at a dizzy height above the docks. On my right, not far away, at the top of his column, Christopher Columbus pointed the way to America. According to Alastair, he ruined Barcelona for years because the New World trade profited the ports far away to the south. It took until the nineteenth century for the city to recover from its local hero's exploits.

Here, in 1937, George Orwell had fought with the POUM Marxists, exchanging casual shots with rival revolutionary groups from buildings on either side of the Ramblas. The cobblestone barricades were up and down so often in those days that the stones should have been numbered for easy replacement. You could always tell when a Catalan revolution was imminent, Orwell said, from the cooking smells—nobody would dream of going to war until a good stock of Spanish omelet had been built up.

Surely Evan will have left by now?

Back in the post office, I was prepared for more telephone treachery, but this time it didn't let me down.

"Has he gone?"

"Yes, William darling, it's all clear. Mrs. Troughton will be in to do her mopping, but that's not for half an hour yet. We can natter on freely. I'm glad you remembered the time difference—I had a sudden panic last night that you'd ring an hour too early. And, a funny coincidence, somebody did ring then, but it was a wrong number, Evan said."

"Is that all he said about it?"

"Yes, of course, why should he—oh *William!* You didn't!"

"Afraid I did. Your nightmare came true. But I handled it with my usual aplomb—our secret is safe."

"I hope so! At least, I think I do."

"You mean, you wouldn't mind if he found out?"

"Oh, I don't know. I really don't. I mean, it's not a bad life here, but no different from the first time 'round except that the house is better."

"A lot better."

"Well yes. Maybe I shouldn't admit it, but things like that do make a difference."

"Everyone needs a base. The Frogs have always understood that. My Frog does."

"Evan wouldn't, even if we could talk about it, which he won't," Ginny said sadly. "It's very frustrating."

"He's got his career, waffling away in hallowed halls. That gives him all the space he needs. You need some space as well—that's only fair. An outside interest. Like me."

"William darling, you're so good at rationalizing. I feel better already. I wish I could come down there."

"What? You *are* coming, Ginny! Don't tell me you've still got dog trouble?"

"Well yes, Molly isn't very keen to have them. They are only puppies, you see."

"Oh no!"

"I mean, they're absolutely adorable, but Molly's worried about the mess."

"Ginny, for God's sake . . . haven't you got a tray for them?"

"Well, you know what puppies are, William darling; they just walk across them wagging their tails and spreading it everywhere. I can see Molly's point of view—it's not as if they were her puppies; everyone has to put up with their own."

"Ginny, Ginny . . ."

"Well I know, it may seem ridiculous, but actually it's a real problem. I've had another idea, though—"

"Oh good!"

"Well, it may not work; it depends on Mrs. Troughton. I'm going to talk to her when she comes in. She's got a daughter of sixteen or so who might look after them if I paid her, and I think she'd be kind to them—"

"Give her a sack of gold. Listen Ginny, I can only be here for a few days. It's a desperate situation."

"I know, William darling, and I'm doing my best. Ring me again this afternoon just after six. I'll probably have an answer by then."

"That means today is gone."

"I know, I'm sorry. I am trying. I've already canceled tennis on Wednesday just in case."

Dogs, puppies, tennis—why are women so hopeless at priorities? I left, feeling uncomfortably second best.

I bought some croissants on the way back to the flat, where I found Pilar and Alastair drifting about in dressing gowns, looking pleased with life. Pilar made coffee, and we sat down to breakfast at the kitchen table.

"Sorry to have neglected you," Alastair said sleepily. "It's all Pilar's fault." He leaned across the table and ran his hand fondly down her sleeve.

"Oh no, Alastair!" Pilar said, sitting up, "why this?"

"I understand him perfectly," I said. "When Englishmen get carried away, you see, it's always got to be someone else's fault. Take no notice. It's a sort of compliment."

"Oh," she said, frowning, "well. He will explain this to me later. But as a guest, you should not be neglected. I am sorry for this."

"Pilar, please! Last night, we had wonderful wine and a fabulous *paella*. This morning I had a delightful stroll by the harbor. I couldn't be happier, believe me."

"Ah," she said, her face clearing. "But perhaps you are too kind . . ."

"No no. It's true. I promise you. And you and Alastair are on holiday—don't let me spoil it for you. In fact, I'd better be on my way; I've got some sleuthing to do. Speaking of which, I saw a strange poster on my walk this morning: does '*Elemental, estimado Watson*' mean what it seems to?"

"It does," Alastair said. "There's a Sherlock Holmes Club in Barcelona. Just the thing for you, William."

"I may need some help," I said, "but it's more likely to be with the Spanish language than the principles of deduction. Can I call on you?"

"Of course," Pilar said immediately, her face lighting up as though she'd been offered a great treat. "We will be *very* pleased. Isn't that so, Alastair?"

"Just let us know," he said. "Perhaps we'll take a trip down to Santa Margarita—there are some places worth visiting in the mountains back from there. Hilltop villages, monasteries—"

"And restaurants," Pilar said, nodding wisely. She leaned back in her chair, blew her cheeks out, and patted her stomach. So I'd been wrong to think she approved of Alastair's new, more opulent outline.

"Oh well, yes . . . look darling, it's part of my *job* . . ."

"Alastair! How can you say this?"

"Because, darling, *because* . . . no, listen . . ."

I closed the door on them, quietly.

Once back on the *autopista*, it took well under an hour to cover the sixty-odd miles to the Santa Margarita junction. The sea had been visible, on and off, for most of the way, inverted triangles of true-blue Mediterranean glimpsed between hills shimmering with heat. Now, as I turned off the *autopista*, the sea rose up before me, windscreen wide, filling the car with light. Blinking, I fumbled in the door pocket for my dark glasses, and put them on.

At a roundabout, I waited to get on to the busy coastal road. The village was clearly visible on the circular hill to my right, a straggle of white houses leading up to a church and a massive fortress, its battlements silhouetted against the sunlight. I shot the Citroën into a space between two trucks, and was carried along the main road into the village.

Alex's house was in a development known as the Villa Club: head for the castle, he'd said, and you can't miss it. I turned off the main road, and found myself in a maze of narrow, dusty streets lined with old, whitewashed houses. Shutters were closed against the heat; dogs scratched or slept against shaded walls; a handful of holidaymakers drifted about with the floating movements of a people adrift in a dreamworld. No Spanish—they'd be indoors, downing the midday meal and avoiding the hottest part of the day. Here, in fact, were mad dogs and Englishmen, out in the midday sun.

I found a small, unofficial-looking sign: Santa Margarita Villa Club. A couple of hundred yards down a side lane, I came to a whitewashed terrace of cottages. Was this it? I stopped the car, got out, and looked about me. There was a Vauxhall Cavalier Estate with a GB sticker parked nearby. And through the open window of one of the cottages a female voice of commanding clarity could be heard:

"No darling—finish it first, and *then* you can have ice cream."

Yes, this was it.

My instructions were to go to number 12 and ask for Jill. I found an arched gateway: inside there were two opposing rows of cottages climbing up the hill, the upper row with tiny gardens overlooking those below. I walked in. It was a picturesque cul-de-sac, paved and planted with mulberry trees for shade, spiky yucca plants, pampas grass, and cactus for decoration. White walls, curly orange tiles, pale blue shutters, and the green of plants made up a picture to lift the spirits of any sun-starved Brit on the run from our arctic isle. No wonder Alex Gordon had bought a piece of this.

I walked farther in. From my left, behind a shrubbery, came sounds of splashing, shrieks, and a subdued heartbeat of pop music. I could see the blue of a swimming pool between the shrubs: figures leaped and ran beside it, their feet slapping wetly on the tiles. I found number 12 at the top end, next to a low, bamboo-screened construction labeled BISTRO. The door was open, but there was a bell push. I prodded it.

A girl emerged from the interior, a large baby on her hip, and came toward the door. About thirty, sensible looking, dressed in a loose yellow shirt, white shorts, and yellow plastic sandals. She had shoulder-length light brown hair, streaked with blond. I thought she looked tired. Our questions collided:

"Jill?" "William?"

"Ah," I said, smiling, "Alex has rung you, then?"

"Sheila, in fact. But I know all about you. Come on in. You found your way all right?"

"No trouble. What a smashing place! You run it, is that right?"

"We try to keep it off the rocks, Sandy and I. This is our sixth year."

"Well," I said, "if you've avoided shipwreck that long . . ."

We had passed a small kitchen and were in a high-ceilinged sitting area at the back of the house. A ladderlike stair led to an open gallery bedroom behind us, over the kitchen. Through wide French windows there was a view over a small garden the width of the house, with the tops of olive trees beyond where the ground fell away steeply. And in the distance, the blue sea again.

"Studio apartments," I said, "that's the phrase I was looking for. The row on this side is best, isn't it?—with gardens on the outside, and the view of the sea."

"Some people prefer the top row," Jill said, "because you can get to them straight off the road without coming all the way in, past everyone else. And if the gardens up there haven't got the view, there's the compensation of being able to look down on the pool and watch all our domestic dramas."

"Which is the Gordons'?"

"Top row, number 10. I'm afraid, if you were hoping to stay there, it's occupied—we act as letting agents for anyone who wants it, and it was too late to cancel. I could probably squeeze you in somewhere else if you don't mind sleeping on a sofa."

"Thanks. I might take you up on that for tonight. Can I decide later? I'll have a better idea of how long this business is going to take." *And of the chances of Ginny coming out . . .*

"Ah yes," Jill said. The baby belched hugely, and she began dabbing at the dribble that was running down its face. I looked away—I'm not good with babies. But you're expected to make some laudatory comment.

"Big, isn't it," I ventured.

She glanced at me, and smiled. "Are you a father?"

"Two teenage daughters," I said. "And a son at architectural college. I suppose they were all babies once, but frankly, I was happy when they grew out of it."

"That's normal," Jill said. "Sandy's the same. As a result, this monster can't get enough of him. Perverse, aren't they!"

"Like cats," I said.

"Like cats." She paused. Then she said: "Tell me about your daughters."

"They're thirteen and fifteen. The older one is in the process of moving on from dear old Dad, to try her claws in the great wide world. She's caught her first victim—our neighbor's son, in France. Could be worse—I think he can cope."

"Ah," Jill said. "Now I understand . . ."

"Understand what?"

"Oh . . . nothing much. What do you think about it all?"

"About Sylvie? Well, mixed feelings, I suppose. But on the

whole, I'm glad. The sooner she's over the experimental stage and joined the grown-ups, the happier I'll be."

"Yes," Jill said, "yes. Tell me something else—how well do you know the Gordons?"

"Hardly at all." I told her about the advertisement, my visit to the *notaire,* how I'd become involved. And then the rest of the story, up to Robert's sighting of Cathy getting into the red Renault 5 with Spanish plates. "So this was the obvious place to come to, first," I concluded.

"Yes. Sheila told me roughly that, but she missed out your illuminating detail. So Cathy skipped happily into the car, did she? That's interesting."

I felt that I'd been carefully, tactfully interrogated, but that it was time for me to ask some questions. "What should I know that I don't?" I said bluntly.

Jill made a face. "Oh well," she said, "here goes. Sheila asked me to put you in the picture—she said to give you her apologies, but she didn't have a chance to tell you herself . . ."

"Tell me what?"

"About Alex," Jill said.

"About Alex." I repeated. Yes. I'd felt sure there was something. He hadn't wanted me to come here—it was Sheila who'd pushed for it. "Right. Let me guess—too strict with Cathy, I feel sure. But that's not so unusual. I guess you mean more than that, don't you?"

Jill said: "Sheila trusts you. She has to."

"Alex is a surgeon," I said, "a professional man. He has a lot to lose. I understand that."

"They've been coming here every year," Jill said. "Sheila and I got quite close. It's been really rough on her."

I sat, silent, taking this in.

"Young girls," Jill said.

Ah. Now we were coming to it. I said:

"Young girls in general? Or Cathy in particular?"

"I suppose, in general. But Cathy had the bad luck to be the one that was available," Jill said. "I don't think he dared to go after others outside the family—too risky."

"Oh, *Jesus!*" I said. "So that's it."

Jill was watching my face. "I suppose you wish you hadn't got involved, now," she said. "Hard to take, isn't it."

"I don't know what to say. My first instinct is *yuk*, how *could* he, all that. But the fact is, I quite liked the guy."

"People do," Jill said. "I did myself. But once you know about this . . ."

"I suppose you have to think of it as an illness," I said. "Maybe that's how Sheila copes with it. How long has it been going on?"

"For years, I believe. I don't understand how he got away with it, though. If it'd been me, I'd have stopped him in his tracks or thrown him out," Jill said.

"I guess the problem is, that these things start with normal fatherly hugs and kisses, and only gradually turn into something else. It must have been difficult for Sheila to decide just when to try to put a stop to it, don't you think?"

Jill gave me an appraising look. "Seems that Sheila was right to trust you," she said. "She did say that if you wanted to back out she'd understand."

"No," I said. "I think I'll stick with it. It makes a difference that she wanted me to know about this—I can see now why she was so anxious for me to look for Cathy instead of Alex or the police. Cathy may have decided to make a break and be hiding from Alex. Jesus!—what a situation to get into with your own daughter!"

"According to the newspapers," Jill said, "there's a lot more of it about than anyone realized."

"Yes. I think if I'd designed the universe I could have made a better job of the human libido. The one we've got has some serious flaws in it."

The baby belched again, and then smiled happily, if lopsidedly, at me.

"Well anyway," I said, "it's the girl we should be thinking about. This could well explain why she went missing. And why Sheila didn't want Alex to go chasing after her. I'd better press on with what I'd already planned, which was to locate her with all possible speed. Then we'll take it from there."

"I can give you a lead," Jill said.

"You can? You know where she is?"

"No, but there's a boy she was keen on, and you might start with him. Better get it straight from the horse's mouth, though, in case I leave anything out. Meanwhile, having fed the monster, I was about to give myself some lunch—will you join me?"

The horse's mouth belonged to a girl called Sue who would be working behind the bar that evening, but was on the beach until then. Partly because of the heat, partly because of a lingering embarrassment at belonging to the male sex as a result of the conversation with Jill, I wasn't in the mood to roam the beach asking strange girls if they were called Sue. So I had a siesta in the shade of a tree in Jill's garden. I went out three times to call Ginny from a telephone kiosk in the village, but there was no reply, so I decided to leave it till the morning, and went back to the Villa Club for a cooling plunge in the pool. Sue's turn of duty in the bar beside the pool began at eight, and I was there in good time, clutching a virtuous glass of plain iced orange juice, watching the spiky shadows of yucca plants lengthen, and hoping that none of the children still shrieking and splashing in the pool would need to be saved from drowning—I was already on my last shirt.

The church clock struck eight, a rusty din such as Don Quixote might have made falling off his horse in full armor, and on the last stroke Sue appeared, a thin girl of about eighteen with blond hair in a ponytail. I followed her to the bar, and leaned on it. "I'm William," I said. "Are you Sue? Good. Jill says you've got some news for me. Can you talk now?"

She looked me up and down, and then said: "It's okay. I'll

have to break off to serve, but this place doesn't start getting busy until nine or so. Are you some sort of private eye?"

"Friend of the family," I said, "and very worried they are. Jill's told you about Cathy's disappearance, then?" She nodded. "How well did you know her?" I asked.

"Pretty well. I used to go to the beach with them."

"Cathy, Sheila, and Alex?"

"That's right. Alex wouldn't let her go alone."

"No?"

"He was funny like that—very strict with her."

"I see. Do you like him?"

"Alex? Yeah. Nice brown eyes. One of those guys that can give you the feeling you're the only one worth talking to, you know?" She smiled reminiscently. I concealed my annoyance at this new example of the Alex effect, and said:

"You liked him although he was so strict with Cathy?"

"He only did it because he was fond of her," Sue said.

"What about boyfriends? Did he let her go out at all?"

"Oh no," Sue said. "He was bananas about that. Even when she was dancing with some boy in the bar here, he sat looking like there was something wrong with his insides."

"So she never saw any boy on her own?"

"Oh, I didn't say that. But he didn't know—she made sure of that."

"How?"

"She used to baby-sit for people—he didn't mind that. Usually it was the Everetts, that've got a house in the bottom row there. He used to climb up the wall from the olive grove and nip in through the garden."

"Alex did? Why?—to check on her?"

"No, not Alex—her boyfriend, of course!"

"What happened?"

"Well!" Sue said with a giggle. "The usual, I suppose!"

"No, I mean, did Alex ever suspect?"

"Don't think so. How could he?"

"He might have gone to check up, see if she was all right."

"He probably didn't think he needed to—his house is just opposite, and from his garden, you can see down to the Everetts' front door. I don't expect he ever thought of anyone climbing in from the back. I shouldn't think Cathy thought of it either. I wouldn't mind betting it was Mark's idea; he's like that, not one to be—"

"Mark?"

"Her boyfriend."

"Mark who?"

"Oh, I don't know that. We're all on first names here. Is it important?"

"Yes, very," I said.

"I could ask around. Somebody might know."

"Would you? No, wait, I wouldn't want him to know that I'd been in here asking after him. There must be some other way to get hold of the name."

"Stephenson," said a quiet voice behind me. I spun around. A red-faced, ginger-haired man stood there. "Hi," he said. "I'm Sandy, Jill's other half. I thought you'd want to know that, so I did a little quiet research to save you some time. The boy's father lives up in the hills behind here, I'm told. He's retired, but at least it's an address. He may be persuaded to tell you where to find the boy."

"Brilliant!" I said, shaking his hand. "I can't thank you enough. I'll go up there tomorrow, and perhaps get this whole thing cleared up."

I suppose I've always been optimistic by nature, but that turned out to be one of my wilder inaccuracies.

$\mathcal{T}$UESDAY

THE VOICE WAS QUIET, BUT INSISTENT. I WAS TRYING to ignore it, but I just couldn't—difficult to say exactly why, whether it was the tone, or . . . well anyway, it was spoiling my lunch.

We were lunching in the Plaça Major at Prades, a little town up in the mountains some twenty miles inland from Santa Margarita. Near here, Sandy had told me, was the villa where Mark Stephenson's retired father lived, though he hadn't been able to find out the exact address. This was just the area Alastair had enthused about, so I'd asked both MacInneses to come along—for company, and for help in asking directions. We'd driven away from the coast, and crawled up the wall of mountains which stands behind the coastal plain. It's a different Spain up here, only twenty miles away from the beaches and bars that most tourists never leave: there are forests and high pastures and dramatic rocky peaks and little, unspoiled villages. *Muy Catalán!* Pilar said proudly. She hadn't been able to resist Alastair's suggestion that a taste of local cooking was essential if I, William, was to get a proper introduction to the region. And it just so happened that in Prades, where we were going anyway, was this little Catalan specialty restaurant, highly recommended . . .

But my lunch was being spoiled.

Pilar could see that something was wrong, but she hadn't picked up the, well, *menace* that lay just underneath the quietly spoken words. English words . . .

"You do not like this rabbit?" she asked, frowning. She felt responsible: the *conill amb all oli quarnico* had been her suggestion.

"This rabbit is ace," I assured her. "This rabbit is perfect. It's only man that's vile. Did you hear him, Alastair?"

"Yes," he said in a low voice, "if you mean the one at the table just behind you. He—"

"Shhh!" I said—"Listen. Listen to that!"

We all heard it this time, a drawling voice, lazily contemptuous, with a force behind it like the casual flicking of a heavy whip. "How many times," it said, "how many times have I got to tell you? *The fuckin' keys are in the fuckin' car.*"

I felt the hair prickle on the back of my neck. My prehistoric ancestors, acting on instinct, wouldn't have bothered to work out *why* their hackles had risen: a threat was a threat. At our present stage of evolution, though, reasons are required. What kind of threat could my instincts detect in a discussion about *car keys*?

I had my back to the room, but there was a mirror on the wall behind Pilar and Alastair. By shifting my chair a little, I could . . .

Yes—that's the one, it must be, at the next table with his back to me. I couldn't see much—just heavy shoulders and the back of a head of short mid-brown hair. But I could see the face of the woman opposite him, her eyes turned downward to her plate, sitting bowed in her chair as if crushed by more than her fair share of the world's woes. She was in her late forties, with graying dark hair forced into unfashionable rolls by an inexpert hand. Her face was pale and lined, without makeup except for a slash of bright red lipstick, a touch of frivolity which seemed grotesquely at odds with her careworn appearance.

His voice again: "Well? Going, or aren't you?"

Watching the mirror, I saw her glance up at him, and then let her eyes slide away, unfocused and withdrawn. She rose from her chair, carefully laid her napkin by her place, and walked out of the restaurant. He sat, Buddhalike, looking at the menu.

Pilar had been watching my face. "What is it?" she whispered.

"I think they've left the keys in their car," I said.

"But," Pilar said, "then why does she go, not him?"

"Because," I said, "because . . . oh, let's take no notice—it's nothing to do with us." We were drinking red Priorato, a local wine of fearsome potency. "I think I'll put some water with the rest of this if I'm driving. Unless you'd care for a turn at the wheel, Alastair?"

"Thank you," Alastair said, "but I fear it's already too late for me. If only I'd known."

"He is disgusting, no?" Pilar said, removing the bottle from Alastair's reach.

"He's Scottish," I said. "They drink to forget."

"Forget what?" Pilar asked, puzzled.

"Never yet met one who could remember that," I said.

In fact, Alastair is as hard-headed as they come, and can absorb vast quantities of wine with no worse effect than an increase in his geniality rating. But his act was a useful distraction from what was going on at the next table; I was glad of it.

We arrived at the pudding stage. I had a *crema Catalána*, Pilar had *postres de music*, and Alastair a *gelat crocanti*. I was just finishing mine when I heard the couple at the table behind me getting up to leave. I turned my head to watch as the proprietor came out from behind the bar and bowed ingratiatingly. "*Gracias, Señor Stephenson, muchas gracias, adios . . .*"

Alastair was saying . . . "a glass of Mascaro, William—you know, the one you liked the other evening, from Villafranca . . ."

"What?"

"Brandy! You must remember, you were—"

"His name's Stephenson!" I interrupted.

"Who?"

"The heavyweight who was at the next table, just going out now. There can't be all that many Stephenson's in this neck of the woods—it may be the one we want."

"Do you want to go out after him?" Alastair asked. "I'll come with you."

"No," I said, "no. Let's not rush this. Pilar—would you ask if that Señor Stephenson lives near here?"

"Okay." She beckoned the waitress, and there was a rapid exchange of Spanish. "She says yes. He comes to eat here once every week—sometimes twice."

"Thanks," I said. The waitress was still hovering. "And I think I'll skip the brandy. Just a *café solo*, please." The waitress took our last order, and left.

"Now something is again wrong," Pilar said, leaning across the table to me.

"It's been a terrific meal," I said. "I'd certainly like to come here again. Thank you, Pilar."

"But?" she said. "Tell me what is wrong."

"When Sandy said Mark's father was retired, I imagined an elderly businessman pottering about his garden," I said. "Not a type like this. Stephenson may be retired, but I doubt if it's from what we'd call business. I think we're in trouble."

"What sort of trouble?" Pilar said.

"Just a feeling I've got," I said. "And I may be quite wrong—the people here were bowing and scraping as if he owned the place."

"That doesn't mean anything, does it?" Alastair said. "He's a regular customer—that's all they care about. Not whether he wipes his feet or beats his wife."

"Oh Alastair!" Pilar complained. She turned to me. "Alastair thinks that all Spanish people are Arse Holes," she explained, in her clear voice.

"Um, darling . . ." Alastair said, looking around at the neighboring tables. "That isn't really a word we use in—"

"But this is what you say! Spanish people are all—"

"Yes, darling, all right . . . Can we discuss this later? And it isn't Arse Holes, it's arseholes, all one word . . ."

"Hah! Who should know this better than you?"

"If I could just butt in a moment," I suggested.

"Of course, William—we are sorry!" Pilar said. "This is not why we are here, for Alastair to be so stupid . . . shall I ask where this Señor Stephenson lives?"

"That's exactly what I had in mind," I said.

The route we'd been given was no better than a track. I'd switched the Citroën's hydraulic suspension to the high position to give maximum ground clearance, but the surface was broken by tree roots and the exposed tops of giant boulders, forcing me to keep our speed down to little more than walking pace. We were traveling along a high ridge, I knew that; but only an occasional glimpse through the dense pine plantations on either side of the track confirmed it, giving a momentary view across an apparently bottomless valley to the next range of mountains on one side or the other. Then the trees would close in again.

"Do we trust him?" I said. "We've been on this track for half an hour, now. Though, at this speed, we've probably only covered three to four miles—I didn't think to check the mileage when we started."

The restaurant manager had said that, although he'd never been there himself, he understood that Señor Stephenson lived at Torrecasim, an old and largely abandoned village on a hilltop to the west. The road was very bad—we would need a cross-country vehicle. Did we have one—no? Then, he said with decision, we should abandon the visit. That was his advice. *Gracias, señora, señores—adiós.*

"Didn't want us to go, did he," Alastair said.

"That was my impression," I said. "I think that Stephenson doesn't like visitors, and he knows it. I thought at the time he was just trying to put us off, but maybe I underestimated him, and he's actually misdirected us."

"Shortsighted, wouldn't it be?" Alastair said. "I can't think many people would be put off so easily."

"Maybe not. But he'd score brownie points for trying."

"Why should he do this?" Pilar asked. "You think he is frightened of Señor Stephenson?"

"I don't know," I said. It wasn't quite what I felt.

A hundred yards ahead, the track turned yet another boulder-strewn corner and vanished out of sight between rocks and trees. How much farther should we go before giving up and turning back? Was this a wild-goose chase, or not? The only thing that persuaded me to go on was the surface of the track: although rough, it was worn as though by regular use, more so than if it had been merely used for forestry. The tree roots that the Citroën had so far succeeded in scrabbling over showed bare patches where other wheels had ground away the bark; every boulder bore two parallel lines which shone in the sunlight where tires had polished the surface. Someone passed this way regularly, and something went on at the end of this track. The question was, who?—and what?

"I think I hear something!" Pilar said suddenly. I pressed the button to open my window, and we all listened.

"A chain saw," Alastair suggested.

"Perhaps," I said. But although the sound was right, there was an extra dimension that didn't fit.

Movement . . .

"Motorbike," I said. We were quite close to the corner now, but there was space on the right, a grassy verge hedged with thornbushes. I pulled over, conscious of thorny branches reaching out at silver paintwork.

The noise of fast-revving engine was very loud now, and approaching at speed from the blind side of the corner. Very loud—more than one, I realized . . .

A helmeted figure flashed into sight, booted feet planted on the jolting footrests of a trail bike. I'd hardly pulled up before the bike screamed past within inches of the car, the rider's helmeted head turning momentarily toward us. A swirling cloud of dust followed, and I stabbed at the button to close my window before the car filled with it. Like a cavalry charge through gunsmoke, other figures burst out of the dust cloud—three, five, six of them. The howl of their engines pained our ears as they passed. A seventh straggler appeared, howled past, and was gone. I looked in the mirror. Nothing could be seen except dust, but the sound of their engines still echoed from the mountain slopes. Then it died away.

"What made you stop?" Alastair said, breathing heavily.

"The noise, I think. Scary, isn't it."

"Good thing you did. Bloody stupid, going that fast around a blind corner."

I engaged gear, and moved off again. Perhaps around this corner we'd see something? No—just another length of track. Interminable track, track that didn't exist according to my map.

Ten minutes later, there was a change in the landscape. The trees began to thin out, and the track became even rockier. We came into the open at the end of the pine plantation, and glimpsed what looked like a village in the distance, but the track plunged into a stony gully with occasional bushes and small trees on each side, and the view was cut off again. Overhead, the sun was a white disk in a cloudless sky of palest blue. Heat shimmered from the rocks. We couldn't see out of the gully, and we couldn't turn around. I drove on.

Then we emerged from the gully.

"Jesus!" Alastair said. "What a sight!" I stopped the car so that we could take it in.

The end of the ridge was in sight a quarter of a mile away, and perched on it was a crumbling group of stone buildings, some of which had shutters and looked as if they might be inhabited. At the nearest end of the village was a mass of stonework which had once been defensive walls, dominated by a broken tower. Beyond the tower and the village was—nothing. Empty sky. Like the end of the world.

"Torrecasim," Pilar said. "I remember now. It was a Moorish stronghold—one of the last to fall."

"With a site as easy to defend as this," I said, "it's not surprising. Do you see the causeway? It can't be more than ten feet wide, and a sheer drop for thousands of feet on both sides. To capture the village, you'd have to cross that under fire from the castle. I doubt it was ever done. The Spanish must have starved the Moors out."

"You'd need a head for heights to live up here," Alastair said. "And, maybe, a good reason, apart from the view. What do you suppose it's like in winter?"

"I'll ask him," I said. "It may be a useful topic of conversation."

"Stephenson?"

"That could be his." I pointed to where I'd seen a splash of white wall, obscured by the gray of olive trees. It was apart from the village, a few hundred yards to our right.

"Could be," Alastair said. "We're supposed to be looking for a villa, aren't we? And there's nothing else in sight that looks new."

I drove on. As we got nearer, I saw that the white walls enclosed the courtyard of a house built on rocky ground between the track and the edge of the cliff which continued along to the left, past the causeway, to the village. The view from that courtyard, I guessed, must be spectacular.

We were near enough now to see an archway in the white wall, with a black iron gate in it. The gate was closed, but through the bars could be seen a graveled area, some red pots with plants tumbling out of them, a rockery filled with cactus plants, a white garden seat—all the normal furnishings of a Spanish garden. It looked reassuringly harmless. Of course, it might not be Stephenson's house, but it seemed the best bet to start with. I stopped the car in front of the gate.

"Shall I come with you?" Alastair said.

"Thanks, but I'd better see if this is the place, first."

"Okay. I'll wait by the gate, in case you need reinforcements. Pilar knows about first aid, don't you, darling?"

"What are you going to do?" Pilar asked apprehensively.

"I'll have to play it by ear," I said. "But don't worry—I intend to keep it cool, no provocation, no dramas. If I'm lucky, I might catch a glimpse of Cathy, who knows?"

I got out of the car, patted my hair, straightened my shirt, and advanced to the gate. There was the usual security system: I pressed the bell push and waited. Nothing. I pressed it again. A man's voice said:

"Yes?"

"Mr. Stephenson?"

"Yes."

"My name's Warner. I'd appreciate a word with you, if you don't mind."

"Yes."

"Can I come in?"

"Yes."

A buzzer sounded, and the gate latch clicked open. I pushed the gate open, turned to nod at Pilar and Alastair, who were still sitting in the car, and went in, leaving the gate open. I was in a graveled parking area, and I could now see a blue Range Rover parked under bamboo shading to one side. The house was a typical Spanish villa: white walls, low-pitched red-tiled roof of rambling outline, etc. There was only one window on this side, fitted with the customary wrought-iron grille. A short flight of steps led up to a massive door of dark stained wood studded with square-headed iron nails or bolts. The door was still shut. I walked up the steps to it, and knocked. Looking around as I waited, I noticed a car's wing mirror attached to the nearby window frame—a neat way to see who was at the front door. Something moved. Looking more closely, I saw eyes reflected in the mirror, watching me. I couldn't resist a smile and a wave—well, I'd been invited in. The eyes wavered and vanished. I waited some more. Then there was a rattle of bolts beside me, and the door opened.

Stephenson close-up fulfilled my worst expectations—and more. I felt the same, electric jolt down the spine that rhino hunters must when they round a bush and come face to face with their quarry. If they're quick enough and have a loaded rifle ready, they may just avoid a sudden role reversal from hunter to hunted. I didn't have a rifle—all I had was words. But I was quick with them, oh yes I was. No matter that I sounded like a door-to-door salesman . . .

"Hello, Mr. Stephenson, good afternoon. I'm glad to have found you in. I'm making some inquiries on behalf of Mr. and Mrs. Gordon, whose daughter Cathy has been missing since a week last Saturday. I understand your son Mark is friendly with her, and I was wondering if, by any chance, you might have some news of her? It's just possible that she may have come back to Spain after her holiday to see him again. Can you help at all?"

I had time to study Stephenson's face while I waited for some response to this appeal. It was some inches above me, not because he was any taller than my own six foot two, but because I was still outside on the steps, one down from him. His was a turnip head, held so high as to tilt backward, from which angle his eyes stared down at me from under lowered lids. The turnip effect was mostly due to his cheeks, which were so puffed out and bloated that his small, pursed-up mouth seemed to float in a sea of flesh. All of this was topped by a curly lock of brown hair hanging over his forehead, which, when he was a boy, might have been admired by female relations. A pretty boy? Well, he'd had, I guessed, thirty-five or more years to grow out of it. And succeeded absolutely.

The rosebud mouth was moving. "You've been followin' me."

"No—I had to find your address, that's all. Can you help about the Gordon girl? That's all I want to know."

There was a long silence. Stephenson had become a statue, still looking down at me, his face expressionless. I was aware of the slight rise and fall of his chest, otherwise he might have been turned to stone. Best to wait, I thought—the ball's in his court. I've said all I need. Be patient . . .

The mouth moved again. "Want to hear somethin', do you?"

"Yes," I said thankful the silence was broken, that I'd done right to wait. "Anything you can tell me—"

I was only aware of a blur of movement as his arms came up. Then my head seemed to explode. I staggered back, clutching my ears as sound and pain threatened to burst them apart. *Jesus!—he's a maniac!* The ground gave way beneath me, and I fell down the steps, landing on my knees in the gravel. Above me, the heavy door banged shut.

Somebody took my arm, was helping me up. Alastair. He was speaking, but I wasn't going to take my hands from my ears, not yet. Suppose my eardrums were burst? Can you do that, by clapping someone's ears hard enough? If so, perhaps they were—nobody ever had their ears clapped harder than that. *A maniac!*

We reached the car, Pilar holding the passenger door open for me. She helped me in. Alastair had gone back to pull the gate shut and now got into the driver's seat. His lips were moving—all right, I'd better know the worst. *Can I hear him or not?* Cautiously, I eased my hands away from my ears. It was like hearing someone at the other end of a drain, but yes!—at least I could hear. "Shall we go, or do you want to have another try at him," Alastair was saying.

Well. It was beginning to wear off, though my head was ringing like Sunday morning. Of course, next time, I'd be prepared, and if Alastair was game to come along . . .

Through the arch, we all saw the heavy front door open again, just wide enough to let out a pair of wildly barking Doberman pinschers, each struggling to be first. They were at the gate in seconds, white teeth snapping between the bars. *Land sharks* . . .

"Let's go."

Definitely a maniac. I needed time to work out how to handle this.

Alastair, at the wheel, seemed to think there was something to smile at.

"What's the big joke then?" I said, scowling.

"Well, William. You did *say* you were going to play it by ear . . ."

$\mathcal{T}$UESDAY EVENING

MY EARS WERE STILL RINGING WHEN WE GOT BACK TO Santa Margarita at about six. Alastair had left his car parked on the top road, and I pulled up behind it.

"You'll stay on for supper? There's a bistro here, or . . ."

"Thanks," Alastair said. "But I think we'd getter get back to the flat—calls to make. Are you sure you feel okay now?"

"It's wearing off," I said. "What makes me mad is that I forecast trouble and still got clobbered. I suppose I didn't believe myself, really."

"Poor William," Pilar said from the back seat. She leaned forward and put her hand on my shoulder: I got a faint whiff of the cologne she often dabbed herself with, a civilized habit in this roasting climate. "It is our fault: we think you make too much of this man. But no—he is what you say, *loco*. I am very sorry."

"What next?" Alastair asked. "Call in the *guardia*?"

"What can I tell them? That I called at the house in case a missing English girl was there—for which I haven't a shred of evidence—and got my ears boxed? Even if the girl's there now, I suspect she wouldn't be by the time we'd got halfway along the track. Stephenson's got eyes in the village, I'd bet on that."

"You think so?"

"He was expecting me, that was obvious. So the restaurant manager or someone else probably rang him. One thing's certain—you could never drive up to that house unannounced: he chose it for the same reason as the Moors who held out at Torrecasim for so long."

All the same, I thought, all the same . . . on foot, and from an unexpected direction . . . but did I really want . . .

"I'll ring Alex now, and see what he thinks," I said. "I've really enjoyed having you two along, even to witness my discomfiture. It hasn't put you off another day out together, I hope."

"Oh no!" Pilar said. "Next time, you come to Barcelona, yes? We will go to the Barceloneta, and eat fish. Okay?"

"Okay."

We got out of the car. "Better luck next time," Alastair said, "and listen—let me know if I can do anything to help. Nothing too athletic, but sheer weight can be useful. I'm a tiger when roused, you know."

"Oh Alastair!—a so fat tiger!" Pilar said, laughing. "Come! See you soon, William."

After they'd driven off, I walked down the road and through the gate into the Villa Club to find Jill and ask if I could use her phone. I was halfway to her house next to the bistro when I heard running feet behind me and Jill's voice calling my name. She came up to me, panting.

"I was in the bar and saw you go past," she said. "Alex rang just after you'd left this morning: said would you ring him as soon as you got back—it's very urgent."

"Right—I was just about to. Can I use your—"

"Yes—the door's open, help yourself; it's on the floor by the sofa. I'll be in the bar."

"Thanks, Jill. Listen, I forgot to ask—does Alex know I've been told the truth about him?"

"Oh!—I'm glad you remembered," she said. "No, he doesn't. Sheila doesn't want him to know she's been behind his back, ringing me about it. Sorry."

"Okay. Well, I'll try to keep it that way."

In Jill's house, I dropped into the sofa, turned up Alex's home number in my notebook, balanced the phone on my lap, and dialed. Whirs, clicks, a pause, and then the ringing tone.

"Sheila Gordon speaking."

"Oh Sheila—it's William." Should I say anything about Alex?—no, I can leave that to Jill. "I got a message to ring Alex—sorry it's taken so long to ring back, but I—"

"Hold on, William—I'll get him, hold on."

I heard her calling—"Alex! Alex! It's William . . ."

"Hello?" Alex's voice, sounding flat.

"I got a message to ring you. Is there some news?"

"Yes," he said.

"Oh—is it . . . ?"

"It couldn't be worse," he said. "No, not true—she could be dead. It's a letter—arrived this morning."

"A letter? What about?"

"I've got it here: I'd better read it to you. It's typed and says: *'Mr. Gordon—your daughter is safe and still pretty, if you want to keep her that way get twenty-five thousand pounds in used notes ready by Thursday night and you will get instructions what to do. No police, no tricks or you know what will happen.'* "

I was silent, playing it back to myself.

"Are you still there?" Alex's voice said in my ear.

"Yes, Alex, I'm sorry . . . I don't know what to say. It sounds unreal, rather than frightening. Do you believe it?"

"I think I do. Who'd want to play a hoax like that?"

"Possible, isn't it. You've kept the envelope, of course?"

"Yes. Postmarked London WC2."

"*London!* Not Spain . . ."

"I've thought about that. It doesn't mean she isn't in Spain—there could be an accomplice here who typed and posted it. Letters take a week or so to get here from Spain, and that's too slow for this business. Also, having a London accomplice to handle negotiations would keep me here, out of the way."

"You're right, yes," I said. "So Spain isn't ruled out. I think in that case I'd better tell you what I've been up to since I got to Santa Margarita yesterday."

Drawing a deep breath, and trying to speak dispassionately,

I started with what Sue had told me about Cathy and her
wall-scaling midnight boyfriend. Even though, in my opinion,
it was a case of chickens coming home to roost, I felt sorry for
Alex. When it was over, I paused to let him take it all in, and
then asked: "Did you know about this lad, Mark Stephenson?"

"Mark Stephenson," Alex said ominously. "So that's who it
was. I suspected something of the sort. But I couldn't believe
that she, that they . . . Oh *Christ!*"

I waited some more. He had to sort this out for himself.

"I'd like to set the police on that boy," he said at last. There
was venom in his voice.

"Well," I said, "you know how it is with these kids . . ."

"Taking advantage of Cathy . . . of her inexperience . . ."

I thought: the man sounds as if he'd have that boy's balls
off—he's positively *Sicilian* about her. I said, to cool it:

"Jill and Sandy are being very helpful. Sandy found where
the boy's father lives, in the hills behind here, and I called on
him today. Now Alex, this may just be coincidence, but—"

"What did he say? Did you see the boy?"

"Nothing; no, I didn't. But listen, the boy's father is a very
rough type indeed, and I wouldn't be surprised if he has a
record in the UK. A proper villain, if ever I saw one. And,
what's more, he sounds like a Londoner. I don't say he must
be behind this, but I'd swear he was capable of it."

"Didn't he say anything? You say you spoke to him?"

"It was a somewhat one-sided conversation. I spoke, briefly.
Then he hit me. I left at speed, pursued by Doberman pinschers."

"Good God! Really?"

"It seemed real enough to me. I had some friends with
me—they could confirm it."

"Oh, I didn't mean . . . I'm sorry; of course, if you say that's
what happened, I don't doubt it. Surely we'd better check it
out right away, don't you think?"

"Yes," I said. "But Alex—how?"

"Ah," he said, "yes. No police, no tricks."

"Exactly. I hate to say this, but I hope it wasn't a mistake to do what I've already done."

"Surely they wouldn't . . . you didn't know about this letter when you went there."

"They don't know that."

"No . . . no . . . I'm afraid I'm not making much sense at the moment."

"I feel for you, Alex, believe me. How is Sheila taking it?"

"Surprisingly well. It seems I'm the one who's going to pieces." I heard a wry laugh. "Never know, do you, until the crunch comes. Hidden strengths—and hidden weaknesses."

Too true! I thought. "Could you pay up?"

"Could I find the money? Oh yes, they've pitched it quite low as these things go, haven't they. I can sell some shares and manage that. I'm going to do it tomorrow."

"Good."

"Will it stop there, do you think?"

"Alex, I don't know. I suppose you should talk to the police: they'll advise you. You could make it clear you don't want any action taken."

"Risky. Suppose they find out? We know they're in London because of the letter."

"Contact the police by telephone—that might be safest."

"Phone tap?"

"Unlikely, surely."

"Yes. But possible."

"I think I'd take that risk. No, listen—of course! Ring from a neighbor's house or from wherever you think is safest, most unlikely."

"That's good, William, yes. Yes, I might do that. But wait! No, no—I won't. Definitely not. I'm going to do exactly what they ask. Get the money and wait for instructions. I'm grateful for your help, but I'm going to ring off now."

"But just a minute . . . Alex—"

"Good-bye."

The telephone went dead. I replaced it, puzzled. Just as we

seemed to be getting something constructive going, he rings off—Why? What had happened?—Had someone come into the room?

What had we been talking about?

Telephone tapping, how to ring the police without being found out . . .

Telephone tapping! Oh yes, of course!

We were talking on the line to his house—the line most likely to be tapped if any were . . . Discussing how to cheat the kidnappers . . .

How stupid can you be?

Well, that seemed to put the stopper on any further activity, at least until Thursday night. Frustrating, just as I seemed to be getting somewhere. I would have liked to have made sure whether Cathy was at Stephenson's villa or not—to have carried on just that much longer. It was vital to know where she was being held—you often hear of kidnaps where the hostage has to be snatched back in a surprise raid after negotiations have gone wrong. But it would be risky—*no police, no tricks!* It would have to be Alex's decision. And from his panicky breaking off of our telephone conversation, I'd guess his verdict would be No.

I went for a stroll around the village to sort my ideas out. It looked like the end of the road for me: Alex would want to get professional help in, now. Did I regret it? Well, I would have liked to have been of some use, and I hadn't really achieved anything yet. But what should I do? Go back to La Sauvegarde, and the unfinished book? Or stay on here awhile, in case I was needed after all? It would feel more of a fiasco to drive back so soon after getting here. I could spend a day at Santa Margarita and a couple more in Barcelona, one part-time unpaid private eye with time on his hands. If only Ginny could have come, but after yesterday's abortive call that must be a forlorn hope.

However . . . there, just ahead, is a telephone kiosk. It'd

be a fainthearted fellow who didn't try one more time . . .

I dialed and waited.

"Hello?" *Her voice!*

"Ginny! What's happening? I rang last night as we arranged, but there was no reply. Did you forget?"

"Oh, William darling, no, of course I didn't, I—"

"Well, what then? That's another whole day wasted—I'm deeply hurt and upset."

"Oh you're not, don't say that . . . listen, William darling—"

"It'd better be good."

"Don't be so foul; I couldn't help it. I fell off Benji."

"You what?"

"I fell off Benji. He balked, you see, but it wasn't really his fault."

"Are you telling me—?"

"I'd left a bucket by the jump, and it frightened him; I expect he thought it was a—"

"Ginny!"

"—dog or something; you know how shortsighted they are."

"I see."

"I knew you'd understand."

"Was it a bad fall? I mean, are you hurt?"

"Only bruises. I came down in mud. But I lost the reins, you see, and it took some time to catch him again: I was afraid he'd jump out; there's a broken piece of hedge that—"

"Well, the main thing is you're all right, Ginny."

"Oh yes, I'm fine really, but I missed your call. Anyway, it's all worked out now, and we didn't really lose a day because Mrs. Troughton's daughter can't take over until Thursday; she's got an interview tomorrow. Oh, I do hope that's not too late."

"You can fly down on Thursday? Really?"

"Yes, I'll be at Barcelona at four-fifteen, from Heathrow."

"Ginny, that's wonderful! I'll be there. But wait—what about the weekend?"

"That's all right too—Evan's going up north somewhere on a case, and he's going to stay up there. You see!—it's not all bad news!"

"It certainly isn't. Thursday—I can't wait!"

"Nor can I, William darling."

Instantly adaptable, fickle creatures we are. Or I am. I found myself humming as I strolled along to the bar for a celebration drink. A few minutes ago I'd been agonizing with Alex. Well, it was out of my hands now, all that. And Ginny was coming on Thursday. Should I book us in to Barcelona, or nearby Tarragona? I wondered. I'd better make a tour of likely look-ing hotels, bounce on a few beds. A balcony for breakfasts, a view of the sea for between times, that's all we need. Roman ruins, musty museums, even galleries of Goyas—no thanks, not today.

"Won the pools, William?" Jill was looking at me curiously from her station behind the bar.

"Oh—some good news from home, that's all." Should I tell her about the ransom note?—better not, for safety's sake.

"And Alex?"

"Well, Alex is very worried, of course."

"He certainly sounded it. So he just wanted to know if you'd made any progress this end?"

"That's about it, yes."

"Did you get anywhere with Mark's father?"

"Completely uncooperative, I'm afraid."

She waited, her elbows on the bar, obviously expecting more. It was difficult not to tell her. I said:

"Let's split a bottle of Freixenet, shall we?—my treat."

"Cordon Negro?"

"If that suits you."

"Sure." She reached into the fridge and brought out the black bottle. "You open it—you're the expert."

"If not, it isn't for want of trying," I said, twisting out the cork. There was only a slight hiss—one does one's best to avoid a vulgar pop by keeping the pressure on, doesn't one.

"Bravo," Jill said. We clinked glasses, and took in a mouthful of golden bubbles. "Are we," she said, "celebrating love?—or money?"

"Ooh," I said, "you're a crafty lady."

"Spend time behind this bar," she said, "and you see it all."

"It's love," I said. She smiled. Oh hell!—of course I could trust her. I looked around: apart from a family group outside the bar, we were alone. "I was being ultracautious about the Gordons. Actually, it's very bad news. A ransom note. So the questions have to stop before the kid gets hurt."

"I don't believe it!" she said. "A ransom note? That sort of thing doesn't happen to people you know. The Stephensons?"

"She could be at the Stephensons', but I daren't go back for another look, not now. In fact the safest thing is for me to clear off, back to Barcelona. We mustn't risk annoying them."

"Christ almighty," Jill said.

"So you see . . ."

"Oh yes, I won't utter a sound. Christ, I wouldn't have thought that the Stephenson boy would let Cathy in for this."

"How much have you seen of him?"

"Well, he's been around this summer, off and on. Good looking boy, seemed open enough, not at all what this suggests. Christ, you never can tell, can you."

"You never can tell." I refilled our glasses. "So, now my mind's made itself up. I'd better collect my things from your house and beat it. Many thanks for the sofa."

"Any time. You'll find some shirts on the line in the garden—I was doing a wash so I bunged them in."

"Oh Jill—that's really sweet of you. I wish I could stay longer—it's a delightful place you've got here."

"Except for the screaming kids."

"Oh well, perhaps . . ."

"The all-night motorbikes."

"Yes, I did notice . . ."

"The everlasting disco beat. The heat. The bloody flies. The sand in everything. The cooking, the cleaning, the endless, all-demanding customers. Oh. Don't mind me—it's the late season blues. Only six weeks more, then peace, perfect peace."

"And money in the bank."

"That's what it's all about. Go and enjoy yourself in Barcelona—come and see us again when this is all over."

"I may surprise you and do that."

"I hope so." As I left the bar, some newcomers were arriving: four large men with American accents, off one of the Mediterranean oil rigs, I guessed. I heard Jill greet them with enthusiastic cries: "Hi! Where've you been hiding? The place hasn't felt the same without you!" Catering, it's called. Show biz, it is.

Back at number 12, I unhooked my shirts from the garden line and began to pack. The telephone rang, but I ignored it—no doubt they'd ring again when Jill had finished her stint at the bar. It rang on. I changed my mind and picked it up.

"Hello?"

"William? Is that you?"

"Yes—oh Alex!—hello. I nearly didn't answer—just off to Barcelona."

"Are you? Oh I see. Right. Well, it doesn't matter."

"What doesn't? Are you ringing from home?"

"No, I've played safe and I'm in a call box. It can't be that easy to tap a phone, but I'm not taking any risks."

"I'm sure you're right—I've seen electronic gadgets advertised . . . What doesn't matter?"

"Well. I was just going to make a suggestion. But if you've arranged to go to Barcelona . . ."

"Forget Barcelona, Alex. What can I do for you?"

"It's a lot to ask."

"Look, Alex—don't hold back. I want to help. What is it?"

"You may well not want to do this after what happened today, but is there anywhere from which you could watch

Stephenson's villa without being seen? That's the important thing—*without being seen*. I've been thinking, and it seems to me that if anything goes wrong—"

"—with the negotiations, you'll need to know where she is? Yes, I had the same thought."

"You did? You see the point, don't you, that if—"

"Yes, I understand; we may have to go in and get her out."

"That's it, exactly. Of course, she may not be there, but from what you say, it's a possibility, and one we can't afford to neglect. Our only one, in fact."

"Right. Leave it to me, Alex. I'll get up there tomorrow morning at first light, and see what I can find out. Where can I contact you?"

"Ring the hospital—you've got the number. If I'm not there, leave a message—I'll ring you back."

So, it's on, then—the plan that's been bubbling away half in, half out of my subconscious.

What do I need? The little Zeiss binoculars I always keep in the glove pocket of the Citroën. A haversack—perhaps Jill can help with that. Clothes—how cold does it get up there when the sun sets? Some kind of weapon would be a comfort—I mean to avoid contact, but accidents will happen. Wire cutters?—no, I won't be getting that close. Food, of course, enough for a full day. And water—vital in that heat. What else?

It takes me back to my time in the army, this military obsession with equipment . . .

WEDNESDAY

IT WAS STILL DARK WHEN I DROVE UP THE VALLEY TO the east of Torrecasim, with the last of the moonlight fading from the mountaintops. If I hadn't acquired an obsession with equipment, I might have set out without the large-scale map that Jill had unearthed; a souvenir, she said, of walking weekends before the arrival of the Monster put a stop to all that. Yes, she had a haversack as well—would I care for a compass? Well, I said, why not—I'm taking this expedition seriously. And a flashlight, too! Ever try to read a compass in the dark? she said. As a matter of fact, yes, I said—and I had some time to regret it while waiting for my tank to be winched out of a marsh. Only National Service, but you learn a thing or two: I can polish brass, wash socks, and iron a knife-edge crease in trousers by soaping them inside. Ah well—no need to fear the Russkies while we have men who can do that, she said. What else do you want? Water, matches, and a couple of corks, I said, that's all. Apart from good luck. Corks? she said . . . oh yes, of course. Bright girl, Jill.

The road I'd chosen was single track, but well surfaced. It ran diagonally through the dense pine forest on the side of the spur of mountain on which Torrecasim was perched, rising steadily to the junction with the main road into Prades. I stopped several times to study the map, the problem being to know exactly where I was. The forest which lined both sides of the road was a black, undifferentiated mass: somewhere below I could hear rushing water, but no stream was visible;

and in any case, there were several marked on the map, any of which could be the one I could hear. What I was looking for was a path or track shown on the map as a thin black broken line leading up across the massed contours to Torrecasim. It could, of course, have fallen into disuse, become overgrown and invisible: footpaths can disappear within a year.

Half a mile short of the point where I intended to start my climb I found a place where I could get the car off the road, and at least partly concealed. Reversing into it, I parked beside a log pile that left a clear passageway for the tractor that always turns up wherever you leave your car in the most deserted-looking countryside.

It was still dark. I walked farther up the road at as fast a pace as I could manage, going uphill, and with years of good living making themselves felt. You can live so long without worrying much about exercise, but after a certain age, it becomes a case of Use It or Lose It. Twelve minutes, which I hoped was half a mile, enough to remind me that I was past that age, and ought to give some thought to the less entertaining forms of exercise. Phew! Twelve minutes up, I squatted on my heels with my back to a tree, taking deep, healthy breaths—well all right, panting. Had to wait for the sunrise, anyway, didn't I?

Fifteen minutes later, I found the track I was looking for. It was still dark, and hard to see much under the trees. I flashed the light to see the task ahead. Jesus! Did I really have to go up there? I checked the map again. If I was at the chosen spot, the map showed that the contours on each side were even closer together, which meant a much stiffer climb than I'd had so far. The angle of the pine tree trunks against the rising ground made that quite clear. No better alternative, though. Better get on with it, then.

I climbed slowly upward, my rubber-soled trainers giving good grip on the rocky ground. Time passed. Then I noticed that I no longer needed the flashlight: the darkness was lifting, turning gray; the trunks of trees gradually taking on color. I stopped to replace it in the haversack, and to ease my aching

knees. Looking around, I could see a sky streaked with pale
yellow, and from behind the high mountains on the far side of
the valley, an orange glow was spreading.

But I'm not here to admire the view. Light is now my
enemy, and I must get up there and into position before the
world is wide awake.

Ten minutes later I emerged above the tree line, paused to take
stock again, and saw the buzzards. A pair of them flapped
above the pine trees, their broad wings searching for lift in the
cool morning air. If I hadn't disturbed them on my climb
through the forest, they'd have stayed at home on the roost,
waiting for the sun to set the easy-rider thermals in motion,
their moving staircase to the sky.

Over to my right, the pines swept over the ridge in a sea of
dark green: somewhere up there, a few hundred yards away,
was the track I'd driven along yesterday with Pilar and Alastair. Ahead was a wide expanse of rock, studded with occasional scrubby bushes and small trees, which we'd crossed
before we'd followed the track into the sunken gully. And to
the left was the rocky outcrop, like a natural castle, that the
track had swerved to avoid. That was where I was headed.

From where I stood, the village, its causeway, and Stephenson's villa were all hidden behind the outcrop. And I was
hidden from them. I made my way along the edge of the trees,
ready to dive into cover if anything moved on the bare skyline.
But nothing did, and in ten minutes, I was opposite the nearest
end of the outcrop, studying its formation for the best line of
approach. From this new position, I could see that it was
longer than I had supposed: more like a wall than a castle. It
was a bare, brownish mass of rock, the upper layers worn
smooth by erosion, the lower part hollowed out where softer
rock strata had been washed away, leaving white streaks which
resembled a frozen waterfall. Some of the clefts and rockfalls
scattered along its length looked climbable. The rock strata
sloped downward in my direction, which not only made it

easier to climb, but should help to conceal me from the view of anyone on the track at the far side. The only problem was its bony bareness: I could see no loose rock, bushes, or anything that would give me shade from the heat that was already starting to make itself felt.

From the shelter of a wiry thornbush, I made a last, sweeping search of the plateau I now had to cross. The broad brown rock appeared deserted: nothing moved on that skull-like surface. A tinny rustle came from dried leaves under a bush to my left: I looked nervously, remembering that adders thrive in hot, dry conditions like this, being thankful not to see the short diamond-patterned body I instinctively dreaded. Something was there, though. I looked again, and as my focus shifted, I saw what I'd thought was an exposed piece of root glitter as it moved. I breathed a sigh of relief: we have grass snakes in France, and although they're much bigger than adders and may grow to three feet long, they're not poisonous and will only bite if cornered. I watched as the slithering ended in a tail, which jerked once or twice before being drawn out of sight. A useful reminder, I thought, not to put my hand in nooks and crannies.

Time to take up my position, then. I moved out from behind the thornbush, and into the open, crossing the gently sloping bare rock to the outcrop. The sun was behind me, and I was treading on the heels of my early-morning shadow, a tall, transparent, stilt-walking, unfamiliar creature, no relation, you might suppose, to the short black confident companion of midday. But he could shift those long legs when he wanted to . . . I was at the outcrop in under two minutes.

It looked higher and more vertical than I'd expected. I slung the haversack farther on my back to leave my hands free, and began to climb, following a fault in the rock. There were areas of loose shale which were treacherous going. I heaved, I scrabbled, I cursed. Then, suddenly, it was all over, and I could see across the top. A final heave, and I was there.

I rolled clear of the edge and stayed flat, aware that a stand-

ing figure would show up against the sky like the Eiffel Tower.
Raising my head, I saw that the surface of the rock had been
burnished by sun and wind to a smoothness you could waltz
across. Where I lay, flat on my stomach, lizardlike, I could feel
the residual warmth of the previous day coming through my
shirt. The sun was already at work, stirring faint shimmerings
of heat from the rock which, before long, would give off mir-
ages, whirlpools of miraculous vision. No oases to reflect up
here, though: nothing but the sky. A distant, plaintive mewing
reminded me of the buzzards: I looked up, and saw the pair
circling farther down the valley, still below the level of my
rock, but balanced now on wings that no longer needed to flap
but rode an invisible column of rising air, each spiraling turn
carrying them up and up. Yes, today was going to be hot.

I wormed my way farther back from the edge of the rock,
and then sat up. From this viewpoint, the rock was an island,
detached from earth, floating in sky. I imagined I could feel it
move—an unsettling sensation. I'd had that feeling before in
high places—the realization of what's true but normally unfelt,
that if the earth stops we all fly off into space. So far, so good,
is all we've got to rely on . . .

All right—so I haven't got a head for heights. Should have
remembered that when planning this expedition. But I hadn't
realized it would feel quite *so* high . . .

Crawl a bit farther from the edge. That's enough. Now stand
up . . .

Yes, well. Sways somewhat, but common sense (or science)
must prevail. An optical illusion, merely. Contrary to appear-
ances, it's the sky that's moving, not the rock . . .

I begin to walk, keeping my eyes on the rock. Faith can
move mountains—but what I want is for this one to stand still.
I need to know what can be seen from the southern end of this
rock, the end which overlooked the old castle and causeway of
Torrecasim. I cover the last few yards on hands and knees. At
last I can lift my eyes from the rock and . . .

Jesus!

There's the causeway, within a stone's throw. Just beyond are the crumbled walls and tower of the Moorish castle. And beyond that, the craggy stone cottages of the village, with smoke drifting from two of the chimneys against the blue background of distant mountains. A stunning picture postcard, it would make.

But if that stone fell short . . .

Well, I'm just not going to look down there. I'd have to get nearer to the edge to do it, and . . . someone might see me. Well, that's perfectly true, they might. So, having done what I came for, I'll withdraw. Hands and knees again, until it's safe to stand up, and walk away.

Funny thing, now—after a glimpse into that abyss of nothingness, the old rock here feels quite firm and friendly. Good old rock.

The observation post I finally chose was about halfway along the rock, on the higher, west side. There was no shade, but there was a change in level of about a foot where a huge flake had broken away, perhaps not all that many years ago because a number of loose fragments were still lying about as if waiting to be collected in evidence. Lying in the fault, I'd been able to rig up a crude shelter from the sun by anchoring my jacket with stones on the higher level and pulling it over my head and shoulders. It was a Lacoste jacket bought for me by Claudine, who likes to get me into trendy clothes; the makers would have been upset to see it so misused, but it did the job admirably. From the sketchy shelter of the semitent thus formed, I focused the little Zeiss binoculars on the white walls and barred windows of Stephenson's house, which lay below my position and some eighty yards away on the far side of the track which led to the Torrecasim causeway, now out of my field of view to the left.

It was just before eight—later than I had intended but, I hoped, early enough to catch a full day in the life of the Stephenson household. So far, nobody had appeared. It was

possible they were having breakfast on the south side of the
house, where there was certainly a terrace—I could see one end
of it—which was angled away from me, an annoyance I could
reduce by moving to another position farther south on my
rock. But at this time of day I was more interested to watch
the front door on the north side, and this was in clear view. I
could see the steps I'd fallen down, and the graveled courtyard
I'd retreated across. I could see the back of the blue Range
Rover, parked under its bamboo shading. I could see the arch
with its iron gates tightly shut. I could follow the line of the
high white wall with its red-tiled coping, dipping around both
sides of the house to follow the contour of the ground as it fell
away to the cliff edge beyond. And I could see one end of a
swimming pool below the terrace on the south side of the
house, close enough to the cliff edge to make you unsure if you
were swimming or flying . . .

Movement!

Something moved behind the corner of the house, at the end
of the terrace; I'm sure of it.

Steady the binoculars. The focus is good. Wait for it . . .

Yes, there it is again. One, then both of the dogs run into
view, and then run back again behind the house. Then one
reappears, turns, and stands, mouth opening and shutting. The
sound of barking reaches me half a second after the event.
What's a bark, then? Is it the effort or the sound? Never mind,
here's something much more interesting!—the ogre himself,
strolling to the end of the terrace, the dogs gamboling heavily
about him. He stops to stretch, to sniff the morning air perhaps.
If I had a rifle with me, and sufficient reason, he'd be a dead
man now. (Or I'd be a lousy shot, which I'm not.) Just speculation, of course, just a thought, the kind of thought that occurs
to men in concealment. Pop! and it's all over. Dash in then and
rescue the maiden.

But is she there?—that's what I really want to know. If
you're holding a kidnap victim, do you let her out of the house
for exercise and maybe a cooling swim, or do you keep her

bolted in the basement? The latter, I'd guess. If so, I'll have a
wasted day. But maybe Mark, the sometime boyfriend, if he's
in on this, would want to make things easy for her, and see she
got some fresh air and exercise. It would be safe enough—
there's little chance of her scaling that wall, and even if she did,
she wouldn't get far in this wilderness.

Back to the binocs. Nothing doing now: dogs and ogre out
of sight, probably at breakfast. Which reminds me: kind sensible Jill gave me a thermos, so I needn't writhe with envy.
Struggle with haversack unwilling to let it go. Damn!—this
movement could give me away. Slide back out of sight for a
moment: defeat haversack, pour coffee, put cup handy, slide
back into position. Have I missed anything? Still no one in
view. Sip of coffee—delicious! Must remember that, even
when I can't see anybody, eyes may still be watching me from
inside the house, through one of those barred windows, impen-
etrable at present because of reflection on the glass. Later in the
day, as the sun goes around, it may improve—but then I'll have
to watch reflection from the binocular lenses giving me away.

What time is it now? Oh my God, only twenty past eight!
At this rate, today is not only going to be hot; it's going to go
on forever.

Eight forty-five: Stephenson's wife appears at the end of the
terrace with a watering can, and makes a tour of the plant pots
there; I can see her arm movements and an occasional glitter
as the water catches the sun. When I last saw her, in the
restaurant, she seemed downtrodden, but perhaps that was
misleading and she's as bad as he is—if the girl's in the basement, she may be the jailer. What's she doing now?—dragging
something about, but I can't see what. Now she's walking back
to the house. A pause, and then a shining net rises from the
ground . . . at this distance, a fairies' cobweb . . . at the bottom
of her garden, too. Will I see the elfin creatures dancing in and
out, all 'round about? Not bloody likely. The hounds of hell
is all—they're back now, both of them, gallumphing like pup-

pies and snapping at the water jets swinging slowly back and
forth. A roar of rage from an invisible Stephenson, and immediately both dogs stop playing and slink obediently back to the
terrace. Episode over.

Nine-five: there's somebody in the pool, but it's very very
frustrating as I can only see the end of it, and all I get is
off-stage effects such as waves and occasional faint sounds of
splashing. I think the steps must be at the far end, which is a
serious snag as it'll be difficult to identify people in the water
at this range, even if . . . wait, yes, I got a glimpse then as
somebody swam into the end I can see, did a flip turn, and
swam back. It was over in seconds. There they are again
. . . useless, it could be anybody. If only they'd come running
around for a dive, as this must be the deep end . . . No, that
seems to be it. Episode over.

Nine-thirty: I don't like what's happening now. The front
door opened, and Stephenson came out with the dogs, walked
straight to the gate in a routine kind of way, and shoved them
out through it. Now he's standing there, in the gateway,
watching them as they rush about, sniffing the ground in businesslike style. If I'd been able to come up that side of the rock
and had chosen to, they'd have got on to me for sure. Now
they're crossing the track, coming this way. No, I don't like
it at all. There's something about the sight of dogs on the trail
that's extremely unnerving: the way they locate and then follow an invisible thread which humans aren't even aware of.
They're not far from the foot of the rock, now—could they
smell me up here, some forty or fifty feet above them? There's
a mere breath of wind from the southwest, coming up the
valley, that should take my scent away. But if they were to
range around to the other side of the rock, the east side where
I climbed up, I think I'd be in trouble. Up here, if they found
me, and if Stephenson decided not to call them off . . . well,
what would I do? It's a bare rock, with nowhere to go. That's

the sort of situation nightmares are made of. I've got no weapon, nothing to defend myself with . . . Where are they now? Oh yes . . . of course! Well, dogs do have to do that, and you don't want it in your garden, so this may be no more than a daily routine for hygienic purposes, and not a sweep for intruders. Yes!—it looks like merely that, as the dogs are making their way back to master now. Through the gate—and he's shutting it.

That sweat I can feel in my armpits is not just the heat . . .

Ten-fifteen: the front door opens again, and it's Mrs. Stephenson this time, coming out to water the pots in the courtyard. Perhaps she's never been told that it's best to water plants in the evening, to minimize the loss of water by evaporation. Perhaps in this climate you have to water plants twice a day. Perhaps she just wants to get out of the house, away from the ogre, and enjoy a quiet potter in the garden. Perhaps I'll take advantage of this pastoral episode to slide back out of sight again and have a quick swig of coffee.

Ten thirty-five: Mrs. Stephenson is tying up some drooping plant which is evidently supposed to climb up this end of the house. It may be bignonia—I think I can just see splashes of yellow, trumpet-shaped flowers, unless it's my imagination filling in gaps. Naturally I'm proud to air this knowledge, the result of timeless trails around garden centers with madame. "What about this one?" I suggest hopefully, as we enter on a third round of indecision. "*Ah non, chéri,* not *yellow,*" she cries, horrified. So it stuck, you see.

Eleven o'clock: this is slightly more interesting—not much, but let's not complain: apart from the false alarm with the dogs, I'm finding it difficult to keep awake. First, I heard a noise that reminded me of yesterday's near miss with the trail bikers: then a pair of them hurtled into view, coming—this might be significant—coming from the direction of the causeway and the

village. They skidded up to Stephenson's gateway, climbed off
their bikes, and after a short wait were admitted. Aha!—I
thought: maybe the bikers are part of the Stephenson setup, as
I'd guessed they might be, and the rest will arrive shortly for
a briefing on whatever misdemeanor is currently being
planned. I waited, hoping to see a cloud of dust come rolling
along the track from Prades, announcing the arrival of the rest
of the gang. Meanwhile, Stephenson himself came out of the
house and stood talking to the two youths in the courtyard,
gesticulating this way and that. Was he, perhaps, describing
some kind of ambush—a pay truck possibly? It's easy to believe
he has that kind of background, and it would also explain why
he's chosen to live out here in this remote place. If only I had
one of those electronic gadgets that focus sound at long distance, to hear what he was telling them . . . ! But no—it would
have been wasted because a minute later both youths were hard
at work with spade and wheelbarrow, building up a rockery
by the side of the front door . . . Well, I have to speculate,
don't I?

Twelve noon: and I've nothing to report, except that the sun
has become an unrelenting enemy, and I'm being fried alive.
The heat haze coming off the rock is obscuring the binoculars,
turning the walls of Stephenson's house and garden into wavering white ribbons, like something glimpsed through running
water. Wherever I look, the scene dissolves: earth, buildings,
trees, rock all seem insubstantial, turned to liquid. Myself in-
cluded—I'm swimming in sweat. I've thought of moving, but
it's most unlikely that I missed a better place when touring the
rock earlier, and the mere thought of useless exertion is enough
to bring on new prickles of sweat. Moreover, the area of rock
I'm lying on is probably the coolest there is, having been
sheltered beneath my roasting carcass all morning: it would be
stupid to let the sun in on it now. I'm so hot I can hardly be
bothered to eat: half a cucumber and lettuce sandwich with a
mouthful of water seems a feast. If there was a breeze, now!—

but there isn't, just a faint movement of air, hot as dragon's breath.

Twelve twenty-five: a rasp of engines again, and I peer through a curtain of sweat to see the bikes take off, their riders heading home no doubt to some cool kitchen behind thick stone walls to drink iced lager and cold gaspacho. The Stephensons are already indoors. It's siesta time—shutters banged up, curtains drawn in every Spanish home. I could leave now, and nobody would see me go. But a man's got to do . . . etc.

One o'clock: the second half of cucumber sandwich and another mouthful of water. Sometime soon, a momentous decision must be made—where, on this island in the sky, to have a pee.

One-fifteen: Well, that's over, and the rocks hissed but didn't fracture. I risked a minute of luxurious pacing up and down to stretch my legs, and transferred a soggy bundle of banknotes from my back trouser pocket to the haversack. It's not impossible that my right buttock now bears a transferred royal portrait of Juan Carlos together with a promise to pay the bearer five thousand pesatas.

Two o'clock: nothing to report except that my friends, the pair of buzzards, are back: so far above me that my eyes have difficulty in holding the focus—one moment I see them, the next I've lost them again. I'm running a competition for the best description of the sky: metallic, certainly, but is it brass, or stainless steel, or—really subtle this—slightly tarnished silver? Who's the expert I should consult? I think I'm in a Coleridge situation here: Alone, alone, all all alone/alone on a wide wide sea. I can't remember what the Ancient Mariner had to say about the sky, but I'm certainly looking forward to: The Sun's rim dips; the stars rush out/At one stride comes the dark . . . (And the cool, the wonderful cool . . .)

* * *

Three o'clock: This must be the worst time of day, with everything heated to maximum. From now on, the sun's in retreat.
Think of it this way—I'd have been almost as hot and bored
on the beach. Of course, that's why I don't go near beaches if
I can possibly avoid it . . . the girls have to drag me there
. . . sheer torture! And a serious risk of skin cancer, I'm told.

Now wait, wait!—don't get too excited . . . There's still a lot
of heat haze, and I could've been mistaken . . . Twenty to four,
I forgot to say, if it matters. Twenty to four, and I think I've
seen, though I can't be sure. I'm waiting for another look to
confirm or deny it, but I certainly had the impression that
. . . Hold on, hold on! No, not yet . . . By the pool, by that
tantalizing end of pool which is all I can see from here . . .
Someone was swimming! It was just like this morning, and I
could see the waves as the sun caught them, hoping that whoever it was would, this time, come running around to take a
dive from the deep end, and then, suddenly, she did . . .
   She did . . .
   I think she did—I mean, it could have been Cathy. Slim,
young looking, a still childish outline . . .
   There! She's come around again, a springy, athletic walk, and
is poised on the pool end, getting ready to dive. And this time,
I really am sure that her hair is blond. So—the right age, the
right hair—*this could be it!*
   How can I make sure?

WEDNESDAY EVENING

WAIT FOR SUNSET, I WAS BEING TOLD. *THEN MOVE IN under cover of darkness. There'll be lights on inside the house; you'll get a good look in through the windows . . .*

It was a crisp, military, authoritative voice from somewhere in my past. Define objective, plan, then execute. Well—get on with it, man!

Yessir. Just like to mention, though, if I may . . .

What?

Er, dogs . . .

Never get anywhere without taking some risk, dammit. Are you a man or a mouse?

Fond of animals, actually. But these are *serious* dogs—urgent carnivores, not just postman nippers. They won't be content with trousers; they'll want the legs as well . . .

No, I didn't see myself slipping over that garden wall in the moonlight. But I had over four hours to think about it before the light began to go: four hours which might produce a better view of the girl or confirmation of some other kind—the boy turning up, for instance, in the Spanish-registered red Renault 5. I ate a salami sandwich and then settled down with the binoculars again.

The sun was now in decline on the far side of the house, and the shadows were growing out toward me. Although the rock surface was still scorching hot to touch, the air temperature was dropping by the minute. But for the dishcloth clamminess of my shirt and the hardness of the rock under me, I was beginning to feel almost comfortable. I lay, watching the tiny figure that was Mrs. Stephenson moving about inside the walled garden, hoeing, raking, watering, adjusting plants and pots, a scene so comfortably and innocently domestic that I began to lose confidence in my reasons for being here. A seedy occupation, spying on people. A woman gardening, unaware that Zeiss lenses were focused on her every movement—that makes me feel a creep. But maybe Stephenson will be about again soon. So, on with the record.

Shortly after five, the two youths turn up on their bikes for a second session of rockery building in the cool of the evening, and I watch as Stephenson comes out to direct them. As before—but I've only just realized this—the dogs stay in the house. There are strict rules about keeping real guard dogs, I've been told: one is that you mustn't let them meet people and make friends: they must be kept in a state of paranoia about all humans apart from their handler. Stephenson's had to make an exception for his wife—perhaps she gets acceptance by feeding them.

I remembered about reflection from the Zeiss object lenses, and am shielding them from the downward sliding sun by cupping my hands around them. I hope it works . . .

Six o'clock: rockery building still in progress. I haven't seen the girl again, and I haven't seen any sign of the pool being used. That's consistent with the girl being Cathy—she wouldn't be allowed out of the house when the workers were there.

Seven o'clock: the workers are packing up now. Stephenson sees them through the gate, and pulls it shut. Then he walks around the house to the terrace on the far side. Mrs. Stephenson follows. Drinks on the terrace, by the pool, to watch the sun go down? A delightful way to end the day. I may be observing an exception to another rule—that crime doesn't pay. I'm trying to see through the windows now that the shine is off them but can see nothing except one or two shadowy angular shapes which might be beds or tables.

Eight o'clock: no sign of anyone—must be still on the terrace or inside starting supper. Feeling peckish myself: think I'll see what sandwiches I've got left . . . one salami is all. Plus some chocolate biscuits, welded into a solid block. Not a wise choice if you're going to lie in the sun all day. There's a drain of coffee left: cold, but still tastes good. I'll keep it for later to wash the rest of the biscuits down with. Something to look forward to . . .

Nine o'clock: the sun has set, and stars are beginning to show as the color drains from the sky. Is that a star or is it Mars, down there to the south? Or a packed British Airways flight to Benidorm?—no, it's not moving; it's a star.

Nine-fifteen: and sudden darkness. But there's a new, cold light from the mountains behind me that must be a full moon on the way up. So—what next? Do I pack up or try for a closer look at the house? There's going to be enough light to move about in, but I'm also going to be visible when I move out of cover. What little wind there was has now died away completely, and it's as silent as the grave up here: I'd have to be careful about noise as a misplaced foot, a slight click of stone on stone, will be audible yards away. Let's have the rest of the biscuits and the coffee while I think about it, and wait to see just how full this moon is.

Nine-twenty: I'm guessing the time without looking at my watch because there's something going on down there in the shadows, outside the villa. I'd moved back from the skyline for a moment (I have to be extra careful now with the moonlight behind me) to pour out the coffee, and then, as I slid back into position, I saw light coming from the front door. No one visible, but the dogs are out, black shadows flitting rapidly about the garden. And now I've just noticed a spark of light under the arched gateway. There it goes again, a miniature shooting star—Stephenson smoking an evening cigarette. He moves, and I can see him more clearly now—a bulky dark shape against the pale gravel beyond. Now I can clearly hear the metallic groan and scrape of the gate opening. And out, into the moonlight, come the dogs . . .

No, I'm not worried this time. They came out this morning, ran about, had a crap, and ran back in. This is the evening session, that's all. I have to be a little more careful, though, because of the silence, and because I'm well aware that, from Stephenson's viewpoint, the rock I'm on is in clear silhouette against the moonlight.

No worries, then, if I keep still and quiet, not really. I don't mind admitting, though, that it's a trifle spooky watching these black dog shadows coursing about. I shan't be sorry when they've gone back to the house. Here they come now, across the track toward the base of the rock, just like this morning. That's all right—dogs have habits, just like humans.

I think, when they've gone, I shall pack up and go home. No one could say I haven't done my bit, lying up here on blistering rock, fried all day and now getting chilly. There's a girl in the house, I've seen that. When I get home, I'll have to sit down and work out some way of finding out who she is.

The dogs are on the way home. So why not me?—I'll slide back slowly, collect my gear, and be off . . .

What the hell is that noise? Tinkle, tinkle, ding, dong—like distant church bells . . .

But it's not church bells, oh no . . .

It's the lid of my thermos, bouncing down the rock face . . .

I should have stayed put; I should have waited just a little longer! But I was moving so slowly, being so careful . . .

Time for that later. The question was, what to do now? No doubt that the dogs heard it—there was a racket like wolves fighting over a kill down there.

Could they get up? I didn't think so, not that side—too steep. But they'd manage the east side, where I came up . . . and where I had to go down.

I knew I'd never make it across the plateau to the woods. And once down there, I'd have to cope with Stephenson as

well. Better wait here. Of course, they may not come, may not
come . . .

I reckoned I had somewhere between one and two minutes
before the dogs could get around to the east of the rock and
find a way up. It was useless to try to hide—they'd sniff me out
in seconds. The best I could do was to stuff some tooth-break-
ing pebbles in the pockets of the Lacoste jacket, zip them up,
and wind the jacket tightly around my left arm. Then I selected a larger stone for use as a weapon. Finally, I moved
along the rock toward the causeway end, where the surface
was smoothest. That was all I could think of—but it wasn't
easy to think at all when, in my imagination, I could see the
black shapes racing around the base of the rock, and scrabbling
their way up. Of course, I kept repeating to myself as I stood
ready: they may not come, they may not come . . .

But they did.

I heard them before I saw anything: a clatter of stones at the
far end of the rock. It seemed to go on forever. Then suddenly,
on the moonlit surface, I saw what seemed at first a whole pack
charging down on me until the last few yards, when it separated into two real dogs and two black shadows.

I tensed, aware that if both dogs attacked at once their combined weight would have me down and demolish my defense
before I'd had a chance to try it. But I stood stock still and kept
silent until they were as close as ten yards. Then, in the fiercest
tone I could manage, I roared:

"DOWN!"

The dogs slowed. Then, six feet away, they stopped.

I took a deep breath. It could only be a temporary loss of
confidence. Both dogs were growling, and showing teeth designed to anchor their full weight securely into a fleeing
quarry. A land shark, that's what a dog is—little more than a
pair of self-propelled jaws.

They were edging nearer. I'd have to try something, but my
mind seemed to have gone blank. The sight of those large
white teeth in the moonlight . . .

A distant shout from down below took the decision out of my hands. What Stephenson's command was I still don't know, but there was no time to think about it. The dogs began to edge forward again, growling as if they meant business this time. Instinctively, I did what I'd been telling myself I must not do—I stepped backward.

The movement acted as a trigger on the larger of the two dogs, who leaped at me, jaws agape. I was just able to avoid contact by sidestepping, and as the dog passed me, I spun to help it on its way with the best kick I could summon up, putting all my weight behind it. I had the advantage of rubber-soled trainers, which gripped the rock and put power behind my kick. The dog traveled several yards down the sloping rock face before crash-landing on the smooth surface. Momentum carried it onward, claws scrabbling uselessly as it struggled for grip. Then it disappeared over the edge.

I heard a long, descending howl, but I was already under attack again. The second dog was smaller, but more intelligent. Its leap was less dramatic but more effective: I felt the teeth clamp into the pebble-loaded jacket wound around my left arm. The dog's weight threw me off balance, and we fell together, dog on top, in a textbook maneuvre that the beast had learned only too efficiently. What none of its previous victims had been provided with, though, was a heavy sliver of stone in their free hand.

"Sorry about this," I said. The dog's face, its coal black eyes and wrinkled brow, was inches from mine. It was a shame, really. The best I could do was to hit hard and try to make it instantaneous. I raised the stone for a second bash if needed, but the dog's grip had slackened, and if there's a Valhalla for Dobermans that die in battle, it seemed to be already there.

I heaved the poor beast aside and got to my feet. From below, still at some distance, Stephenson's roars were echoing around the rocks. He was going to be crosser than ever when the dogs failed to appear; it'd be wise to conceal this second corpse. I bent to grasp its back legs, and dragged it to the edge of the rock. In the moonlight, the causeway below was a pale, spidery bridge over a bottomless void. I sat down and pushed the dog into space with my feet. Several seconds later, there was a dull crash from far below. I retreated some distance on my backside before standing up again. The stone sliver still lay on the scene of the crime, and I sent that spinning into space. Then I unwound the jacket from my arm, and inspected it. Though the dog's teeth had made puncture marks, it was still wearable; I put it on, leaving the pebbles in the pockets for the moment. It was time to be on my way, before Stephenson arrived to see what his dogs had had for dinner.

I collected the haversack from the observation post, and ran back along the rock, watching the eastern edge for Stephenson's emerging head and shoulders. I guessed he'd probably come up at the northern end, taking the shortest route as I'd done myself this morning. But there were other climbable points along the east side—I'd noted that. I found one, a cleft in the rocks that would give me some cover, and began to climb down.

A thought struck me: Stephenson might well have decided to wait below, keeping watch while his dogs were busy up aloft. By choosing a position some distance out from the rock, he'd have a good view of anyone coming out from the moonlit east face onto the bare plateau.

Yes—but he'd be visible too. Even if he was waiting in cover, he'd have to come out onto the plateau himself to chase after me.

Better get on down, I decided, keeping to the cleft, and review the situation when I'm near the bottom.

I had time, during the climb down, for some silent self-castigation. No police, no tricks, the note had said, or you know what will happen. I'd gone through a long and uncomfortable day without ever forgetting that threat, treating my task with the care of a professional, only to bungle it at the very end. By knocking over a thermos top, for God's sake! If Stephenson had the girl, and carried out his threat, it would be my own stupid clumsiness that was to blame. No matter that Alex had asked me to come up here—in accepting this job, I'd known that it was one of those that doesn't permit failure.

What should I do now, then? There were two options.

First, I could clear off, taking care to avoid Stephenson, in the hope that he wouldn't hold an unexplained mystery against the girl. But it would be fairly obvious that he'd been spied on—even if he didn't find the dogs, he would have heard the shouts and growls up there, and that long, last howl. Then there'd be the evidence of the thermos top, plus any crumbs and other signs I'd left behind in my retreat from the observation post.

Second, I could take advantage of the dogs' demise to take a closer look at the house, and even—if it was Cathy I'd seen— to snatch the girl back. Risky, yes—but I could take it in stages, and I had the initiative at present since Stephenson didn't know both dogs were dead. I could try to get around to the house without being seen, and take it from there. If it looked too risky, I could still retreat and no harm done. But following this option, I just might score a positive identification or even the jackpot of getting the girl away to safety.

What would Alex want?

I stopped behind a large boulder to debate the question. In any case, I might as well make use of the corks and matches: it was now more important than ever to play the invisible man. I shielded the flare against the boulder as I charred one of the corks and blacked up, face and hands. My clothes had been chosen with concealment in mind, and although dark blue wasn't so good as black, they'd do.

A surgeon has to take risks. Alex must have to, every day. So that decides it.

Option Two . . .

I moved cautiously, taking advantage of every rock and surface contour that would conceal me from a northern viewpoint, sometimes moving at a crouching walk, sometimes having to crawl, as the cover dictated. There was no sign of Stephenson. Doubts assailed me: could he have passed the gully while I was still climbing down, and be waiting for me around the next corner of rock?—had that shout come from *this side* of the rock, and not, as I'd thought, from the west . . . ? There are times when one pair of eyes seems horribly inadequate.

I got to the trees, and worked right around the plateau until I arrived at the point from which I'd first seen the rock that morning. Now I felt sure I'd lost Stephenson, and I cut across the scrub, over the sunken track to approach the house from the west, the side I hadn't seen yet. Soon I could see the pale luminosity of the white garden wall ahead. I made the final approach with care, helped by a small grove of ancient olive trees whose twisted trunks were thick enough to give a comfortable feeling of security as I slipped from one to another. Then I was at the wall, taking deep slow breaths as I recovered from my efforts.

I pushed up my sleeve to check the time. Ten-fifty. Not bad going.

Now, perhaps, for the payoff . . .

WEDNESDAY NIGHT

THE TOP OF THE WALL WAS ONLY A COUPLE OF FEET above my head. I could jump, perhaps, and get a grip on the tiled coping to pull myself up. I took a pace back to see it.

On top of the coping, a wire had been stretched between neat, green-painted steel brackets to support more of Mrs. Stephenson's climbing plants when they grew high enough to reach it. So far nothing but the bare wire was visible against the moonlit sky. Her husband might be an ogre, but he was evidently a handyman as well. They had gardening in common, that was clear. And he was an expert handyman: not many could stretch a wire so straight, or would bother to run it through . . .

Insulated sleeving . . . ?

Come to think of it, I'd never seen a plant-support wire quite like this. Not a single wire on *top* of a coping, no. It's more likely an electric fencing wire, to stop the dogs from jumping out. Or . . .

Trained dogs, electric fencing, security system on gate, mirror by front door—of course, there are a lot of burglaries in Spain, especially of foreigners' villas. But to go to all this trouble . . . ?

Am I wrong about the wire? Well—easy enough to test it. I found a long strand of grass, licked one end to wet it, and touched the wire with it. Uh-huh. Only a tingle, but a tingle as sharp as that at my end means high voltage at the other. Good-bye to the keen gardener theory.

This unexpected setback, at the end of all my energetic cross-country work to arrive unseen at this point, had me hopping with frustration. On the other side of this wall, only a few yards away, were the lighted windows of the villa. Surely there must be a way to get a view of them?

The gates? With the dogs out of the way, there was nothing to prevent me hiding *inside* the garden, if I could get through or over the gates. They looked solid enough, but you never know—there must be a weak point in Stephenson's defenses somewhere.

I reached the corner of the wall, and lay flat, edging forward on my elbows until I could see enough. To my right, the northern section of wall stretched away toward the track, with the shadowed bulk of my rock beyond.

Where was Stephenson? I searched the silver landscape with its indigo moon shadows. He could be still out searching for the dogs. But if I slipped along to the gate in the shadow of the wall, I'd be able to see him in plenty of time to retreat unseen around the corner of the wall while he approached, spotlit, across the silver landscape. Yes!—this was more like it.

I reached the gate and looked through. The front door was shut, but the single window near it was uncurtained: inside I could see the beamed ceiling of a large room, and the tops of a flower-patterned sofa and two chairs arranged around a stone fireplace; the room was lit by rustic wooden wall brackets fitted with yellow candle lamps. Someone was sitting in the chair with its back to me: a head moved, and I recognized the graying hair of Mrs. Stephenson. Her head was tilted forward, and moved slowly from side to side as she followed something on her lap, a book perhaps. She looked up from time to time, and I had the impression that there was someone else in the room. Then I heard a voice which might have been hers, and someone else replying—I couldn't make out the words, but I could have sworn it was a girl's voice. Oh yes!—this *was* more like it. Perhaps in a minute or two the girl would move into view, and at this distance I could surely . . .

But other things could happen in a minute or two. Like Stephenson turning up, or the girl leaving the room to go to bed. It was a moment to be seized, not left dangling.

I looked at the gate. Anything metal could be wired into the circuit. I brushed it quickly with a fingertip—it wasn't. Gently, I grasped the handle, turned it, and pushed.

I didn't expect it to open, of course. A man who surrounds himself with high walls, dogs, electrified fences, and barbed wire doesn't leave his gate unlocked. Unless, when he stands by his gate watching his dogs take their evening run, he gets distracted by seeing them chase off after a possible intruder, and goes after them . . .

So Stephenson is still out, then, or the gate would be locked. But where is he? and how long have I got?

Crouching in the shadow of the wall, out of the moonlight, I stared across the open ground toward the shimmering black bulk of the rock beyond. Nothing moved. I looked up, to the top of the rock, a hard outline against the sky. I followed the outline along, searching for irregularity, a movement. Still nothing. Unless . . . had there been a small boulder near the edge there, not far from my watching post? I didn't remember one. Of course, things would look different from this angle. There could have been a boulder . . .

But not one that moved.

It had to be Stephenson, searching for his dogs. What I'd seen had been his head and shoulders, above the line of the rock. Then the shape had shortened and vanished, as though sinking into the rock.

And now was my chance to nip in through the gate and across the courtyard for a look through that window. Even if the search for the dogs was over, I had fifteen, maybe twenty minutes in hand while Stephenson climbed down from the rock and made his way back here from the far side.

The gate groaned. I had to waste some seconds easing it open to minimize the noise. Then I was inside, keeping to the edge of the graveled courtyard, where the stones were a sparse sprinkling on bare earth, making only an occasional faint crunch under my trainers. The windowsill was high: the house must have a cellar. But—once again, this was more like it!—I could, by stretching, see into the room.

Jackpot!

I could see the girl, now! And it has to be Cathy!—the age is right, and I recognize the blond hair. Now that I'm looking at her in the flesh, I can see she's certainly pretty enough for boys to climb walls for. She's lying on the sofa: that's why I hadn't seen her before. It looks domestic enough, but she must know there's no hope of escape from this place. She doesn't know the dogs are dead and gone. She's probably been shown the electrified wall. So there'd be no need to keep her in the cellar. Oh yes!—*this is it!*

I look around at the gate: an instinctive movement, since I'm safe enough for the moment. But speed is essential. How do I get her out? The window's barred, the front door shut. But of course, I needn't assume it's locked; the gate wasn't.

Up the steps, quietly, and try the handle. It turns—but what happens when I push, very, very gently?

It opens . . .

I almost laugh aloud. When your luck turns, it often does it in a big way, but this . . . !

I push it open wider. There is a narrow hall inside, ten feet long, four feet wide, tiled floor with mat, blank wall at the far end with a gory bullfighting poster hanging there in a wide gilt frame and, on the right, a glass door that must lead to the sitting room. Safe enough. I'll step inside, creep to the sitting-room door, then burst in and snatch the girl. All hell may break loose: Mrs. Stephenson scream her head off, the ogre come running to stop us, but hell—*let's do it!* Just one more look around to check everything, and then . . .

"Don't move if you want to stay alive," said a quiet voice from the sitting-room doorway.

I turned my head to see Mrs. Stephenson standing there. Her eyes widened at the sight of my blackened face.

"Don't be alarmed, Mrs. Stephenson," I said quickly. "I mean you no harm . . ." It was a unilateral sentiment, I realized that. I could hardly bear to let my eyes travel down from her face to the shotgun that she . . .

I stared. Not a shotgun that she held, but—

Knitting?

A brief, wild fantasy flashed through my brain—Gloria Stephenson, the notorious knitting-needle killer, deadly at twenty paces . . .

No no. But what did she mean, then?

"If you step on that mat, it'll be the last thing you do," she said. "You'd better believe it."

I looked down. My right foot was already halfway to the mat. I withdrew it. Then I felt stupid—not even Stephenson could be as mad as that.

"What will happen?" I asked disbelievingly.

"Look up," Mrs. Stephenson suggested.

I looked up. In the ceiling above my head, a recessed panel some three feet square was visible. The surface of it appeared to be studded with something like six-inch nails, the points filed to an awesome sharpness.

"If you step over the mat, you'll be all right," Mrs. Stephenson said in a matter-of-fact tone.

"Are you sure?"

"Oh yes."

I looked at her, but her face was a desert, empty of expression. I took a deep breath and stepped. Nothing happened.

"Is that thing set all the time?" I asked, breathing again.

"Only when the light's on," she said. I turned and saw a small red bulb glowing above the front door, invisible from the outside. "Suppose you forget to look?" I said.

"Well. You don't, do you."

"I suppose not. Or only once, anyway. I suppose you realize your husband's going to kill someone before long, if he's not careful."

She looked at me with weary eyes, but said nothing. She didn't need to—at that look, my words suddenly sounded as naïve and meaningless as a missionary's sermon from the cooking pot. I'd been telling myself that Stephenson was crazy, without quite taking it in. But his wife, clearly, *knew it* . . .

"I suppose you've come about the girl," she said.

"That's right."

"Can't help you. If I knew where she was, I'd tell you—he's made a big mistake; I told him so."

"Oh now, Mrs. Stephenson—she's in there with you, isn't she. I saw her. That's why I came in."

Her eyes rested for a moment on my face. Then she shrugged again, and said:

"You'd better come right in. See for yourself."

"Look," I said, "I saw her. So if you've . . ."

I followed her into the sitting room. The flowery sofa was empty. "All right," I said, "but I know she's in the house—"

Mrs. Stephenson called:

"Come back here!"

A girl came into the room from a door at the far end, her bare feet silent on the tiled floor. She carried a pair of espadrilles in her right hand. Late teenage, blond hair long enough to swing across her face—the girl I'd seen through the window, I was sure of that. But now that I saw her standing . . .

"Hi!" the girl said, inspecting me curiously. A strange sight, I suppose—apart from the blacked-up face and hands; the Lacoste jacket, in a proper light, was a lot more ripped than I'd thought.

"Hello," I said. "Please tell me your name."

"My name?" the girl said with a giggle. "Well, it's no secret, I s'pose. You want my telephone number as well?"

"Just tell him," Mrs. Stephenson said.

"I'm Sharon, of course," the girl said.

"Sharon who?" I prompted.

"Well, what d'you think? *Stephenson* . . . Isn't that right, Mum?"

"Satisfied?" Mrs. Stephenson asked.

I nodded. This couldn't be Alex's daughter. Every gesture, every word told me that—not Guildford, but Guildhall. I should know: when I'm working, I'm down that end of London every other day, at my warehouse. *Oh God—Alex, I'm sorry, but it's the most unkind of coincidences.* Well, I'll just have to try to salvage what I can from the situation. I said:

"All right. But you know who I'm looking for, don't you, Mrs. Stephenson?—surely you must have some idea where she is? You've got a daughter—you can imagine what her parents are going through."

"Is it Mark's girlfriend?" Sharon asked.

"Cathy Gordon, yes. Twenty-five thousand pounds or else. How do you feel about that?"

"And you think Dad's got her?"

"Ask your mother," I said. "You know he has, don't you, Mrs. Stephenson?"

"Is her dad going to pay up?" Sharon asked.

"Is he going to get her back unharmed if he does? You know your dad better than I do," I said.

"Oh," the girl said.

"Yes—'oh'. I wouldn't bet much on her chances, either, from what I've seen of him. Would you, Mrs. Stephenson?"

"What are you going to do?" the girl said.

"Find her, get her back—what else?"

"She's not here."

"All right—so where is she?"

"Do you know where she is, Mum?"

Silence. I let it lie for a moment, and then urged:

"Come on, Mrs. Stephenson. I know you'd like to see an end to this—I'm asking for your help. Where is she?"

"Dad needn't know you told him, Mum," Sharon said.

"That's right. I'll guarantee to—"

"Shut up!" Mrs. Stephenson stood as if at bay, something like emotion trying to find expression in a face that seemed to have forgotten what to do with it. "I told you—*I don't know!* That's it. Now you'd better clear off."

"It's going to be worse, now I've been here," I said. "Your husband has threatened to kill the girl if any attempt is made to find her."

"Well, that's your fault, isn't it. You should have kept away; you've only yourself to blame . . ."

"I thought I'd found her—"

"Well, you hadn't—"

"No, but wouldn't you—"

"No, I bloody wouldn't."

Silence. Mrs. Stephenson suddenly dropped her head into her hands, and began to weep. I went across to her, and put my arm around the shaking shoulders. Sharon watched, her eyes wide. "I'm sorry." Mrs. Stephenson's voice came in gasps. "I'm sorry, I'm sorry . . ."

"I believe you."

"Oh no, no. You don't know the half of it. Not the half of it . . . I've had enough . . . I can't take any more."

"Mum!"

"There's got to be an end. It creeps up on you, see. I know what you must think, but it wasn't like this at first . . . he had a regular job, you know . . . he was an army man, that was before—"

"Look, Mrs. Stephenson, I know what you're saying, and I think I understand, but I—"

"—and afterward, see, he wasn't the same, it all—"

"—must get out of here. Before he gets back. Then he might not realize I've been in, talked to you and Sharon. Don't you think?"

"—got to be an end."

"Mrs. Stephenson?"

"Oh yes. Yes, you'd better go."

"I think so."

"Both of you."

"What?"

"You go too, Sharon. You'll look after her, won't you?"

"Take her with me? You want me to?"

"He won't touch that girl, then. You'll go, Sharon, won't you?"

"Mum! What about you? You know we've always . . ."

"Yes I know. But this is different. I don't care what he does to me now; I'm past caring. All I know is, I've had enough."

My thoughts were whirling. Would it work? Would we get out of here in time? I looked at the girl.

"Is that all right with you?"

"If Mum really means it—are you really sure, Mum? I mean, like *really*?"

"I mean it."

An idea struck me. "Shall we lock you in somewhere, Mrs. Stephenson—make it look as though you were forced into this?"

"If you like—"

"No—if *you* like. Might help, mightn't it, when he gets back?"

"Yes. Yes, all right. Have to be the boiler room—there's no window there."

"Let's go, then—no time to waste."

"Follow me," she said. "And Sharon—you'll need some things; you'd better pack your—"

"No time for that," I said. "I'll get her anything she needs. Just put some good shoes on, Sharon—we've got some way to walk."

Mrs. Stephenson led the way along a corridor and down a short flight of stairs to the basement. She opened a door, switched the light on. It was a small room, part store, part boiler and drying room.

"Will you be all right?" I said. She walked in, and turned to face me. Now, she seemed almost cheerful: I hoped it would last. "Get on with you," she said. "And listen—take the car."

"The Range Rover?"

"Key's in it. Go on!"

"All right. I'll leave it—"

"Never mind—just go!"

"Well—good luck then."

"Don't mind me. Look after Sharon. Now lock the bloody door and be off."

I ran up the stairs. Sharon was waiting in the sitting room: she'd put on trainers, and a pale blue quilted jacket. I said:

"Are you sure the key's in the car?"

"He always leaves it there," she said.

"Right. Let's go." We went out into the hall.

"Mind the mat," she said, stepping over it to the door. I glanced up at the red light, and the spiked panel waiting in its recess for a victim. The man was insane—must be, even if the thing was just for show.

"Does it really work?"

"I dunno. Think so. Why?"

"You open the gates and jump in the car," I said. "Be with you in a moment."

I stood in the doorway, looking up. Was it real, this horror-movie contraption?

On impulse, I held the door half open, and put my foot out momentarily to stab the mat with my heel.

Above, there was a click, and then, with a shuddering crash that resounded in the little hall, the spiked panel fell . . .

And embedded itself in the hall floor. Well well—so it did work! But it'll take you a while to sort that out, Stephenson, old chap. Chuckling, I sprinted to the car, where Sharon's small face was looking anxiously out at me.

"What were you doing?"

I climbed in. "Giving your dad something to keep him busy," I said. "And it'll look as though I broke in, won't it."

"Oh. Look—who are you, anyway?"

"Call me William. Four gears, aren't there? I've driven one of these, but it was some time ago. Ah—here we go, then."

The waffling roar of the V–8 engine was comforting—I'd
been using my feet long enough for one day. With power like
this, we'd be away from here in no time. I wound the car
around, through the arch, and—

"Look! There's Dad!"

"So it is. Are you scared?"

"*Yeah!* If you knew my dad—"

"That's just what I want. You're being kidnapped, remember? That's what we want him to think. I'll drive quite close,
and if you could shriek a bit—help! help!—you know, stuff like
that—and keep on looking scared, that'd be just fine? Will you
do it?"

"Well, I don't know . . ."

"It's to help your mother. Give some extra color to her
story."

"Yes, I s'pose. All right then. Oooh, I don't know, though . . ."

"Come on, Sharon. Do it . . . *now!*"

Stephenson must have thought the car was coming to fetch
him; he stood patiently, waiting. Then, as I didn't slow, but
drove past at speed within a couple of yards of him, his bulk
was suddenly galvanized by realization, and rage. His roar
mingled with Sharon's reedy attempts at screaming and the
waffling of the big engine. Then we were past. In the mirror,
as the dust cleared, I could see him running for the house.
Whatever firearms he might have there, we'd be out of range
before he could bring them to bear. A close thing, though—
another minute, and we wouldn't have been driving away in
comfort like this.

The Range Rover's headlights were hardly needed in the
bright moonlight, but I saw no reason to switch them off—the
games of hide-and-seek were over now. We reached the main
track which led to Torrecasim, and I turned left, away from
the village, heading for Prades. Once there, I only had to drive
down the eastern valley to where I'd left the Citroën. But we
had a bumpy half hour or so ahead of us before we reached the
main road at Prades. No need to hurry and risk bursting a tire:

even if Stephenson managed to borrow another car in Torrecasim, he'd have a job to catch up with us now.

Sharon was saying something.

"What's that?"

"Was I all right?" she said again.

"The screams? Oh yes, fine. Superb. Just what was needed."

She smiled, pleased, but said nothing. I said:

"Not really scared, not now, are you?"

"No. I'm really worried for my mum, though. That's why
I never left home before, see."

"I can't think why you didn't both go," I said.

"Are you joking? He'd have killed her!"

"Why?"

"*Why?* Well, she's his property—I mean, like he owns her.
He'd never let her go. He'd kill her for that."

"She believes he really would?"

"She'd better! You know why my dad's out here, don't
you?"

"More or less," I said carefully.

"Well, there you are then."

"But she could have—you could have both gone back to
England. He couldn't follow you there, could he, without
getting arrested for . . . what happened in the past?"

"No. But he's got friends—if you can call them that. If he
wants a job done—no problem."

Ah yes. Like a letter delivered . . . But why choose Alex's
daughter? If Stephenson was some kind of gangland Mr. Big,
£25,000 was just petty cash, not worth the trouble . . .

We bumped on down the track, and I let my mind drift in
and out of the growing complexities of this affair. If somebody
had told me about Stephenson, if I hadn't seen him and, more
particularly, the spiked booby trap for myself, I don't think I'd
have believed them. What makes a man spend so much time,
effort, and mental energy on building himself into a kind of
do-it-yourself death trap? Perhaps this kid will throw some
light on it: I'll have to go easy, though, draw her out gently

because, although it seems he's a monster and ought to be behind bars, he's still her dad, his blood in her veins, all that. She's talking again:

". . . the police, are you?"

"Me? No, I'm not police. Can't be extradited, can he?—there's no agreement. You said yourself, that's why he's here."

"No. Well, what then?"

"What d'you mean?"

"I mean, who are you from?"

"I'm not from anyone. Just a friend of the family."

"Oh yeah. Well all right—*don't* tell me."

"Sharon—I *have* told you."

"It doesn't matter, forget it. I suppose you're not allowed to say."

Silence. Then she said:

"What happened to the dogs, then? They weren't with Dad."

Should I tell her? Why not. "They came up onto the rock where I've spent the day watching your house. That one over there. I had to . . . deal with them."

"You did them in?"

"Afraid so. They attacked me."

"You never!"

"I had to. I'm sorry."

"We didn't hear no shots."

"I didn't have a gun."

"How d'you do it, then?"

"Look—does it matter?"

"With your bare hands—just like that?"

"Well, I know a bit about dogs . . ."

"You must do, and all!"

"I didn't enjoy it—let's just leave it there, shall we? I think I can see lights behind—your father didn't have another car hidden away, did he?"

"No."

"Then I'm going to stop and take a look. Just stay there, Sharon—we may have to be off again in a hurry."

I snapped the lights out, grabbed at my haversack, which I'd thrown onto the back seat, and pulled out the binoculars. We had reached the spot from which Pilar, Alastair, and I had had our first, distant glimpse of Torrecasim yesterday. Through the binoculars, I could see the village, which looked dark and abandoned. In front of the village was the spidery link that was the causeway, and there were lights dancing on it like Halloween candles, crossing it, a stream of them, coming this way. I jumped back into the car, shoved it into gear, and put my foot down.

"What is it?" Sharon said, clutching at the dashboard as we jolted along the track.

"Your dad's private army. At least I'm assuming that. A bunch of trail bikes coming over the causeway from the village. What do you know about them?"

"Some of the boys who live there do jobs for him, I know that," Sharon said.

"Yes. Well, they're doing overtime tonight. And on this track they can make twice our speed. I'm afraid we're going to have to bail out and take to the woods. Do you know any of these boys?"

"Dad never lets them in the house. And he won't let me go across to the village."

"No, I suppose he wouldn't. How do you manage to amuse yourself, locked up in there?"

"Sometimes we go away, to hotels. He likes that. And there's the telly; we've got a big one, really huge. I help my mum some of the time. That's about it since I finished school."

"Where did you—no, never mind, we can talk later. Just hold on—I've got to do ten minutes driving in five."

I had the headlights on again—it was more important to keep the speed up than to hide our position. We were chasing the track through the forest now, crashing over tree roots that

seemed to have doubled in size and number since yesterday.
Somewhere along here, surely, unless I'd got things mixed in
my memory, was the blind, boulder-strewn corner where—
Yes!—surely this was it!

I stopped the car with a jerk in the middle of the track, and
jumped out to check. Good enough! Yesterday, I'd pulled into
the side when we'd heard the bikes coming: this time I wasn't
feeling so generous. The square, utilitarian stern of the Range
Rover filled the track like a cork in a bottle. It was time to leave
the rest to fate.

"Come on!"

Probing ahead with the torch, I led Sharon down the steep
slope to the east, in and out of the pine trees. Our feet skidded
on moss and the slippery carpet of needles—we almost skied
downhill. No bike could stay upright on this.

"Can you hear them?"

She nodded. From the track to the south, already high above
us, came a sound like angry hornets, becoming louder even as
we listened.

"Let's get on down."

Another fifty yards, and the sound was almost above us.
Question—would bikers on foot be able to catch us down this
slope? The pine needles wouldn't show our tracks, good. But
perhaps it was too obvious to head straight down—perhaps I
should head off at an angle . . .

"Listen!"

We heard a crescendo of hornets immediately above us.
Then there came a sudden, short series of shouts and bangs.
We listened while a solitary survivor, revving out of control,
screamed itself to bits. Finally, a kind of silence. Last time we'd
met, they'd been well equipped with crash helmets and leath-
ers—so maybe it hadn't been too bad. In any case, nobody was
going to convince me they just wanted to wish us good night.

"We'd better get on down. Okay?"

Sharon nodded again. For a chatty sort of girl, she wasn't

saying much at the moment. Of course, real life can taste a little raw if you're used to television.

"Let's go then. There's a car at the bottom of the hill, and I don't know about you, but I think I've had enough for one day. What's that?"

"Glad to hear it," she said.

By the time we had scrambled down the hill, found the road, and walked to the forestry track where the Citroën was tucked away beside the log pile, I really was feeling I'd had enough. Once it was clear that the pursuit was over, however, the girl got more and more chirpy. She stood, watching, as I wiped the cork off my face with a handkerchief moistened with wind-screen-washer water, and got a clean shirt and trousers from the boot.

"I don't believe you're just a friend, doing all this. You must be Special Branch or something. You can tell me—I won't let on. You are, aren't you?"

"Oh, stop it, Sharon. Too much television, that's your problem. In any case, Special Branch looks after national security, spies, and so forth. They wouldn't be interested in your dad."

"Ah-ha! But you know that, don't you!"

"Everybody does who reads newspapers. Go on, into the car, and let's get out of here."

The headlights showed the way, up the rutted track, and onto smooth, soothing, civilized tarmac. Virtually home and dry, surely.

"Where are we going?"

"Barcelona."

"What for?"

"I'll work it out before we get there. A hotel, probably."

"Are you going to stay there too?"

"I told you, I don't know yet. Look, why don't you put a tape on—I need to think. They're in the glove box."

What was Alex going to think about this? Personally, I was afraid it would turn out to be one of those spur-of-the-moment

decisions that Seemed A Good Idea At The Time . . . but if
I'd left the kid there, we'd have nothing. Worse, Stephenson
would have been annoyed, and that wasn't a comfortable
thought, bearing in mind what the ransom note had said . . .

"There's nothing but classical stuff in here."

"There's some jazz—try that."

Wednesday night now, and Alex had been told to get the
money ready by Thursday evening. The contact might be by
another note, either pushed through his letter box or arriving
by Friday morning's post. He couldn't bargain with a note;
he'd just have to do what it said. To bargain this girl for Cathy,
there'd have to be some kind of meeting or discussion. How
much bargaining power did we have, anyway?

A sudden blast of Louis Armstrong filled the car. "Turn it
down, Sharon, *please!*"

"Which is it?"

"The knob on the left. Listen, what's your father going to
feel about you being snatched away like this?"

"Him? Well, what d'you think!"

"I can guess. Are you the apple of his eye?—that's what I
want to know."

"S'pose I am, sort of."

"He's fond of you, wouldn't want you harmed, of course."

"Harmed? What do you mean?" Her voice was suddenly
shrill.

"Don't worry!—you're perfectly safe. You know that, don't
you?" I cursed the trap my one-track mind had laid for me.
"I'm just trying to work out what he'll be thinking, that's all."

"Oh." Relief, poor kid. As if I'd . . .

But, but—that's the problem. Stephenson must know that
our side, the good guys, don't do things like that. Hence, no
threat, and no bargaining power . . .

On the other hand, good guys don't usually go in for reverse
kidnaps, either. That brings in an element of uncertainty
which we could, perhaps, build on. Scenario: Alex, desperate
father, resorts to hiring heavies to redress balance. Always

difficult to control heavies—Stephenson knows that. Things could get out of hand. So—call the whole thing off: swap daughters and all go home. Yes—*it's possible* . . .

"When we get to a motorway service station, I'm going to stop and phone ahead to some friends in Barcelona. And pick up something to eat. Don't know about you, but I'm starving."

"I quite fancy some crisps," she said. "And a Pepsi."

"Right."

"I've been thinking."

"Yes?"

"The car doesn't fit. It ought to be a Ford or something like that. Not a foreign car."

"Exactly," I said. "I told you—I'm just a friend of the family."

A pause. Then:

"Of course, I s'pose it depends how high up you are."

"Sharon," I began. Then I stopped. Who can argue with almighty telly? Shut up and drive.

Barcelona at one o'clock in the morning was still humming. I found the underground car park Alastair had directed me to, and Sharon and I walked from there, down the Ramblas seething with nightlife, past the guard with slung machine pistol, to Alastair's flat.

"*Si?*" said the entryphone.

"It's me, Pilar—William."

"Okay."

The door lock clicked, and we were in.

Upstairs, Pilar and Alastair were waiting by the open door of the flat. Sharon's relief at the sight of their normality was obvious. I realized that the collapse of her chirpiness over the last part of the drive here hadn't been due to tiredness, as I'd supposed, but to an attack of second thoughts: made worse, probably, by my giving in to Alastair's insistence on the phone that we stay at the flat rather than at a hotel. God knows what sinister ideas must have passed through her mind, but they

now seemed forgotten, and she allowed herself to be led off by
Pilar to the kitchen, from where a cheerful chattering could
soon be heard.

"I expect you could do with a drink," Alastair said.
"Whisky?"

"I'd love one. Listen, I'm sorry about this."

"Don't give it a thought. We're happy to help."

"Tomorrow, I must install the kid somewhere safe. I haven't
really had time to work it all out. Depends on Alex, largely.
I must ring him."

"Do it now," Alastair suggested. He handed me a large
cut-glass tumbler with the lovely liquid sparkling in it like
jewels. Crown jewels. Oh yes! I took a swallow of it. Camels
must feel like this after a waterless week in the desert. Oh wow.
"Take it into the study—the phone's there. Make yourself at
home."

"Well, that would be—"

"Go on. Then food. Pilar's defrosting a chicken. I'm about
to open a bottle. You're among friends now, you know."

"Do I look that bad?"

"Pretty rough, to be honest. You've got black in your ears
and all along the hairline. No decent hotel would've taken you
in. I look forward to hearing all about it."

He showed me into the study, and shut the door on me. The
telephone sat waiting on the desk. I sank into Alastair's chair,
and looked at it. What time was it in dear old Ingleterra? An
hour earlier—that made it a quarter to one. Should I leave it
until the morning, when my thoughts had cleared? No, better
get it done. I pulled the telephone toward me and dialed Alex's
home number. Remember, remember someone may be listening . . .

"Hello?" He sounded wide awake but edgy.

"Alex, this is your man in Spain. Sorry to wake you, but—"

"Who? Oh yes, I'm with you. I wasn't asleep. What's happened?"

"I'll keep this short, in case we're being overheard. The

operation was successful, and we now have Stephenson's daughter in safekeeping."

"*What?*"

"I knew you'd be glad to hear that. As you know, her name is Sharon, she's seventeen, and we've now got the bargaining position we were aiming for. You'll want to consider the implications before we discuss this further, and I'll ring you at eight tomorrow to give you a number to ring. Better not say any more now."

"Just a minute . . . wait . . ."

"I think I'd better ring off now."

"Wait! Let me just think for a moment." A pause, in which I hear Alex making anxious tut-tutting noises. "Yes, all right. I agree. Eight tomorrow?"

"Yes. Good night."

A forlorn hope, but at least, as he lay awake, he'd be able to turn over this new angle. And if there had been anyone listening in, Stephenson would shortly be getting a call that would keep him awake, too. I awarded myself a mouthful of whisky.

There was something else I ought to be doing. What was it? Oh yes—ring Ginny! I'd have to put her off now I'd got the girl to look after. Oh hell!—all that persuasion, all those arrangements, expectations, all up in smoke. And women being what they are, it would be held against me, no excuse accepted. It would take a lorry load of best butter to get over this. Plus a ton or two of red roses.

Leave it until the morning? There'd still be time to catch her before she left for Heathrow. And there just might still be a way to avoid calling it off—I'd know after the talk with Alex. All right, then. I'll ring her tomorrow.

I opened the study door. The living room was empty, but there were voices in the kitchen. I swallowed some more whisky. A bath would be bliss—perhaps food afterward. I walked along the corridor to the kitchen.

". . . with his bare hands! Dogs like that!" Sharon was telling them.

Oh no, no. Would she never let up? I leaned in through the doorway. "Any chance of a bath?"

"Here he is!" they all cried.

"Has she told you," I said, "about how we had to swing across a bottomless chasm on a dead snake?"

"No!"

"Well, she will, she will. Is there a towel I can borrow in there?"

$\mathcal{T}$HURSDAY

IN THE POST OFFICE THE NEXT MORNING, I SAT IN THE telephone cubicle waiting for Alex to call me back. These precautions were probably a waste of time, but if Stephenson's associates in England were able to tap Alex's telephone, today was the most likely day for them to be at it, with negotiations due to take place this evening. At last the call came through.

"William?"

"Yes, Alex—is it okay to talk?"

"I hope so. I won't tell you where I'm calling from, in case I want to use this line again."

"No, don't. Well, this is a turn-up, isn't it! I hope you don't disapprove."

"Frankly, I don't know what to think. Would you fill me in on exactly what happened?"

"Of course." I gave him a blow-by-blow account of yesterday's events.

"Good God!" he said. "I never expected anything like this. I thought you were just going to watch the place."

"So did I. But one thing led to another. I think, on the whole, we've ended up with a net gain. I hope you agree."

"Well, I must say it's a relief you took the girl away with her mother's approval. From what you said last night, I thought you'd gone mad, quite frankly."

"Carried her off, screaming and kicking? No, not at all. I thought I had to give that impression last night, in case anyone was listening in. In fact, it was her mother's idea, as I've just said."

"Yes, I've got that now. The trouble is, William, I don't see how we can make use of it—this fellow Stephenson isn't going to believe that we'd harm the girl, is he? He may just refuse to deal until we hand her back."

"Quite possible. But suppose we refuse?"

"I don't think I could—the risk to Cathy . . ."

"Yes, I realize that. Of course, I'll do whatever you want, Alex. But I'm afraid there's a risk in any case, isn't there?"

"Yes. Yes, I'm afraid there is. Even if I pay up . . ."

"That's why I thought that you might take a tough line. You're desperate, and you've hired professional help. People do, you know, to collect debts, dispose of unwanted husbands and wives, scare off blackmailers. Why not this?"

"Well, without wanting to sound pompous, I'm a professional man, William, and—"

"So you can afford it. That's credible."

"And Stephenson's seen you—you're not the type, either."

"He may feel differently about me this morning."

"Ah. Yes, it seems you left your mark. Do you really think it could work?"

"All I'm suggesting is that, since this has fallen into your lap, you go into these negotiations in the character of a man who's decided he's going to take the law into his own hands and give as good as he gets. No threats, no bluster—just very firm, quiet, confident. It could rattle them: they won't be expecting it. I think you could do that, Alex."

"I feel savage enough, that's for sure."

"Right. This girl is, apparently, Stephenson's one weakness—she says he dotes on her. Okay then—let's have a straight swap and call the whole thing off."

"You don't think I ought to offer the money as well?"

"I think it might look like weakness. Have you got it?"

"I'm collecting it this morning."

"Has it struck you as odd that it's so little? Twenty-five

thousand pounds is peanuts by comparison with what you see in the newspapers—a quarter of a million is more usual, I think."

"Thank God—I couldn't have raised that."

"No. But in that case, why did they pick on you and not some rich industrialist?"

"I agree—it's odd. I said so, before."

"So you did. Well, I suggest you keep the money in reserve until you see what their attitude is . . . Oh Alex—I don't know why I'm sounding off like this. I could be horribly wrong. The other thing is just to do exactly what they say and hope for the best."

"That's what I thought at first. But I had doubts about whether they'd keep their end of the bargain, of course—that's why I asked you to keep a watch on Stephenson's villa."

"And I messed it up. I'll never forget the sound of that thermos top rolling down the rock face."

"It always was uncertain, William. What we've got now is a different set of uncertainties—better for us, I hope."

I hoped so too. Well, that's how it was. I said:

"Have you thought any more about bringing the police in?"

"Oh yes. But what you've told me about Stephenson now makes me glad I didn't. If we knew where Cathy was, then I wouldn't hesitate—but we don't."

"I could ask Pilar if it's possible to talk to them on the quiet. There's some sort of a lead, now."

"Your Spanish friend? Ah, yes. We'd have to tell them about Stephenson's daughter, though. It'd be awkward, but . . . look, that's a good idea, but I'd like to get this evening over, first. See how it goes. To be honest, I'm quite looking forward to it, now. The buggers aren't having it all their own way, are they!"

"Stay cool, Alex."

"Oh sure. You're quite right. I'll be negotiating peace terms, not declaring war. That's it, isn't it?"

"That's it. Shall we say, same time tomorrow? I'll have to ring you first, as this phone booth may not be free."

"Could you make it later, say at ten? That'll give time for the post to arrive, and for me to think over anything that may be in it."

"Right, ten it is."

"And William—I can't tell you how—"

After we'd rung off, I sat for a moment, hoping that he'd still feel the same when this affair was over. A negotiated peace would be just fine, if it came off. I couldn't say I felt confident about it, though: events so far were too reminiscent of the risks and uncertainties of war.

Ah well. Now I had to ring Ginny, and shatter that idyll. I suppose I *had* to? Opportunities don't come up often these days: it was a frightful waste. Suppose Alex had finished with me, anyway? Yes!—install Sharon in a hotel room, with color TV and a room service instructed to keep up a supply of favorite foods: surely that would keep her happy for a day or two?

No—I couldn't just leave her on her own, all sorts of things might happen. She was only a kid, and I was responsible for her.

Ginny, my love—the fates are against us, and it will have to be Some Other Time. Sighing, I picked up the telephone again, and dialed the number.

"Hello?"

She sounds breathless. "Ginny?"

"Mrs. Duff-Jones is not here."

"She's out?"

"Gone away for a few days. Who is it calling?"

"Er, *Time* magazine. When did she leave?"

"She caught an early train up to London."

But her flight isn't until this afternoon . . . "Can I get hold of her anywhere?"

"I don't think so. She said she had some shopping to do."

Damn . . . or perhaps not . . . "I see. Never mind, it wasn't important. Thank you."

"You're welcome. Good-bye."

Well, I did my best. No man can do more. So—

> *"O frabjous day! Callooh! Callay!"*
> *He chortled in his joy.*

"It will be hot again today, I think," Pilar said. (It's a myth that only the English go on about the weather.)

"After being roasted on that rock all yesterday," I said, "some nice, cool showers are what I'd order up if I had the choice."

"Not today, but soon, perhaps."

Pilar pointed. From the balcony of the flat, where we were just finishing breakfast, I looked between the giant stone pineapples on the roof of the civil governor's palace to the ring of mountains beyond. A pale gray smudge of cloud hung just below their tops, like a single sweep of watercolor.

"It'll be hot and sticky," Alastair said, "until there's a storm to clear it. Have some more coffee?"

"Please. You learn to move slowly, I suppose."

"That, and showers two or three times a day. Help yourself, William, whenever you feel like it. You too, Sharon."

"Can I have one now?" Sharon said. She sat, hunched in an inappropriately stylish red silk dressing gown of Pilar's, her hair tangled, her small-featured face still bleary with sleep, looking more like an O-level schoolgirl than the seventeen she claimed to be.

"Of course!" Pilar said. "And I will try to find you some clothes. But I think you are smaller than me, no? We will see."

"Sharon and I have got to do some shopping," I said. "And find a hotel—any suggestions?"

"Oh!—but I will take Sharon shopping," Pilar said. "That will be better, no? And you must stay here—we invite you! Don't we, Alastair?"

"You're very kind," I said. "But there are complications.

Suppose Sharon has her shower now, while I talk to Alastair?"

"Okay. Come with me, Sharon. Perhaps, if we try something loose . . ."

When they'd gone, I said:

"I've got a friend flying out this afternoon."

"Oh, I see. Reinforcements?"

"A girlfriend—someone I've known for years. I rang this morning to put her off, but I was too late—she'd already left. She's not going to be very pleased about all this."

Alastair gave a snort of laughter. "Sorry!" he said. "But I see what you mean. Complications!—yes."

"I can't break it to her just like that, and wave her off on the next flight home. She's got to be here for one night at least, so that I can explain things gently over a champagne supper et cetera. It's going to take careful handling."

"It sounds like it," Alastair said with interest. I began to regret telling him.

"So," I said firmly, "what I'd like to do is this. If you and Pilar could possibly put Sharon up here for tonight, I'll take Ginny off to a hotel for candlelit explanations. Then tomorrow, after I've heard from Alex about the negotiations, I'll take Sharon off your hands. Now, you must tell me if—"

"No, that's fine," Alastair said. "Leave her to us."

"Can I really? What's Pilar going to feel about it? Is she going to write me off as a dangerous subversive?"

"I'm not with you, William."

"Well, being French, Claudine's attitude to marriage is that outside interests are to be expected, and accepted, as long as the rules are observed. But things may be different in Spain."

"Would Pilar get on with your . . . er . . ."

"Ginny. Yes, I'm sure she would. As far as you can ever be sure of that."

"Then let's all have lunch together tomorrow. Pilar will forgive anybody anything if she likes them."

"Of course! Good idea, Alastair!"

"*Elemental, estimado Watson,*" he said.

* * *

Alastair's advice on hotels was to work my way up the Ramblas, where there were many. I picked the Oriente, and the room was on the fourth floor at the back, reasonably quiet, thick carpet, and a marble-tiled bathroom. I prodded the bed, and looked at the stock of drinks in the little fridge. Then I tapped the walls, a habit formed by years of traveling in France, where you're not expected to mind cries of *ooh ahh chéri!* coming through from next door. But the walls were solid enough: yes, it would do.

Booking completed, I strolled up the Rambla de Sant Josep toward the Plaça Catalunya, where I was due to meet Pilar and Sharon after their shopping expedition in Barcelona's biggest department store, El Corté Inglés. I felt we were all quite safe. In fact, I'd decided the night before that to drive straight here was the safest thing I could do: you can disappear much more successfully in a big city than in the country, where strangers are noticed and newsworthy.

I kept my eyes open, all the same. In the bright midday sunlight, dark glasses were normal wear, and I made the most of mine, scanning the sea of faces for one that looked out of place. But I saw nothing suspicious, and I reached El Corté Inglés still in ebullient, confident mood. And earlier than expected. Should I have coffee? No, perhaps I'd see if I could find something for Ginny in this Spanish Harrods while working my way up to the café on the top floor, where I was to meet Pilar and Sharon.

There was a man on duty at the entrance with *Seguridad* on the shoulder tabs of his dark blue uniform. A holstered pistol, truncheon, and handcuffs flapped on his belt. There'd been guards in the bank, in the post office, and now here—security seemed to be a thriving trade in this newly democratic, post-Franco Barcelona. I passed him, getting a cursory glance up and down, and went inside.

What would Ginny like? I'm not going to hang around the airport with a bunch of flowers—too operatic. Scent then, in case nothing more original turns up—but there's no sign of any on the ground floor. Let's escalate.

Going up, there was time to look around. The escalators crossed each other at midpoint, with no barrier between. In the triangle formed by the crossing, descending shoppers appeared for a few moments before dropping out of sight. Standing at attention, we meet, then part, like statues on conveyor belts. An elderly gent, coming under scrutiny, smiled gravely and inclined his head in salutation. "*Señor* . . ."

The counter I was looking for was on the second floor. There were all the tints and perfumes of Arabia plus a scented painted houri who seemed to be wearing them all at once. What does she look like in the mornings?—a blank canvas I shouldn't wonder. I point, proffer my wrist. Smiling, she shoots. Ugh—smells like fly repellant—no thanks! How about this? Oh, so *that's* what it is, I'd forgotten the name . . . and now, let's face it, the name of the girl who used to wear it . . . Could I try that one? Yes well, *where* is becoming a bit of a problem. I know, on my handkerchief, thanks. Mmmm, wow. Of course, with our vanishing ozone layer, one shouldn't buy aerosols, but I think I've got to have it. How much? Wait!—divide by two, move the decimal point—it can't be! Can it? It is? Oh well . . . Yes, thanks, *gracias*. Yes, Barclaycard, or Visa as you Continentals call it—here you are. *Muchas gracias—adiós.*

I turned away from the counter feeling a glow of achievement. Byzance, it was called, by Rochas. Where scent is concerned, no one gets near the French, you've got to admit it. Along the counter, a swarthy chap in an expensive black leather jacket was drifting away, shaking his head. I thought: you're making a mistake, my friend!—she'll love it, and if she doesn't, then you're wasting your time anyway. The silent message must have got to him, as he drifted back to the counter farther along.

I left to find exotic chocs: the consuming mood was on me. Down to the ground floor again. Turkish delight!—better than chocolate, which is a wine killer. Demi-sec champagne—that's what I need now. On the escalator going up, I passed my friend in the leather jacket on the way down, framed in the triangle between the two escalators. Shall I give him a cheery grin? No, it'd be a waste of time; he's got an expression like frozen granite, what I can see of it around gold-rimmed shades as black as mine shafts. Down he goes. *Adiós* to you too. On up to the seventh floor.

French scent is unavoidable, but French champagne . . . no, I really ought to brush up on my Spanish. I bought a Codorniu gift pack of three bottles: sweet, semi-dry, and extra dry. Barclaycard, and *gracias* again. Now I'm ready with a proper reception!

There was still some time before I was due to join the girls in the café on the top floor. I decided to go down to the fourth floor, to buy a couple of spare shirts.

Well well. There's Black Leather Jacket going up! He must be as erratic a shopper as I am. Except that . . .

Except that he doesn't seem to have bought anything. No packages, shopping bags. Could be something in his pocket, there. Is it the same guy? Granite face, black black shades . . . Yes. I'm sure of it.

Ho hum.

Got to check this.

I escalated on down to the ground floor. There was a counter some ten yards away—scarves, that's fine. I riffled through them, watching the escalator out of the corner of my eye. Granite Face didn't appear. I riffled and watched some more. Still nothing. Overactive imagination, that's all. He's just a hopeless shopper, faced with the yawning elephant trap of someone's birthday, a prospect that gives many a poor sod an expression like that . . . no, wait!

Here he comes. Down the escalator at a run, drawing attention to himself, tut tut. He's looking around; he's seen me. Now he's moved to a counter on the far side of the escalator, from where he can watch it and the exit. Right. Now I'm

heading for the escalator, to go up again: I can almost feel him
groan. Why doesn't he stay here and watch the exit? Because
there are other ways out—I've seen them—and there's bound
to be a staircase somewhere for when the escalator breaks
down.

Arriving at the second floor, I return to the perfume counter
and hang about there, watching and waiting. The houri is
hovering hopefully. Maybe I should buy myself some mascu-
line fragrance to counter the rather too natural hot weather
effect I've been aware of lately—a Vichy underarm stick would
certainly add to the quality of life in this climate. Or shall I
indulge in some Lapidus Pour Homme, a "rich, rare, mysterious fragrance encapsulating a very virile originality"?

I may need it; I may need all the virility and originality I can
get. Because here comes Granite Face, stepping off the top of
the escalator. I feel sorry for him, just at present, because
nobody could handle a job like this on his own.

How did they catch up with me? Stephenson must have
more clout than I realized. Did he . . . no, this isn't the time
for academic speculation.

What am I going to do? That's the question.

I've got to lose him and get the girls away. But how?

Time!—I need time to think. I can't hang around this
counter any longer. And I can't dash for the exit and come
back in another way—too easy to follow. Up, then. Six more
floors above this one. I'll browse through them until an opportunity comes up.

Third floor. Ladies' fashion: knitware, underwear, nowhere
to hide in that lot.

Fourth floor. Gents' fashion. Perhaps Barclaycard would
buy me a quick change into Barcelona businessman? No—not
quick enough; he's too close behind.

Fifth floor. Glass, china, gifts. Not much opportunity here.
If only these antique pistols worked . . . but that would be too
drastic, as well as too noisy.

Sixth floor. Furniture, household goods. And almost deserted—useless. I've noticed, though, that there's a loo on every floor, always in the same place, next to double doors labeled SORTIDA EMERGENCIA.

Seventh floor. I've been here before: wines and spirits, and delicatessen. No use, skip it. Though I'm running out of floors and opportunities now. I'm going to have to do something, and soon.

Eighth floor. Toys and games. Also sporting goods—track suits, footballs, fishing rods, and—look!—a gun counter. Well, I couldn't, you need a license. Anyway, I can't walk around Barcelona carrying a shotgun. Forget it. How about a large knife, the sort you disembowel deer with? Or *this!* . . . no, it's a toy, isn't it? Though it's very well made, with calibrated sights . . . and silent, of course. The fact is, I'd feel safer with it than with nothing: when in danger, I like to be armed. I believe I *will!* . . . fourteen thousand pesetas!—that's hardly a toy. All right, I'll have it. Is he watching? Can't look around, too suspicious. So point, snap down Barclaycard, and walk away to browse elsewhere while the salesman wraps it up.

I've got to chase Granite Face away, now, so I can nip back and pick it up unobserved. Walk toward him. It's like being a sheepdog with a single sheep: I advance; he retreats. I steer him into a far corner, behind a display of ski gear. From there, he can see the escalator, so perhaps he won't bother to move while I slip back to the gun counter. I sign, snatch up Barclaycard and the plastic shopping bag that's held out to me, and then head for the loo. He can see me going in there, but I hold the shopping bag in front of me to conceal it from him—you should never throw away the advantage of surprise. Into the gents', which is empty, pick a cubicle, shoot the bolt, and sit down to inspect the purchase in comfort and temporary safety.

Am I mad to blow the equivalent of £70 on this? It's neatly boxed, with a drawing on the cover that would certainly upset the Animal Rights people: if it can do that to a rabbit, it should easily puncture a leather jacket, should that unfortunate necessity arise. Inside the box, the parts are laid out for easy assembly, together with instructions in several languages. Take the butt, attach the blued steel bow and then the lever action cocking device, place the bolt thus. Richard the Lionheart's career was terminated by one of these at the siege of the castle of Chalus: crossbows were new then, and he thought he was out of range. This is only a pistol version (with extension butt for long-range use), but hi-tech and surprise may again win the day.

There's a clip to hold the bolt in place. I slide my new ally, cocked and ready, into the shopping bag.

And there's another secret weapon I've just thought of: I'll have that ready as well.

Right—let's go.

No, wait!—someone's just come in: I heard the hiss of the door close. Footsteps, hardly audible on the tiled floor, are coming closer, coming level with my cubicle, have stopped. I can see a shadow in the wide gap under the door that wasn't there before. Now he's moved on. I hear the cubicle doors being pushed open, one by one. Mine is the last, and the only one that's shut. If I could make Spanish bowel trouble noises, he might give up and go away . . . Let's have a go: might confuse him, and I've got nothing to lose. A troubled sigh, then, and mutter:

"Aie, aie, caramba . . ."

I wait. Ten seconds, twenty, half a minute. There's no sound; he's just waiting there. Maybe I didn't roll my r's enough.

Nothing for it, then, but confrontation. I get to my feet. Out of your bag, crossbow: this is your debut; let's hope your technology impresses. No need to set the sights—this is going to be at zero range. Ease back the door bolt—he must have heard that. Are we ready?

Waiting, I feel like a man-sized mousetrap. But I want *him* to open the door. Surely, he won't be able to resist taking a closer look—

The door is opening . . .

Quite gently, smoothly, so that he can say he's sorry if he finds an innocent citizen in occupation. Standing back, I let the door swing open, all the way.

The black glasses do a little dance as they take everything in. Then they become very, very still, as the crossbow's pointed presence makes itself felt.

This is going to have to be in sign language. Let's have the right hand out of that pocket, first. Good.

Now let's move back against the wall, easy does it. Just a little more. Splendid.

I'll have the shades off now. Don't move—I'll take them off you with my left hand. I've got two reasons for doing this.

The first is a traditional gesture of ill will. I drop your shades on the floor and grind them under my heel. What d'you think of that, eh? I'm twice as horrible as you and several inches taller. Don't you forget it!

But that was just a bluff, so that I can now . . .

"AAARGH!"

No, I hadn't shot him. Just given him a blast of Rochas Byzance in the eyes. Well, it was quite humane really, in the circumstances. Minimum force, to allow me to grab up my bags and get clear away, out of the gents', and in through the doors of the SORTIDA EMERGENCIA.

I ran up the concrete staircase. It had to have doors onto the ninth floor as well as all the rest, unless the architects had made a complete cock-up of their plans. Yes, here was the ninth floor—and over there beyond a hairdressing salon was another short flight of stairs leading to the cafeteria. Pilar saw me and waved. I sank into a chair beside her.

"Hello. Hello, Sharon. How's the shopping going?"

"You are like a steam train!" Pilar said. "Puff, puff . . ."

"I suddenly realized I was late. Ran up the stairs. Well, this is nice. What are we having?"

"Shrimp salad," Sharon said. "You've been doing some shopping too, then."

I pushed my bags under the table. The champagne bottles clinked.

"Presents for my friend," I said.

"Oh, yes," Pilar said noncommittally. She didn't want to know. That was a help, just at the moment, with the bag containing the loaded crossbow leaning against my leg. I looked at the menu, more for practice than information.

"*Ensalada de gambas*—is that it?"

"Yes. You want this?"

"Please. So, tell me about your morning."

"Sharon—you do it."

"Well," Sharon said, "first, we . . ."

I thought: how are we going to get out of here? It may be a mistake to stay on for lunch, but I hope Granite Face will assume I left in a hurry after the confrontation. If so, no problem—but how can I be sure? He could keep watch downstairs, call up assistance. We could chance it and be lucky, but I prefer to give luck a helping hand.

". . . really great!" Sharon said. "I hope you like them too."

"Sure I shall," I said.

What was the child on about?

$\mathcal{T}$HURSDAY AFTERNOON

IT WAS CLOTHES, OF COURSE. I'D ASKED PILAR TO KEEP Sharon happy, and she'd obviously succeeded: at what expense I didn't dare to ask. I hoped Alex would think it was justified. Of course, if we'd needed to alter her appearance . . .

Ah! But that's just what we did need! I watched Sharon shoveling in ice cream: she looked up and smiled. On the whole, I thought, we'd managed the situation rather well, apart from that awkward moment in the car last night. I had to keep reminding myself that she was supposed to be a kidnap victim: of course, she had her mum's approval to fall back on in moments of doubt or distrust. No worse than the situation of an au pair, really. Without the washing up.

The victim finished her ice cream, and wiped the remains away with a paper napkin. "Is there a toilet?" she said.

"Over there," I said. Good—this was the opportunity I needed. I put a restraining hand on Pilar's arm in case she felt inspired to follow: women are like lemmings on these occasions. As soon as Sharon was out of range, I said:

"I'd better tell you that I had some trouble with a man who was obviously trailing me. That's why I was late."

"Oh no!" Pilar said. "Where is he now?"

"I lost him. The problem is, he may be waiting downstairs."

"Oh! Oh William! What will we do?" She stared at me with big, worried eyes.

"It's all right," I said. "The worst that can happen is that

Stephenson gets the girl back. But we don't want that if we can
help it. So here's the plan: we make her look as different as
possible. Can you do that with the clothes you've bought?"

"I think so. Perhaps we buy some dark glasses, no?"

"Certainly, yes. That blond hair is the problem—a scarf,
perhaps?"

"Over there is a *peluquería*—she could—"

"Yes! If she'd like to try one of those punky very short cuts,
that'd be ideal; she'd look completely different."

"Okay. I ask her."

"If not, just do the best you can, Pilar, will you? And take
as long as you like: the later you leave here, the more chance
they'll think they've missed her."

"But listen, William!—perhaps they have already seen her?
Perhaps they are watching us now?"

"Perhaps. But you came here by taxi—I think they got on
to me because I walked here. In any case, don't worry about
it. When you're ready, go down by the escalator, and say
something to the security guard at the main entrance, to make
sure he watches you while you get a taxi. Okay?"

"Okay. And then?"

"Go straight back home—you'll be safe even if followed,
with that guard in your street. Then I'd like you to ring my
hotel—the Oriente: I've got her booked in for tomorrow, but
I'd feel better if she moved in tonight. If they can take her, ask
Alastair to put her in a taxi and send her 'round at eleven this
evening, with my bag, please, to be left at reception."

"But she can stay with us!"

"Pilar, it's very kind of you, but I've changed my mind about
that. I don't understand how Stephenson traced me to Barcelona so quickly, and it makes me uneasy: suppose they tried
to break into your flat? I just don't know what might happen
next."

"You think this?"

"Who knows. The first thing is to get you out of El Corté
Inglés and home, undetected if possible."

"But William!—she will not be so safe at the hotel!"

"Can't be helped. If they get her, they get her. They're supposed to be contacting Alex this evening—that's as far as I can think, at present—and I'll do what I can to keep her hidden away until I've talked to him, tomorrow morning. Then we'll see. Look, I've got to go; I'm supposed to be at the airport by four-fifteen. I'm sorry to land you with all this, I really am."

"It's okay. I put her in the taxi at eleven."

"No, Pilar!—*Alastair* does it. Please!"

"Don't worry! Alastair, okay." She smiled.

"You're terrific!" I said, bending to kiss her cheek. "And I'm still hoping we can have lunch tomorrow. Then we can settle up for all this, though I owe you a lot more than money."

"*Nada, nada.* Listen—suppose they follow you now?"

"That's what I'm hoping, if they're still here. A long taxi ride to the airport will keep them busy while you and Sharon slip away. Good luck, Pilar."

"And you," she said.

There are a variety of dangers to be avoided in Barcelona, I was discovering, and a ride in one of the city's black-and-yellow taxis came fairly high on the list. The one that swerved out of the traffic swirling around the Plaça Catalunya to pick me up was an elderly SEAT, conducted by a black-bearded cheroot-chewing Spaniard who, by his driving style, might have been a matador for relaxation. No signals—they give other drivers a competitive advantage. Better still, deliberate misinformation—ha! nearly caught him, see the rubber on the road! A collection of St. Christophers obscured the middle of the windscreen; a hanging roof lining intermittently beat the driver on the head; and whenever the brakes were applied, the broken driver's seat was forced back for support against my right knee: a painful event, but one I soon learned to welcome. At the airport, I refused what looked like an offer to wait for me. With a shrug, cheroot at full cock, he blasted off.

One consolation—I could be sure we hadn't been followed. Only a motorcycle could have kept up with us, and I hadn't seen any that looked as if they were trying to. Limping, I went to check the arrivals board.

The Heathrow flight was listed as on time. Twenty minutes to wait. I bought a *Times* and sat on a bench near the arrivals entrance, a lone Gibraltar surrounded by shouting Spanish, to read it.

The doors opened, releasing a trickle of pale-faced Brits. Was this it? No, according to the board, it was a delayed flight from Manchester. A blue-suited courier harried them past, and out to a waiting coach.

Some minutes more. Twenty past now. Just my luck—French air traffic controllers on strike again . . . no, hold it! Greeny beige baggy trousers and jacket, pale cream shirt, seemingly smaller, but the sleek dark head is just as I—

"Ginny!"

Are we shy? Seconds only—then the old magnetism snaps into action. "Mmmm . . ." *And to think that I . . .*

"Let me take that."

"Oh thanks. Give me your shopping bags then. What's this: El Corté Inglés?"

"Some champers, Ginny, and, er, one or two other things —I can manage, thanks. Oh, I'm so glad you could make it!"

"Champers, how lovely. Me too, William darling."

We walked through the swinging doors and onto the pavement. I looked along the stream of taxis and chose a Renault 12 with a gray-haired driver of uncompetitive mien who was just dropping off his passengers. We got in.

"Where's the limo, then?" Ginny said. "I was expecting to be swept up in air-conditioned comfort, William darling. Have you bent it?"

"No, I had to leave it in a garage. This town's a bit tough on cars; you can't leave them on the street . . . Rambla de Sant Josep, *por favor.*"

The driver nodded, and we were off, with Ginny settled in my encircling arm. "Well well. Here we are again."

"I hope it's a good idea," Ginny said.

"Of course it is! How can you say that?"

"Well, I do think it is really."

"That's more like it. I say, Ginny—you seem to be into the haute couture. What happened?"

"Not the usual me, is it? I wasn't sure but you see, William darling, I felt it was time I went upmarket a bit. A mistake, you think?"

"No no, I don't mean it doesn't suit you—it's just that it makes you look different."

"Well, it's meant to. I can't go around in old jeans forever."

"As far as I'm concerned you could. But anyway, you look wonderful. We're going to have a marvelous time."

"Tell me about it."

"Well, first we're going to this hotel in the middle of the city, not far from the harbor and the old quarter. We'll have a few drinks and settle in. Then we'll have dinner and decide what next."

Ginny sighed. "I can just relax and leave it all to you?"

"That's the idea."

She stirred and moved closer. "You're a rotten sod, you know that?"

"Well, I . . . yes, if you say so. But we are going to have a marvelous time."

Ginny giggled. "Yes," she said, "I think we are."

I'd like to have been a fly on the wall, people say. Perhaps it comes off the tongue better than "a fly on the ceiling"—which is where, like most flies, ours was. A solitary fly, strolling in circles to relieve the boredom of a sudden and mysterious celibacy (the window was shut), an unnatural state for all God's creatures. Two by two we're meant to go, but circumstances had been against me, lately. Until an hour ago.

"Ginny?"

"Mmmm?"

"We got it wrong."

"Oh William darling—seemed all right to me."

"We were supposed to have drinks first."

"So we were."

"So now it's champagne time."

"Oh goody."

"And Turkish delight."

"What made you think of that? I'm not going to entertain you with belly dancing, if that's what you had in mind."

"Wow! Could you?"

"No."

"Just a little wobble?"

"I'm sorry I mentioned it."

"The idea is, you have a lump of Turkish delight, and it makes you thirsty. So you drink some champagne. Then you have another lump of—"

"I think I've got it."

"Right. Here—sit up and have some."

"Must I? It's horribly sweet."

"Sugar. For energy."

"Just one lump, then. Ugh! No wonder they all get so fat. Give me that glass—um, that's better."

"We could forget it and just drink the bubbly."

"That's the best idea you've had yet. William darling . . ."

"Yes?"

"Tell me something nice."

"You're perfect, Ginny."

"Am I?"

"Totally. Are you glad you came?"

"Mmmm. Are you glad I did?"

"Of course I am. Do you doubt it?"

"Not seriously, William darling. I just like to hear you—"

"It's, well, obvious really."

"Obvious?—oh! Yes I see. It is, isn't it."

"Will you have some more bubbly?"

"Um—what time do they serve dinner here?"

"Not for hours yet."

"Then let's save the rest of the bubbly for later."

"My thought exactly. Oh, and here's a little something for you. It's called Byzance."

"Darling, how sweet of you! Oh, I'm shocked at myself, but it's wonderful to be pampered, just sometimes. Look—they don't exactly give you a full bottle, do they!"

"I had to test it, of course. Pretty effective, I thought."

"Um yes, I agree. Yes very. In fact, I think it's time for you to have your wicked way with me again."

"Let me take your glass, then."

"How kind. Thank you, William darling."

"Not at all."

It was one of those evenings. Even the shower worked. We went down to dinner at nine-thirty, or rather, floated. Stephenson and all his works were somewhere in the cellars of my mind, with the door shut. We ate, drank, smiled, talked (not a lot, but easily), and let the rest of the world take second place. At the pudding stage, I surreptitiously glanced at my watch: ten forty-five. Time for a *crema Catalán* each, after which I steered Ginny into the lounge for coffee. From there, I planned to watch the entrance lobby inconspicuously to see Sharon safely checked in.

"Brandy?" *That would spin out the time.*

Ginny shook her head. "Not for me."

"I've been having a local brew called Mascaro—it's very mild. Try it?"

"No thanks, really."

"Well, I think I will. The night is young, by Spanish standards." *Five past eleven.*

"You're not planning to go out?"

"No no. Back to bed."

"Do remember, I'm not terrific, touristically."

"There may have to be intervals of it, Ginny."

"I'll endure them bravely."

"Where's that waiter got to? Perhaps I'd better collect my brandy from the bar."

"There he is."

"Ah yes. Yes, he's coming. *Brandy Mascaro, por favor.*"

"Impressive accent, William darling."

"I feel a bloody fool: it makes it worse, being so at home in France. Odd how a shift of a few miles can make such a difference: language, customs, everything." *Ten past. I told Pilar to send Sharon over at eleven. Any moment now.*

"But you sell Spanish wine?" Ginny said, yawning.

"Oh yes. But Alastair, my agent out here, does it all for me. I've never bothered to learn the language."

Through a wide archway, I had a good view of the hall. *Surely I hadn't missed her?*

The waiter was crossing the hall now, carrying a tray on which reposed a single glass: my brandy. Well, I could spend ten minutes or so sipping it: if Sharon hadn't arrived by then, I might start to worry. Now the waiter has halted politely to allow a girl in a stunning yellow dress to pass. She's looking around on her way to the reception desk, she . . .

Has given me a big smile. Surely I don't know her?

But that's my bag she's got! My God . . . *it's Sharon!*

Ginny had noticed my expression and had turned to see the cause of it. Together, we watched Sharon hand my bag over the counter, accept a key, turn, and give me another goddamn big smile. Well, I was the one that watched: Ginny's gaze was more on the lines of a naturalist studying a previously unsuspected form of life. Sharon walked away toward the lift. I was spared more smiles, but the swing of her hips in the new yellow dress, the bounce of her freshly cut hair, the looks she collected from a pair of waiters standing by the dining-room door, were shovelfuls of clay on my grave that I was going to have to scrape off, piece by piece, during the long night to come.

"William darling . . ."

"Yes," I said, "I know the kid. She's dropped my bag in for me—nice of her."

"She seems to be staying here," Ginny said. "Who is she with, I wonder? This nice kid."

"I meant this to wait until morning," I said, "but I see it won't. I have got something to tell you—but it's not what you're thinking. Not at all."

"I don't think I'm unreasonable," Ginny said, "but couldn't you have waited until I'd left before moving this bimbo in?"

"She's not a bimbo—well, perhaps she is, now. But she's not *my* bimbo."

"Well, whose is she, then?"

"Does she have to be anybody's?"

"Of course she does! All bimbos are somebody's. There's no such thing as an ownerless bimbo. From the way she smiled at you, William darling, I'd say you were it."

"I'm not!"

"Are you paying for her room?"

"That's not the point—"

"I see. Oh shit, you really are a stinker—"

"Ginny, just listen a moment—"

"—me, of all people, after all this time. Well, what?"

"You know I'd never do this to you. Don't you?"

"Well, I thought not, but—"

"I wouldn't and I haven't. Let's go up, and I'll tell you what it's all about. If I don't convince you that I'm whiter than white, I'll stand in the shower all night. With the cold tap on."

She looked me up and down. Without an effort, I'd have fallen into two halves. I said:

"You want to believe me, don't you?"

"Maybe. But it had better be good," she said.

We sat on the bed, side by side, my story concluded. Through the open door of the marble tiled bathroom, I could hear the shower dripping, plip, plop, plip . . .

"Oh no," Ginny said, "oh no."

"You don't believe me?"

She studied me, her head on one side. I thought: it's odd, I mean, I like the *idea* of blondes, but both the ladies in my life are as dark as . . .

"I suppose I've got to," she said. "Either that or you've gone completely off your nut. What makes me think you may not be lying through your teeth like the evil hound you are is that this isn't the first time you've got yourself caught up in a situation of this sort—and me, to boot. How do you do it?"

"It wasn't my idea," I said. "Claudine offered me. Alex and Sheila accepted. I could hardly refuse."

"William darling, the idea of refusing never crossed your mind, did it? You're in your element, admit it."

"Well, perhaps I . . . but listen, all I agreed to do was make a few inquiries after their missing daughter: we all thought she'd done a bunk with the boyfriend, that's all."

"And now it turns out to be a kidnap. Aren't you lucky."

"Oh now, Ginny . . ."

"All right; I know, I know. But I'm feeling bitchy—well, my God, who wouldn't! You persuade me to fly out here, and then, the moment I arrive—blam, I get dropped into this. You can imagine how I feel."

"Of course I can. I tried to put you off, although I must admit I was glad I was too late. If you hadn't gone shopping . . ."

"Yes. Well, I suppose that's true."

"Of course it is."

"Oh well, anyway. I suppose that's it. I'll just have to go back tomorrow."

"Hold on—let's discuss it first . . ."

"Well, what else can I do? I'm not going to sit here like a service widow, waiting for you to have time off."

"It may all be over tomorrow morning. I'm expecting news from Alex about the hand-over deal."

"Really?"

"Yes," I said. "really."

"Oh all right, don't get touchy. I'm still trying to take all this in."

"Sorry, sorry—of course you are. Listen, Ginny—why don't we just let it ride for a while—make the best of it? For tomorrow at least. There's a lunch planned with Alastair and Pilar—that should be fun. Don't decide anything now."

She considered. "Well . . ."

"See how it looks in the morning?"

"Oh William. Why couldn't I have had a nice, normal bloke to have an affair with, someone who made me feel special, cared for, et cetera. Instead of . . ."

"I do care for you, Ginny."

"Well, I suppose you do, in a way. When you can spare the time. When's this Alex going to ring?"

"I've got to ring him, at eleven. Until then, we can relax."

"Did I hear you right? You said 'relax'?"

"Yes. Relax. Anything wrong with that?"

Ginny sighed. "Now I *know* you're a nutter, William darling," she said.

FRIDAY

CROUCHED ONCE AGAIN IN A STUFFY CUBICLE AT the post office, I listened to Alex's extremely English intonation. Did it, perhaps, conceal just a trace of underlying Scots, of whisky in his water? I hadn't noticed that flavor before, but perhaps it was more noticeable today, now that he was in optimistic, almost confident mood.

". . . agreed to give them the money. I'm afraid you'll not be too pleased about that, but the fellow sounded so unexpectedly reasonable, I decided not to make an issue of it."

"You're the best judge of that, Alex. So, the phone just rang, and there he was. What did he sound like?"

"Perfectly polite. It might have been a business discussion; he could have been selling double glazing. No, even that gives the wrong impression—there was hardly any pressure, any persuasion. Apart from right at the start when he said something like: we have to come to an agreement; it would be unthinkable not to."

"That was firm enough."

"Yes, but he left it at that. 'Shall we say,' he suggested—it was more like a suggestion than anything else—'shall we say that you'll bring the money out today? The sooner, the better; I'm sure you'll agree.' "

"Smooth."

"Very. Not at all what I was expecting after what you told me about this Stephenson character."

"No, it certainly doesn't sound like his style. I thought you'd be getting a roughly typed note saying 'Do this, or else.' Of course, it could be clever stuff: the sweet-and-sour technique."

"What's that?"

"According to my van driver, who's had a spot of bother in his time, the police have an interview system: first you get the rough questions; then they wheel in a nice bobby with cups of tea—well, all I'm saying is, let's proceed with caution. But it's a relief that they seem to be taking a professional attitude. That's reassuring."

"I thought so. But I take your point about caution. I'm not going to this next meeting without taking every precaution I can think of. I hope there'll be a chance to discuss it with you beforehand."

"When are they going to let you know about it?"

"After I get to Spain, he said."

"But how will they know where to contact you?"

"I've been given the name of a hotel in Barcelona. The . . . hold on, I wrote it down; it's on the pad."

"Well, never mind, tell me when you get here."

"No, I might as well—ah!—here it is: the Oriente."

"Christ!"

". . . William? Are you there? Hello?"

"Sorry, Alex. Yes, still here."

"What's the matter? Do you know the place?"

"I'm staying at it."

"*What?*"

"Alex, I'm staying at it. And I've got a feeling this isn't a coincidence. It's done to impress. They're playing with us."

"How could they know that?"

"How could they know I was in Barcelona, even? But they do: I found myself being followed yesterday. I thought I'd lost him, but evidently I hadn't."

"You think we've underestimated them?"

"Kind of you to put it like that. I'm sure *I* have. I don't understand it, unless Stephenson's got a much larger organization than I assumed. That's possible—he's been out here for some years."

"Doing what?"

"Developing an information network, for one thing. That's becoming uncomfortably obvious."

"No, I meant—"

"I know you did. And I can't tell you what he does, Alex, apart from kidnaps. Perhaps he's got a new, supermarket approach to crime: there seems to be a lot of petty crime going on here, and a large number of small deals could net as much as the Great Train Robbery while attracting much less attention. I don't know. I'm trying to make sense of the twenty-five thousand pounds, which we agreed was just petty cash by comparison with the ransom demands you read about. I've always felt it was odd."

"Yes," Alex said, "it is. And here's something else for you to think about which is just as odd. This polite fellow said he would appreciate it if, with the money, I would hand over a ring he's convinced I've got. I said I hadn't got it. He then suggested, with respect, that I knew where it was and to be sure to bring it with me. After which, he rang off."

"What ring? Is it worth a lot?"

"It's a plain gold wedding ring."

"What's it to do with you?"

"Nothing. It belonged to an old man who lived in Santa Margarita. I happened to be called in when he had a thrombosis—the local doctor wasn't available. Look, I'll tell you the rest when I see you. But it was ages ago, ten years, maybe more."

"What happened?"

"Oh, he died."

"But what's all this about his ring?"

"He gave it to me, that's quite true."

"But you haven't got it now?"

"No, of course I didn't keep it—I handed it to his wife as I left."

"But she says you didn't?"

"Apparently. I must go now, William. We'll meet at the hotel, then?"

"Unless I . . . no, there doesn't seem much point in moving. Yes, at the Oriente."

"I should be there about eight. Good-bye."

I put the telephone down, feeling dazed. Also—what's the word?—*marginalized!* These people were running rings around us. They'd had no trouble at all in keeping up with me, and I'd just been wasting my time trying to . . . Oh shit! If they knew about the hotel, they could have just been waiting for me to slip out and make this call. Better get back there fast! I jumped out of the cubicle.

And there, as if to emphasize their control of the situation, was Granite Face's leather jacket, waiting: I caught the movement as he quickly turned his head away.

He was a lousy sleuth! They were winning by sheer manpower, weight of numbers, that's all! It was positively insulting to be followed around by this goon! But I'd dealt with him once, and I could do it again! I strode over to him and tapped the leather shoulder . . .

All right, so it wasn't him. *"Perdoneme . . ."* I said, spreading my hands apologetically. The man stared. I left.

I had the ten-minute walk back to the hotel to get a grip on myself. Things were falling apart: it was a very uncomfortable feeling. I went straight to the reception desk, where they gave me the bad news I was expecting.

"How long ago?"

"Perhaps ten, fifteen minutes, sir."

"Who with?"

"A señor. There is something wrong?"

"Maybe. What did he look like?"

"Look like?"

"His age, his clothes?"

"The age, like yourself, sir. The clothes: he wear . . ."

"A suit? A leather jacket?

"*Sí sí.*"

"Which, for God's sake?"

"*Una chaqueta . . .*"

"Color?"

"I think . . . black. Yes, I think so."

"Shit."

"Excuse me?"

"Never mind, sorry . . . The key to my room?"

"Certainly, sir . . . ah no. Is not here. The *señora* perhaps is still . . ."

"I hope she is. Thank you."

"Thank you, sir."

The lift seemed to stick in the shaft. Eventually it arrived at the fourth floor. I leaped out, pounded along the corridor, and rapped on the door. A pause, a heart-stopping pause, and then Ginny's voice said:

"Who is it?"

Thank God! "Me, William." The door opened. Ginny's smile faded as she saw the expression on my face.

"What's happened?"

"They've got Sharon."

"Oh?"

I shut the door and folded her in a hug—best not to say how relieved I felt that she was safe and still there. We crossed the room to sit on the bed. "How bad is that?" she asked.

"Maybe it doesn't matter now. Alex has decided to pay the money. He's probably right; it may be the safest way to get Cathy back. Stephenson is a lot better organized than I'd thought possible."

"How much did you say it was?"

"Twenty-five thousand."

"Can he raise it?"

"He already has: he's flying out today with it."

"Oh!—and what then?"

"There'll be a meeting—an exchange."

"Oh William!—how horrible for him. Suppose they—"

"Quite. I've got to think about what to do if they don't keep their side of the bargain."

"And you can't call in the police?"

"It's a gamble Alex doesn't want to take. Not yet, anyway."

We sat in silence for a while. Then Ginny said:

"There's something I can do, which might help. See what's known about Stephenson."

"Can you . . . oh yes, of course you can! Why didn't I think of that?"

"Probably," Ginny said, "because I wasn't being exactly supportive. I feel differently about it now: the thought of that poor man being put through this makes me embarrassed to remember how I was last night. Such a selfish bitch . . ."

"Dear Ginny. Perhaps you should trust me more."

"Don't get carried away, William darling. I am not to be taken for granted."

"No no. Of course not. God forbid."

"All right. Now, you think this Stephenson has a record back home?"

"According to his wife and daughter, yes."

"I'll get my agency to check the news files, then. If there's nothing there, I know someone who might agree to get the name run through the computer at Criminal Records Office: we'd have to provide him with a good reason."

"It would have to be done on the quiet. Is that possible?"

"He works for the *Police Gazette:* it would get lost in the mass of stuff they go through for publication."

"Right! That sounds ideal."

"It may be useless, of course."

"Well, it's worth a try. We just might strike lucky and gain a bargaining point. When will you do it?"

"What time is it?"

"Midday. Eleven in England."

"Good enough. I'll do it now." She reached for the telephone.

"Ginny, no! Not from here."

She pulled her hand away as if the phone was hot. "Takes some getting used to," she said. "Where, then?"

"We'll find a booth on the way to lunch."

"Lunch! Is that still on?"

"Why not?" I said. "Stephenson's taken his daughter back. He knows I'm staying here. Alex is coming here this afternoon—"

"Here?"

"He was given the name of this hotel by the man who rang him last night, coolly, without comment. It's not coincidence, because Sharon's been picked up from here. So I think we can assume there's a sort of truce in operation. We'll be followed, but there's no point in trying to shake them off until we've made new plans. So let's make the best of it, have a fishy lunch in the Barceloneta as arranged, and talk things over. Very good for the brain, fish."

"Well," Ginny said, getting up, "I suppose we've got to eat. Do you think I'm all right to go like this?"

I watched her as she frowned at the long mirror. Blue jeans, a white, short-sleeved T-shirt. Her bare arms were smooth and brown.

"What are you worrying about?" I said. "Those things suit you; that's all there is to it. Always have, and always will."

"What do you think Alastair's wife will be wearing?"

"This is a waterfront shack we're going to, nothing ritzy. You look just right."

She went on frowning at herself in the mirror. Why can they never believe it?

In fact, it was fairly swish as shacks go: a long, low room with a single, windowed end facing the sea. Blue, sunlit water reflected onto white painted paneled walls decorated with green trellis and hung with signed sketches of past patrons. It was crowded, and for a moment, I thought Alastair had forgotten our arrangement. Then I saw him and Pilar waving from a table near the far end.

"There they are!"

I led the way down a narrow aisle between busy elbows. Introductions over, we all sat down and menus were passed around.

"I've got news," I said to Alastair, "but let's get the ordering done first."

"Shall I tell you what you can have?" Pilar offered.

"Oh, please," Ginny said. "My ignorance is total. Are *chipirones* anything to do with chips?"

"Oh no," Pilar said, "no chips. Little squids."

"Well, there you are then," Ginny said, laughing. "Please go on, Pilar."

"*Navajas*—this is razor fish. *Sepia*—cuttle fish. *Langostinos*—you know this one, like in French."

I let the litany drift over my head while I looked around the room. Any sleuth who followed us here must count this his lucky day. Of course, he could be waiting outside, but even sleuths have to eat. Me, I would have combined business with pleasure. In that case, who might it be? In the center of the restaurant, what looked like an office party was in full swing: the men wore expensive designer jackets; their hair was neatly trimmed; large, slightly tinted horn-rimmed glasses seemed to be obligatory. If Barcelona has yuppies, these were they.

Should I suspect the lottery ticket sellers, who were squeezing past the tables brandishing their wares? Or the little dark man, very gaunt, who has suddenly appeared behind a huge guitar and is skipping about, giving a lively rendering of *Viva España*—the din is incredible. Or the free-lance photographer, passing from table to table, snapping the happy, sweating faces: no avoiding him, but then They already know what we look like . . .

Forget it. What are we going to eat?

"Are we all agreed?" Alastair asked.

"Sorry—I missed it; I was miles away."

"*Parrillada*—many sorts of grilled fishes," Pilar said. "You will like this, William, I promise. Yes?"

"Yes. And lots of *vino de la casa.*"

"Ah yes, yes—*vino de la casa!* You say this with very good expression, William. *Muy bien.*"

"He learns the essential phrases first, of course," Ginny said. "It's a good way to discover what they're really interested in, don't you find?"

"Oh yes! Alastair is like this! I will tell you . . ."

No problems there, I noted, catching Alastair's eye: his plan was working. Once girls start ganging up, it's a sure sign they're going to get on. The grilled fishes and the wine came, and we got down to it. Some time went by. Then Alastair said:

"Tell us your news, William."

"Are we all ready? Right, then." There was so much noise in the restaurant that we couldn't have been overheard, not even at the next table. I told them first about Sharon's disappearance: I'd had time to get used to the idea now, and in any case, her usefulness to us had been overtaken by events.

"But," Pilar said, "what will her father do to her, the poor girl?"

"He thinks she was kidnapped. She'll be all right as long as she sticks to that story."

"But how did Stephenson find her?" Alastair said.

"Well, that's really today's big news," I said and recounted the telephone conversation with Alex.

"A *ring?*" Pilar said.

"That's what he said. It's got to be nonsense. English doctors don't steal wedding rings from dying Spaniards."

"Maybe the old boy didn't have medical insurance," Alastair said. As I'd noticed before, amusement set his whole bulk in motion: now I realized what it reminded me of—Yogi Bear. The wine in his glass rocked to danger level and back.

Pilar watched him anxiously. She probably had nothing worse on her mind than the risk to the tablecloth, but on a face as mobile as hers, it registered as a potential major disaster. She glanced at me and must have read my thought, as her expression switched instantly to a brilliant smile which seemed to wrap all four of us in warm complicity. Not for the first time, I realized why Alastair had chosen to marry her and live in Barcelona, her place not his. Girls don't smile quite like that in England.

"And anyway," Alastair said, "doctors can be bent: it's not unheard of."

"Oh come on! Would he bother? A plain gold ring, worth ten quid at most?"

"A sudden temptation . . . a souvenir . . ."

"I don't believe it."

"What's he like?" Ginny said. "You're the only one who's seen him so far."

"Well of course, I haven't seen much of him myself, but he seems quite upright to me. He's a surgeon now. You can't get much more upright than that. Can you?"

"All right," Alastair said. "So he's not guilty. Then we believe him when he says he returned the ring to the wife?"

"That follows, I suppose."

"So the wife is lying when she says he didn't."

"Oh Alastair, you're too bloody logical for a wine merchant. Especially at this stage of the meal. Yes—is she lying? If so, why?"

"This poor woman," Pilar put in. "I think if she have the ring, she will put it back on her husband's finger, no? So he will go to his grave with it."

There was a thoughtful, respectful silence. I said:

"We can assume that the old man wasn't wearing the ring when he was buried. Or Alex wouldn't have been asked for it."

"Then," Pilar said firmly, "I think his wife never have it. No."

"Perhaps she kept it," I suggested. "Wouldn't that do?"

"No, William," Pilar said. "First thing: why should she tell lies about this? Second thing: she would want *him* to have it, her husband. Believe me."

They both looked at me, then. Alastair with his ready belief in petty thieving doctors. And Pilar with her knowledge of Spanish wifely virtue, to the grave and beyond.

"Oh God," I said. "If you're right, we've got trouble in the camp. If you're right, it means that there's more to Alex than he's cared to let on—and I think it must go beyond what I told you about his being overfond of his daughter. This stuff about the ring is really over the top—of course it is; I can see that now. This time, he's deliberately trying to mislead me. I swallowed it because by the time he fed it to me he'd got me into the habit of believing him. So what's true, and what isn't? Stephenson exists; I've seen that for myself. And I know his daughter was driven off from the Cubzac fête in a red, Spanish registered Renault 5—I believe the French kid who says he saw that. Otherwise, everything I know is based on what Alex told me."

"You think he cooked it all up?"

"I think I'd like a large brandy," I said. "Who'll join me?"

The telephone woke me, but I wasn't complaining: the lunch and the afternoon that followed had left me in a mood as beatific as any I could remember: put to the stake I'd have felt nothing but a gentle tickling from the flames. Hotel reception was calling to tell me that Dr. Gordon had arrived and was asking for me—well, fine, even that I could cope with now. I had a quick shower, dressed, and went down to the lounge.

He didn't look like a doctor on holiday anymore but was suited and serious. Preliminaries over, I asked him if he'd heard about the meeting.

"There was a note waiting," he said. "It's to be in the cathedral of Santa Maria, somewhere near here, at nine tomorrow morning."

"Well, that's bright and early. I think we can take comfort from it." He looked slightly puzzled. "Hard to imagine dirty deeds being done at nine in the morning," I explained.

"Oh, I see."

"It's the hour of simple toil. Mail opening, diary checking, all that. An honest hour, before the worm of avarice awakes."

"Yes? Well, I hope you're right."

"I'm sure of it. And in a cathedral, too—that can't be bad. Why don't we go along there this evening—now? They'll probably watch us all the way, but it's a natural thing to do. I'd like to study the ground."

"All right." Alex looked at his watch. "It's half past eight. I suppose we'll get in."

"If not, no harm done. We can walk—it's only a few minutes from here."

"Good."

"I'm with a friend who might like to come with us."

"I don't see why not."

"I'll go and ask her. Meet you here in ten minutes?"

"Her? Oh, I see, I'm sorry . . ."

"You'd rather she didn't come?"

"No, no, of course not . . . Ten minutes, then."

Going up in the lift, I wondered how noticeable my changed attitude to Alex and all his works was. We'd decided, by a unanimous vote toward the end of lunch, that I should go along with his story, and not try for a confession until I'd collected some better clues to what the affair was really about. So, since Alex had arrived at the Oriente, I'd been quite enjoying the game, and the relief from responsibility—he was back in the driver's seat, and I was now just a passenger on his mystery tour. He'd have to think up something a lot more convincing than tales of missing gold rings if he was to keep me on board.

"Who's that?"

"Me."

"Come in, you."

Ginny's smiling face reminded me of the old times, the good times. Around and around we go, hoping for moments like this, the brief times of contentment that make all that well-worn maneuvering seem worthwhile.

"Some siesta, Ginny darling. Wasn't it?"

"Mmmm . . . it was."

"Mmmm . . . sure?"

"Mmmm . . . positive."

After which, she retreated to the bathroom, and splashing sounds ensued. I called:

"You want a stroll before supper? I've got to go with Alex to the Santa Maria, where he claims the deal is to be done tomorrow."

"Is it far?"

"Maybe fifteen minutes."

"I might just manage it."

"Dear Ginny, please try. I want to make the most of you."

"Promise we won't get shot at, or anything. Can I trust you that far?"

"Of course! You can hold my hand."

"Oh wow."

"Plus you may hear Alex reciting the next installment of The Golden Ring, a fairy story for naïve wine merchants."

"Now, that would be interesting."

"Wouldn't it. What are you doing in there?"

"None of your business."

"Oh. Well whatever it is, we ought to go."

"Coming, coming. I don't know which is worse, mental or physical knackeredness. Can we have a little calm tomorrow?"

"*You* can. *I've* got to be Alex's minder. Well, that's the role I'm playing. You can stay here and—"

"That reminds me! William—there's something really horrible in a shopping bag in the wardrobe, I presume it's something to do with you?"

"Ginny!—you mustn't touch that."

"Don't worry, I wouldn't dream of touching it. Whatever it is. Do you have to—"

"It's only for self-defense. All I could find, not having a gun license."

"Couldn't you keep it somewhere else? It makes me nervous, just being in the same room as a thing like that."

"All right, all right—I'll put it in the car tomorrow. Come *on*, Ginny."

"I'm ready now," she said, emerging.

We walked along the corridor to the lift. "I suppose," Ginny said, "you've explained me to Alex."

"Yes. Not that it's—"

"He's met Claudine, hasn't he?"

"Yes. It's all right, though. We're not breaking the rules, are we?"

"Aren't we?"

"No, we're not. Alex isn't a family friend nor likely to be. Discretion is preserved."

The lift arrived, and we got in. There was a middle-aged couple at the back: Americans by the look of them.

"I don't feel like a scarlet woman," Ginny said cheerfully.

"Er, good," I said.

"How do you suppose the French worked these rules out in the first place?"

"Er, Ginny, perhaps we could discuss this—"

"Of course, they've always been more keen on sex than us British. I suppose, after centuries of—"

"*Ginny* . . ."

"—around it's become second nature to them, this famous discretion. Is it really true—you're not just building on a fable?"

"Well," I said, giving up, "you've met Claudine. What do you think?"

"She seemed to take it in her stride, that time, yes. But perhaps you were clever in your choice of wife, William darling. What about the other French you know—are they all at it?"

"All the time, Ginny, I promise you. What we're doing is par for the course, French marriagewise."

The lift stopped. I stood aside to let the American couple leave first. "Thank you, sir," the man said heavily. When we were all outside the lift, he turned.

"Excuse me. I believe we met once before? Two, maybe three years ago, in Paris?"

I looked at him. Bells rang—yes! In a café near the Sorbonne, what an extraordinary coincidence! The evening that Dominique . . . uh, just a moment . . .

"I'm afraid not," I said. "No. Must be someone else."

"Oh, really? I could have sworn . . ."

"Sorry."

We watched them go.

"He was sure about that, wasn't he," Ginny said.

"Yes, seemed to be. Isn't it odd, all American tourists seem to be like that. Why don't we ever come across wisecracking New Yorkers?—can't they spare the time from making films for Woody Allen? Now Ginny, you did that deliberately. What got into you?"

"I just felt like it," she said.

"But—"

"A short sharp attack of Francophobia, you could say."

"It came on pretty suddenly."

"Oh yes. It does. Without warning."

"Is it over now?"

"Yes, William darling. All over now. For the time being."

"I see. Well . . . here's the lounge. Let me introduce Alex."

"Hello," Alex said in a hushed, conspiratorial voice, "so here she is!" His eyes flickered as nervously as a schoolboy's. What did he expect?—high heels, black stockings, plunging neckline, the traditional trappings of naughtiness? For God's sake, what's the matter with the man?

"Hello," Ginny said. Her voice left me in no doubt that she'd received the same message. Time that we—

"Let's go, before the shop shuts," I said, "if I won't be struck down by speaking thus about the House of God."

I could try a prayer. Bloody hell, I've tried everything else I can think of. O Lord, give us a break, *please!*

We walked through the dark, narrow streets of the Barri Gotic, across the Vía Laietana, to the little cathedral of Santa

Maria. We stood in the square before the west end, looking up at the tall facade, sandwiched between medieval houses. I'd been here before, I realized, walking back to the flat with Alastair that first evening after putting the car in the underground car park. Once again, I watched the pale shapes of pigeons swooping over my head. There were lights on inside the building, and we could hear the deep throaty rumble of an organ.

"Sounds as if there's a service going on," Alex said.

"Let's look." We climbed the steps to the pointed doors, and I pushed one, tentatively. It swung heavily open. We filed through, into a dark paneled lobby, and through a padded inner door. As I opened it, the organ sounds rushed out to greet us.

"Bach!" I hissed happily. "We're in luck. Surely they won't mind if we sneak in and sit at the back. Okay?"

"There's nobody here," Ginny said. "It's not a service, then."

"Organ practice. What could be better?"

We went quietly into the shadowy, cold interior, and slid into a pew. Ahead, the cavernous stone vaulting marched toward the spotlit high altar, which seemed to float in the gloom. Behind the altar, a palid Christ hung motionless on a carved screen of painted wood which rocketed upward almost to the roof, glinting with gilded decoration. The broad side aisles lay in darkness, except where a pyramid of guttering candles flickered in the hope of special consideration from the Virgin Mary . . . No, not my scene. But here, tomorrow, at nine A.M., Alex's troubles would meet their maker. If there was any such person outside his imagination.

Well, we'll see. Meanwhile, we're getting a free live performance of a Bach prelude and fugue. It's a break all right, not quite the sort I was praying for, but it'll do. Just listen to that!

SATURDAY

AT NINE IN THE MORNING, THE CATHEDRAL HAD A much more matter-of-fact air. The light had lost its mystic quality. The sounds now weren't courtesy of Bach, but of Hoover—distant, but distinct. I stood in the north aisle, partly concealed by the mahogany bulk of the confessional, the shopping bag containing the crossbow dangling from one hand . . . Yes, I know that carrying a weapon in cathedral precincts might seem, all right, *was* a monstrous thing to do, but Ginny had insisted I remove it from the bedroom, and I was going to put it in the Citroën just as soon as I had the chance. Anyway, if there was trouble, it would probably erupt outside, on secular territory. That's one thing Catholics and Protestants usually manage to agree on.

I watched Alex pacing up and down the aisle opposite. We were not alone: apart from cleaners, the occasional priest appeared and disappeared about some clerical task, cassock swinging, big black shoes clopping on the stone flags. Tourists passed my post from time to time, heads turning, cameras dangling. From somewhere far above, a harsh clang sounded: the first stroke of nine. I looked across at Alex again: he was still there, still apparently convinced that something was going to happen. He was standing, now, with his face turned to the doors at the west end.

On the last stroke of nine, two figures appeared. Not a difficult feat: they only had to wait in the lobby. No reason to be impressed by that, I told myself. They stood, looking around. I shrank as far as possible behind the confessional. They saw Alex, and walked toward him with purposeful tread. Now: was this going to be a genuine encounter or a performance for my benefit? I intended to note every gesture.

The problem was that, from where Alex had chosen to take his stand opposite me, they would be able to see around the confessional. The nearest statue was a painfully skinny saint—which saint, I couldn't say, but he'd certainly taken *cuisine minceur* to the limit, leaving nothing much for my fuller figure to hide behind. The columns would do to conceal me, but not to look out from—and tourists might stop to wonder what I'd found of such compelling interest in the unadorned stone-work. I looked across to the south aisle again. The gap between Alex and the visiting delegation was rapidly narrowing, and the meeting was imminent. If I was going to move, it had to be now, while their attention was fixed on Alex.

You could say I did it without thinking, but that wasn't quite true. It was instinctive, yes, but I was also aware that it was the best I could do in the time available. I was in there and had the red velvet curtains pulled across with seconds to spare. Leaving, of course, a crack to peer out of. It was perfect, really, except for the guilty sense of trespass.

Having been brought up Church of England, it was my first time in a confessional. There was a hard little seat to perch on; set in the partition, at face level, was a wooden grille closed by a shutter on the far side; there was an overpowering smell of furniture polish. Through the join of the curtains, I watched the two men walk up to Alex. The one in the leather jacket was, I felt sure, Granite Face. The other had on a dark suit which looked at this distance to be of expensive cut: he had short dark hair, and an indefinable Mediterranean air. Perhaps it was the way he walked, the deliberate, upright strut of a man of honor, the sort of honor that gets defended to the death, usually with knives . . .

Mafia?

I clutched the velvet curtains. Perhaps I should be over there

with Alex? It was two to one. But they might not have come
in if I'd been with him—the instructions were that Alex was
to be alone . . . Of course, from here I could be fairly sure of
winging one . . .

What am I saying? That's out of the question while on these
premises!

Well then. What's happening now?

Alex is handing over a bulky envelope—he's being quite
open about it; he wants me to see. Now there's a discussion
going on. The mafia type is doing the talking: it looks polite
but firm, just as Alex said about the man on the telephone. But
now what?

The mafia type is handing the package back again . . .

If only I could hear what they were saying! Alex is . . . but
now a tourist has blocked my view, no, a priest, well whichever; I wish he'd move on. Ah—he has . . .

*But into the next compartment of the confessional. The center
compartment, where the priests . . .*

Click. And the little shuttered grille is now open . . .

I looked through at the profile of my new neighbor. A young-
ish man, his close-cropped hair still dark, steel-framed specta-
cles perched on a pudgy nose in front of eyes which (I was
relieved to see) were directed away from me. His right hand
supported his brow in the classic pose of a patient listener. He
said nothing.

I looked out of the curtain again. Alex and the two men
seemed to be arguing. If I left the confessional now, Granite
Face would almost certainly recognize me—he had reason to. If
only I could hold on in here for a few moments—surely I could
be forgiven that, in a good cause? But what to say? What *could* I
say, in Spanish? Best to come clean, well, partially . . .

"*No hablo Español,*" I said.

"*Ah, sí. Deutsch?*"

"No. *Inglés . . .*"

"*Inglés, bueno.* You may speak, I understand."

Just my luck: young, keen, speaks English . . . "I'm afraid this is very wrong . . ."

"You will be forgiven, my son. How long since your last confession?"

"No, really—normally, you see, I don't . . ."

"One year? More?"

"Oh yes, much more . . . I'm not even a—"

"Five years? You must tell me. Have no fear."

"—Catholic."

"You are not of the Church?"

"To be honest, no."

"But you have troubles."

"Yes."

"God will help you, if you will let Him. You have been waiting here one hour, I see this."

"Yes, as a matter of fact, I have. I'm sorry."

"You would like instruction?"

"Perhaps, well, if you had a leaflet . . ."

"This is not the place. You must see your own priest, where you live. He will give you instruction."

"Yes. Thank you."

"Bless you, my son."

Click.

I heard him go, looked out, and saw the black shadow pass. Over in the south aisle, Alex was standing alone, looking about him. I checked that the coast was clear, stepped out through the confessional curtains, and went to join him.

"So that's where you were. Good Lord."

"I'm beginning to think so. What happened?—wouldn't they take the money? Where's Cathy?"

"They say they must have the ring as well. I don't know where Cathy is, but they put a lot of effort into persuading me that she's come to no harm. And they gave the money back as a gesture of good faith."

"What does that mean?"

"To show that they mean what they say. They don't want the money without the ring."

I'd had enough of this. I said sharply:

"Look, Alex—why don't you tell me what it's really all about? Isn't it time we had all the cards on the table?"

Alex looked at me. Then he shrugged, and began to walk toward the exit.

"Well? Isn't it?" I persisted.

He didn't reply. I put a hand on his arm and stopped him. He turned. His face was grim.

"I'd do anything to get Cathy back," he said. "I'd sell the house, pay every penny I own. I offered them more money, but they wouldn't take it."

"They want the ring?"

"They want the ring. And I haven't got it."

"It really exists, then?"

"Well, of course it does. I told you."

"Yes, I know, but . . . frankly, Alex, it doesn't make sense. You're sure it's just an ordinary wedding ring of no real value?"

"Yes."

"And you gave it back to the old man's wife?"

"Yes."

"And she says you didn't?"

"So they say."

"But she's still alive, and living in Santa Margarita?"

"I believe so."

"Well, we'd better collect Pilar and get over there."

"I suppose you're right," Alex said.

Ginny let me in, and then slid back into bed, where she sat, hugging her knees. There was no sign of a breakfast tray—I'd been hoping to get back in time for some coffee. What time was it? Just after ten—perhaps the hotel catered for late breakfasters? Or should I open a bottle of—

"Well? Did it go off all right?" Ginny asked.

"Yes and no. Mostly no. I don't know what to make of it, quite frankly. Perhaps a little refreshment would help."

"I need something to eat—I'm starving," Ginny said. "This luxury life stirs up my appetite. What do you mean, no?"

"No deal without the ring," I said, reaching for the telephone. "They handed the money back, and told him to—hello? This is room four one six: we'd like a tray of cakes, please. Well, I don't know what sort—would you just send up a selection, whatever you've got? Thanks, *gracias.* Told him to find it."

"So it's true, then? About the ring."

"I don't know, Ginny: I didn't actually hear what was said, but I did see them hand the money back. I'm afraid it'll have to be the semi-dry; we drank the sweet yesterday."

"William darling, you won't get any complaints from me. Listen, so what next?"

"How do you feel about a little trip down the coast? The old man's wife is still going strong, and I've suggested to Alex that we pay her a visit."

"Alex is coming too? I suppose he has to."

"Well yes, I think he has. Do I detect a certain lack of enthusiasm for the good doctor?" I handed her a fizzing glass of the Codorniu.

"The man's a creep," Ginny said with decision. "Umm, thank you, darling. Champagne breakfasts, yet. I shall think of this when I'm back, mucking out the stables."

"A creep? You'd pitch it as strong as that?"

"A creep. He's a long mackintosh merchant, darling, take it from me. Dirty books in the desk drawer."

"How can you be so sure?"

"A woman knows."

"She doesn't, not always. I've read about women who've lived with spies for years without knowing a thing about it."

"I'm not talking about spying, William darling. I'm talking about sex, S–E–X."

"As a matter of fact, you're right—he's got a thing about

young girls." I didn't want to tell her the whole of it, not yet. "You're to keep it to yourself, mind."

"There you are! I knew it."

"Yes, but how?"

Ginny considered. "It's a crawly effect down the spine," she said. "You just know you wouldn't like him to touch you."

"I see. But Ginny, girls seem to go for him. My Sylvie said so. And there's a girl at the Villa Club who—"

There was a knock at the door. I opened it and took charge of a tray covered with a napkin. "Thank you, very kind." I carried it to the bed and took off the napkin. "Oh, brioches, good. And those sticky almond things: this'll restore the old blood-sugar level . . . So, how do you explain that, Ginny?"

"I can't darling. You need to ask a shrink. All I know is what I feel as a mature and not inexperienced female: crawly down the spine. My glass seems to be empty."

So, as we bowled down the motorway in the Citroën, Alex sat, all unsuspecting, in the front, and Ginny was in the back with Pilar, safe from contact and crawly feelings. Did Ginny really mean what she'd said? I wondered. Or was she just getting her own back on Alex for the way he'd looked her up and down last night, clearly seeing her as a piece of merchandise, a married man's optional extra? (Ginny had got distinctly more peppery on the subject of female independence over the last year or two.) No, she'd probably meant it. It was one more in the growing collection of oddities that clung to Alex: the worried wife, the background of sexual perversion, the hardly credible affair of the missing wedding ring. I had a monster sitting next to me! It was hard to remember that when face to face with him; so easy to be taken in by those polite phrases, that conventional mask. I should do some probing . . .

"Tell me again, Alex," I said, "how long did you say you've had the house at Santa Margarita?"

"Nineteen seventy-two," Alex said.

"Oh, I see. A long time."

"Yes. Not so good an investment as I hoped, but perhaps now, with Spain joining the Common Market . . ."

"Bound to make a difference. People will pay more for a place in the sun, if the political uncertainties are removed."

"I hope so," he said. "Mind you, it's not happening overnight. Franco's gone, and Spain has opened up, that's true. But now there are new uncertainties: the Basque separatists, and even, I'm afraid, the people here . . ." He glanced over his shoulder, but Pilar was engrossed in conversation with Ginny.

"The Catalans. Yes, Alastair was telling me about that. Relatively harmless, though, aren't they?"

"Harmless? Bombings and robberies?"

"I said, relatively. They're demonstrations, aren't they?—not true terrorism. People aren't meant to get hurt."

"So far, but it's intensifying. And the authorities have had to react—you must have noticed the number of security guards around the place: not only in banks, but in post offices, the big Pryka supermarkets . . ."

"Not just a passing phase, you feel?"

"I'm afraid not. The new, post–Franco freedom's gone to their heads. When I first came here, people were afraid to talk openly in case the secret police were listening. There was strict censorship, with everything under tight control from Madrid: the country was virtually run by the army and the church. Now, since Franco died, the lid's off, and anything goes: politics, religion, books, films, whatever you want, up to and including live sex shows—it's an unbelievable change in such a short time. But you must have heard all this before."

"Interesting to hear it from you, though," I said, "as you were out here before the change—Alastair wasn't. When did Franco die?"

"Two or three years after I bought the house."

"Nineteen seventy-five," Pilar said from the back seat.

"Thank you, Pilar."

"You're welcome."

"It's hard to imagine how it used to be," I said. "I didn't

come to Spain in those days. Sitting in a café, having to be careful about what you said."

"Nobody was mugged," Alex said. "It was a much safer place. Less traffic, too. Much quieter."

"You make it sound almost idyllic, Alex," I said.

"Well, the changes aren't all to the good," he said. "But it had to happen, of course—I'm not denying that."

"How did Franco manage to hang on so long?" I said.

"Some say they needed him to hold things together, really, and knew it," Alex said.

"Who says this?" Pilar said.

"Well, I've even heard Spanish people say it."

"Oh yes! We still have many fascists, you know."

"I'm sorry," Alex said hurriedly, sounding embarrassed. "I didn't mean to upset you. My apologies."

"It's difficult for us Brits to remember that there are still these deep political divisions here," I said, "when all we see is sun, sand, and package tours. But we were on your side in the Civil War, Pilar. A handful of us, at least, in the International Brigade."

"Oh yes," she said. "I do not forget this. But you know, every year, in Madrid, there is still a big demonstration to remember Franco. There are many, many people who want to bring back those times."

"They haven't got much chance, surely?" Ginny said.

"I hope not," Pilar said, "but they can still make trouble. They have money, and some of them are high up, especially in the army. I think they like to take control again if they can."

"Who are the Spanish people you've heard talking in favor of Franco, Alex?" I asked.

"Well, I've already upset Pilar once."

"No, Alex, no," Pilar said. "You tell me. It's okay."

"Then she can get out the old Browning automatic from the bottom drawer and deal with them," I said.

"Oh no, William!"

"Browning?" Alex said with a nervous laugh.

"I'm only guessing. Might be a Beretta. Tell us, Pilar."

"No, William, really . . ."

"I see you as a beautiful revolutionary, Pilar—famed throughout the Free World. *La MacInnes,* making passionate speeches and leading attacks on post offices . . . where is the Free World, does anyone know?"

"William darling, you've never risked stepping outside it," Ginny said.

"I have, I have."

"When? Where?"

"I haven't. Look!—Santa Margarita. I assume we're all going to drop in at the Villa Club bar, first? Perhaps Jill can do us sandwiches. And you think she might be able to take us to see the widow, Alex?"

"Yes. The old man used to drink in the bar occasionally: that's how I first met him, and there's still some contact with the family. The house is very near the Villa Club: I don't know what its proper name is, but at the club it's always been known as the Big House."

"The Big House. And the old man's name was?"

"Miguel Delgado."

"So we're going to see Señora Delgado."

"No, William," Pilar said. "She will have her own names: first her father's and then her mother's."

"Oh? You mean, a Spanish girl doesn't change her name when she gets married? You're not La MacInnes?"

"No. I am Pilar Perales Lopera."

"Quite right!" Ginny said. "Why *should* girls have to—"

"But the old man only had two names. Miguel Delgado, you said, Alex?"

"That is for short," Pilar said. "He must also have one more, his mother's name. Like, you see, my children, God willing, will be called MacInnes Perales."

"Then, all Spanish people have three names?" I said.

"Oh yes. Unless they have a first name like Jose Maria. Then they have four."

In the silence, the sound of grinding brains could be heard.
"Is very simple," Pilar said.
"Give us time," I said. "And a few drinks. Here we are."

It was late afternoon when the message came to say that Señora
Morales would be pleased to receive us. I didn't see who
brought it. The four of us walked along the narrow dusty
street, through the lengthening shadows, to the Big House. I'd
expected a tall villa, closed off behind iron gates, but the reality
was nothing like that. The house was simply part of the village
street, indistinguishable from its neighbors except for the extra
weight and elaboration of the window grilles, and the massive
molding of the iron-studded double entrance doors. One of
these doors stood open; inside, we could see a dark, square,
tiled entrance hall, without any windows, lit only by the sunlight reflected on the white plastered ceiling from the pavement outside. It was furnished with plants in brightly glazed
earthenware pots. At the back of the hall, an iron-railed stone
stair could just be discerned, leading upward into an almost
total darkness. There was an incongruous modern plastic bell
push fixed to the door frame. I pressed it, and we waited.
    After some moments, as I was beginning to wonder if I
should give the bell a second prod, a shuffling could be heard.
It came from the top of the stairs, and soon a pair of floral
slippers worn by sturdy legs in coarse brown stockings de-
scended slowly into the light. Smiling and gesturing, a small
white-haired old woman in a black dress came into full view.
Pilar stepped forward to speak for us. There was a rapid exchange of Spanish, with some laughter. Then the old woman
started back up the stairs.
    "What was all that about?" I asked.
    "She invites us to follow. Señora Morales is upstairs, in her
room," Pilar said.
    "Then who was that?"
    "I think you would say, a companion."
    "Ah."

"I'm sure I shouldn't have let you persuade me to come,"
Ginny said to me. "Perhaps I'll wait here."

"No, come with us, Ginny. We need your journalistic eye
and memory."

"Don't expect too much, darling—I used to rely on a tape
recorder. When I forgot it, my interviews were rather low on
facts, if high on creativity. Editors used to—"

"Ginny! Are you coming, or not? If so—"

"All right, all right. Sorry."

Upstairs, a low wattage bulb hung from the ceiling of a large
but windowless landing, throwing a dim yellow light on the
brown painted walls and doors. The claustrophobic effect was
increased by the sinuous dark mahogany furniture which
lurked in every available corner, the sort that seems to move
the moment you take your eye off it. I passed a blackened
mirror in a gilt frame: in it, as through a window from another
world, a startled face loomed toward me. *Mine!*

"Look!" Ginny said, nudging me. "A painting of him."

"No no. An ancestor, surely, in those clothes . . ."

"And those whiskers. Hoo hoo . . ."

"*Shhh.* This was a pirate village, you know. Wreckers, perhaps, putting lights out to lure ships to their doom."

"And handy with a cutlass, I'd say."

"But a fine-looking old boy."

The old woman was standing by a door at the end of the
landing, still smiling, and beckoning us to go in. Here, at last,
there was daylight: a single French window, narrow and obscured by net curtains, but looking over a bright garden.
Beyond was a gray-green haze of olive trees—the orchard
which lay between the back of this house and the gardens of
the Villa Club.

A broad figure in black was struggling up from a high-
backed chair beside the empty fireplace at the far end of the
room. Pilar darted forward to dissuade her, but she was determined to stand: Pilar took her arm to help her and, having
succeeded, leaning on a stout stick, she greeted each of us with

a stately inclination of the head. She must, I supposed, be in her eighties, but her face was as round and smooth as an apple. The black dress was almost as wide as it was long, but the impression was of sturdiness rather than overweight. Like her companion, Señora Morales wore her white hair pinned up behind her head like a Victorian grandmother.

"Señora Morales invites you to be seated," Pilar said. The old lady smiled and waved us to take our places on hard chairs that looked as if they'd been brought in from the dining room for the occasion. There was no sofa, although the room was full of furniture: cupboards of various shapes and sizes, tables loaded with memorabilia, a bulbous mahogany wall clock, its brass pendulum hanging inert behind a glass door. I glanced at Alex, who was sitting on my left, but he was biting his lower lip, his face withdrawn, and gave no sign that he was expecting to open the discussion.

"Shall I . . . ?" I prompted quietly.

He gave a start. "Oh yes. If you would."

Did he already know that nothing useful would come of this? If so, why had he agreed to come? I said:

"Please tell Señora Morales that we are grateful for the opportunity of this visit. And also that I very much regret not being able to speak to her in Span . . . in her own language." *A near one, that!—Catalan was surely spoken here.*

Pilar translated. The old lady listened, and then smiled approvingly in my direction.

"*Lo siento . . .*" I ventured. *I'm sorry . . .*

Another smile. For a moment, I caught a glimpse of the young girl who had once inhabited this grandmotherly body.

"I think it's your turn, Alex," I said.

"Yes. Well, can't be avoided, I suppose."

"That's what we're here for, isn't it?" *He's on the spot; he knows it . . .*

"Yes. Well, she can only throw us out. Pilar, would you ask Señora Morales if she remembers me?"

Pilar translated, and the old lady replied. Pilar nodded and

turned to Alex. "She says, yes, you are the doctor who attended her husband when he died. She wants you to know that
she has always been grateful for this."

Gracious smiles were now being directed at Alex. He made
an attempt to smile back. There was an awkward silence.

"Haven't you seen her since?" I asked him in a low voice.

"I don't think she ever leaves the house," he said. "Maybe
by car, but I haven't . . . look, I'll simply put it to her about
the ring. Pilar: would you ask her if she remembers this?
On the day I attended her husband, as I left the house, I gave
her the ring that her husband wore, which I understood was
what he wanted me to do. Ask her if she remembers that, and
if so, what she did with it."

*He's squirming in his chair. Is it nervousness, embarrassment,
or . . . ?*

"She says no; she does not remember this," Pilar reported.

"But she must!"

"Shall I ask her again?"

"Yes . . . yes. Say to her, that I remember it very clearly."

"Okay. I try again."

I watched the old lady as Pilar spoke. She listened calmly,
then shook her head. Now, as she looked up and toward Alex,
her round face was not smiling, but wore the stubborn expression of the very old, survivors against the odds, chin up and
corners of the mouth turned down. Then she looked away, and
spoke to Pilar, who bent forward to listen.

"Señora Morales says, why do you ask this?"

"What shall I say," Alex said urgently, looking at me.

"Tell her the whole thing."

"William, how can I?" His face was a picture of indecision.

"Tell her your daughter's been kidnapped, and in order to
get her back, you've got to produce this ring," I said in as
neutral a tone as I could manage. *Now for it!*

Alex's eyes searched my face. Then he said:

"I can't do that."

"Why not?"

"It's . . . too much to put on an old lady. I don't see how I can say it in a way that'll make sense to her."

He knows he'll be blown out of the water . . . "I think it's got to be your decision, Alex."

"I'll try it another way. Pilar—"

"Yes?"

"Ask her if there was anything special about that ring."

"Okay." Again, the old lady listened and then made a brief reply.

"Señora Morales says, yes, it was a very special ring. It was her husband's; he wore it always."

"No, Pilar, that's not what I meant. Was it anything more than a wedding ring?"

"She says, no."

Silence fell. Señora Morales sat with her hands in her lap, eyes on the floor, lost in her thoughts.

"Ask her," Alex said abruptly, "if her husband was buried with a ring—with that ring."

Pilar bent forward again. She spoke gently, and seemed to have to repeat herself. The old lady was absorbed in thoughts of her own and made no reply. I followed her gaze across the room, to where a collection of silver-framed photographs stood on a side table beneath a larger, portrait photograph which hung on the wall behind. Then she spoke to Pilar, at length, in a voice that started firmly enough, but gradually got weaker until it was barely audible. At last, Pilar put a hand on her arm, and the wavering voice fell silent.

Pilar bent forward until her hair brushed the old lady's cheek and said something which sounded like comfort. Then, after a pause, she got up quietly, and came over to us.

"Señora Morales says, she would like us to go now. But she says we may take a book from the drawer over there, which will show us what sort of a man her husband was. We must take great care of it, and return it soon."

We got to our feet obediently. Alex said:

"But Pilar—excuse me—did she answer the question?"

"I ask her this," Pilar said, "but she did not say yes, or no. I think the book is her answer."

"But—"

"I am very sorry," Pilar said firmly, "but I cannot ask her this again. No."

She went to the side table where the photographs were displayed, opened a shallow drawer, and took out a large flat volume bound in red leather. Señora Morales made a small gesture of approval with her hand. Then, with awkward bows and nods, like children on best behavior, we trooped from the room.

SATURDAY EVENING

"IT'S GEORGE ORWELL!"

"William darling, you've got George Orwell on the brain. You can't be sure, not with a fuzzy old snapshot like this."

"Well, see for yourself. That wide, narrow mustache, that odd short-back-and-sides barbering with thick wavy hair on top, the desperado expression—it is! Isn't it?"

"Certainly could be," Alex said.

"Barcelona, December, nineteen thirty-six," read Pilar. "The Civil War began in the summer, you know, and Barcelona was very soon taken over by the socialist and anarchist groups."

"Which is Delgado?"

"I think this one," Pilar said. "Handsome, no?"

"He looks about forty: that would be about right," Alex said. "He was in his mid-seventies when he died."

"Somebody was busy with the Box Brownie," Ginny said. "You'd hardly think they had time to take all these snaps with bullets flying all over the place. I suppose they knew they were making history. They look conscious of it, don't they, posing with their rifles. Where are these sandbagged buildings?"

Pilar bent to look more closely. "I think, the Plaça Catalunya. There was a lot of fighting up there, to win the Telephone Exchange."

"Occupy."

"Thank you, William. Occupy."

"Newspaper cuttings, too. I suppose they must refer to events that Delgado took part in, though he's not mentioned."

"I should think so, William, yes," Alex said. "It isn't a war scrapbook, is it, but a memorial to the old man. Everything must have a personal meaning. Why do you suppose Señora Morales wanted us to see it, exactly?"

"She is very proud of him," Pilar said. "She is saying to us, look what he was!"

"A bank robber, among other things," Ginny said.

"What?"

"Look at the picture in this cutting—it's a blown-up bank, isn't it? If William is right, Delgado had a part in it."

"Read it, Pilar."

Pilar looked at it. "Oh, is all right," she said, laughing.

"All right?"

"Yes, quite all right. This one was full of fascist money, from rich people and big landowners. I think Delgado blow it up and take the money to buy guns."

"Or perhaps he just kept it," Ginny said, laughing. "Oh!— I'm sorry, Pilar. I keep forgetting." She leaned forward to see if Spanish sensibility had been touched off again.

"Is okay," Pilar said abstractedly. She was still reading the cutting. "Perhaps you are right, Ginny. Perhaps this is how he becomes a big man in Santa Margarita."

I groaned.

"William!—why do you do this?" Pilar asked.

"Because," I said, "this affair is complicated enough already. I smell trouble."

"What trouble?"

"Money trouble, probably," I said. "But give it a day or two, and that will emerge. Bound to, isn't it."

"Are you all right, William darling?"

"Apart from a feeling of impending, inescapable doom, absolutely fine, Ginny."

They were all looking at me, blankly. They didn't see what I meant. All right, maybe it was all in my mind. But again, maybe it wasn't. I certainly had that feeling, of something big, something threatening, just offstage. And of being used, for some purpose still obscure to me. Somebody, somewhere, was pulling the strings . . .

"I'd like a word with you, Alex," I said. "Shall we walk up the lane together?"

He looked wary, I thought. But he said:

"If you like."

The dusty tarmac lane out of the village led past three or four newly built villas and the football field before turning into a rough, unsurfaced track. It was Saturday evening, and down the hill, on the other side of the main road, I could see and hear the tiny, hurtling toylike shapes of go-carts, endlessly circling the new track Jill had complained about. Once clear of the village, the landscape was one of parched brown fields and orchards, divided by low, drystone walls. Up to the left, I could see a high white enclosure that had to be a cemetery, judging by the rows of dark, pointed, sad cypresses that stood there. Farther away, perhaps a half mile to the north, was the Black Bull silhouette of an Osborne Brandy advertisement: the motorway must be just beyond. The heat had gone out of the day: it was nearly six o'clock.

"Shall we go to the next corner, and then decide whether to go back or around by the cemetery?"

"Suits me," Alex said.

We walked on a little farther in an uncomfortable silence, until I reckoned he was either softened up or impervious.

"All right," I said, "I'll put it plainly. What's going on that you haven't told me about?"

"Ah," he said. "I knew this was coming: I could see it in your face the moment I got out here. You were different."

"Well, Alex. Put it this way: I think you could have fed me a tale in order to get my help in getting Cathy back. All that stuff about the ring!"

Alex shot a glance at me. "Why should I want to do that?" he asked, frowning.

Because you couldn't tell me the real reason for her disappearance, her need to escape from her father . . . The thing I'm not supposed to know about. "I'm asking," I said. "I want *you* to tell *me.*"

"Everything I've told you has been perfectly true," he said stiffly.

"Uh-huh. Nothing else I should know about?"

"Not that's relevant," he said. *No, he wasn't going to tell me. And I'd gone as far as I could without spelling it out.*

"You still expect me to believe that Cathy's being held hostage in return for a gold ring?" I said. "I do find that very hard to take. Why on earth should—"

"Quite. I can assure you I feel the same myself."

"You're still convinced you gave it to Señora Morales?"

"Yes. It was a long time ago, but it's not the sort of thing you forget."

"But she says she doesn't remember it."

"I'm sorry to say I don't believe that."

"Then she's lying."

"I'm afraid she is."

"Why?"

"That's where we're up against it. I have no idea."

"You say 'we'—are you sure you want me to go on being involved in this?"

He stopped me, and said earnestly:

"William, I'm very grateful for all you've done, and I think I've been extraordinarily lucky that you turned up to help me. I hope very much that you'll help me a little while longer, but if that's dependant on my telling you more than I have already, it can't be done. That's all I can say."

After a pause, we walked on again. I said:

"I don't know what to think, Alex. I really don't. Nothing seems to add up, but I suppose I'd rather be had for a fool than leave you in the lurch, if that's what it amounts to."

"I appreciate it, William, believe me."

"Well, okay. I suppose we'd better plan what to do next."

We reached the place where the track turned a sharp corner to the north, and stopped.

"Shall we go on or turn back?" I said.

"Oh, let's go back—I'm not in much of a mood for walking," Alex said. We did an about-turn. "There's a son, I believe."

"Delgado had a son? Do you know where he lives?"

"No, but Jill might—she knows this village inside out."

"Ah. Well, that's something. He would have been at the funeral, surely."

"Let's find out," Alex said. "And William—I hope this has cleared the air to some extent, if not completely."

When we got to within a hundred yards of the Villa Club, I could smell burning; a haze of smoke was coming from behind the bar. I looked at Alex to see if he'd noticed it, but he merely smiled, and said: "Saturday evening barbecue."

On the terrace overlooking the olive grove, a charcoal grill was being coaxed up to operating temperature. Ginny and Pilar were talking to the cook, a perspiring Spanish boy minimally dressed for the occasion in swimming trunks and apron. On a table nearby, racks of spareribs lay ready for the chopper.

The girls looked at us inquiringly.

"We've come to an understanding," I said. "And we're going to crack this thing and get Cathy back, no messing about. Have you seen Jill?"

"She's in the bar," Ginny said.

"I'll go and talk to her," Alex said. We watched him march off.

"So," Ginny said, "you're in military mood. He convinced you, then?"

"Not exactly, but I'm going to go along with it," I said. "What I feel now is that the story's too crazy not to be true. He could easily have invented something better."

"Yes, I agree with this," Pilar said, nodding. "Much too crazy."

"Unless it's a double bluff . . . oh hell, anyway, I'm in it now. And apart from helping Alex, I want to know the answer; I'm hooked. Ginny, I think we must have a talk, now."

"If you're proposing to pack me off home, darling, forget it," Ginny said.

"Oh? But I thought, because of what you said about not being prepared to be a service widow . . ."

"William darling, that was *days* ago. Things change, you know. And I've got my new friend here to keep me company when you're at the front."

"Oh yes!" Pilar said. "You don't need to worry about her now." They smiled at me in unison.

"I see. Well, that's wonderful for you both."

"Yes—there are lots of things we're planning to do."

"Are there?"

"Oh yes! You can come with us, when you've got time off."

"Ginny!—am I about to become surplus to requirements?"

"Oh no, darling. You're not upset, surely?"

"Of course I'm not. It's just that . . . oh, nothing."

"You do want me to stay?"

"Yes, of course I do."

"Oh good. That's settled, then. Now, we were thinking that it would be nice to have the barbecue supper, unless we have to rush back to Barcelona. Do we?"

"I guess not. I'll have to talk to Alex."

"Sure you do. And perhaps, if you're going to the bar . . ."

"Red wine? A bottle?"

"Perfect, William darling."

I left for the bar, feeling that it was about time *I* gave some orders around here. How had I got myself into this position, being manipulated by all and sundry? It was going to have to stop . . .

"Hello, Jill."

"How's it going, William?"

"Chin up and soldier on, I think is the phrase."

"Putting you through it, is she?"

"Forces in temporary retreat. But we shall regroup and re-gain control, never fear."

"That's the boy."

"May I ask what on earth you're talking about?" Alex said.

"Jill is a witch. She sees all, knows all."

"She knows a lot about Delgado. Apparently, he was more famous than I realized."

"A legend in his lifetime," Jill said. "You know he was a Civil War hero?"

"We've just been looking at the scrapbook—you've seen it?"

"I should think everyone in the village has, at one time or another: Señora Morales makes sure of that. She's the queen of this place, and she likes you to know it."

"I got that impression," I said.

"Yes. It's not just a front, either: she owns maybe half of it. The old man bought up masses of property over the years, a field here, a house there. Think what that's worth now, with all this development going on. Alex can tell you about that, can't you, Alex?"

"Oh, I don't know," Alex said.

"Yes you can: you must be quite an expert by now."

I turned to Alex, groping for words. *How long had our new understanding been in existence—ten minutes? And already, a new duplicity was being pinned on him.* "You're into development here? I didn't know that."

"Didn't you? I thought—"

"You know I didn't. Look here, Alex—"

Jill said:

"Steady on, chaps. Sorry if I said something I shouldn't, but it's no secret, is it, Alex?"

"No," he said, "no secret. But I'd rather you didn't make too much noise about it, Jill. Prices tend to go up when it's a foreigner buying."

"From now on my lips are sealed."

"It's a Spanish company," Alex said to me. "I just put a bit of money in from time to time when I've got some to spare."

"Could you sell me a decent bottle of red?" I said to Jill. "I've just remembered I'm supposed to be taking some to the girls out there."

"It's got nothing to do with what's happened to Cathy, I promise you," Alex persisted.

"Tres Torres good enough for you?" Jill asked.

"Fine. And four glasses, please."

"I hope you believe that," Alex said.

I shrugged. "What's one more thing among so many."

"No, William, I mean it. I don't know of any connection."

"You mean, you've bought property in this village, but not from Delgado?"

"I can't actually tell you that: it's the company that does the deals, and I don't see all the papers."

"Okay, all right. Can we spare the time to stay on for the barbecue, or do we have to get back? Ginny wanted to know."

"We can talk and make plans here as well as anywhere, so yes, let's stay . . . I think I see what you're getting at, William: you're suggesting that my company might have bought some of Delgado's property. Yes—it's possible, isn't it. That's a connection of a sort, I suppose. But then, you might just as well say that there's a connection with the bank raid because Delgado may have used some of the money to buy the property in the first place. Do you think that's significant?"

"Alex—I didn't suggest that . . ." *But somehow, I'd known that he was going to . . .*

"What's this?" Jill said, putting an opened bottle and four glasses on the counter. "Are we into the legend of the missing millions?"

"Alex is," I said. "So it's still talked about, is it?"

"No," Alex said. "I was only—"

"It dies hard, that one does," Jill said. "I wonder what did happen to it, in the end?"

"I have to leave you two fantasists a moment," I said, "if you'll excuse me." I took the bottle and two of the glasses, and steamed out of there.

"Darling!—why are you stamping about like that?" Ginny asked, as I put two glasses down and sloshed wine into them.

"Because," I said, "because—look, didn't I predict that god-damn money would turn up?"

"It hasn't!"

"It has."

"Where?"

"Only in Alex's fairy tale so far. He's now feeding me the line that he's put money into a property company here. The company *may* have done deals with Delgado. Delgado *may* have kept the money from the bank raid to buy the property in the first place. And any minute now he's going to suggest that there *may* be some of the money left over, hidden away somewhere, the cause of all our problems while assorted villains go through Machiavellian maneuvers, involving us, to find it. Jesus!—do I look an idiot?"

"No, darling, of course not."

"Well then . . . Now you're supplied with drink, I'd better go back in for the second installment. I wish I knew why he feels he can do this to me. And why he wants to."

Back at the bar, Alex said:

"I've been thinking. It would make more sense of what's been happening if there's money in the background. The Delgado family were always buccaneers, and proud of it. There could be some of the money still hidden away somewhere."

"Gosh," I said. *Shall I hit him?* "And the ring?"

"Well, I don't know how that comes into it . . . These days, I suppose it's more likely to be something like stock certificates than actual money."

Jill said:

"How does that old Sherlock Holmes thing go? 'When you have eliminated the impossible . . .' "

" '. . . whatever remains, *however improbable,* must be the truth,' " I said. "Not you, too, Jill?"

"Just think," she said. "Suppose there *was* still some left, hoarded away, and we found it . . . I could get shot of this sodding place. You don't suppose . . ."

"No," I said, "I bloody well don't. Have you and Alex talked about the old man's son and where to find him?"

"Yes. He's quite a big wheel in Barcelona."

"Mafia, doubtless, on current form?"

"No no, very legit. I've just agreed to give him a buzz on your behalf, to ask if he'll spare you a few minutes of his valuable time on a very important matter, unspecified."

"Oh Jill, that's really big of you."

"That's okay, partner. Just remember me at share-out time."

"Do you think he'll agree?" Alex asked.

"I'll do my best. I can be quite persuasive, you know."

"I'm sure you can."

"Meanwhile, my nose tells me the spareribs are ready. You'll go wild over our new, secret recipe, marmalade sauce. All four of you?"

"Yes."

"Then you owe me three thousand six hundred pesetas. If only it was as much as it sounds."

SUNDAY

JILL'S POWERS OF PERSUASION WERE AS EFFECTIVE as I had imagined they would be. The result was that, at midday the next morning, Alex and I found ourselves on the Moll d'Españya, walking past the lines of yachts on our way to meet Delgado at the Real Club Maritim. It was Sunday: the early clamor of church bells had given way to a drowsy hum as Barcelona relaxed under a hot, holiday sun.

"Have you been here before?" Alex asked.

"No, but I've seen it across the harbor from the city wharf. If it's like an English yacht club, with at least a few genuine scruffy sailors come ashore for a shower and a break from tinned soup, we won't look too out of place, but from what I've seen of the boats tied up here, it's likely to be somewhat more glossy. Are you a sailor?"

"Dinghies," Alex said. "I've got a Firefly. Cathy and I used to . . . used to . . . ."

"You raced it?"

"We weren't all that good. But she enjoyed it."

A black Porsche 911 Carrera growled past us and stopped at the yacht club entrance. Was this Delgado? No, it was a young couple, straight off the set of *Dallas*. Padded shoulders came even bigger and better in Barcelona!—I watched the girl go striding in through the smoked-glass swinging doors followed by her well-tanned summer-suited escort. My trousers felt more like potato sacks than ever. Why hadn't I got the hotel to press them? It was all Ginny's fault: last night, she'd been in demanding mood, and this morning we'd overslept . . . Yes, it was time I asserted myself, got a firm grip on things. Especially Alex. And starting now.

"You'll do the talking, Alex, won't you."

"I suppose I'd better."

"Yes. And please—the whole story this time, embarrassing or not. Too bad if he thinks it's a joke. We've got to get some answers this morning—we're running out of leads. Aren't we?"

"All right, all *right!*" He pushed ahead of me, through the swinging doors. I followed, feeling a surge of frustration. Perhaps I should ring Sheila, tell her I couldn't go on like this, pussyfooting around Alex's problem. *If* what she'd said about him was true! Though it must be: Jill was certain, and she'd struck me from the moment we met as an unusually perceptive person. I'd adopted her matter-of-fact attitude to Alex and tried to see him as a man with a hang-up rather than a monster, but it didn't get any easier. My revulsion would grow in the intervals between seeing him, as my imagination got to work. Then, when face to face with him again, I found it difficult to remember what he was—he looked so normal. As he does this morning.

A large portrait of the king, Juan Carlos, hung in pride of place on the polished paneled wall opposite the entrance. We crossed to the reception desk, and I hung back to let Alex speak to the dark-suited clerk. "Señor Delgado, *por favor.*"

"Señor Delgado? *Sí señor, momentito.*"

He pressed a button, and a uniformed porter appeared. We followed him up a wide, curving marble staircase to a landing lined with nautical paintings. To one side I saw into a long dining room, where groups of beautiful people were graciously accepting the attentions of waiters armed with menus and napkins. A sudden craving for lobster salad and chilled Chablis swept over me. No Alex, just a solitary table by the window would suit my present mood. Perhaps when this interview with Delgado was over . . . We were being led through a

spacious lounge with a bar at one end and out to a splendid
balcony, the width of the whole building, from where yacht
owners could look down at the harbor full of floating expense
accounts. A light steel framework carried a blue canvas awning, through which the filtered sunlight fell on white steel
chairs and tables sparkling with glasses of iced drinks.

The porter halted, and bent to speak to a man who sat by
himself with his back to us, studying the harbor, a tall glass at
his elbow. Dismissing the porter with a nod, this person rose
from his chair and turned to face us.

"Delgado," he said. His grave smile and a dignified inclination of the head immediately reminded me of Señora Morales.

"Alex Gordon," said Alex. "And this is a friend, William
Warner."

"I am delighted," Delgado said as he shook hands with each
of us in turn. "Delighted. This is a beautiful morning: you see
Barcelona at its very best. Please be seated."

He remained standing, smiling at us as we sat down. A fairly
big wheel, Jill had said, and I could believe that. He was a tall
man of stately, upright carriage, with an air of unforced, natural confidence: a clipped, gray, military mustache added to this
impression. I guessed his age to be in the late fifties; his hair
was a neat gray fringe surrounding a bald brown head, which
he held with the chin up, surveying us with soft brown eyes
from beneath hooded lids. If the porter had introduced him as
General Delgado, our minister of defense, I would have believed it.

"This is very kind of you," Alex said. "I'm afraid this is an
unwelcome interruption of your Sunday."

"Not at all. You will have some refreshment?"

He raised a hand. A waiter arrived at the trot and took away
an order for two gin and tonics, with lemon.

"I understand that, like me, you have a house at Santa Margarita?" Delgado said politely.

"Hardly like yours, but yes, a small holiday house in the
Villa Club," Alex said.

"And you are the same Dr. Gordon who was called to my father when he was ill?"

"Yes. It was a long time ago."

"Twelve years, yes. I hope that my mother expressed our thanks for the kindness of your visit to my father."

"She did," Alex said. "Though I'm afraid I was unable to do anything except to make him as comfortable as possible."

"Although I am so many years too late," Delgado said, "I also wish to express my thanks. It was unfortunate that I was not in our country at the time."

"You were abroad, I seem to remember."

"Abroad, yes. In the United States, where I had business interests at that time. Otherwise, I would have called to thank you personally."

"No need," Alex said, "really. It must have been very upsetting for you and your mother. I quite understand."

Now's the moment, Alex! Were you at the funeral?—ask him!

"Do you, er, still have business interests in the United States?" Alex said conversationally.

"Yes, I have interests still, but I have agents who look after these interests for me," Delgado said in his courteous voice.

Now Alex was taking a swallow of gin and tonic. *Get on with it, man!*

Nothing happened. Delgado looked from Alex to me, his face, with the smile and the soft brown eyes, all polite inquiry.

All right, then! If you can't, or won't . . .

"If I may put a word in," I said.

"By all means," Delgado said.

"May I ask if you attended your father's funeral? I'll explain the reason for this odd and, perhaps you may think, impertinent question in a moment."

"Why should you not ask this? Yes, I was at my father's funeral: I flew back from the United States the day before."

"Where did it take place?"

"As you would expect, at Santa Margarita, in the tomb of my family."

"Of course. An even odder question now, I'm afraid: did your father wear a ring?"

"A gold ring, yes. Always."

"His wedding ring?"

"Yes."

"Can you remember if he was buried wearing it?"

Delgado's eyebrows lifted. "Now I must say you surprise me, Mr. . . ."

"Warner. I'm sorry, I will explain. But do you remember that?"

"As Dr. Gordon said, it is a long time ago . . . Is it important?"

"Excuse me a moment. Alex—I think you must now explain the situation."

Let's see how you avoid this one!

He couldn't, and he didn't. I sat back and listened without interrupting as Alex told Delgado the whole story, starting with the Cubzac fête, my entry into the affair as a result of the advertisement in the *Sud Ouest,* our discovery of the boy who'd seen Cathy get into the Spanish registered car, my first inquiries in Spain, the meeting with Stephenson, the arrival of the ransom note, my day on the rock watching the Stephenson house, the fake abduction of Stephenson's daughter, the episode in El Corté Inglés when I found we were being followed, the telephone call from the kidnappers when they demanded the Delgado ring in addition to the £25,000, the loss of Sharon, the meeting in the church and, finally, yesterday's expedition to Santa Margarita to call on Señora Morales, which ended in failure.

"And which is why we are here now, taking up your time," Alex concluded.

"My dear Dr. Gordon," Delgado said, "this is, I think a most extraordinary story."

Alex's face now wore a look of wooden obstinacy. "I can assure you," he said, "that every word of it is true."

"Forgive me! I did not mean that I do not believe you."

Alex shrugged. I said:

"It would be easier to understand but for this demand for a ring that Alex hasn't got. Señor Delgado: can you think of any reason why anybody should be so keen to get hold of your father's ring? Did you ever get a close look at it, yourself?"

Delgado leaned back in his chair and let his eyes rest on my face. "To answer your second question first," he said. "As I told you, my father always wore this ring. When I think of him now, of his hands coming to lift me up when I was a child, and later, all through my life, I can still see this ring. It was big. I think—I am *sure*—there was nothing written there. But I never saw him take it off. If you ask me, was there anything written inside, no, I never saw it."

"So there could be an inscription inside?"

"It is possible. But it is perhaps more likely, that these people, who have taken your daughter, *think* there is something inside."

"But what?"

Delgado said: "May I ask you, *señores,* have you ever had the chance to speak with criminals?"

"One or two," I said.

"Ah, Mr. Warner. One or two. You are, perhaps, a businessman?"

"A wine merchant."

"I see! *Bueno!* In the course of a lifetime in business, we must meet some dishonest persons, unfortunately. And you know what I think? I think they are often not so clever—*but we try to explain what they do as if they have good reasons for it, not bad ones* . . . I am afraid I express myself badly."

"I think I understand you," I said. "I don't know why we tend to overestimate them, but we do. The truth is that most criminals live in a different world from the rest of us, one without consequences. They always think they're going to get away with it—that the stolen goods won't be traced, the tax fraud never found out, the insider deals never detected. It's a dreamworld, hard for us to understand."

"I think you understand this very well, Mr. Warner."

"I had a close friend who turned out to be one," I said. "That's why I spoke with feeling."

"Some must get away with it," Alex said tersely.

"Oh yes, Dr. Gordon, you are quite right, of course. Some must, some do get away with it. But all *believe* that they will— is this what you mean, Mr. Warner?"

"Yes. However crazy the scheme."

"May I ask," Alex said, "what all this has to do with our visit here today?"

I made an apologetic gesture to Delgado. "I'm afraid I interrupted you."

"Oh no. I apologize to Dr. Gordon—we talk and talk, and meanwhile his daughter is missing. Excuse me. What I want to say is very simple. These people *think* the ring is important: that is all you need to know."

"You mean, we shouldn't bother about the motive?" Alex said.

"Exactly."

"Well, I felt you needed an explanation," Alex said.

"Dr. Gordon, I am already in your debt for your kindness to my father. If you need my help, you have only to ask."

"Unfortunately," I said, "the only thing that can help is the ring."

"You do not think that the police . . . ?"

"I daren't risk it," Alex said. "I'd rather pay up; I can afford the money—it's the ring that's the problem."

"Perhaps you are right, Dr. Gordon. If you think you can trust this man, Stephenson . . ."

"I'm not dealing with him direct, but with a Spanish contact who seems very businesslike: I hope I can trust him."

Delgado nodded. "That, at least, is good."

"Well," Alex said, "there's been no trouble since he took charge—they've apparently decided to allow me some rope

and see where I go with it. No doubt they're close behind—
they seem to be expert at that."

"You think you were followed here?" Delgado said, looking
away from us, along the balcony.

"I think we can be sure of it," I said.

Delgado's gaze returned to the tall glass in his hand. Raising
it, he said:

"Let us have another drink—the same again?"

"Very kind," Alex said.

"You too, Mr. Warner?"

"Thank you."

The waiter was recalled. We sat in silence for some moments. Then Delgado said:

"Very well. The ring must be found. I will ask my mother
if she knows anything more than she has told you."

"She denies that I gave it to her," Alex said. "But as I've just
said, I am sure that I did. What puzzles me is why your father
should have wanted me to take it to her in the first place."

"But he was dying, Dr. Gordon, he was confused in his
mind, perhaps," Delgado suggested.

"He was very weak, certainly," Alex agreed.

"Perhaps he wanted to make sure he wasn't buried in it," I
said. "That would make sense if there was something special
about it. But from what we saw of Señora Morales yesterday,
that would be the last thing she'd agree to, if she had any say
in the matter."

I looked up to find Delgado's hooded eyes turned full on me:
his expression was thoughtful. He nodded approvingly.

"Very good, Mr. Warner. Yes, I think you have something."

"Unfortunately," I said, feeling encouraged, "if she still denies—or rather, has forgotten the episode, there's absolutely
nothing we can do to prove that Alex did, in fact, return the
ring to her."

"No?" Delgado said, looking surprised.

"Well, I can't think of anything. Short of opening up the
tomb, and that's obviously out of the question."

"Why do you say this, Mr. Warner? Ah!—here are the drinks: *gracias,* Antonio. Perhaps, *señores,* you will stay to eat with me?—it would give me great pleasure."

"Well—" Alex began.

"I think that would be delightful," I said, aiming a kick at him under the table. There are times when business and pleasure coincide, and this had every indication of being one of them. Why couldn't the idiot see that?

"Very good." Delgado spoke rapidly to the waiter, who bowed and hurried away. We lifted our drinks.

"*Salud!*"

"Cheers!"

"You were saying?" I prompted.

"Ah yes. We were discussing what to do: I think this is now very clear," Delgado said. "We will do as you suggest, Mr. Warner."

Lobster salad and chilled Chablis, so nearly in reach, seemed suddenly to lose its savor. He *couldn't* mean what I understood him to say! . . . no no. He couldn't mean picks and shovels behind canvas screens . . . men with screwdrivers, applying them to the lid . . . who could *look* in there? . . . and of course, the police standing by . . .

"But surely," I said, "it can't be done, can it? Not just to recover a ring? In England, it means an application to the home secretary and police involvement."

"The police? Oh no, Mr. Warner, not here, not in Spain— why should they be concerned in what is a family matter? No, there is a formality, a permit from the *ajuntament,* but that is easily obtained. Shall we say, tomorrow afternoon, at half past two?"

Was he serious? He appeared to be.

"You mean, you would like us to be there?"

"But of course! Dr. Gordon, I imagine you will wish to see for yourself?"

No need for me to go—this was Alex's affair . . .

"This is most kind of you," Alex said. "I never expected you to go to such lengths. But if you're really sure? Most kind." He looked across the table at me. "We'll be there . . ."

Oh now, wait a moment—this may be all in a day's work for a surgeon, but—

". . . myself, and witness," he said.

$\mathcal{M}$ONDAY

"WHAT TIME IS THIS GRUESOME EVENT?" GINNY said, reaching for another croissant from the breakfast tray.

"Two-thirty. We'll have to be on the road by eleven, to allow time for a fortifying drink at the Villa Club."

"Two-thirty. Pour me some more coffee, William darling, will you. Thanks. Will they have him already dug up, do you suppose? Or will you have to wait while they—"

"Oh, don't go on, Ginny! I had nightmares all last night, when I wasn't lying awake trying not to think about it. I've got to ring Maggie at the office before I go, and while I'm over at Santa Margarita, you're going to ring your contact about Stephenson—let's concentrate on that, shall we?"

"You can always not look," she said.

"Well, I'll have to, won't I. I can't stand there with my hand over my eyes; I'm supposed to be a witness. Alex will *make* me look: it's my comeuppance for not believing his story."

"Do you believe it, now?"

"I don't know. Delgado seems prepared to: listening to him, I could feel my English skepticism draining away and being replaced with Spanish gothic."

"Sounds like an oil change, darling."

"Well, a country gets to you, doesn't it. And here, they've got this morbid dark side, all relics and catacombs and death in the afternoon. A family vault is used as if it was a sort of spare room for the old folks—let's pop in and see how they're getting along."

"It's a Mediterranean thing," Ginny said, wiping butter off her fingers with a paper napkin. "Or Catholic, whichever. *Memento mori.*"

"Obsessed with it, if you ask me. Anyway, I can't back out; I'll have to go and make a show of paying attention. As long as I don't have to *touch* anything—Alex can bloody well do that; he's used to doing ghastly things on the operating table. I think I'll get up and have a shower."

By the time I'd showered and dressed, it was just after ten, and I called the shop in Church Street, Kensington, on the bedside telephone. Maggie, my long-time manager, prop, and stay, answered. After we'd gone through a mercifully short list of business matters, she said:

"Pedro Masana found you all right, did they?"

"Who?"

"Somebody rang from Pedro Masana—they'd heard you were in Barcelona, and wanted to get in touch. I gave them Mr. MacInnes's address, and—"

"I haven't heard from them, no."

"Oh. That's odd—they were very anxious to contact you."

"Perhaps I should ring them. What's the name, again?"

"Pedro Masana. He said they wanted to invite you to visit their cellars at Tarragona."

"Perhaps they rang Alastair, and he forgot to tell me," I said. "I'll chase it up. Anything else, Maggie?"

"No, not for the moment."

"Right. Well, the figures don't seem too bad, then, for summer trading." I looked around: Ginny was in the shower. "Will you be in touch with Claudine?"

"She's due to ring this afternoon."

"Oh good. This is one of those times when I wish we'd had a telephone put in at La Sauvegarde so that I could ring her myself, but give her my love and all that. Has she told you why I'm here, apart from seeing Alastair?"

"She has," Maggie said, sounding disapproving.

"Maggie—it was her idea, you know."

"Was it, Mr. William?"

"Well, anyway—will you tell her that I'll be here a few more days, yet? The affair is more complicated than we'd supposed, but we're making progress . . . Maggie? Are you there?"

"I'll tell her," Maggie said. "I suppose it's no use my suggesting that you—"

"No, Maggie—it isn't. Sorry."

"One of these days I'm going to wish I made you listen to me," she said, in the doom-laden voice she uses when she's pointing out the error of my ways. "I know I shouldn't talk to my employer like this, but at my age—"

"Dear Maggie, don't worry. Everything will be all right."

"Well, I certainly hope so. When will you ring next?"

"Later this week. Will that be okay?"

"You're the boss," she said, ringing off.

Ginny emerged from the bathroom, rubbing her hair with a towel. "All right?" she asked.

"I suppose so. I wonder what it'll be like when Maggie leaves. She can't go on forever, and she's starting to get quite crabby at times."

"William darling, you know you love it when she gives you a talking-to."

"What a ridiculous notion," I said. "What on earth would be the point of that?"

Ginny gave me a pussycat smile. "Well," she said, "when Maggie goes, you'll be promoted to senior citizen. I can guess how you'll relish the role."

Oh my God . . .

"So don't waste too much time on tombs," she said. "Gather ye rosebuds—that's the thing. What time do you think you'll be back?"

Not for the first time, I thought: they're really weird . . .

*　　*　　*

I was still thinking it, as I piloted the Citroën out of Barcelona and onto the southern *autopista*. Then my mind drifted back to the more tangible, less universal mystery Alex was dragging me through. It wasn't that there was no solution in sight: the problem was that there were *too many* . . .

We arrived in time for an hour's sinew-stiffening in the bar of the Villa Club. Alex asked for a gin and tonic, and took it to one of the outside tables. I stayed to consult Jill privately.

"What do you recommend for an occasion of this sort?" I asked, when I'd outlined what was in store.

"Ah! That's a new one," she said. "Births and marriages—champagne, obviously. Deaths—well, assorted hard stuff, according to taste. But exhumations—no, haven't come across them. Would you say you were of a nervous disposition?"

"Today, yes. One of your more powerful potions is called for, definitely."

"Mustn't overdo it, though," Jill said. "It might be thought bad taste if you were stretched out alongside the—"

"Don't, Jill—just start mixing, please."

"Right. Here goes, then. Orange juice, tequila, a dash of brandy, plenty of ice—that should fix you. Try it."

The effect of that tall glassful was still blooming in my brain as Alex and I trudged after our hard-edged, blue-black shadows up the track to the cemetery. Soon, we could see the high white walls and lines of pointed dark cypresses. I checked my watch and said:

"I make it almost half past. There's no sign of Delgado."

"Perhaps he's inside," Alex said.

We reached the arched gateway. The tall iron gates stood open. Inside, it was like a walled garden, with a grid of neat graveled paths between flower beds. The central path led between a twin row of cypresses to a niche in the far wall, from which a statue of the Virgin Mary looked back at us. There were no tombstones, but the high walls were lined with marble fronted vaults, row upon row—a filing system for dead people.

A quiet chipping sound of steel on stone came from somewhere behind the cypresses.

We walked slowly down the central path. The high walls cut off all air movement: I became aware that, outside, we'd had the benefit of a slight cooling breeze, now excluded. The graveled path and the white, vaulted walls shimmered with heat. I could smell herbs—thyme, rosemary. Looking up, I saw small birds swooping across the deep blue sky—swifts and martins. The sound of stone chipping was louder.

"There." Alex said.

I looked to where he was pointing. Framed by a pair of cypresses was a homely scene of two workmen in faded blue overalls, chiseling at the marble front of one of the vaults in the third row up from a low, scaffolded platform. A barrow containing long-handled implements stood to one side.

"Let's wait here," I said, feeling we were close enough.

"I'll ask if they're expecting Delgado," Alex said. "You wait here if you like." I watched him approach the men, who stopped work to speak to him. Then he turned and beckoned.

Reluctantly, I followed the path he'd taken. The workmen had resumed their chipping.

"This is it," he said as I approached.

"Oh. Well, don't you think we'd better wait somewhere else until Delgado turns up?"

"Why?"

"Alex, it's his father in there!"

"I don't think they'll take the front off until he get's here," Alex said.

"You don't *think* they will! You're not sure?"

"What's the matter, William?"

"Well, I . . . look, Alex, it's a question of respect for the dead, surely."

He looked at me. His face wore what I supposed was his professional expression—politely solicitous. "I don't think you need worry," he said.

"No?"

"Well . . . to put it bluntly, after—what is it?—twelve years in that oven, there's not going to be a lot left."

"You don't think so?"

"That's the system, with aboveground vaults like this. We're mostly liquids, you know."

"Have you seen, er, into one of these?"

"No, no I haven't. But it stands to reason."

"Does it. Well, I'd rather wait for Delgado, if you don't mind. There may be some sort of ceremony; we don't want to upset anyone. Do we?"

"All right."

We walked back to the cypress avenue, and stood in the shade, waiting. Jill's potion was wearing off. I wished Delgado would arrive so that we could get this over.

A car outside the gates. A door slamming, and a tall, dark-suited figure hurrying down the path toward us.

"I am so sorry," Delgado called. He came up to us, and we shook hands. "Our bureaucracy is, I must admit, one of the slowest in the world. I had, eventually, to call for the papers myself." Seeing his expression as he said this, I had a mental picture of some clerk cowering behind his counter as Delgado bore majestically down on him.

"No matter," Alex said. "But it's all right now?"

"Oh yes. To save time, I telephoned ahead to the *sepulturero*—I hope he is already at work."

"Yes. We thought we'd wait for you here. Will a priest be coming?" Alex said.

"A priest? No! Why should we need a priest? We are not going to bury anyone, are we?"

"I see."

"Let us see what progress has been made." Delgado led the way to where the workmen were still chipping at the edge of the marble slab. They stood up, and greeted him with respect. There was some conversation in Spanish, and then Delgado turned to us and said:

"Five minutes more. Then we shall see."

Five minutes . . . Alex was speaking:

". . . different from ours, and I can't help a certain curiosity. There's a minimum time limit, I suppose?"

"Yes, Dr. Gordon. Eight years are usual. After that, the . . ."

"Vault?"

"Thank you . . . the vault can be used again."

"I see. It belongs to the family, then?"

"This one, yes. But alternatively, you can rent one."

There was a hollow, grinding noise, and one of the workmen called to Delgado, who said:

"Ah. I think we are ready. Let us go near." He led the way onto the scaffolding.

"After you, Alex," I muttered. "Let me know when you want some witnessing done."

He shot a glance at me, and then followed Delgado. I brought up the rear.

The marble slabs that closed the front of the vaults were rather more than two feet square, with arched tops. Some had faded photographs attached in glass frames—the occupant as he or she had been in life, often with a happy smile. Little bunches of flowers were tucked into metal holders. The slab at the center of our attention was of gray marble, the surface dulled by weather. It bore a carved and gilded inscription:

MIGUEL DELGADO GARCIA
1897–1975

The workmen were easing it from the opening, letting the top swing out first. Chips of cement fell from the edges onto the planked platform. The first crack of darkness appeared and grew wider.

I have to look. But what will I see? Bony feet? Or the end of a coffin? No, nothing yet. The slab is half open now, letting in the first light for twelve years, but the vault is deep, and the depths are still as black as night. The slab is hinged right down, and now the workmen are taking the full weight and are lowering it to the

platform. The vault stands open. They reach in, and start pulling
something out . . . this is the bit I've been dreading. It slides out,
a thin shape, into the glare of sunlight . . . Oh well, that's all right,
nothing but a sliver of wood, the coffin's broken up, evidently. More
wood, parched and crumbling. And more! Where's the . . . the old
man? That seems to be the last of the wood. I can't really see; it's
still pitch dark in there beyond the sunlit entrance, but it seems to
be . . . empty? One of the workmen has gone to the barrow, and
is coming back with a white linen bag, a long-handled broom, and
a . . . Oh no, this is ridiculous! Miguel Delgado Garcia is about
to be tidied up by a dustpan and brush . . .

"You were right, then, Alex."

"Interesting, isn't it," he murmured.

We stood together, behind Delgado, who was instructing
the workmen. The long-handled broom was being used to
reach right into the interior: some small, dusty, angular ob-
jects were brought forward and placed in the white linen
bag. Then one of the workmen exclaimed, picked something
out of the dust, and handed it to Delgado, who turned to us.
He was frowning, but as he turned, the frown was replaced
by a wry smile. He held up his closed fist, and said dramatically:

"Well, Dr. Gordon—here it is!"

"The ring?"

"The ring. Take it, please." He lowered his fist, and opened
it like a conjurer. And there it was, lying on his palm.

"Thank you," Alex said, with a glance at me. He took the
ring, and held it between his thumb and forefinger. It was plain
gold, quite thick, but otherwise unremarkable. He peered inside it. "Some initials and a date," he announced. "That seems
to be all."

"Oh. The mystery's still unexplained, then." We'd have to
think this out, but not now—it wasn't the time or place for it.

Alex held the ring out to Delgado. "It seems we're none the
wiser. But I'm really very grateful to you for—"

"No, Dr. Gordon, I said 'take it.' You have a use for it, I believe."

"Oh, but . . . really?"

"Excuse me one moment," Delgado said. He turned to the workmen, and gave instructions. They smiled, and nodded. Delgado turned back to us and said:

"They will close the vault. We can go, now."

We stepped down off the platform and began to walk up the path between the cypresses. Alex said:

"Do you mean that I can take this ring and hand it over?"

"In exchange for your daughter, Dr. Gordon. That was why we opened the vault, no?"

"It's extraordinarily kind of you," Alex said, sounding as though he wasn't sure if he could, or should, accept.

"No, no, not at all. The ring is not valuable. You need it more than I. Think nothing of it."

"Well, in that case . . . Thank you very much. I hope I will be able to repay you some day, though I can't see how."

We walked on a few paces. My mind was, of course, whirring. Well, it's a wicked world, and few things come free. But what was the catch? So far, there didn't seem to be one. There didn't *have* to be one, of course—from my brief dealings with Spain and the Spanish, I had noticed the pleasure they took in making courteous gestures.

"There is one thing I will ask you," Delgado said to Alex. *Aha, I thought, oh yes—here it comes! Well, I suspected as much . . .*

"This is, not to tell my mother," Delgado said. "I asked the *sepulturero* to keep silent about his work, and I think this will be best. She might be upset, you understand."

"I understand perfectly," Alex said. "Of course we'll keep quiet about it. I suppose, in fact, it's her ring."

"She may think so," Delgado said. "But I take responsibility for giving it to you. Mr. Warner, you are a witness of this."

"Of course," I said, "and with pleasure. Señor Delgado—some refreshment before you return to Barcelona?"

"Most kind," he said, "but I have to call on my mother. Some other time, perhaps. Your car is in the village? Then let me drive you down. No trouble, I am going there myself."

Back in Barcelona, I returned the Citroën to the underground car park, and then walked with Alex to the hotel. We went to the reception counter to collect our keys: mine was missing, which meant that Ginny was back from her lunch with Pilar. Alex was given his key, and also a small sealed envelope. As we walked toward the lift, he tore it open, and found a note inside, which he read and then handed to me. He was politely instructed to be in his room at nine that evening to take a telephone call.

"Well," I said, "at least it's convenient. I wondered how you were going to contact them." I pressed the lift call button.

"They said they'd contact me after the weekend," Alex said.

"Did they? You didn't tell me that. Well, so they have. Now we can arrange the exchange—are you going to stick out for what we agreed in the car?"

"Yes," he said. "It's got to really happen, this time. I've got the money, I've got the ring, and that's all they're asking for. But they've got to hand Cathy over first."

"Right. This must be the end of the line. Well, good luck, Alex. And call me in my room as soon as you've heard from them."

"I will. And thanks for today—I know you'd rather not have come."

"Oh, I wouldn't say that, exactly." The lift arrived, empty, and we stepped into it. I pressed the button for the fourth floor: the doors closed smoothly, and we started upward. A thought struck me; I said: "Look, lend me the ring to show to Ginny, will you? She might have some ideas about it."

"Well . . ."

"I won't lose it."

"No . . . here you are, then."

"Thanks. I'll wait for your call, Alex."

The lift doors opened, and we went our separate ways. Ginny took some time to open the door of our room.

"What were you doing?" I asked.

"I was asleep," she said. "We had champagne for lunch, and I seemed to drink most of it. It's your evil influence, William darling. What time is it?"

"About half past six. Why don't you get back into bed, and I'll join you. Here's something for you to look at."

She sat up in bed, inspecting the ring, while I pulled my clothes off and dumped them on a chair.

"So it exists, then," she said.

"Apparently."

"Well, isn't this it?"

"That's the question. But before we go into that, how did you get on?" I climbed into bed beside her.

"With Pilar?"

"No, with your London call."

"Oh yes!—sorry, I'm still half asleep. Yes, Stephenson has a long entry at Criminal Records. He was a sergeant in the Royal Engineers—explosives expert. The army had nothing against him, but after he came out he became a kind of consultant safebreaker. Then he went into business on his own account—they think he was behind that spate of security van holdups a few years ago. But when they got close, he did a runner and ended up here. Now they can't touch him: all this happened before the extradition treaty of nineteen eighty-six."

"Which isn't retroactive?"

"That's it. He seems to have got away with it—not the only one, either. The rozzers have a list as long as your arm of people they'd like to interview who are alive and well and living on the Costa del Crime. But that's nothing new—it just confirms what we thought, doesn't it. Tell me about this ring."

We lay back against the pillows while I described my day in as much detail as I could remember.

"I see," she said. "So the workman picked the ring out of the dust and gave it to Delgado—you saw that."

"I saw the movement, to be precise."

"Ah yes, you saw the movement. So he might have handed him anything—or nothing?"

"Not nothing—I saw something glint. And I saw the workman dust off his hands afterward—that seemed quite normal; there was a lot of dust in there."

"All right. So what are you saying?"

"That when Delgado took the ring from the workman, he had his back to both Alex and me."

"Aha—he could have swapped it! But why should he want to do that? And what makes you so suspicious?"

"Well, Ginny, he's so bloody helpful, I can't believe it. Look at what's happened: Alex and I turn up, complete strangers, at the yacht club, and immediately he's arranging to disinter his dad for us. Plus, he treats us to drinks and lobster salad . . . all in all, it's too good to be true, surely."

"Alex was there when his father died. You told me he kept saying how grateful he was."

"True, true—I keep forgetting that. But then, why wait twelve years to show his gratitude: that's the sort of slow-burn which would be excessive even in cold-blooded England, isn't it?"

"The opportunity didn't come up?" Ginny suggested.

"The Big House is minutes from the Villa Club—he could have popped 'round while visiting his mother. Or simply written a note, for God's sake."

"William darling, it's not difficult to explain. Perhaps he missed the first opportunity, and then was embarrassed and let it drop. Or language difficulties might have put him off."

"He speaks almost perfect English. But your first point, yes, that's possible. Why else should he go out of his way to help Alex—any other ideas?"

Ginny thought for a moment. "Why not," she said, "that he believed Alex's story and simply wanted to help him get his daughter back? He'd have to have been very hard-hearted to refuse, wouldn't he? *You* didn't—and look what you've been doing for Alex."

"And I didn't owe him anything, even."

"No. There you are, you see."

"I'm afraid it's more curiosity than compassion that drives me on now," I said. "But you've got a point."

"Then, of course, there's—but you won't like this," Ginny said.

"What? Go on, I won't bite."

"The money angle."

"Ginny darling, it's worth ten quid at most . . . oh, I see. *That* money."

"Yes. The ring exists. Maybe the money does, as well."

"Oh sure. It's buried on a lonely hilltop, somewhere, and the ring bears the key to it. Fifteen paces nor'nor'east o' the crooked pine that's like a man dangling from the gallows; dig, and there ye shall find . . . doubloons, doubtless. Come off it, girl!"

"William darling. There *was* a bank raid—"

"You read it in the paper. Ginny! And you're supposed to be a journalist!"

"Most stories have a basis of fact—it's the detail that gets distorted. Anyway, just suppose it's true. That would be interesting, wouldn't it?"

"I always knew you were a romantic, Ginny."

"Stuff belonging to rich landowners, Pilar said. Cash and jewelry I'd guess. Stolen, and then hidden while the war was on, here in Barcelona . . ."

"You've only got to look at the ring to know it isn't. Look, here—a perfectly plain, ordinary wedding ring, right? With his initials inside, MDG, and a date, 31.11.21, which is obviously when they got married . . . let's drop it now, shall we? It's nearly seven, and unless you've changed your mind, we have a prior engagement to fulfill . . ."

* * *

Funerals are supposed to turn some people on. For the record, disinterments can, too. Relief, of course, at not being in the principal role. Afterward, Ginny said:

"May I speak, now?"

"Why this formality? Are you going to lodge a complaint?"

"No, William darling."

"No? Is that all you can say, no?"

"I mean, certainly not."

"That's better. What, then?"

"I've been thinking. It isn't a date."

"What isn't? Oh, *that* . . . but of *course* it's a date. They must have got married about nineteen twenty-one; I've worked it out. He would have been twenty-four, and she a few years younger. Of course it's a date, the date of their wedding."

"Tell me," Ginny said, "what were you doing on the thirty-first of November, last?"

I thought for a moment. "I can't possibly remember."

"No," Ginny said. "Nor could anyone. Thirty days hath September . . ."

". . . April, June, and November! I see what you mean."

"So this ring may have some special significance and be the real McCoy. And as Delgado handed it over, he must be genuine."

"Right!—he hardly looked at it. Ginny—you might have something here."

"Might? Such enthusiasm, darling!"

Too much applause, and they can get out of hand . . . "We'll check it—could be an engraving error, couldn't it."

Silence.

"What are you thinking now?" I asked.

"Just running through synonyms for 'stingy sod,' " she said.

$\mathcal{T}$UESDAY

 WITH LUCK, I THOUGHT, THIS SHOULD BE THE LAST drive down this now too familiar piece of *autopista.* This evening, we should be driving back with the girl— not in triumph, exactly, because Alex would be £25,000 worse off, but mission completed. He'd be more than happy with that, he said.

He said, he said. Too much still depended on what Alex said, for my peace of mind. If it hadn't been for what Stephenson's wife had admitted, I'd probably have broken with Alex by now. Well, think about it! I'd never heard any of these tele-phone conversations that seemed to happen so conveniently whenever he needed to talk to the opposition—you might conclude, from this, that *he* was telephoning *them.* He'd shown me the original ransom note, true—but anyone could have typed that, including Alex himself. There was the meeting in the church, which looked genuine enough—until you realized that he could have hired a couple of sinister-looking Spaniards to meet him there and go rhubarb, rhubarb, while I looked on from a safe distance, as instructed by him. He hands over the envelope; they hand it back; a simple piece of theater to add verisimilitude to his narrative. Oh yes, I'd met one of them before, of course—Granite Face—but his brief could have been to follow me around until he got noticed: paid a bonus, proba-bly, for getting assaulted. All to support the story Alex wanted me to believe.

But *why?* All this had to have a purpose, and Ginny and I

had debated what it might be for much of last night without getting anywhere. The only thing that seemed certain was that he had some essential role for me in his plans because, if it were otherwise, he could easily have waved me good-bye. We'd had a couple of theories, but in the cold light of day, they looked less than convincing. Ginny's favored notion, after talking to Pilar about the Civil War, was that Alex had—well, I'm embarrassed to put it down; it's so second feature—had happened to acquire a property which happened to have the stolen money bricked up in the basement: hidden away by old Delgado after the bank raid of 1936, and never taken out because a few months later the government had sent in troops to restore order in Barcelona, which was in the hands of half a dozen rival revolutionary groups, the CNT, the POUM, and the rest of them, as described in George Orwell's book . . . all right, it was possible, and it would make an exciting film, but really! Real life isn't like that, is it? Well, Ginny said, it is *sometimes* . . . and it would explain everything: Alex knows the money is there or else has smuggled it out, bit by bit, and that's why he seems rather too well-off, and can raise £25,000 without batting an eyelid, but now this gang has got wind of it (she was into the phraseology, too!) and is pressuring him, hence the kidnap. The business with the ring is just a red herring to keep you hooked while you help him get the girl back. Look, Ginny, I said, with all that loot to hand, he could hire heavies, a whole army of them. No no, she said, he wouldn't know how, and anyway why should he, when he's got you for free? Brilliant, Ginny, I said; you've even got the Scottish background to fit!—never spend a muckle when a mickle will do . . . I can't think why I don't believe you—but I don't. Sorry. Well, work it out yourself then, she said, miffed.

All right, I said, how about this: he's got a grudge against the Stephenson family for besmirching his daughter, of whom he's abnormally fond, and he's been to the police in the UK to get Stephenson, who's on the wanted list there, but has been told that nothing can be done because the crimes were commit-

ted before the extradition treaty came into force in eighty-six
as you've confirmed with your contact at the Criminal Records
Office. Right, thinks Alex, I'll fix him with another crime
now—and then the UK police can get him. So he invents this
kidnap, gets a friend—someone she trusts—to pick up the girl
from the Cubzac fête in a Spanish-registered car at a place
where it's bound to be noticed, types the ransom note in case
I ask to see it (which I haven't, yet, but I'm sure he'd instantly
produce it if I did), invents the telephone calls but for added
realism leaves himself a note at the hotel reception desk, and
does everything possible to create a kidnap atmosphere in
which Stephenson is implicated. The only thing that really
made me believe in the kidnap was that Stephenson's wife
admitted she knew about it—but Alex could have rung the
house as a hysterical parent and left her with that impression.
My part in this is easily explained and also essential—he needs
a witness, and I seem to be a suitably gullible idiot. Look how
easily I fall in with his idea of keeping watch on Stephenson's
house—where nothing, you remember, actually happened except when I provoked it . . . There's the ring to explain—well,
as we've agreed, £25,000 is a small sum for a ransom, so a
mysterious extra needs to be added: it doesn't diminish the
crime much, but *it reduces the cost of Alex's revenge*—he's actually got to put up real money for this, and might lose it. But
the tricky bit's still to come—he's got to stage a rescue that will
convince me that the girl was actually kidnapped by Stephenson, and I can't see how he's going to do that. Also, of course,
there's the problem of what the girl herself is going to say when
she's rescued, but it would be easy enough to take care of that
by keeping her locked in a hotel room somewhere, and letting
her overhear people talking about Stephenson. The police are
going to be only too pleased to believe what they're told,
because of his previous record. There!

Well, Ginny said, it's a lot of risk for small returns, isn't it?
Ah, I said, you've got to remember how he feels about that
girl—he's obsessed with her, nothing less. Strange chap,

Alex—it's hard to see what makes him tick; it's all under the surface, but these quiet people are the ones to go overboard for an obsession. And he worries his wife—you can see that. I don't think she's in this, but I think she suspects there's something going on. Anyway, tomorrow, we'll see—can Alex stage-manage this meeting with Stephenson convincingly enough to—

With Stephenson? Ginny almost shrieked. You didn't tell me that! "A meeting," you said, not—

Didn't I? Oh yes, we're insisting that Stephenson be there; we're not going to be fobbed off with underlings; we want to deal direct with the boss. That's why I'm borrowing Alastair's shotgun.

Oh . . . my . . . God, Ginny said. Here you go again. William, you are the—

It'll be all right, I said. The shotgun's only a precaution against Stephenson getting out of hand. But I'm Alex's witness, remember? His plan must include my safety, mustn't it?

I turned off the *autopista* at the Santa Margarita junction, and drove up through the village toward the cemetery, on the little road we'd walked along yesterday. Once again we passed the new villas on the outskirts of the village, and the sites waiting to be built on. The road continued past the cemetery, but the surface was much rougher: I slid the Citroën's suspension lever to the high position to give us more ground clearance, and we jolted on our way toward the conical hill on which was mounted the giant cutout shape of the Osborne Brandy firm's Black Bull.

This was my choice of venue, which Alex had agreed to on the drive back, yesterday. Towns are notoriously dangerous places for confrontations: who knows what may lurk behind every door or around every corner? Give me open country, where you can have a clear view of the opposition, at least within pistol and shotgun range. The Black Bull looked an ideal site for a potentially dangerous meeting. From its isolated hilltop, we ought to be able to see what was coming long before it arrived. In case of trouble, we could use the slope for cover, lying flat to defend ourselves or crawling away to safety. And a few hundred yards away was the *autopista*, an escape route if needed, but one would mind its own business meanwhile.

The road became a narrow farm track, wide enough for only one vehicle, running between stone-walled fields, parched and dusty, on which it looked unlikely that anything useful could ever grow, let alone thrive. The earth was poor, patchy stuff: yellow here, reddish there, with small stones scattered over the surface. We reached a sort of neolithic crossroads, where three walled tracks converged, and there was a small open space wide enough to park on. I said:

"Better stop here, and walk the rest of the way. There may not be anywhere else to turn."

"All right," Alex said. He got out of the car, and guided me while I reversed it as close as I dared to a bramble patch, off the track. There was a screech of brambles against paintwork: I winced, and stopped.

"Sorry," Alex said. "Didn't see it."

I climbed out, stretched, went around to the boot, and opened it. Alex watched as I slid Alastair's ancient Aya Yeoman boxlock out of its case, broke it open, and took a quick look down the barrels. Best Toledo steel, they say, but I've heard of old Spanish guns bursting when they're fired, and that's something to avoid. But it was clean, and if well looked after, it was probably safe.

"Is that a good idea?" Alex said. "You didn't say you were bringing a gun."

No. I hadn't. And now it was too late for him to adjust his plan, if he had one. "Just a precaution," I said. "I'm not Stephenson's most favorite person, remember, even if he managed to get his daughter back."

I broke open the box of cartridges I'd bought that morning, dropped a handful into my pocket, shoved a couple more up the spout, and snapped the gun shut. Automatic safety—that's okay then. I reached into the boot again, and lifted out the shopping bag from El Corté Inglés.

"Perhaps you'd carry this," I said.

"What is it?"

"The crossbow."

"Oh, surely we don't need that as well," Alex said.

"If we don't need it, we won't use it," I said firmly. "Take the bag, Alex, please."

He took it, reluctantly. I shut the boot, locked the car, and we set off along the track. I looked at my watch: five past three, and the meeting was arranged for four. Time, I hoped, for a short reconnoiter of the ground before the other side turned up—unless, of course, they'd had the same idea. Well, you can't cover everything.

After five minutes we left the track and followed a path which led directly to the hill. At the start, the Black Bull was still visible, but as we neared the base of the hill, it sank below the slope and out of sight. We passed a grove of carob trees, with their curiously small, fat oval leaves and black-and-yellow beans: I pulled one off and bit it, but it was tasteless, and I spat it out again. The track led through a gap in a boundary wall on to the rough, open hillside: there were heather and clumps of gorse bushes: in one of these there was a giant spider's nest, the sort somebody had once warned me about: if you brush into it and break it, you can get painfully bitten. It wouldn't do to blunder about here at night.

Above us, the Bull's horns were coming back into view. We climbed on, the sun on our backs. Alex was sweating more than I was: was he nervous? or was I becoming acclimatized? We could see the whole height of the Bull, now: it was larger than I'd supposed, perhaps thirty feet high: from our angle of approach, it looked thin and foreshortened: the width of it was aimed at the *autopista* beyond. Closer still, and I could see the steel sheets it was constructed of, and the framework of steel that supported it.

There was nobody else in sight. We walked slowly around

the Bull, looking in all directions. Still nobody. Three or four hundred yards away, on the far side of the hill, cars, trucks, and coaches sped with surprisingly little noise along the motorway.

"It's not yet half past," Alex said. "What do you want to do, now?"

"You wait here," I said, "and I'll take a look around. And I'll relieve you of the shopping bag, now. Thanks, Alex."

"Right." He moved into the vast shadow thrown by the Bull and sat down in the heather.

I looked again at the Bull itself. Black-painted, quarter-inch steel plate, enough to stop a bullet. But the lower edge of the body was six feet off the ground, and the legs were too thin to give much shelter. No use, in short. Well, not for me, though some people had found a use: *Oscar y Miriam* wanted the world to know they loved each other most sincerely, in white chalk. On another tack, someone was urging LIBERTA PER ELS PATRIOTES CATALANS in red paint . . .

Come on!—work to do.

Maybe it wasn't such a good idea to meet here. Standing in the shadow of the Bull, we had a clear view of about sixty yards all around, before the ground dropped away: in that dead ground, anything might be going on. I'd planned for *us* to use the dead ground if we needed to escape, but at this stage, before the opposition arrived, we were at a disadvantage: we couldn't see who was coming, or how many. We could be surrounded by a regiment of villains, and not know it.

I decided to move out from the Bull, far enough to see down the slope to the track. If Alex stayed behind, watching the rest of the skyline for movement, we'd be covering the ground as well as two pairs of eyes could and would still be able to join up in case of trouble. I explained this to Alex.

"The main thing is to keep within sight of each other," I said. "Point and shout if you see anything."

He gave me a wry smile.

"Is there anything wrong?" I asked.

"No. I admire your professional attitude to this."

"A meeting with Stephenson is a high-risk venture," I said with feeling. "I'm just trying to secure every possible advantage. I think, when you meet him, you'll be glad of it."

"I'm not criticizing," he said, "quite the contrary. You carry on, William: I'll do my best to follow instructions."

I looked at him sharply, but if he felt resentment, it didn't show on his face. I supposed I had rather taken charge without his agreement, but my skin was as much at risk as his.

"If you'd rather . . ." I said.

"No! I meant it—you carry on."

"Well, all right. You take the shotgun now, and I'll keep the shopping bag—I don't want to be seen waving a gun about on the skyline."

I handed him the gun, and I began to walk away. After a few paces, I looked back. Alex was standing there, already surveying the horizon as I'd suggested. I moved on, feeling uncertain. The trouble with Alex was that he seemed as bland as butter, but I didn't trust him, and that sometimes made the most ordinary things he said, and did, seem full of hidden intent. Why trust him with the shotgun, then? Because I planned to get it off him in good time before war broke out: meanwhile, it would look as though I took him at face value.

Rabbit tracks criss-crossed the heather. I followed first one, then another, until I was about sixty yards from the Bull, far enough to be able to see the track below. Alex's head and shoulders were still visible up there, above the slope of the hill. I gave him a slow, horizontal wave—nothing in sight—and after a little hesitation, he returned it. The time on my watch was ten to four.

I spent a couple of minutes collecting some gorse twigs and loose earth together.

A sound from below set me searching the track. It was coming from the low ground just this side of the *autopista,* but it didn't sound like a car, and I expected Stephenson to arrive from the opposite direction. I waited. After a while a moped came into view, trailing blue smoke, and laboring under the load of a fat Spaniard in a white vest. A small brown dog trotted beside. They disappeared in the direction of the village.

At three minutes to four, I heard the throaty waffle of a V–8 engine approaching from the left. Moments later, I saw Stephenson's Range Rover. It jolted along the track and stopped at the foot of the hill. I turned to signal to Alex, who waved acknowledgment. Three figures got out: Stephenson's bulk was easily recognizable, and the other two could be Granite Face and the smoothly dressed mafioso I'd seen at the meeting in the church. There was some discussion, and then the two started up the hill toward me, leaving Stephenson behind with the car. He began to walk up and down, impatiently. It was then, as he moved, that I saw a fourth figure, still sitting in the car, and caught—yes!—a flash of white pullover and yellow hair.

So they'd brought her, then! And this was to be a genuine exchange!

So—was Alex genuine?

Leave it, leave it! That'll become clear, soon.

Very soon, in fact. I could now see the two approaching figures well enough to identify Granite Face and the mafioso.

I bent down out of sight to hide the crossbow under a clump of heather and to scoop the twigs and earth I'd collected into the shopping bag. Then I retreated up the hill, back to where Alex was waiting at the Bull. I said:

"There are two coming up. Stephenson's staying down there with the Range Rover. Cathy's in it."

"She is?" Alex took a step forward. I caught his arm.

"I saw her—but we must wait for them here or my plans will be upset. It seems they mean to make the exchange, though. Now listen, I'll stand off a few yards with the gun. Don't, whatever you do, get between me and either of them. Let's have the gun, then, and you hold this bag—you can tell them the money's in it, if they ask."

He ran his tongue over his lips nervously. "Right," he said. "My God, I hope this comes off."

Granite Face and the mafioso were coming up, and were twenty yards off.

"Stop there!" I called. "That's close enough." I held the shotgun with barrels pointing to the ground, but ready for use.

They stopped. The mafioso called back:

"You, señor—what is your name?"

"Warner. And I know how to use a gun. We want no trouble."

"There will be no trouble. But you must put down the gun."

I looked at Alex, who looked back at me blankly. Up to you, he seemed to say.

"First," I called, "hold out your guns so that I can see them. Then we will all put them down, together. All right?"

"I have no gun, señor," he said with dignity, pulling his jacket open to show me a bare expanse of dazzlingly white shirt.

"No, but your partner there has. Tell him to hold it out—carefully."

Well, he has to have one. And—yes, he has, a small automatic, tucked into the belt. He draws it, slowly, and holds it so that I can see. His face is as much like granite as ever, and he has reason to dislike me—I must be careful . . .

Slowly, cautiously, we bent to place our weapons on the ground and straightened up again.

Granite Face moved closer to the mafioso, and spoke briefly in Spanish. The mafioso nodded and then called:

"Señor Gordon—you must put down the bag, please."

"Not until you hand over my daughter," Alex said.

"Is the money in there, señor?"

"Yes," Alex said.

Granite Face spoke again. The mafioso frowned and said:

"I think this is not true, Señor Gordon. My friend has seen a weapon in that bag. Please, no games—put down the bag."

Alex looked at me. "Better do what he says," I advised. Alex leaned the bag against one of the Bull's steel supports. "Now call my daughter up here," he said, a new edge to his voice.

"One moment, señor. You have the ring?"

"Yes." Alex reached inside his jacket and brought out the bulky envelope of bank notes. He tipped it up, and the ring slid out into his hand, glinting in the sunlight.

"Come forward, please, Señor Gordon. Put it down there, with the money. *Gracias.* Now go back, and I will come forward to look." It was like a courtly, old-fashioned dance. Examining the ring, the mafioso said:

"I see . . . yes . . . very good. I think we can do business . . ."

"Put it down," Alex said tersely.

"Señor?"

"Put down the money and the ring. You can't take the ring until I've got my daughter."

"I regret, señor, that is not possible today."

Alex stared at him. Something seemed to snap. He shouted: "You *bastard*! Call her up here, *now*!"

"Señor, please believe me, she is not—"

"*Now!* Or I'll—"

"Please, señor—"

It was a moment of truth, all right, if I ever saw one. Certainly it was a new, wild, enraged Alex who charged his tormentors with as much blind fury as any beast of the bull ring. Suddenly, the web of threat, bluff, and counterbluff that held us in our places was ripped apart, and we all exploded into action. Alex's charge sent the mafioso flying, and as soon as I got over my surprise, I dived for the shotgun to give him support. But I was too slow—there was a crack, and a bullet kicked up a puff of dry earth just in front of my hand; I looked up to see that Granite Face had already snatched up his automatic and had it trained on me. I flung myself backward and rolled aside, my flesh quivering as it anticipated the shock of a bullet. But nothing happened: on seeing me roll away from the shotgun, he'd turned to deal with Alex, who was on him like a tiger. A second shot went harmlessly into the air, a reflex of the trigger finger as Alex struck aside his gun arm and knocked him onto his back in the heather. It all happened in seconds and then, ignoring the fact that Granite Face still had his automatic, he was off down the slope toward Stephenson and the Range Rover with Cathy in it.

I checked my chances of getting to the shotgun while Granite Face's attention was elsewhere. Nil!—he glanced around, saw me, and waved the pistol threateningly. All right—I'd been lucky he missed me the first time. It would have to be Plan B, a retreat to where I'd hidden the crossbow.

I rolled a couple of yards farther away and then got up and ran. It's not that easy to hit a running target, especially if it's moving fast, and believe me, I was. Some distance ahead and to the left, Alex was bounding over the heather for his next death-defying deed. My God!—this wasn't the diffident doctor I thought I knew!—this was the sort of nerveless character who gets Mentioned In Dispatches for wiping out a machine-gun nest single-handed. It was his show, now, but I could tag along and try to be supportive. Granite Face was also up and running after him, automatic in hand—BANG! and again BANG!—thank God he was missing, so far. Now, where was the bloody crossbow, somewhere here under this clump of heather—no!—*that one* . . .

I grabbed it and ran across the slope to put Granite Face between me and the Range Rover. I couldn't hope to catch up to him, but I could make the shot easier by firing down the direction of his movement. First, a warning shout . . .

He must understand STOP!—it's universal . . . But if so, he's ignoring it. And BANG!—he's loosed off another shot at Alex. Well, that's it . . .

I huddled the crossbow's extended butt against my shoulder, took aim at the diminishing back, and squeezed the trigger. There was a metallic thud.

Nothing. Then I saw Granite Face stumble . . .

He stopped, swayed, and sat down heavily.

Jesus! And I'd only half believed the thing would work.

A shout from behind: I looked around. The mafioso was on his way with the shotgun.

It seemed to take an age to cock and reload the crossbow with a bolt from the clip of three spares on the side. I dropped flat, worming my way into the rough ground for cover, and took aim. He stopped, put up his hands.

"You make a mistake, señor!"

"I don't think so. Put down the gun—*now!*"

He complied. *Ha! What a wonderful little weapon this is!*

"Let me pass, señor. I am worried about Señor Gordon."

So polite, so thoughtful, these Spanish . . .

"Get back," I said. "Go on . . . farther. Good. Now, don't move." I rose from the heather and moved to pick up the shotgun. The mafioso said urgently:

"Señor Stephenson is, you know, a man of much anger and also . . ."

"I'll deal with it. Stay here—if I see your face, I'll blow a hole in it. *Entendiente?*"

"Listen, please, señor—"

But I was running down the hill with a weapon in each hand, skirting clear of Granite Face, who sat huddled in the heather and had apparently lost interest in the rest of the world. And there, by the Range Rover, was Alex confronting Stephenson, who also, *oh no!* had a gun, and was using it to emphasize whatever it was he was shouting. Alex was shouting too, but no shots had been fired yet, and with luck I'd get there in time to—He's hit him! Stephenson has clubbed Alex across the side of the head with the pistol, a heavy blow, and Alex has crumpled at the side of the track. He's not moving. Now there's a scream from inside the car, no wonder!—the poor kid seeing that happen to her father. She's opening the door on the far side to—

"Stephenson!" I shout. "Drop the gun or I'll blast you . . ."

What am I saying?—he's got a pistol; he can blast me just as well . . . Panting, I come to a sudden halt, ready to drop flat again. Range thirty yards—he could miss, but some of the shotgun pellets must score . . . as long as the girl doesn't get in the way . . . she's coming around now to go to her father . . .

What???

It's not Cathy; it's Sharon . . .

We've been had. They intended us to make that mistake, by giving us a glimpse of white pullover and fair hair. They never meant to make the exchange . . .

Stephenson is glaring. I've got the shotgun leveled, but the girl's a problem . . . Or is she, now? She's *Stephenson's* daughter, and he won't want to risk her getting hit by stray pellets.

"Throw your gun over there, into the heather!" I shout.

And slowly but surely, he does . . .

Now I can move closer.

"Don't shoot, señor," says a voice from behind. I look around—oh, not him again. Señor *this,* señor *that*—I'm pissed off at him . . . But I suppose I won't shoot him.

"What?"

"I warn you of this," he says. *Cheeky sod!—as if Alex getting hit was my fault rather than his!* Sharon has been bending over Alex and now straightens up. "He's not moving," she tells her father. "You've maybe killed him!—what did you do that for?"

Stephenson scowls. "Get in the car," he says.

"But Dad—"

"*Shuddup!* I told you—"

"I'm coming to look at him," I tell Stephenson.

"Who's stoppin' you."

"Well, move back."

He moves a little, reluctantly, a circus big cat. I bend over Alex. He's breathing, but the side of his head is streaming blood, and his eyes are closed.

"Pardon me, señor." The mafioso takes a look. "This man must go to hospital," he announces.

"Where?"

"Is one in Tarragona, señor. We take him now, at once."

What the hell is going on? First they practically kill him; then they take him to hospital . . .

"How do I know you will?"

"You have my word, señor."

The word of a mafioso . . . Rich, that is. But what's the choice?— Alex does look bad, and my car is half a mile away.

The mafioso is applying a large white handkerchief to the side of Alex's head. It makes me think that, perhaps . . .

"All right. I'll follow."

Stephenson is opening the boot, folding down the back seat. Alex is loaded in, a coat pushed under his head.

"I'll sit with him, Mr. Warner," Sharon says to me. It's the first word we've exchanged.

"Thanks. Try to stop his head bumping as you go down the track."

"Of course. I'm . . . I'm sorry. For what my dad did."

"Not your fault." *But she had a part to play . . .*

"I didn't know, you see. I still don't understand . . ."

"Nor do I, Sharon. Go on, you'd better be off."

Stephenson is at the wheel, the mafioso beside him. Someone's missing . . .

God almighty! *Granite Face!* Here he comes, walking wounded, the automatic dangling from one hand and something else in the other. He comes up to me, and my hand tightens on the shotgun stock. But all he does is give a slight bow, wincing as he straightens up, and then hands me—

—the crossbow bolt!

Then, moving stiffly, he squeezes into the car next to the mafioso. *And I thought the stiff-upper-lip was a British invention . . .*

The Range Rover lurches out of sight. I start to make for the Citroën. Then I remember the money and the ring. Cursing, I pound up the hill to where I saw them fall in the scrimmage.

WEDNESDAY

"YOU MUSTN'T LET IT GET YOU DOWN, WILLIAM darling," Ginny said, reaching for another croissant from the breakfast tray.

Nice of her to try to cheer me up. But useless. This morning, we had Alex in hospital and had lost both the money and the ring.

"It wasn't your fault, was it?" Ginny said. "I mean, he went berserk, didn't he?"

I thought I'd got it all worked out—the ideal place, contingency plans, right down to weaponry and fields of fire. The professional approach, as Alex himself had acknowledged—but with a wry smile which, in retrospect, said it all. I had tried to cover us against disaster. In spite of which, disaster was what we'd ended up with.

"Berserk, yes. But if I hadn't misled him about the girl in the car, he wouldn't have gone charging off and got clobbered. As his caretaker, I should have anticipated that. I knew he had hidden depths—said so, didn't I?"

"You did, William darling. You certainly did."

Ginny was doing all she could to sooth me. I ought to snap out of this mood and do something. Yes, I ought, and I would—as soon as I could decide what.

"There's one good thing to come out of this, anyway."

"Oh yes? There is?"

"Of course, darling. You know that Alex is genuine now,

don't you. He wouldn't have charged at Stephenson otherwise.
Shot at all the way, you said."

"By Granite Face, yes, until I stopped him. And missed—
three or four shots, and they all missed. What do you make of
that?"

"Rotten shot, darling."

"Maybe. He'd have to be—he was firing down the direction
of movement."

"I don't know what that means."

"Well, it's much easier than shooting at someone who's
crossing your line of fire. That's how I was able to hit Granite
Face with the little crossbow."

"I'll take your word for it, William darling. It seems to be
built into men, the technology of beastliness."

"Let's not start on that; you're quite pleased to make use of
us at times . . . Was Alex just going for the girl or did he see
his plan going wrong and lose control of his suppressed hatred
of Stephenson? That's the question. He really went for Stephenson, you know—who, I'm sure, doesn't need much excuse to indulge his psychopathic tendencies. It was a very, very
dangerous thing to do. Even his own employees tried to stop
him—that's what I think now. Granite Face didn't miss: he was
firing warning shots."

"Oh my God, William! And you . . . !"

"Yes. Not my day, was it. I think, in the circumstances, he
was remarkably restrained about it. Pulled the bolt out himself:
I suppose the leather jacket stopped it to some extent."

"Why didn't they shout to warn you off?"

"They didn't know I'd hidden the bow in the heather—
thought it was in the shopping bag. Well, let's move on. What
next?"

Ginny looked at me and suddenly giggled. "Some lucky
girls have lovers who propose a day on the beach followed by
candlelit dinner and a stroll in the moonlight," she said.
"What's on your program, William darling, I wonder? Target
practice? Hospital visiting?"

"That's not quite fair, is it?" I said. "But as a matter of fact, we ought to visit Alex, of course. When I went with Jill to the hospital last night, they told her he'd probably be in a fit state to be visited today. She's going to ring and let me know. You needn't come if you'd rather not."

"I didn't mean that," Ginny said, taking my arm and squeezing it. "You know I didn't. Of course I'll come. I won't be able to stay much longer, you know. I think I must be back to greet the old stick at the weekend. And there are the dogs—"

"Go back? But you've only just arrived! Oh Ginny—"

"I've been here almost a week, darling."

"Have you? Oh shit—I thought, you see, I'd just get this business wrapped up, and then—"

"—I'd have all your attention? That'll be the day. Not that I haven't enjoyed the times in between."

"Oh God."

"It's all right. You can invite me again, somewhere, sometime."

"But will you come?" I said.

The telephone rang. "Well, will you?" I demanded.

"Hadn't you better answer that?" she said, smiling.

I stared at her, but she just went on smiling. The telephone rang again. "I'll deal with you later," I said, reaching for it. "Hello?"

A man's voice said heavily: "Mr. Warner?"

"Yes. Who is it?"

"Mr. Stephenson here."

My brain seemed to swirl, and then settle into an unnatural concentration. I said:

"Yes, Mr. Stephenson. What is it?"

"It's about the Gordon girl. We've got what we want now, see. So you can come and get her."

"Where?"

"At my house. She's at my house."

"Mr. Stephenson—why should I believe that? Especially after what happened yesterday?"

"Yeah, sorry about it. He shouldn't have said what he did."

"You shouldn't have hit him like that."

"Said I'm sorry, didn't I? Listen—d'you want the girl back or don't you?"

"Of course we do."

"Well then. Be at my house, two o'clock. Right?"

"All right. I'll be there."

"And listen, Mr. Warner—"

"What?"

"Be on your own. I'll know if you're not. I'm doing you a favor, and you'd better not try and take advantage. There won't be a second chance—know what I'm saying?"

The phone went dead. I put the receiver back. Ginny said:

"Was that who I think it was?"

"Stephenson. I've got to collect Cathy from his house at two this afternoon."

Ginny said nothing, but her thoughts were almost audible. So, no doubt, were mine. Then she said:

"Don't go. It's time to send the police."

"Ginny, I can't. There'd be one hell of a battle if they tried to break in there, and by the time they got in . . ."

"You think he'd do that?"

"I think he would."

"But surely, once he saw what he was up against—"

"He's not the sort of man to reckon the consequences. He knows he's going to be caught up with sometime, and he'd relish a last, bloody holocaust. I'm sure of it."

Ginny was silent again. Then:

"Don't go. There must be another way."

"Like what?"

She didn't answer. "It's half past nine," I said. "I might as well get up, and get showered and dressed."

I pushed the breakfast tray over to her side, and swung my legs out of bed. "Tell you something useful."

"What?" Her voice was sullen with disapproval.

"I've got Stephenson's automatic," I said. "I made him

throw it away into the heather at one stage in yesterday's drama, and he went off without it."

"Won't he have others?"

"A whole arsenal, I should think. But I'm glad to have it, all the same. It'll be a comfort, having that in my pocket."

"Would you take this bloody tray off my legs," Ginny said abruptly. "I want to lie down."

I lifted the tray, carried it to a side table, and went back to the bedside. "Ginny? Are you all right?"

She pulled the bedclothes up, and didn't reply.

"Ginny?"

Still no reply. I said:

"Well . . . wish me luck, at least."

Her voice came muffled through the bedclothes:

"Stupid bastard . . . do you think I don't?"

The little square in the center of Prades was emptying as people finished their shopping and headed home for lunch. I had a few minutes to spare before I needed to set off on the last stage of the drive to Stephenson's villa, and I bought a *boca-dillo*—two large slabs of bread rubbed with olive oil, tomato, and garlic, with a slice of ham hanging out all around. The garlic gave me a breath powerful enough to send most English-men reeling for cover—it might help to keep Stephenson at arm's length. I sat in the car on the shady side of the square, munching and watching the world go by.

I was worried about motorbikes. The town seemed to have a plague of trail bikes which were roaming the narrow streets aimlessly. The noise of their exhausts brought back vivid memories of my last, moonlit escape from these parts with Stephenson's daughter. There was no way I could tell if any of these were of that band, but if I got buzzed on the track to his villa, I was prepared to call the whole thing off: I had enough doubts already about today's expedition, and if the bikers were about, that had to be a sign of bad faith.

Lunch over, I brushed the crumbs off my lap, tucked my

escaping shirt back into my trousers, and drove off. I watched the driving mirror carefully, but none of the bikes left the town limits to follow me: so far, so good. Soon, I was on the track along the high ridge, jolting slowly over the rocky surface between the pines once again.

The track seemed even longer than I remembered. But at last, I emerged from the forest onto the bare, rocky plateau, and saw the crumbling walls of Torrecasim on its vertiginous perch. I drove into the final stretch of sunken track across the plateau. Then the view widened out again, and before me were the white walls of Stephenson's villa—or, as I now knew it to be, his crazy castle. I was sweating: was the day really that hot?

I pulled up before the iron gates, got out, pushed the button of the entryphone, and waited. Not for long.

"Yeah?" said Stephenson's voice.

"Warner," I said.

"Wait there."

Across the entrance courtyard, I saw the front door open. Stephenson came out, leaving the door ajar. He came down the steps, and across the yard toward the gate, the gravel squeaking under his weight. He was wearing a short-sleeved, pale blue sports shirt, the buttons strained across his belly, and white cotton shorts that barely contained his massive thighs. I watched his approach with a growing sense of alarm at the sheer size of him. Then we were face to face, the bars of the gate between us. *This is how you ought to be,* I thought—*safely behind bars . . .* But he was unlocking the gate.

"Come in."

"No need for that," I said. "Just bring the girl out."

"You'll have to give me a hand," he said. "She's not been too well. Nothing serious, but it's left her a bit weak, like."

I tried to repress the feeling of foreboding that swept over me. *Mustn't get angry, mustn't shout, accuse . . . must keep calm . . .*

"What is it?"

"Nothin' much, nothin' you need worry about. Some sort

of flu, that's all. High temperature. She'll be all right once you get her home and into bed. I'll help you carry her out. Come on."

"Has the doctor been?"

"Doctor? Oh yes. Yes. What d'you think we are? Course we had him in . . . What are you waitin' for?"

"What did the doctor say, exactly?"

"I dunno, do I. Wasn't here. My wife let him in."

"I'd like to speak to her, then."

"Why not. She's inside. Come on."

"Perhaps you'd ask her to come out, Mr. Stephenson."

"Come out? Well, I dunno about that; she's washin' up."

"Well, I'm sorry, but I'm not coming in."

Stephenson stared at me, his small mouth pursed, his eyes screwed up almost to invisibility in his turnip face. Then the corners of his mouth flickered slightly. He said, very quietly:

"I know what you're thinkin'—been in the house, haven't you, and seen how I've fixed it up. I got enemies, you see—I got to live like this. But you've nothin' to fear, nothin' at all. You did in my dogs, didn't you. Well, that's all right; I understand that, and I don't bear you no grudges—fortunes of war they call it. So I reckon we're quits, eh? What do you say, Mr. Warner?"

"I'm not coming into the house," I repeated. "Sorry, but no."

"Oh dear me. That's not very friendly now, is it? But I can see your mind's made up. You don't trust me, that's what it is. All right, all right, I'll say no more. You can come 'round through the garden, and I'll bring her out."

"Why not all the way, if you can carry her that far?" I said.

"All the way? Well, to be honest, Mr. Warner, I don't think she'd like it—doesn't trust me more than what you do, although I've tried to treat her right. On the way through the garden now, you can stop for a word with my wife at the kitchen window: she'll tell you what the doctor said. All right?"

I hesitated. Anything to do with Stephenson was a risk, of course, but he didn't know I'd got his automatic in my pocket.

"All right. You lead the way, Mr. Stephenson, and I'll follow."

"Well, you are a cautious one, Mr. Warner! Not that I blame you; this house has got some very nasty surprises for people that come in uninvited. So, we'll go through the garden. This way."

What booby traps can you have in a garden? I follow Stephenson's bulk across the courtyard and to the left, around the east side of the house, where I'd seen his wife tying up bignonia to the frame against the wall. We're walking on a graveled path, and I keep two paces behind Stephenson, watching where he puts his feet. *A pressure mine?*—ex-army explosives expert, wasn't he! But we're close enough for him to be blown up as well. *A trip wire to a concealed shotgun!*—no, he'd have to go through it first; I make sure I step over anything he steps over . . . *What else?* Maybe he meant what he said, and the game is played out. But I don't believe he called in the doctor. His wife might have done, though, that's true. Where is she? Ahead is the swimming pool terrace, and we're now going around the corner of the house to the south side, the side I've never seen . . .

Careful, then!

But there's nothing alarming to be seen. A long terrace of marble slabs in a random pattern, equipped with a swing seat, the awning a flower-patterned fabric in violent colors, two white plastic reclining chairs with matching tables, a leaf net such as I clean our pool with. And that's it.

Through a picture window to my right, Mrs. Stephenson can be seen washing up in yellow rubber gloves. She takes plates from her left, washes them, and stacks them on the right. I look straight at her and wave, but she's got her eyes on her job, the yellow of the gloves moving rhythmically from side to side behind the glass . . .

*   *   *

Stephenson stopped outside an open glass door. I stopped too, keeping my distance.

"Take a seat, Mr. Warner," he said. "I'll bring the girl to this door, right? And I'll tell my wife you'd like a word."

"I'm quite happy standing here, thanks all the same."

"Suit yourself. You look about to melt away, you know: my wife'll bring you somethin' to drink."

"Not for me, thanks."

"Oh, come on, Mr. Warner! You've no call to be like that, not now. It's all over, I told you. How about a nice cold beer?"

"I'm not thirsty, thanks."

"No? Well, you're hard to please, I've got to say that. Tell you what—have a dip while you're waitin'. I've got some spare trunks you can have a loan of, just about your size."

"Look, Mr. Stephenson," I said, "all I want is for you to bring the girl out. She'll want to get home: this isn't the time for drinks or swimming, thanks all the same."

"You're sweatin', though. I can see that."

"Maybe—it doesn't matter."

"You could do with a cool off—sure you could."

"I told you—*no thanks.*"

"You shouldn't refuse a good offer, Mr. Warner."

"Sorry. Just bring the girl out, *please.*"

Stephenson stood, looking at me. The rosebud mouth was twitching again. Then he said:

"Afraid I've got to insist on it, Mr. Warner."

His rush took me completely by surprise; by the time I knew what was happening, I was already airborne. It was a short flight in terms of distance, but I had time to think: *it's the pool, the pool; it was that all the time, so large and obvious I didn't see it. What'll it be? Has he filled it with acid, stocked it with piranhas; is he going to use me as a floating target? Will I be killed or just horribly injured . . .*

SPLASH!!!

Now what, what shall I do?—dive down or try to scramble out?

I came up to the surface, gulped in some air, and snatched a quick look around to see what was in store for me.

Then I heard Stephenson's laughter. It sounded rusty, but otherwise quite ordinary. From my watery situation, I glared at him.

"Oh dear," he spluttered, "oh dear, oh dear. Sorry about that, Mr. Warner. Can't think what come over me."

No acid. No piranhas. No bullets. Just an ordinary revenge— usually known as the last laugh . . .

"No hard feelin's, I hope," Stephenson said, still chuckling. "They was expensive dogs, you know. I reckon I was due a bit extra. But you're a good sport; I'm sure of that. You climb out over there, Mr. Warner, and I'll fetch you a towel. Oh dear, oh dear. What a laugh, eh?"

Treading water, I felt in my jacket pocket for the automatic, grasped it, and brought it to the surface. Stephenson's chuckles died away as I took aim at his stomach.

"Thought you could take a joke," he said.

"Oh yes," I said. "I can take a joke, all right. And improve on it, too. Your turn to cool off, Mr. Stephenson. Jump!"

He stood there, eyes on the gun, considering disobedience.

"I'm only an amateur compared to you," I said, "but I know how to use this, and I will. You've got three seconds to jump before I put a bullet in your right shoulder. Starting . . .*now!*"

He didn't jump—he dived.

Where is he? Somewhere down there, streaking sharklike for my legs . . . to seize and pull me under . . .

I struck out for the shallow end and the security of steps under my feet. To stay in the pool with Stephenson was not what I'd had in mind: I wanted *him* in there, immobilized, while I got out and spoke to his wife.

Behind me, I heard Stephenson breaking the surface, snorting to clear water from his nostrils. He didn't sound too close. I felt for the pool bottom with my feet, found it, and turned to face him. I needn't have got so panicky: he was at the far end, treading water, apparently unperturbed.

I lifted the automatic to make sure he saw it, and called:
"Stay in the pool. I'm going to talk to your wife."

"Why not," he called back. "And the best of luck."

He watched me as I waded to the steps, an expensive-look-ing teak ship's ladder with brass handrails, and hauled myself out. Dripping, I stood for a moment to take my jacket off. Stephenson's head still bobbed on the water at the far end of the pool: he was scowling now.

"I'm warning you," I said. "Stay in the pool, right?"

He said nothing. I'd have to watch him, but it isn't easy to get out of a swimming pool in a hurry, and I thought I was safe enough for the moment. I dripped along the terrace to the glass door, and glanced inside. It was a dining room: beyond was a passage, which I thought must lead to the living room at the far end. On the right, behind a counter, was the kitchen, where Mrs. Stephenson was still busy at the sink as though she had no interest in what had been going on just outside her kitchen window. That, I supposed, was what life with Ste-phenson had done to her: it was hateful, so she'd trained herself to ignore it. I put my head in through the doorway, and said:

"Mrs. Stephenson—you remember me?"

"I remember you," she said in her flat voice.

"Is Cathy Gordon—the missing girl—here? Your husband says she is."

Outside, Stephenson was swimming slowly toward the shal-low end of the pool, an easy sidestroke, his face toward me.

"Watch it!" I shouted.

Mrs. Stephenson's hands in the yellow gloves were busily scouring a saucepan.

"Please tell me," I urged.

She looked out of the window, along the pool.

"You'd better let him get out," she said. "Tell him to take you down to the basement."

"Is she all right?" I said. *What would I find down there?*

"I don't think you need worry," she said.

"Can I go down by myself?"

She considered. "If you like."

"But is it safe?" *And could I trust her?*

"Oh yes. Quite safe."

I looked around to see where Stephenson had got to. He was treading water again, halfway along the pool. It would take him some time to realize I was no longer watching and climb out.

"Go on," she said. "Come inside and lock the door if you're worried about him. Here—let me do it."

A satisfying click, but it was only a glass door.

Oh come on!—*let's risk it . . .*

I moved to the door at the back of the dining room, yanked it open, ran along the corridor, and found the stairs to the basement. I tore down them, into the basement, and flung open the door at the bottom of the stairs.

Empty! A trap! Shit—she's in it with him! I was a fool to trust her . . .

Gripping the automatic, I ran up the stairs again, sure that Stephenson would be up there by now, and that I was going to have to shoot my way out of this hellish house. I reached the top of the stairs, looked cautiously around the corner into the corridor. No one there! *Make a run for it, then!*

I pounded across the dining room to the outside door, wrenched at the key, pulled the door open, and fell out onto the terrace. Where was Stephenson? Ah! Just in time!—he's in the act of climbing out.

"Stop there!" I bellowed. "Or I'll . . ."

Something odd going on. He's got his foot stuck in the steps . . . or he could even be having a heart attack; he's gripping the handrails and shaking all over . . .

"Mrs. Stephenson!" I called. There was no reply. I looked inside, into the kitchen.

She was back at the sink, mopping down the stainless steel draining board with meticulous sweeps of a dishcloth. The metal shone like silver in the sunlight that came through the window overlooking the pool.

"Mrs. Stephenson!"

The yellow gloves never paused. She didn't look around.

"*Mrs. Stephenson!* I think your husband's having a heart attack!"

She looked at me then, but her face was expressionless, and she didn't move or even glance out of the window.

I looked out of the doorway again. Stephenson had sagged against the steps. I started to run along the terrace toward him. As I ran, I saw his hands slide down and then off the brass handrails, his body collapsed into the water. His *body* . . .

"Mr. Warner!"

I spun around. Mrs. Stephenson stood just outside the glass door, peeling off the yellow gloves. "I shouldn't touch him, if I were you."

We both gazed at the body in the water. It was turning slowly over to float facedown, drifting slowly away from the steps. The wooden steps. With the metal handrails. *Oh yes.* I turned back to Mrs. Stephenson, still standing there with the gloves now off and dangling from one hand.

"I think," I said, "I owe you my life. The switch is in the kitchen, I suppose?"

"I wouldn't know," she said. "He always told me never to touch anything of his. And nobody can say I ever did."

She went inside. I followed, and found her sitting at the dining-room table with her back to the window.

"Bound to be an accident, sooner or later, with all these lethal gadgets around the place," I said.

"Yes," she said.

"And the girl isn't here? Never has been?"

"No. I'm sorry."

"You can't tell me where she is?"

"I would if I could."

"Can I ask if your son is with her?"

"He goes his own way. I haven't seen him for two weeks or more."

"But he could be with her?"

"He was keen on her. He could be."

"Oh Christ."

"He's not like his dad," she said defensively.

"Mrs. Stephenson—we think he took her away. And she hasn't been seen since, for the same two weeks or so."

"I don't believe he'd try to make money out of her. Not Mark—he just wouldn't."

Well, I thought, after what she did just now, I have to believe her . . . I said:

"What would you like me to do?"

She was sitting at the table with her hands folded in her lap and didn't look up. "I think . . . just go," she said.

"Not ring for the ambulance or tell anybody?"

"I'll do that. You weren't here, were you," she said.

"You'll be all right?"

She looked up then. Our eyes met. How had a woman like her ever got caught up by Stephenson in the first place? Ah yes, I remember. She'd told me—*"It wasn't always like this . . ."*

"Right as rain," she said.

WEDNESDAY EVENING

WHEN I'D FINISHED MY ACCOUNT, I STOOD FOR A MINute or two looking out from the flat's west-facing windows. Beyond the Barcelona roofscape, the mountains glowed with the last of the sunset. Alastair came back into the sitting room and handed me a tall glass, three-quarters full of golden liquid. A column of bubbles streamed upward, waving like river weed. "Try this," he said.

I took the glass gratefully. Ginny and Pilar watched, smiling, as I tilted it. I never need much excuse to down a glass of bubbly, but if I did, this afternoon's narrow escape was as good as you can get. And although I'd come back empty-handed, the search for Cathy Gordon seemed more hopeful with Stephenson no longer part of the opposition.

"I don't think I know this, Alastair," I said. "What is it?"

"It's not well known: Ferret, *brut nature*. Does it meet with your approval?"

"Certainly does. From around here?"

"Yes—Alt Penedés."

I took another mouthful. Spanish *cava* never has the depth of French champagne, but there are occasions when its delicacy and lightness seem just right, and this was one of them: not a celebration, more of a restoration. "What's the matter with the rest of you?" I said. "I haven't got to get through this on my own, have I?"

"We're glad to have you back, William darling," Ginny said. "We're just checking you over to see there's no harm done. It seems, from the way you're tipping that down, there isn't."

"Oh!" I said, touched, "well. I don't know what to say. Thank you all. *Salut!*"

"Just one thing," Pilar said, "because, when it comes to electricity, I know nothing. It was the steps that kill Stephenson, right? So why not you?"

"Mrs. Stephenson was watching from the kitchen window, and switched the current off."

"Oh yes! And then on again . . ."

"Forget all I've said," I warned. "And I wasn't there. That's the agreement. An accident—and I can't think of anyone who'd want to spend time trying to prove otherwise, can you?"

"Poor Mrs. Stephenson!" Pilar said. "What will happen to her now?"

"She'll live happily ever after, darling," Ginny said. "Won't she, William?"

"By the time I left, she was already showing signs of it," I said. "Personally, I feel the same as when I read that a terrorist has blown himself up with his own bomb—that's one less to worry about. I know I shouldn't, but I do. Oh, thank you, Alastair—how kind. Mmm—it really *is* good, isn't it!"

We all stood around and sipped. Something was nagging for my attention. Something else about wine that I'd meant to ask Alastair. Oh yes—

"Have you had a call from a firm called Pedro Masana?"

"No," he said. "Should I have?"

"Maggie said they'd rung the London shop, and she'd told them you'd know where I was: she gave them your address."

I felt my words run into the sand. Of course!—that's how Granite Face got on to me. So easy—all he had to do was watch the flat until I turned up. Why I didn't see it at once?

"Something wrong?" Alastair asked.

"It doesn't matter now," I said.

"Stay to supper?"

"Well, there are things we should discuss," I said. "So if you're sure, Pilar?"

"Of course! I am very pleased. And William—ask Ginny to tell you what we have been doing this afternoon. I think he will like to hear it, Ginny—no? Now, Alastair will look after you while I go to the kitchen."

"Make yourselves comfortable," Alastair said. We settled into the sofa, and he began to move around the room, switching on lights and closing blinds.

"Not so exciting as your afternoon," Ginny said, "and I don't know if what we did will be any help toward finding Cathy Gordon, but we are feeling rather pleased with ourselves, Pilar and me. Those numbers inside the ring—they aren't the date of old Delgado's wedding."

"How do you know?"

"We rang Jill and got her to ask at the Big House. Their wedding was in May, nineteen twenty-three, not in November, twenty-one."

"So what happened in November, nineteen twenty-one?"

"We think, nothing. We don't think these numbers—three-one, one-one, two-one—*are* a date because, as I reminded you, there is no such day as November the thirty-first."

Ginny paused and looked smug.

"All right, all right. Spare me the suspense," I said. "Let's have it."

"We thought of all the things it might be, and decided that the most likely was a deposit box number."

"Could be, I suppose. But why? And where?"

"And we thought that, if we're looking for a deposit box, the place to start must be old Delgado's bank. So we asked Jill to see if she could find that out, as well."

"And she did?"

"You know Jill. Yes, she did," Ginny said. "And guess which bank it is? You've seen it yourself."

"I have?"

"You've had money from it."

I thought. *Oh yes, of course!* "Caixa Catalunya! Obvious isn't it!—what other bank would a Catalán patriot be more likely to go to!"

"That's it, William darling. Caixa Catalunya—the branch in the Plaça Catalunya, just up the road from the hotel. Furthermore, they have a vault where you can hire deposit boxes. And still further furthermore, the boxes have six-figure combination locks, not keys. Not a bad afternoon's work, I feel."

"How did you find all this out?"

"Pilar rang up and said she needed a safe place to stash away some jewelry. They were happy to give her all the details. But there's a snag—two snags. If the number is the safe combination, then we don't know which box it refers to. And we can't go in and try them all in turn because the vault is supervised by an armed guard."

"Bank vaults, armed guards," I said. "You're still thinking about the money from the bank raid, Ginny, aren't you?"

"Well . . ." she said, and stopped.

"Ah-ha," I said.

"All right," she said. "Well, we could just forget it. If there is still a deposit box in Delgado's name there, Stephenson's bunch have had twenty-four hours to clear it out since they got the combination. We'd probably be wasting our time. On the other hand . . ."

"Yes," I admitted. "It'd be nice to have a look. But now that I've come back without Cathy Gordon, I've got to concentrate on finding her. I've been hoping for a call—they've got all they wanted from Alex now—but there's a chance they may decide it's safer . . . not to return her."

"That's what I've been thinking. But what can you do?"

"I've got nothing left to bargain with," I said. "That's the problem. All we can do, bluntly, is to hope they prefer not to have a murder on their hands as well as a kidnapping. I haven't given up hope yet—the mafia type seemed to have a spark of humanity, and if he's in charge now, I may get a call to pick her up. I left this number at hotel reception, just in case."

Alastair's bulk was slumped in the sofa opposite. "Won't there be a point," he suggested, "at which, if she doesn't turn up, you might as well bring in the police?"

"Yes. I was thinking the same, but it's so hard to decide when. It ought to be Alex's decision, don't you agree? I'd better go to Tarragona tomorrow, and see if he's up to it."

"You said we'd got nothing left to bargain with," Ginny said, "and I expect you'll think I've got a one-track mind, but wouldn't it be worth just trying to check if those numbers do fit a deposit box in the Caixa Catalunya?"

"Why not?" I said. "What have we got to lose?"

"Have you ever seen inside a Spanish jail?" Alastair asked ruminatively. "I met a man who had, not long ago. He said—"

"We're not aiming to break in, Alastair!"

"Not your deposit box though, is it, William."

"No, it's . . . Ah! If it exists at all, it's supposed to be old Delgado's box, isn't it! So, the answer's simple—I explain the problem to *young* Delgado and ask him to come with us."

"Is there any chance he'll agree?" Alastair said. "I don't mean to be depressing, but why should he agree to let you see what's in his father's deposit box?"

"Because we'll have *found* it," Ginny said. "There's nothing to show he even knows it exists—William said he handed the ring over with hardly a glance at it, didn't you, darling?"

"There certainly wasn't time for him to note the numbers inside it," I said. "So maybe he'll be delighted to come with us to the bank, or, if it's technically his box now, to let us go with him. Anyway, how can we get at it without him? Any ideas? No? Well, I might as well see if I can get him on the phone now and save on mental effort. I'll try to arrange a meeting at the bank first thing tomorrow morning. Okay?"

"Let me get through for you," Alastair offered, heaving himself to his feet. I followed him into the office off the sitting room, and stood at his side while he looked up Delgado in the telephone book and keyed in the number. A pause, and then he spoke in Spanish, glancing up at me. I waited impatiently.

Then he replaced the receiver. "He's away until tomorrow evening on business."

"That's leaving it too late. If we're going to do this at all, it ought to be tomorrow morning."

We went back into the sitting room, and broke the news to Ginny. "A whole day lost," she said. "Too much, isn't it. We don't have to consult Alex to know what he'd feel about that."

They were both looking at me. Clearly it was time to be decisive, masterful . . . not easy when your mind's a blank.

"Right," I said, "we'll get over there tomorrow morning."

"What's the plan, darling?" Ginny asked.

"It's a question of alternatives. I haven't decided which is best yet."

They bought it. Alastair came over and refilled my glass. Well, I'd sort something out by the time we got there . . .

$\mathcal{T}$HURSDAY

ALASTAIR STAYED BEHIND. I WAS RELIEVED BE-
cause he had no particular role to play, and four of us
would have made up too large and noticeable a party.
So Pilar came alone to the Oriente at eight in the morning, and
when we were ready, we set out to walk the rest of the way
up the Ramblas to the Plaça Catalunya. Sunlight sparkled
through the trees lining both sides of the broad central pavement: street sweepers and delivery vans were hurrying to finish their work before the crowds built up: it was a smiling day,
but smiles can be deceitful, and I'd had too narrow an escape
the day before to feel as confident as I was trying to appear.

The project was fraught with uncertainties. Was it a crime
to open someone else's deposit box if you'd been given the
number? That, presumably, would depend on Delgado's inter-
pretation of our motives, if and when he got to hear about it.
We might run up against an opposition party on an identical
mission: we could claim to be acting on Delgado's behalf, but
of course, they might try the same trick. One way or another,
there seemed a good chance that Alastair's pessimism would
turn out to be justified, and we'll be in a Spanish jail before the
morning is over.

In spite of all that, we'd decided to have a go. So—on to the
central problem. This seemed to have two stages: first, how to
get into the vault, and second, how to locate the box (if it
existed) once we were inside. There was very little information
to go on: therefore, the first part of the plan which I'd evolved

during the night was to send Pilar in alone to talk to the official in charge of the vault and find out as much as she could about the rules that governed access—in effect, a continuation of the telephone call she'd made yesterday. She was dressed for the part in a discreetly expensive suit and extra makeup—a girl with a rich husband who liked to decorate her with diamonds in the old-fashioned way. Luckily she didn't have to display any—nobody would want to tempt Barcelona muggers that far—but just look the part. We'd had some fun over that. The final scheme consisted of a very plain, dark red dress which showed off her hips, and a heavy investment in makeup. "More lipstick, darling!" Ginny had encouraged. "And lots more stuff around the eyes, go on! You need to look more obvious, and less *real* . . . that's what they like." It was a revelation to me. "I didn't realize you had such a feeling for this, Ginny!" I said. "What does it mean?" "I was going to be a goddess, once," she said, "but journalism was more fun. You look stunning, Pilar! Doesn't she, William?"

And she did. Out on the street, Spaniards stared after her as though girls had only just been invented. We paraded up the north side of the Plaça Catalunya, past El Corté Inglés (whose shopping bag, now empty, I'd brought to put our winnings in, if any), and arrived outside the Caixa Catalunya.

"We walk in as if we own the place," I instructed, "and Ginny and I will park ourselves somewhere while Pilar interviews the staff to see if the facilities are up to her standards."

We passed the guard on the door and entered the banking hall. It was large and properly lavish. There were leather chairs to wait in: Ginny and I chose a couple and watched Pilar approach an official behind a desk, undulating discreetly. He stood up, beamed, and gestured her into a chair.

"It's looking good!" I whispered.

"Don't we rather let her down?" Ginny said.

"We're British friends of hers on holiday" I said, "and by Continental standards, Brits are normally scruffy. As long as we stand up straight and speak with confidence, we'll pass."

A few minutes later, we saw that the interview was over. Both parties stood up. The official took Pilar's hand, bent over it, and then watched her come all the way over to us before sitting down again. Obviously she'd made a big impression. There wasn't an empty chair near us, so I vacated mine. Pilar sank onto it graciously.

"You are *so* kind," she murmured. "Okay, listen. First, anyone can go down to the vault: no permission is needed."

"*Anyone?*"

"Yes. This is because, when you take a deposit box, you do not give your name—you must pay rent in advance, that is all, for however long you decide you want the box. Then they tell you which is your box, and give you your combination—six figures, I check this again. The bank does not keep a list of names, only of rent paid."

"Anonymous!" I said. "Of course! I remember now—there's a lot of tax-free loot tucked away in places like this. There was a raid on a vault near Harrods recently, and a large proportion of clients didn't dare to claim their stuff."

"I tell him that both I, and my so rich English friends, may like to have boxes," Pilar said. "I ask if we can visit the vault to see if we like the arrangements, and he says, no problem." She smiled at each of us in turn, and then across the hall. Range, getting on for twenty yards, but smack on target.

"Leave the poor sod alone, Pilar—he'll be running after you down the street," I said. "Now, is there any way we can be left alone down there to try this combination on the boxes?"

"What!—*all* of them?" Ginny said.

"Have you got any other ideas? We can't find out which box we're after, can we, because they don't keep the names."

Silence. Then Ginny said:

"If they don't record names, who's to know we don't already rent a box? Or that we're collecting something for a friend?"

"It can't be that easy, can it?" I said.

"The guard will be watching, of course," Pilar said. "I think he will stop you if you try to open more than one box, no?"

"Then you'll have to distract him, Pilar."

"Yes, but William! How can I do this? He will not be so stupid, I think."

"You'll need a story. Listen—how about this? We all go down there. Ginny and I get ready to try as many boxes as possible as soon as the guard's back is turned . . ."

"Yes, but . . ."

"Wait! You tell him that what we are getting out of the box is very private. Like . . . well, of course, you don't *tell* him what it is *because* it's private, right? That's better left to his imagination. If he follows us about, you say: 'I understood that these boxes could be opened in privacy.' Make a big play of that, get indignant if necessary. Can you do that?"

Pilar looked doubtful. "I will try," she said.

"If it doesn't work, we'll have to retire gracefully and think up some other plan."

"The trouble is," Ginny said, "Pilar's already told her admirer over there that we don't own a box."

"Yes—but the guard doesn't know that, and he won't, if we can get someone else to take us down. Which way is it, Pilar?"

"I am sorry—I forgot to ask," she said.

"Well, it would have looked odd at that stage. Let's wait until your friend is occupied—he is now!—and ask at the counter. Let's go, before he's free again: he might be tempted to play host. Don't look his way; it might encourage him."

We rose, and headed for the securities counter, Pilar in the lead. There was no one there: she pressed the bell imperiously. A clerk appeared. Pilar spoke briefly. He nodded, and pointed. Pilar turned to us.

"We have to go to that door," she said. "There will be a guard there to take us down."

I cursed—the door was at the far end, and we'd have to pass the desk of the official Pilar had spoken to. But he was occupied with another client, and we swept safely past.

The guard at the door was young, good looking, and bored. Pilar smiled; he opened the door and led us down a steep flight

of carpeted stairs to a carpeted lobby with an office opening off
it. A second guard emerged, straightening his jacket, and took
charge of us. He was an older man, from the sergeant-major
mold. The first guard went back up the stairs.

Facing us was a steel door with a peephole in it. Pilar spoke
to the guard, who smiled, and began to unlock it.

"I tell him you are English, and just married: you are going
to show your new wife the things you have put here for her,"
Pilar murmured.

"I should be so lucky," Ginny said.

"Smile!" I said. "Think of diamonds, rubies, pearls the size
of pigeons' eggs."

"All I can think of," Ginny said, "is that we're likely to be
carted off to you-know-where any minute now. Can you remember the number?"

"Three-one, one-one, two-one."

"That's what I thought, but I'm glad we agree."

We began to file through the door. But the guard stopped
us, and said something to Pilar.

"What's he say?"

"Only two can go in," Pilar translated.

I thought fast. "Ginny and I go. You try to keep him with
you, outside the door and away from that peephole." If he
insists on coming in with us, what will we do . . . ?

The vault may have had walls of reinforced concrete six-feet
thick, but it looked like an ordinary room, white painted, with
a plain blue close-fitting carpet. The two longer walls were
completely covered by rows of small doors: in the center of
each door was the calibrated knob of a combination lock. My
heart sank. We had a hopeless task, surely.

I looked around. The guard was closing the door.

And he was staying *outside* . . .

Could Pilar distract him from looking in through the peephole, or would she find a way to block his view of it?

Got to take a chance. I looked at the box numbers. Columns
were numbered one to twenty, rows were lettered A to E . . .

one hundred boxes. On each side! No, wait—the boxes on the right were lettered F to K and looked newer. Let's leave them.

"You work from this end, Ginny."

"Shouldn't I do the other side?"

Women, women . . . "No! The old ones are more likely."

"All right, all right. Turn the knob left first?"

"That's how my office safe works. Hope these are the same."

Left three-one, right one-one, left two-one. Pull—still locked. Try the next . . . *left three-one, right one-one, left two-one, pull—no good. Left three-one, right one-one, left two-one, pull. And again* . . .

It was taking well under ten seconds to try each lock. Say twenty a minute . . . five minutes for a hundred or two-and-a-half minutes if Ginny's working at my speed. Maybe she's faster . . .

Left three-one, right one-one, left two-one, pull. Left three-one, right one-one, left-three one, pull. No no!—bloody fool, you got that one wrong; do it again . . . *left three-one, right one-one, left two-one, that's better, but it still doesn't open. Maybe this wasn't such a good idea of Ginny's, after all* . . . *Now, now, you wouldn't be here if you didn't think it was at least possible that those numbers fit one of these locks* . . .

I'm really hopeless at these repetitive jobs; after a while my mind goes numb, and I make mistakes all the time; I'm sure I'm dialing some of these numbers wrong, but I daren't stop. How many's that? Two columns, plus two more of Ginny's, leaves—oh Jesus—sixteen columns still to go . . .

Left three-one, right one-one, left two-one, pull. Left three-one, right one-one, left two-one, pull. Left three-one, right one-one, left two-one, pull . . . *it's hypnotic. I think I'll be doing this in my sleep tonight* . . . *Left three-one, right one-one, left two-one, pull, and again* . . . *and again* . . . *and again* . . . *and again* . . . *that's two more columns finished* . . . *twelve to go and almost halfway now* . . .

Is he watching us? Or has Pilar persuaded him to let us gloat over our wealth in private? How could she keep him from the peephole without it being obvious? Any moment now, the key may rattle in the lock, and we'll have an angry guard on our necks, demanding to know what the hell we're up to!

Left three-one, right one-one, left two-one, pull. Left three-one, right one-one, left two-one, pull. Left three-one, right one-one, left—

"William!"

I can hear it too—a key in the door. Prepare for trouble! "All right, Ginny, I heard it. Play it cool, okay?"

"No—look!"

I looked. Then I looked again—*at an open box!*

"Jesus! Ginny—you've done it!"

"I have, haven't I."

"Señor! . . ."

And here's the guard. Is he angry or just worried? Where's Pilar? I'll make apologetic noises . . .

"Terribly sorry—couldn't remember which box it was. No harm done, though—got there in the end. Thank you so much, most grateful."

Be calm, smile—but not too much . . .

Pilar speaks from the doorway: I think she's telling him what I just said. Well, you can be rich *and* stupid . . .

"Clear it all out, Ginny—here, into the bag. What have you got?" Oh wow! Maybe all the jokes about diamonds will—

"One folder, dog-eared," Ginny said flatly. "And that's all. Haven't looked in it yet."

"Let's assume it's full of amazingly valuable share certificates and get the hell out of here."

"Do you think it is?"

"For *his* benefit, it's *got* to be. Smile, Ginny! You're over the moon, mercenary bitch that you must be. That's better. Take my arm and swear eternal love until the cash dries up . . . good. I hope he's convinced. He seems to be calming down a bit. Darling!—shall we go?"

"Yes darling. Please please let's."

"Is it all right, Pilar?"

"I hope so; I think so. He only had time to see you try maybe two or three boxes. I will tell him good-bye for you."

"I hope he accepts it. Everybody smile . . . good-bye, good-bye!"

Outside, the pavement crawled under our feet, slowly, slowly. Once around the first corner, we allowed it to speed up and bolted back to the hotel. I collected my key from reception.

"A letter for you, Mr. Warner."

"Thank you."

I stuffed it into my pocket, and we almost ran for the lift, the shopping bag bumping against my leg. Then we were at the bedroom door. I got the key in, turned it, and we were home again. Home and dry. Home and dry, and as high as the sky . . . My adrenaline level is up up up . . . One last time—oh *wow!*

Ginny held out her hand for the shopping bag. Well, it was hers by right—yes! It was her triumph from start to finish. She should be the one to unveil the mystery. I surrendered the bag to her with a ceremonial flourish.

"As I was saying," she said. "One dog-eared folder, foolscap, muddy green in color." She threw it on the bed.

"Well, go on!—have a look," I urged.

"I just know it's going to be a disappointment: I can hardly bear to. Oh well—here goes." She picked it up. "Told you so. A list of names . . ." She flipped through it. "And that's all."

"Ginny, it wouldn't have been there if it wasn't valuable."

"I know that, you fool. Once upon a time—but is it worth anything *now?*"

"Let me see, please," Pilar said. She held it up, and began to read the list to herself, frowning. I looked over her shoulder. The list was in large, old-fashioned type on plain white paper, yellowed at the edges. Some of the names had been crossed out by a single stroke of a pen. Right at the back, there was a handwritten sheet, with virtually all the names run through.

"A revenge hit list from the civil war," I suggested idly.

"Just a minute," Pilar said. She'd returned to the top sheet. "I think, maybe, I know some of these names."

"Who are they?"

"Well, I think maybe you have the right idea."

"Really? A hit list?"

"No, not that. The opposite. A list of supporters: people who were working for the revolution *against* Franco. Important people: this one is an army man, and this one also—and it was Franco's army then, remember! This one was in the government—"

"Terrific," Ginny said. "A list of revolutionaries, reds under the bed—and the revolution's over. When did Franco die?"

"Nineteen seventy-five."

"Then that's when this list's value took a sudden nosedive. I knew it!—it's useless."

"Old Delgado couldn't have thought so," I said.

"No. But—when did *he* die?"

The room was filled with calculation. Then the memorial plaque rose up in my mind. "Also in seventy-five," I said.

"Ah. But before or after Franco?"

"Franco died in November," Pilar said. "As I told you, there are still these big demonstrations for him in Madrid every November."

"We'll have to check," I said, "but my guess is that Delgado died earlier than that, in August maybe, because that's when Alex would be likely to be out here on holiday. If so, Delgado died at a time when this list was still dynamite."

"Not anymore," Ginny said. "Now it's just paper."

Pilar handed the file back to me. I closed it and dropped it onto the bed. Mind you, there was still—

"Who was the letter from?" Ginny asked.

"Letter? Oh, yes." I pulled it from my pocket and looked at it. No stamp—*delivered by hand! Just like*—

I tore it open. Something fell to the floor, and I bent to pick it up. A snapshot of a blond girl, this time against a background of blue water. "It's Cathy!" I looked in the envelope, found a folded note, and hurriedly spread it out. We all looked. It bore a single line of typing, no signature:

"*Fuente luminosa de Montjuic, Sábado 21.00*"

"This is a big fountain in the Plaça de Carlos Buigas, in front of the Palacio Nacional," Pilar said. "They mean that she will be there at that time on Saturday, no?"

"I suppose so. I hope so. Yes, surely it does. But who the hell is it from? Stephenson's dead!"

"Then his men will want to get rid of her, no? I think she look okay, thank God."

"We don't know when it was taken."

"No. But I think this is what they mean, that she is okay."

"Let me see," Ginny said. I passed her the note and photograph. "They're not asking for the file, then."

"No," I said. "But I'll take it along, just in case they find out it's missing meanwhile."

"No need to let me down lightly, darling. Let's face it, this morning was a waste of time."

"I'm not so sure," I said. "But if nothing else, it added a few extra stitches to life's rich tapestry, didn't it?"

Pilar thought she should go home, and I went down to the street with her. "Sure you don't want a taxi?"

"Oh no, it is not far, and I like to walk. So now you can have a peaceful time together, you and Ginny."

"I'll have to go down to Tarragona to consult Alex, but otherwise yes we can, until Saturday. I'll be in touch, perhaps tomorrow morning. Pilar—thanks for everything."

"Oh, you are very welcome. See you soon."

I watched her set off down the Ramblas and then went back into the hotel. Ginny let me into the room. She looked apprehensive. Behind her, on the bed, was her suitcase. It was open.

"Ginny! You're not—"

"William darling, I must. There's a plane at three-fifteen, and I can easily catch it. I *told* you, darling . . ."

"But it's only Thursday! Why not go back tomorrow?"

"I've got to get things ready for the weekend. I can't leave all that to Mrs. Troughton."

"But Ginny—how can you leave now, just when everything's about to be wound up? Stay over the weekend to see it through."

She hesitated. Then she said:

"I've got my own life to run, you know. I don't want to get across everybody and spoil it. Please don't be difficult."

I sat on the bed, next to the open suitcase. It was already half full of her things: soon it could swallow the lot, be zipped, belted, and gone . . .

"I'll drive you to the airport early tomorrow," I said. "You could be back home by midafternoon, in time to do essential shopping and see everybody."

She looked doubtful. But not determined.

"See how reasonable I'm being," I said.

"Think of me mooning about here on my own," I said.

"A last glorious evening together," I said. "Until the next time, of course . . ."

"William," she said, "if I miss that plane, I am going straight out to get the largest, sharpest knife money can buy, and I am going to make sure that you never again—"

"I'll help you unpack," I said.

FRIDAY

PARTINGS, AND DESCRIPTIONS OF THEM, ARE BEST got over quickly, so I'll just say that, in the morning, Ginny flew away on the ten-fifteen plane out of Barcelona. My loss would soon become another's gain—but we won't dwell on that. Anyway, it was her four-legged friends she missed the most; of course it was. And I drove on to the hospital in Tarragona to see Alex.

He thought he'd be well enough to come back to Barcelona in the morning, if I could collect him. So when we'd said all we needed to say and agreed that nothing could be done until after the Saturday meeting, I called at the Villa Club to see if Jill could find me a bed for the night, to avoid going back to my half-empty room at the Oriente.

My memory of what followed is as black as the night itself, starred with disconnected incident. It started as an extended evening in the bar. I can recall parts of Jill's advice to the lovelorn, in return for which I told her the superfast way to boil eggs: bring a *quarter-inch* of water to a boil in a saucepan with a lid, and then put the eggs in for the usual four minutes— they cook in the steam! But after that, a velvet darkness, plagued with faces which laughed like demons before being banished by a pale figure that must have been a dream . . .

So we'll cut to Saturday morning, if you don't mind. Or even, goddamnit, if you do.

SATURDAY

I WOKE ... WITH DIFFICULTY. THE BEDROOM WAS unfamiliar; peeking through the venetian blind, I saw that it was in one of the houses in the top row—Alex's, perhaps. How did I get here? And whose was the Mexican hat by the bedside? My short-term memory seemed to have been wiped from the slate. I tottered into the shower to see what cold water could do.

Nothing. Incontinent Night refused to be brought before the Court of Day—admission of guilt, you bet. And yet such are the mysterious workings of the subconscious brain that explanations of all that had happened in the two weeks *before* last night were now fairly shouting for attention. It never fails to amaze me, how much better we think when we're not even trying. Well *I* do, and I've read that others are the same.

As my head cleared, I was even getting a kind of mental printout of jobs to be taken in hand: things to be done, people to be moved from this category to that, accused, apologized to. Alex was high on the list: I could talk to him in the car. Stephenson had crossed himself off. I ought to clear things up with Delgado, whose property I had, in effect, stolen. There were others, but they'd have to wait until later in the day. First things first.

I pulled on my crumpled clothes and went down to Jill's house. She greeted me amiably as a fellow survivor of the night before and offered breakfast. Then it was time to get down to business.

Jill made the call for me.

"Just a moment, please," she said, handing me the receiver.

"Señor Delgado? Ah, you're back—I hope you had a pleasant trip . . . good . . . I'm glad to hear it. I was hoping you'd be in a good mood because I'm afraid I've a confession to make. Yes, a confession. Did you know that your father had a deposit box in the Caixa Catalunya? No? I see . . . well, the fact is I discovered that he had and that the numbers inside his ring weren't a date, but the combination of the lock. I telephoned you on Thursday night, but you were away, so I'm afraid I went there and opened it . . . Yes, she's still missing, you see, and I thought . . . yes. Quite. Well it might have . . . Yes, we did, there was a folder. I haven't looked at it very closely, but it's a list of names . . . No, I've still got it: it's quite safe, I assure you. There's a new factor, now—the people who've got Cathy Gordon are apparently proposing to hand her back tonight— the meeting place is the Montjuic fountain in Barcelona, at nine o'clock this evening . . . ah, you know the place, good. The problem is this: these people must know about the safe because otherwise why would they have been after the ring, and if they go to the safe and find it empty before the meeting this evening, they may refuse to hand her over unless I give them the folder . . . yes, I'm glad you see what I mean. Yes. I do appreciate that, Señor Delgado; you're being very understanding . . . What do I suggest? Well, I have got an idea, but you may feel it's rather more than you'd care to take on: if it is, you must say so, of course . . . Yes, right, I will. It's to set up a, well, a kind of trap. What it needs is some plainclothes police in the crowd, so if I have to hand over the folder in return for the girl, they can get it back for you afterward. Plainclothes? I mean, not in uniform. They'd have to follow the contact man until it was safe to grab him—that's to say, until the girl was safely in our hands. That means hand-held radios, cars perhaps. In other words, a job for the police. But they must be discreet, or the girl may be harmed . . . Yes . . . yes. That's right. What I'm asking is that *you* arrange this with

the police because they'd listen to you. I don't think I'd stand
a chance, not in the time available . . . You would? Oh, that's
really marvelous; Dr. Gordon will be so relieved, I can't tell
you . . . Had you heard he was in hospital, in Tarragona? Yes,
it was Stephenson: I saw it, but I couldn't prevent it; I felt very
bad about that. And now Stephenson's . . . yes, quite extraordinary. I can't say I was sorry to hear about it—in fact I think
it's what we call poetic justice . . . yes. Señor Delgado, I don't
know what we'd do without your help . . . no, really, I mean
it most sincerely. Just one more thing: how will the police
recognize me? I don't want to brandish the folder in case they
don't know I've got it, so I'll have it in a shopping bag, but
there may be other people with shopping bags—it's so easy to
make mistakes in a crowd. Also, unfortunately, it's Saturday
night; there'll be a lot of people there I suppose . . . You *will?*
To be honest, I was hoping you'd say that. With you there, I
feel the whole thing will be in safe hands. Yes. Yes. Well, I
certainly do; it's probably the last chance . . . Thank you very
much indeed. Yes, I'll pass that on. Good-bye, Señor Delgado.
Until this evening, then."

I put Jill's telephone down, feeling that I'd done a good job.

"Success, then?" Jill asked.

"Yes. I've asked him to get the police to cover the meeting
this evening—you heard all that. You said he was a big wheel,
and having met him now, I should think he can do it with a
flick of the wrist."

"What about your little bit of safebreaking?"

"He bore it bravely. As Ginny said, he ought to be pleased
that we discovered the safe. And of course he'll get the contents
back—he's quite interested to see the folder."

"Only quite?"

"It can't be important, Jill, not anymore. It's all ancient
history, as dead and dusty as the old man himself. Well, I'd
better go and collect Alex. What do I owe you for the call?"

"After the profit I made on you in the bar last night? Forget
it."

"Oh God. Just another drunken Brit. And I've always despised them."

"With a difference. They're not usually trying to sing opera."

"Oh no! Did I?"

"*Rosenkavalier.* But you've got a long haul ahead before you make Covent Garden, to be frank. You didn't think to bring my hat back, did you?"

"A Mexican hat? Yours?"

"Mine."

"Jill! Surely I didn't, I mean, we didn't . . . ?"

Jill smiled, leaned over, and patted me on the arm. "Nothing untoward," she said. "Very nice and friendly, it was, even if you kept calling me by another name. Good luck, William. Let me know how it goes."

Well now, um . . . mustn't waste any more time on these incidentals. Best get on.

Alex wasn't talkative on the drive to Barcelona, and when we reached the Oriente, he said he was feeling groggier than he'd supposed he would and had better go back to bed. Should I call a doctor? I wondered—how ill was he? With a head injury, you can only go on what the patient tells you. But then he ought to know. So I saw him up to his room, tucked him in, and let down the blinds. It was two o'clock: I had several hours to kill before it would be worth setting off for the Montjuic fountain. I put the car back into the safety of the underground garage, and then strolled down through the Gothic quarter toward the harbor.

Watching boats is as pleasant a way of wasting time as any I know. I bought my second *bocadillo* of the week, and sat on a bench, enjoying, once again, the glittering display in the yacht basin. It's almost a public service to go to such expense for the entertainment of the passersby: let's not listen to those who think all forms of expensive display are obscene, whether beautiful or not.

If I'd been one of those, my digestion would have been seriously upset by the sight of one of this afternoon's arrivals—a vast white motor yacht, whose swordfish bows appeared, house high, in the harbor entrance. I watched her glide across the basin to the main quay on the city side, reserved for larger vessels, a yellow-and-red Catalan flag swinging lazily over the stern. A lithe young crew in white trousers and singlets performed the tying up rites with smooth efficiency. I would have liked to watch the privileged persons she carried coming ashore, but it would have meant moving to another bench, and I couldn't face the effort—last night's junketings were catching up with me. I knew the delayed action would take full effect by five o'clock, by which time I, too, ought to be back in the hotel and getting some sleep. Meanwhile, some minutes more of sitting and staring would do no harm. In a perfect world, an ice-cream seller would come by right now. But if not, too bad—I could stop and buy one on the way back. Which, philosophically, I did.

"Time I went, Alex."

He sat on the edge of the bed, visibly drooping after the effort of letting me into his room. The shaven patch with the six stitches on the left of his head gave him a Frankenstein appearance.

"I'd really like to come," he said.

"I'd rather you didn't. You're not going to be any help in your present state, and you might be a hindrance."

"Well, that's plain enough," he said ruefully. "But I feel that Cathy—"

"Leave it to me, Alex, please. She'll get less of a shock if she sees you here, in bed."

He sighed. "All right. Listen, William, I don't know how I'm ever going to repay you for all this."

"Always useful to have a surgeon in stock," I said. "You'll get your chance sooner or later, I'm afraid. And now, I really must go: I like to look over the ground before a confrontation."

"So you do. What's this?—the third, isn't it?"

"It is. And it's going to be third-time lucky."

"Dear God, I hope you're right," he said.

With Delgado's folder in the shopping bag and Stephenson's automatic in my jacket pocket, I took a taxi to the foot of the Avenue de la Reina Maria Christina. The rendezvous was to take place by the gigantic fountain at the top of this broad boulevard. Gigantic it certainly was: walking slowly up the boulevard toward it, I could see a mountain of colored water, shining under the night sky, constantly changing shape as a variety of movable jets came into play.

As I got nearer, I could hear the roar and splash of the water. It was easy to believe the figures I'd read in the guide book about the Carlos Buigas masterwork: thousands of liters per second, pumped to a height of fifty meters—a hundred and fifty feet. Concealed lighting made this liquid castle glow like ice, changing from blue to green, through yellow to pink. On a small scale, it would have been merely pretty, but the sheer size, the weight of water being propelled upward into temporary escape from gravity, gave an impression of a solid structure, a liquid architecture.

Behind the Buigas fountain was a dark hillside—the gardens of Montjuic—surmounted by a turreted classical building, the Palacio Nacional. Below the palace, a cascade many yards wide poured out of the darkness down several levels to the fountain: it was lined with steps and crossed at each level by a stone balustraded bridge. I reached the paved *plaça*, which was thronged with strolling people, skirted around the fountain, avoiding the mist that drifted from it on the lee side, climbed the steps to the first of the bridges, and turned to look back.

From up here, as if on a saluting base, I could see down the cascade to the fountain, which even from this elevation rose high enough to interrupt my field of view from time to time, and beyond, along the mighty axis of the boulevard. I stood there for a while, the hum and glow of nighttime Barcelona all around me, playing dictator and admiring the shifting shape of the fountain. Then I went to check the side streets.

When I had the layout clear in my mind, I went back to the fountain and, in its glacial light, looked at my watch. It was five minutes to nine. Mingling with the crowd, I waited. With the shopping bag in my left hand, I slid my right into my jacket pocket to check that Stephenson's automatic was still there. Water, water everywhere—but my throat was dry.

Something made me look up, toward the cascade.

Delgado had kept his promise. There he was, his tall, military figure clearly visible in the center of the first bridge, just where I'd been standing a few minutes before. A saluting base, I'd thought—but perhaps it was more like the bridge of a ship. He leaned forward to place his hands on the balustrade, and I had a sudden vision . . . Captain, no, *Admiral* Delgado, at the controls of this great city-ship, Barcelona.

A low rumble of new sound came from the fountain. Then, without more warning, it burst into song—music, at least. It was a piece I'd heard a thousand times without ever wanting to know the name. It seemed a pity they couldn't have chosen something better—the magic of the water structures was ruined by these banal fairground noises. I looked at my watch again: just after nine. We got music on the hour, apparently. And regrettably.

But it was zero hour—time to ignore the thing, anyway. I stood with my back to the fountain, searching the crowd. A mass of dark Spaniards circulated under my stare, laughing, shouting, waving to friends. Was I watching for a blond girl— or would one of these come up to make the contact?

I saw him then. A man with a grave expression that set him apart from the laughing crowd. The mafioso, carrying a small black briefcase.

He walked toward me, unhurried, wary. Then we were face to face. The noise of the fountain folded us into a bubble of privacy. I said:

"Have you brought the girl?"

"*Sí*, señor. Please follow."

"Wait."

He was turning away but stopped and faced me again. I said:

"Listen carefully. I have Stephenson's gun in my pocket, and it is pointed at you. You know that I will shoot if I have to, but you will not get hurt if you do as I say. Do you understand so far?"

He nodded slowly, his black eyes resentful. I said:

"We are going for a short walk. You will keep on my right and a little in front—so. All right—let's go."

He said:

"This is a mistake, señor. I have brought the girl; you do not need to worry."

"I'm not worried. Walk!"

He walked. Around the fountain. Up the steps.

"We turn right here, onto the bridge."

Almost there . . .

"Stop."

Look around quickly. There's a tourist couple at the far end and some Spanish men scattered about . . . leather jackets. They could well be police if Delgado did what I asked.

"Good evening, Mr. Warner," Delgado said. He looked from me to the mafioso, his eyebrows slightly raised. "Who is this?"

"Someone who's going to get shot if he doesn't do exactly what I tell him," I said. "He claims to have Cathy Gordon with him."

"That is good news. But why have you brought him to me?"

"There's been a change of plan. I want to turn him over to the police now and pick the girl up afterward."

"But Mr. Warner—why?"

"Kidnapping is a crime."

"What I meant to say was—why have you changed your mind?"

"It's a little complicated to explain. You call the police to take charge of him, and then I'll try."

"Are you sure this is not a mistake, Mr. Warner?"

"That's what people keep suggesting. But the answer is yes, quite sure. And getting surer by the second. I should perhaps mention that I shall insist on going with him to the police station. To see that everything is as it should be."

"Ah."

"I think you understand me, Señor Delgado."

A slight frown appeared on his face. "I think I do, Mr. Warner. You have the idea that I am not to be trusted. This is a disappointment to me."

"I've had that idea since I realized why you made such a show of handing the ring over without inspecting it, as if you weren't interested."

"Mr. Warner, I—"

"It wasn't natural in the circumstances. It meant that you were sure of seeing it again—after Dr. Gordon had given it to the kidnappers."

Delgado's hooded eyes studied me. "So small a thing, and you are so sure?"

"I wasn't. That's why I asked you to arrange for the police to be here this evening. You've only got to call one of them over to prove his identity, and I'm proved wrong."

There was a silence. It seemed to drown out the hiss and splatter of the fountain below. The fairground tune was over, I realized. But the music wasn't: I recognized the opening bars of *Swan Lake*. What else. Delgado said:

"Very well. The comedy is finished. Perhaps I may tell José that you are not going to shoot him?"

"Yes. But he must stay here while we talk. Then he can lead me to the girl."

"There is nothing I want to say, Mr. Warner: I will wish you good night."

"One or two questions first," I said.

"Questions! Our business is over, I think."

"Señor Delgado—whatever your reasons were for what's happened, I don't feel that we are enemies. Do you?"

His eyebrows lifted. Then he spread his hands and said:

"I did not expect this. But . . . *muy bien!* What are your questions? I do not promise to answer, of course."

There are better backgrounds for collecting thoughts than the "Dance of the Sugar Plum Fairy" . . . Struggling, I said:

"I suppose you saw that your father wasn't wearing the ring when he was buried?"

He nodded. "My father always intended me to have it, of course, but I was in the United States when he died, so he could not give it to me as he had meant."

"Yes. I could see no other reason for your father wanting Dr. Gordon to take the ring—he knew that your mother couldn't be trusted to give it to you because it was also his wedding ring, and she was strongly sentimental about it." *Pilar: ". . . she would want him to have it, her husband. Believe me."* "But Dr. Gordon misunderstood what your father wanted and gave the ring to your mother. Has she now admitted it?"

Delgado nodded. "And also that she put the ring, not on his finger, but hidden in the coffin, so that I would not see it and take it. This was the start of the trouble, that she did not tell me this."

"So Dr. Gordon got the blame. You thought he'd kept it. Why did you wait so long before trying to get it back?"

Delgado shrugged. "At first, I did not think it was important. Our movement seemed to have died with the revolution, and I did not want to draw attention to the ring or accuse the doctor. Then, when our movement came alive again, the document became a danger to us. I had to get it back and without exposing myself. It was difficult, very difficult, but then at last I saw this opportunity."

"The chance to kidnap the girl?"

Delgado merely smiled and shrugged again. Hard to understand how he could think so little of it! I said:

"An opportunity provided by her boyfriend, Mark Stephenson. How did you know about that?"

"He works for me, Mr. Warner."

Of course. "And his father?"

For the first time, Delgado looked less than imperturbable. He said:

"A very dangerous man, Mr. Warner. I will admit, before this, I did not know how dangerous."

"At the start, you let everybody think he was behind this, a man with a rough reputation, to put pressure on Dr. Gordon and to keep suspicion away from yourself. But when you realized he was too rough to be trusted with the negotiations, you took the affair out of his hands and put in your own men to control him. I thought that they were working for him, but in fact, after the early stages, it was always José here who was in charge and Stephenson who was being told what to do."

"You must remember I was convinced that Dr. Gordon had kept the ring, and I felt entitled to put pressure on him," Delgado said, a shade defensively.

"I'm surprised that you had any connection with Stephenson in the first place."

"I never met him, Mr. Warner. But he had . . . certain skills that were useful. This is, I think, an area where you, who are not Catalan, cannot judge."

"Explosions in empty offices? Did Stephenson make the bombs and the biker gang, led by his son, plant them? Is that what you mean?"

"Mr. Warner, I did not guarantee to answer all your questions. I think that is enough." Delgado made a sign, and I felt a pressure in the small of my back: it could have been a finger but for a certain metallic hardness. I slowly took my right hand out of my jacket pocket and then felt another hand slide in, grasp the automatic, and withdraw that comforting weight. Perhaps, as everybody kept telling me, I *had* made a mistake. I looked along the bridge, one way, and then the other. Apart from the man who'd come up behind me, there were at least two others in each direction, casually watching the fountain. And the tourist couple had gone . . .

"You have no need to worry," Delgado said. "But as you

guessed, these are my men. Let us think of them as a peace-keeping force. And this, I hope, will be accepted by Dr. Gordon and yourself as a peacemaking gesture." He beckoned to José, who held out the small briefcase: Delgado took it and then offered it to me.

"Dr. Gordon's money?" I asked.

"Yes. With interest and expenses. And also, if you will accept them, my very sincere apologies."

I hesitated. I wanted to believe him, but the image of Stephenson sprang into my mind, the man with . . . certain skills.

"Perhaps you'd open it," I suggested.

"Here?" Delgado didn't understand.

"And then shut it again," I said.

Now he understood. "Ah." He did not look pleased.

"After the experiences of these last two weeks . . ." I said. But Delgado had balanced the briefcase on the balustrade. He snapped the latch, swung the lid fully open and back again. Then he looked at me inquiringly.

"Thank you," I said.

"What you were thinking would not be worthwhile, Mr. Warner. You have nothing much to complain about now, I believe."

"*What?*" He was too calm by half. "You can't think that," I said. "It's possible that Dr. Gordon may be so relieved to get his daughter back that he won't want to pursue you, but—"

"We shall see," he said. "Good-bye, Mr. Warner. Please wait here. José will bring the girl to you." He held out his hand. Automatically, I shook it. I watched him stride down the steps and away. After a while, the two men on the bridge, and several others I hadn't previously noticed in the crowd below, drifted after him in ones and twos. What would happen if the girl didn't turn up now? But I knew she would. It wasn't surprising he'd chosen to make use of Stephenson to put a threatening face on the operation. These Catalans were still as Orwell had described them: still shouting, still demonstrating, still kicking at outside authority and sometimes each other, but they hadn't—so far—been infected with the cynical malevolence, the homicidal destructiveness of real terrorists.

The fountain had finished with Tchaikovsky and was quiescent. I searched the *plaça* for the figure I was expecting, but could see no one that might be her nor any sign of José the mafioso. Of course, I knew who was responsible now, but it wouldn't be easy to get at him. Had I been too gullible? A rich revolutionary!—perhaps I should have realized that was a contradiction in terms. But his father had been just that. And another thing—what ever did happen to that loot from the bank raid?

A deep chord from the fountain. It sounded familiar: I stared down at a ring of huge arches, slowly rising up in solid water, glittering green. Was it . . . ?

A second, stately chord convinced me. Yes! *Ah, this is more like it!*

Fantastic!—you'd think there was a giant organ in there. Teeming scales and arpeggios now, to set the key. *To which my spine responds . . .*

The fountain sends up more arches . . . and more. The structure grows and lifts, higher and higher, becomes a whole, vast, incredible *cathedral* of water . . . Oh yes, this is it, this . . . is . . . *it!* Hold everything while I watch and listen. I really think, if old man Bach could have seen this, he would have been . . . he would have felt . . .

Prelude over. Now the fugue . . . rockets of mingled sound and water . . . who would have guessed it would work, would combine so well . . . Oh yes! . . . and now sound and water sink before the last, long, build up . . .

"Excuse me."

. . . a new and even more enormous cathedral being built before your eyes, as you watch, water supported on sound, sound . . .

"Excuse me!"

... climbing on water, to the last peaks and pinnacles of both. And so, at last, to the final major chord . . . Well, that *was* a surprise . . .

"*Excuse me!*—are you Mr. Warner?"

Oh my God!

I spun around. She was standing there, a blue canvas grip slung over her shoulder, smiling uncertainly. "Yes," I said, "yes, that's me. I'm sorry, I was just . . . You're Cathy, of course. I'm very relieved to see you. Are you . . . all right?"

"All right? Yes, of course I am."

She looked tanned, a little older than I'd expected, less of a child, more of a young woman. She shook the blond hair out of her eyes and added:

"It was really marvelous."

"*Marvelous?*"

"Yes. Why do you look like that—is there something wrong? Oh!—is my father—?"

"No, nothing wrong. Well, he's had a bump on the head, that's why he's not here to meet you, but . . . look, let's start walking, find a taxi, and I'll take you to him. Give me your bag—ouch!—what have you got in here?"

"Just some souvenirs," she said.

We walked down the steps, around the now quietly trickling fountain, and to the boulevard where taxis prowled. I agreed to a price, and we got in.

"Tell me, Cathy, where was it, this marvelous place?"

"Didn't Dad tell you?" she said.

"Tell me? No—how could he?"

"But I sent him simply stacks of postcards. Mum as well, of course."

"Where from?"

"Well, some from here. And lots from Minorca, when we got there . . . I don't understand it."

"Did you post them yourself?"

"Oh no, the crew did that. They did everything: it was

amazing, I didn't have to lift a finger. Must be really nice to be that rich."

The crew . . .

Bells were ringing. And a yellow-and-red Catalan flag was waving . . . I said:

"Was it a large white motor yacht; came in this afternoon?"

"Yes, absolutely enormous. And just for us. I don't know exactly whose it was, but—"

"You and . . . ?"

"Mark. I know, I know, but Dad's just going to have to come to terms with it. That I'm not a child anymore, that he can't . . . We haven't met before, have we? Do you mind my asking how well you know him?"

"Fairly well, now. I think I must tell you that he's been frantic, not knowing where you were. You'd better be prepared for that."

"Well, I don't understand about the postcards. I didn't want to hurt him, but I had to do it, make the break, you know. It was really heavy this summer, and I was afraid that, that . . ." She broke off. I looked across the cab and saw that she was looking out the window, biting her lip.

"That it would all start up again?"

"Oh, so you do know, then. It's been two years since it was supposed to be all over: but he's never really accepted it, and I just couldn't bear . . ." She grabbed a handkerchief out of her sleeve and mopped fiercely at her eyes with it. "I didn't think I was going to be like this. It's just the thought of what I've got to go through, now."

"We only met five minutes ago," I said, "but my guess is that you can handle it. You've made a break, which is maybe the hardest part. And if I may suggest, wouldn't you be better off away from home, for the time being, until he gets used to the idea?"

"That's what I thought," she said. "I'm going to try for a course in nursing—I've got the qualifications."

"He should be pleased about that. Or at least, find it hard to object."

"I hope so." The taxi swerved to change lanes, and she fell against me. "Sorry."

"Murderous driving in this town," I said. "And it's not too safe for pedestrians, either. It's recommended to leave everything valuable in your room when you go walking."

She gave a dry little laugh. "You have to look out for yourself whatever you do, don't you. I should know that."

"Well, you don't sound as if you've taken against him too badly. That's something."

"Against him? No, not really, not anymore. I used to hate it, of course, when he . . . but I didn't know what to do, I felt so helpless. But at other times I loved him; he was my father—a good father too, in all other ways. It was Mum that came off worst—I can see that now, and it doesn't make me feel any better, I can tell you that."

"She's not a strong character, is she?"

"She's not strong, no. I don't know what'll happen to them now. They're poles apart in some ways: Dad's got so much more energy, more everything. Oh, I'm really upset about those postcards. Why would the crew not post them?"

"When we get to the hotel, Cathy," I said, "we'll find a quiet corner, and I'll tell you all about it, before you see Alex. It's a long story: we've been quite busy here in Barcelona."

She looked across at me, but said nothing. Poor kid, I thought—but maybe the affair would prove a useful distraction, if Alex would let it.

So, that was that, except for loose ends. One of these was propped against my leg—the El Corté Inglés shopping bag, now looking a little the worse for wear. A crossbow, it had held, and £25,000, and a gold ring, and now—the dog-eared folder! Oh no, I hadn't forgotten it; I'd been ready to hand it over as soon as Delgado asked me for it.

But Delgado hadn't asked.

Now, that was interesting, wasn't it? Well, I mean, if you're a big wheel in the revolutionary process of separating Cataluña from the rest of Spain, you wouldn't forget to ask for your list of comrades, would you? *Not unless it was out of date and worthless.*

And that was the tale he'd spun. I'd been prepared to believe it, that even after twelve years, there were still plenty of live supporters on that list, people who had been ready to keep the red flag flying over the barricades against the Franco regime, and it had occurred to me that they might well be needed again if things went on hotting up between Cataluña and the central government and if the Franco fanatics that turned up in their thousands every November for the Madrid demonstration began to edge back into power as Pilar had said was possible.

Yes, I'd been prepared to believe it. But not now, not any longer. The list had to be worthless because Delgado hadn't bothered to reach out and take it from me.

But that raises a new question, doesn't it. *Why had he been to all that trouble to get hold of the ring and the deposit box combination?*

Aha. Now we're getting to it. And there could only be one answer—*there'd been something else in that deposit box, which he'd removed the day before we got to it!*

Away on business, as he said? Don't give me that! He'd been waiting twelve years to get into that box: he'd have been bursting with impatience to get in there, of course he would! No, the only reasonable conclusion is that he went to the box the day before we did, took out whatever was valuable, and left the folder because it wasn't. Clever to leave something to mislead us, in case we got there. But not quite clever enough!—he'd blown it all now, by carelessly letting me walk away with the folder.

So what had been in the box?

It's a shame Ginny isn't here to watch her chicken flying in to roost. What else was left but *the proceeds of the bank raid!* If not the actual stuff itself, then the location, and maybe the deeds, the *escritura* of the actual property in which the loot still lies!

We'll never see or touch any of it, of course. But it's good to get at the truth at last. And it's the proper thing to find at the end of a search like that, after all the sweat, dirt, and danger—not a grubby folder, but a glittering fortune stolen from the rich—jewels, heirlooms, gold maybe! Well well. So that was it, after all.

The taxi swerved away from the waterfront and was driving up the Ramblas. Nightlife was in full swing and . . . *caramba!*— look at that!—the things these girls do to attract customers! . . . here we are, outside the Oriente. We pull up behind a ship-sized dark blue Mercedes. The taxi driver names a sum. I give him what we agreed. He doesn't like it: what does he think I am, a tourist or something? *"Vamos, hombre!"* Yes, I'm coming to grips with the language at last. I collect the bags, and we make for the hotel entrance.

"Señor! Señor!" Running feet. I stop, spin around.

It's the mafioso, looking worried.

"This could be a mistake," I josh him—well, they were always saying it to me.

"Sí sí—mistake! Please, señor—the papers!"

The papers, the list, the folder. So Cataluña is on the march again, and Delgado *does* want it. There he is, watching from the rear window of the Mercedes. He simply, unbelievably, *forgot* to take it from me. There *isn't* any loot. He *was* away for the day on business. And everything George Orwell said about them is true.

"Here you are," I said crossly, reaching into the shopping bag for the folder. "And tell your boss from me—this is no way to run a revolution."

MARTIN SYLVESTER was educated at Harrow and, after national service in Germany, became an architect. He ran a successful house and furniture design practice for many years before closing it to take up writing full time. He still, however, retains directorship of a modern furniture store in Oxford and is a consultant wine buyer to the family-owned delicatessen in Devon. Martin Sylvester currently divides his time between Oxford and his farmhouse near Bordeaux.